From
BIRD MOUNTAIN

LYLE FUGLEBERG

iUniverse®

FROM BIRD MOUNTAIN

iUniverse books may be ordered through booksellers or by contacting:

iUniverse
1663 Liberty Drive
Bloomington, IN 47403
www.iuniverse.com
1-800-Authors (1-800-288-4677)

Because of the dynamic nature of the Internet, any web addresses or links contained in this book may have changed since publication and may no longer be valid. The views expressed in this work are solely those of the author and do not necessarily reflect the views of the publisher, and the publisher hereby disclaims any responsibility for them.

Any people depicted in stock imagery provided by Getty Images are models, and such images are being used for illustrative purposes only. Certain stock imagery © Getty Images.

ISBN: 978-1-5320-5104-3 (sc)
ISBN: 978-1-5320-5106-7 (hc)
ISBN: 978-1-5320-5105-0 (e)

Library of Congress Control Number: 2018907070

Print information available on the last page.

iUniverse rev. date: 06/25/2018

Chapter 1
GUNNAR
In the year 982

Gunnar didn't see them until he was halfway from the barn to the manure pile. He dropped the handles on the cart and straightened up, a curse forming on his lips.

The three who'd ridden to the corral railing nearby were just sitting, and probably wouldn't have been noticed if one of the horses hadn't snorted. Behind them 100 feet away at the smithy, Vilhjahn stopped pounding and also straightened, the silence bringing everything about the yard to a standstill.

Aarni nodded, not smiling. He was a weasel of a man with a narrow, pock-marked face and spaced teeth that even the well-fashioned tunic and matching cape couldn't dignify. On each side of him, larger men, simpler dressed and well armed, were also expressionless.

"Sorry to bother you, Gunnar, but you know why we're here," Aarni said.

Gunnar puffed and turned red. He looked around, as if for something to throw, then turned back. "Ya . . . I know. And also know that I've given enough.

"Do you happen to see Ingvald around here?"

Aarni shifted in the saddle, knowing the answer.

"I've given enough," Gunnar repeated, trying to find the right words. "And you can tell the bastard that sent you . . . that I've given enough. And if he wants more, tell him to come and get it. I'll give him some of this," he said, raising his fist with an obscene gesture.

1

The next afternoon, after a sleepless night and a grumpy morning, Gunnar left the work he was doing, which was continuing to get the barn and pens ready for winter, and hitched up a horse instead. But getting up and on wasn't easy. With the third try he made it, grunting and cursing and swinging clumsily into the saddle. What made it so difficult were the unstrung bow angled across his body, the bulky sheath of arrows likewise hung, the rigid battle-axe jammed through the back of his belt, and the sword at his side.

The weaponry was unusual. This wasn't a time to go hunting, and there wasn't a battle about that anyone knew of, so to anyone watching, what he was carrying didn't make sense. And someone was watching. Gurtha, his wife, had stepped out and walked toward him as he struggled by the corral gate, and now stood alongside, glaring, with two-year old Sigurth in tow. Rather than ask what he was doing, even though curiosity piqued because of Gunnar's recent behavior, she said, "Why don't you take the boy along? He's been cooped-up and would love to go."

"The weather's turning cold . . . it might rain, even snow."

"*Pshaw*, what else is new. He's well wrapped. He'll be fine."

Gunnar clenched his teeth. He started to speak, but didn't. He didn't want to explain, explain that he'd dug a hole and was in it and didn't know what to do. He looked away and was about to spur the horse when Gurtha butted against him with a look that asked *What's going on?* She handed him Sigurth, who oblivious to the tension, bubbled with excitement.

Gunnar sighed, grudgingly settled Sigurth in place, and nudged the horse's flanks. With that they sauntered away, moving along the corral which was at the tail end of the homestead complex.

The only structure separated from the complex was the smithy, which was apart because of the fire, smoke and noise generated there. On this day, like the day before, it was busy, as clouds of smoke and sounds of metal on metal had filled the air since first light. The sounds stopped as they passed as Vilhjahn and his helper gawked at the odd combination plodding by. Vilhjahn sighed and shook his head.

Gunnar ignored the stares and steered into the expanses that made up the bulk of the farm. Off in the distance he saw Sven, his oldest surviving son, and a number of field hands hard at work haying. He likewise ignored Sven when the boy stood straight, leaned on his scythe and watched them pass. Moving on, he went through a pasture where he could see that the cattle were no longer scattered as they'd been all summer, but were now bunched, which was possibly an indication the animals knew something about the weather he didn't.

He ignored them too.

Eventually, past cleared fields and more remote grazing areas, Gunnar stopped near the boundary of the farm at its southeastern corner, which was the point he had in mind all along. From there, the end of the gentle ridge they'd climbed, the land dropped to a convoluted valley before rising again in the distance. Here he had a panoramic view of not only the topography, but also the winding trail that was the shared roadway for most of the area.

It was the roadway Gunnar wanted to see. Holding the horse in place, he scanned it and the surrounding area for movement of any kind, somewhat relieved and settling back when there wasn't any—none except for the crows that always seemed to be around. So they sat, just sat, on a horse that munched at everything in reach, occasionally taking a step or two to do so but generally remaining in place. Sigurth, whose eyes initially darted to everything about, remained quiet through it all, finally nodding off. After a while, enough to convince Gunnar there wasn't going to be anything to see, he exhaled, beginning to feel foolish—foolish because he didn't have a plan if he did see anything to be concerned about, like a group of men on horseback coming his way. He wondered *so why the weapons?* He was still on edge, though, for when Sigurth, who'd awakened when the horse made another shift, jerked, babbled and pointed at the trees nearby, he froze. But it was just a doe and two fawns wandering into the clearing, who sprung back and disappeared when they heard the babble on the ridge.

Gunnar exhaled again, squeezing Sigurth, even chuckling. Tugging at the reins, he turned and started back, giving the valley one last glance. Instead of retracing the way he'd come, he turned north to the rough back-trail circling the plateaued heights that extended from the forests on the east to the cliffs along the ocean on the west. The plateau was called Bird Mountain, and separated his farm from another larger one belonging to his older brother Gyrth. The trail was rarely traveled because it really wasn't a trail; it was more of random meandering way with trees and boulders throughout the uneven terrain of its length. The way passed along a small creek that gouged a shallow, rocky, winding gully, beginning in the woods and running along much of the eastern side. With only a trickle in it at the time, the creek still had pools that had an appeal; so there were stops and dismountings, with Sigurth chasing frogs and splashing stones and taking cool, slurping drinks. Somewhat settled now, he plunked on the ground and even laughed while watching Sigurth, whose antics drifted from the water to the horse, where he circled around and between its legs, giggling all the way.

Gunnar groaned, an unconscious reaction, because what Sigurth was doing reminded him of Ingvald, his first son, years before in the same place doing the same thing. At the sound, Sigurth left the horse and crawled onto his lap, his face in childish concern, and said, "Ouwie?"

Gunnar teared-up for a moment.

Because of these distractions, along with the difficulty in working the horse while juggling Sigurth once they'd gotten back in the saddle, Gunnar almost forgot what had been bothering him.

Almost.

An hour later, they broke into the clear and descended across scenes much like those they'd left. He spotted Gyrth at the barn, where he was pitching hay side by side a few others, and saw him stop as they neared, sticking his fork in the ground. That the two were brothers was obvious. Gunnar was the taller with broad shoulders, while Gyrth was more stocky; but there were similarities, like dark blond hair, scuffy beards and strong chins, the way they sounded, and even the way they walked.

Wiping hands and dusting off as he moved to meet them, Gyrth said, "How are things with you, then? What brings you here, especially from *that* way?"

"Oh," Gunnar said, beginning to reply, but then he shrugged and flicked a nervous smile, not knowing what to say.

"Well, what do we have here?" Gyrth asked, as if not noticing the hesitation. He reached up and took Sigurth, giving the boy a shake and a hug, to which Sigurth squealed. "If it isn't my favorite dragon slayer. Just look at you. You look like your Pa just chewed on something and spit you out." Then, while still cradling him, he grabbed the reins as Gunnar dismounted and led them away, adding, "Damn I'm glad to see you two. I could use a break."

The Gyrth homestead was an assembly of buildings much like Gunnar's, which was fairly typical throughout the area. As they moved on, they circled the corral, empty at the time, then came to a garden, which was active. Ingibjorg, Gyrth's wife, and several others, were busy, with Sveyin, their son, same aged as Sigurth, tagging along and generally making a mess. When the tots saw each other, Sveyin stopped his imitations of work, and Sigurth broke free, the two hopping with excitement and scampering off.

"What brings you here?" Ingibjorg said, straightening up and wiping a dirty hand across her forehead. Then, "What's this?" Running her fingers across her chest. "You out to kill somebody?"

Gunnar laughed, "No, Sigurth was being a handful for Gurtha, so I thought I'd take him out for a bit and have some fun."

"Well, good to see you, and I understand. Sveyin's been driving me crazy, too."

After a few more words, the brothers turned away and drifted back to the corral, tying the horse to one of the railings.

"So what brings you here?" Gyrth asked, probing.

"Nothing special," Gunnar said, still trying to put to words what was on his mind.

"Glad you brought Sigurth along," Gyrth said after not getting an answer. "Just look at them go . . . They love to play together and don't see each other nearly enough."

Gunnar smiled, nodded, kicked some dirt around. "Where's Hrolf? I didn't see him when I crossed."

"He's way up in the north end checking out the stock. They're starting to bunch up."

Gunnar nodded, "Ya, same over our way."

A little more of the conversation going nowhere and Gyrth lost patience. He'd been understanding of Gunnar's occasional oddities ever since the accident. Gunnar had been hard at work a few years ago, building a shelter in the upper pasture, when a misstep sent him tumbling off an edge into rocks. He'd broken a leg and suffered a blow to the head that knocked him senseless for days. Fortunately, the leg healed well enough, and his head eventually did too; but at times his actions seemed different than before, particularly under pressure. Gyrth looked at him now and repeated, with an edge to his voice, "What's up? This isn't making sense, Gunnar. You ride in from the back side of the mountain, toting Sigurth, which is the good part, but armed to the teeth for no apparent reason. You look like a dog that's been kicked. You're worried about something, aren't you?"

Gunnar looked away, looked down, finally said, "Ya, I may have fucked up big time."

"How? With who? Oh let me guess. With Skuli, the high and mighty jarl to Earl Hakon."

"Ya . . . The high and mighty."

"What happened?"

"It's that latest levy that's been imposed."

"Oh ya, I know about that. No-one around these parts has been happy about it."

"Did you pay it?"

"Ya da. Everyone else I know has too."

Gunnar whistled, his features seeming to collapse. "Why should we have to? Why? Because some asshole assembles enough of a hird to call himself King, or says that because of some screwing in the past he has this bloodline that makes him "royal"? For this we have to kiss his ring and pay? Why?"

"You sound like Pa."

"That might be 'cause he had a snoot full of it too. But ny, I'm talking for myself about not only this tax, but also about that battle Earl Hakon had to have. You were there and I wasn't, so you know first hand."

"Ya, sure, I know, and know that Ragnfroth had landed with an army there and was trying to take over Hakon's kingdom, so he had to do something."

Gyrth looked around to see if anyone was close enough to hear, then said, "And you've never stopped feeling guilty about not being there. Look, I've told you a dozen times, you couldn't be there, you had a broken leg when that war-arrow arrived, remember? So your Ingvald and a couple hands from your farm went instead."

Gunnar shuddered. "That's another thing. Why should we have to go and fight someone we don't know every time someone we don't care about says so. As for Ingvald, I didn't ask him to go; he jumped at the chance as if it was some great adventure."

"He was just a kid, Gunnar," Gyrth said. "Like all of us, he'd grown up hearing about the Gods and the heroes all winter long, then playing games with swords and shields imitating them during the summer. He was full of piss and vinegar, and you couldn't have held him back with a team of horses. I had my hands full keeping Hrolf out, but he was just too young at the time, so I went."

There was no more to say as this was a story that had been hashed over many times. Finally after another lapse, Gyrth said, "You should be proud. As I've said before, the last I saw Ingvald, he was fighting like a banshee with blood spatters all over him; but when the fighting finally ended, he wasn't among those standing. My take on this is that he's been in Valhalla ever since, having more fun than working these fields ever was."

Gunnar snorted, "The Gods are what they are, and I'm okay with that; but this eagerness to fight and kill, and even to die in battle, particularly by the young, is something I'm no longer into. And I'm certainly against fighting for somebody else's glorified whim anymore."

"It's just the way it is," Gyrth said. "We grow up with it. When we get older and get some sense, most of us would rather stick to family and farming and live in peace. So I understand what aggravates you, Gunnar . . . It does me too.

"But there's more . . . there's the plundering that goes on. It's awful. A boatload of guys you wouldn't mess with on a dare goes out, and the ones that get back are loaded with the things people like you and me in some other place have worked for." He shook his head. "People are killed, some are enslaved and dreams are shattered, and that's supposed to be okay. I'm not sure that's what the Gods have in mind. But as far as I know, and from what Pa told us, it was like that as far back as he knew, so it probably always will.

Gyrth was worked up now, and had more to say, but something beyond Gunnar caught his eye and he stopped . . . He calmed and said, "Gunnar, turn around."

Gunar did and looked. There in a pen a short distance away Sigurth and Sveyin were giggling in some silly game with a young kid goat, and all three were into it, thoroughly enjoying themselves.

The men laughed and Gyrth said, "I don't know if the world's ready for what those two can do."

Relaxed now, Gyrth said, getting back to what had been bothering Gunnar, "Look, if it'll help, I'll go see a few of our neighbors, like Einar Jonsson, you know, next over, and other friends from farms nearby, as soon as I can. We'll get together, ride over, and accompany you in for the satisfaction of the levy. It won't hurt to have some backing, as well as witness to what happens, since there's no telling what Skuli will do if he has a free hand."

On the way back, Gunnar rode the easier way, passing below the cliffs that dramatically shaped the west side of the mountain. For most of its length the cliffs were an airshow of terns, sweeping and diving in the continual cycle of their world, and in a way, he was now with them. Gyrth had done that. He always seemed to see things with such clarity. Because of his counsel and pledge, a weight had been lifted so now Gunnar felt like one of those birds, soaring and catching the wind and gliding without a care. Halfway home, he dug in his heels that sent the horse into a gallop. He kept spurring while Sigurth bounced and giggled, the hooves churning dust which fanned out and drifted past when they came to an abrupt stop at the gate where they'd started.

At the longhouse, the atmosphere was markedly different from what it had been earlier in the day. The change began with the first thing Gunnar did, which was, as light was fading and most hands were returning from the fields, to have one of the sheep slaughtered. He did so in a simple sacrifice to Thor, the God of rain, fair weather and produce of the soil, with appropriate words of praise to him and also to Frey, the God of the seasons who made the fields fertile, for the good fortune they'd enjoyed.

Then, after a few end of the day details and the usual cleaning-up, both family members and hands drifted into the longhouse, where the fire provided a simple comfort in contrast to the chill building up outside.

The longhouse, the main feature in the complex, was neither large nor impressive, but it was the place where most aspects of living took place. It consisted of a central, dirt-floored aisle running the length of the building, which was used not only for circulation, but also heating, cooking and entertaining. Paralleling the aisle on both sides were wide benches, or platforms, for all else. Attached to the longhouse, mainly on the north side and extending eastward, were a string of other structures for assorted functions. These were tied together and although juxtaposed, were such that it was possible to travel from one to the other, including areas where animals were sheltered, without going outside, a characteristic appreciated in winter. Interior spaces were dark, with the only illumination being a central smoke-hole over the fire-pit in the longhouse, and scattered swing-out panels for light and ventilation elsewhere. Since light sources were limited, oil lamps and candles were used throughout the year. Another characteristic of these spaces was that each component was identifiable by the smells it generated, with smoke from the fire and odors from food, sewage, silage and animals providing a rich organic combination. Because of all of these—light, ventilation and aroma—being outside was preferred except during winter and the worst of the weather.

Normally a meal and some relaxed conversation would have been the extent of the evening; but this night it was different. This time there was mead. The drinking started before the last of the workers shuffled in and never stopped. Horns were filled and emptied and filled again.

Gunnar was at his station, the high seat in the center of the room. With more formality than usual, Sven was beside him on the right, with Vilhjahn on the left; but that was it for any order. After a settling down of sorts, Gunnar made toasts to the Gods, toasts to anyone who'd done well, and even toasts to some who had goofed up in some way. He directed attempts at singing, which didn't go at all, and then poetry, when he got emotional and recited, as if he'd been drinking Sutung's Mead, what a skald had written after the battle with Ragnfroth.

> Stern the struggle, ere the
> stalwart bonders' leader

under eagles' beak could
eftsoons thrust three hundred.
Seaward sailing then his
sloops of war, the active
gold-dispender grim—a
gain was that—his foes dogged.

Along the way there was food, better than usual with skewered meat, fresh bread and a stew of grains enriched with vegetables and spices. The women were all about keeping food and drink on hand; but except when Gunnar acknowledged his young daughters, Rogna and Solveig, or drank a toast to Gurtha for all she was doing, they were mostly in the background.

The evening, which was a celebration for no announced or apparent reason, went on well into the night before finally ebbing away. The young went down first, curling up in the far corners of the benches; then a few farm hands, who'd labored hard hours before, retreated to bunks near the stables. Those still in the innermost circles were fading too, slumping and yawning and dozing off.

Then Gunnars's mangy hound, lying curled at his feet, bolted up, fur on end, and snarled . . .

The door burst open, followed by a flood of screaming, armed men, who at first bunched, blinded by their own torchlight in the dim interior where most lamps had burned out, and then recoiled as the dog charged with fangs bared and snapping. One of the hands, bundled and almost asleep to the side near the entry, jumped to his feet in a stupor, and before realizing what was happening, was bludgeoned and chopped by others not involved with the dog.

Gunnar's jaw dropped, eyes wide . . .

But Vilhjahn, seeing first blood, jumped to his feet and reached for a shield and sword from the array of arms hanging on the wall behind the bench. Moving forward and growling himself, he joined the dog, first dodging the body of another man just awakened, who reeling of wounds, crashed into the fire-pit, spraying ashes and embers and pots and cook-stands in all directions. He met the leading attackers and the first semblance of a fair fight resulted, with swings and thrusts and blocks and scores.

Gunnar finally stood. Moving at first in a stupor, he grabbed a battle axe and another shield, and stumbled forward to join Vilhjahn into a melee of rising, guttural grunts and groans and sounds of metal on metal.

Then among the blurred images in the dim light he saw behind the closest attackers a gleam from spaced teeth—and knew who it was. Knowing the man also told him what this was about, so with kindled anger and bellowing like a prodded bull, he pushed those before him to the side, and with a sweeping chop spaced the teeth further. As he grabbed the falling body to free his axe, however, he was clubbed on the side of the head and stunned. He dropped to his knees.

A large, whiskered raider, the one to the rear who barked orders, reacted immediately. Stepping forward, he raised his sword and stroked. Blood flew in all directions, Gunnar's body slumped to the side, and his head rolled down the aisle.

"Kill them, kill them all!" the large man bellowed. *"We want no witnesses!"*

When Vilhjahn, the last of those able to up a fight, sagged and fell with multiple wounds, the rest in the room fled into the string of attached buildings, hoping to exit where they could in a desperate attempt to escape. This had been anticipated by the attackers, who had men waiting on horseback at each door with torches and lances. The one person who made it into the open became a game before he was skewered.

The moon had hardly moved in the sky since the dog snarled when the last of the men in the farm fell, some trapped in the farthest reaches of the stables. The attackers then finished killing where there was still life, gathered their own dead and wounded, and began to pillage. While doing this, they opened a door to a storage room and found it crammed with terrified women and children.

"Do you want these killed too?" They asked.

The large man nodded. "Everyone but the two young girls and that boy. Tie them up and gag them. I have a use for them."

On the other side of the mountain, it took time for Gyrth to make rounds to the farmers he'd mentioned who he felt would accompany Gunnar in solving his problem. The difficulty wasn't in getting cooperation, it just took time. Being so, it was past noon on the second day after meeting with Gunnar, that he, along with the farmers and a dozen well-armed companions, chosen to emphasize solidarity, reached the end of the cliffs near the lane turning towards Gunnar's farm.

All had been fine along the way with nothing out of the ordinary; but then they winced at a smell wafting their way. Moments later, upon making the turn, they were met by a similar body of men, also on horseback, heading their way. This group was led by a large, black-bearded man, immediately recognized by Gyrth as Skuli. Even though Skuli was dressed about the same as the rest of his men, he was still an imposing figure, with a confidence that left no doubt who was in charge. Beside him were three others who Gyrth knew to be noted farmers from the eastern side of the district, and behind them a dozen armed men similar to those in his own group.

The two groups stopped, and for a moment stared at each other, both at a loss. The most that happened at first were nods of recognition. Then Skuli broke the silence. "Gyrth, we were on our way to see you. We have some very bad news."

"Is that awful smell part of the news?"

"It is."

"Where's Gunnar?"

"That's also part of the news . . . He's dead."

Gyrth's jaw dropped, his face contorting, unable to speak for a moment. Then he asked, his voice breaking. "This can't be. What happened? Where's Gurtha? Where are the others—the girls, Rogna and Solveig?"

"They're dead too."

Gryth groaned, *"Oh nooooo!"* He hesitated, fighting for words, finally adding in almost a whisper. "And Sigurth, the boy?"

Skuli slowly shook his head as if he felt Gyrth's pain. Then seeing the news was hitting not only Gyrth, but also everyone in his group like a tidal wave, with reactions including the sound of swords being drawn even exciting the horses, he said with almost a soft, sympathetic tone. "Now everybody hold on. Don't do anything foolish. This whole thing's horrible enough the way it is without getting worse. Let me explain what I know."

Gyrth twisted in his saddle, his mind reeling. He wasn't armed, nor were his three farmer friends, so his urge to grab a weapon wasn't an option. The lack of arms, at least for the four up front, was decided upon because it was felt being otherwise would be disrespectful. So with anger rising to boil, he was forced to silently vent until he was able to say, "Okay . . . Explain."

Skuli waited until everyone quieted. "Well first, did Gunnar tell you he hadn't paid his taxes and levies?"

"Yes, he told me; he told me just two days ago. We're here because we were going to accompany him to get that matter resolved. He was going to pay."

"Oh my, this makes what happened even worse. We didn't know."

"So you slaughtered a community, over a dozen people, *a whole farming family including women and children?*" Gyrth said, his voice rising with each word.

"No, no." Skuli answered. "That wasn't the intent, anyway. Calm down, all of you, please.

"Did Gunnar ever tell you he insulted me in public, and threatened that if I ever came on his property, he'd hang me by the balls from the nearest tree?"

"He never told me that."

"Well, he did; the gentlemen behind me were witness to it.

"Now, you know I work for Earl Hakon, right? And you know Hakon depends on me to represent him in this district. Well, no-one likes a collector, but that's one of my duties."

"That doesn't include killing."

"I agree. As I said, nothing like this was intended, but I couldn't let the tax matter go without some action. So yesterday, I sent Aarni, you remember him, along with a dozen others, just like you're doing now, to reason with Gunnar.

"Unfortunately, Gunnar didn't reason. From what I've been told, he must have been drunk. Anyway the first thing he did was reach behind his back, pull out an axe, and split poor Aarni's head to his shoulders. Then as the other men made a move to help, that big blacksmith of his came out with a sword and chopped up the nearest one. Well, the men accompanying Aarni went crazy with that, and you know how crazy it can get, and how hard it can be to stop once the killing starts. They charged, chasing Gunnar and the smithy back into the lodge where all hel broke loose. When things took this turn, one of the men had the good sense to leave. He almost killed his horse getting to me to tell what was happening. By the time I could put together another group and get here, a day had passed and it was too late . . . all the damage had been done.

"I know you want to see everything first hand, so let's turn back."

They did, Gyrth numb in the saddle. When the farmstead came into view, faces pinched and heads turned at the intensity of the essences streaming from the smoldering pile in what had been the corral. Seeing little that could be identified among the horrors there, Gyrth and his friends dismounted, and moving from one stench to another, entered the longhouse. They found the interior a mess with spatters and ashes and broken weapons and furniture, none of which was a surprise after what Skuli had told them. There weren't bodies or even body parts, however, so obviously there'd been a cleaning of sorts. Whatever the cleaning, there was still a large pool of blood yet to dry on the floor near the high seat.

The group snaked its way through the longhouse into the annexes, finally exiting at the end of the barn, where the normally fetid air was more pleasant than what they re-experienced outside.

"So all the bodies were burned on that pile," Gyrth said, pointing to where the corral had been.

Skuli was waiting. "Ya," he said.

"Why?"

"Just common practice after a battle, I guess. The burning was done before I got here."

"Are the men with you now the ones who did this?"

Skuli shook his head.

"Then where are they? I want to talk to them. Where are their wounded? Where are their dead?"

"The dead are a part of that pile. The rest left right after we arrived. In fact, I ordered them to leave. When I heard what happened I was furious, so I understand some of what you feel. Although they were by that time embarrassed at how things had gotten so completely out of hand, to me that wasn't enough. There wasn't much I could do about it, however. Besides, they had only been along with Aarni on what was to be a quick trip helping out, and had to get back. They're crew members of a ship that by this time has sailed away."

Gyrth looked about, grim, sagging, and not knowing what else to do or say. He walked back to his horse and mounted, the others following suit.

"Look Gyrth," Skuli said, "I know all this is hard to swallow. I'm stunned too, that things could go so wrong. I'll schedule a hearing before a Thing as soon as it can be arranged. If there's more to learn about what's happened here, it should come out then and appropriate recourse taken. You're entitled to that. There's one thing more, though . . ."

"One thing more?"

"It's the farm. Since it appears no one in the direct family survived, there are no heirs to ownership."

"Don't I count?" Gryth said, his voice rising again.

"Your tie isn't strong enough. It's not as strong as the King's, who has a lien on the property because of unpaid levies."

"That's crazy!" Gyrth screamed, almost coming out of the saddle and making his horse shy to the side and rear-up. Regaining control and turning to face Skuli, he said through gritted teeth. "That farm has been in the family for generations. On his deathbed, Pa divided his holdings, which included the farms both sides of Bird Mountain, between Gunnar and me. There's no way I'll let Gunnar's share slip away on some technicality. I'll pay your god-damned taxes or levies or whatever they are! *But you're not taking this farm!"* This said to a chorus from the friends who once again stirred and rattled arms.

"*Ny o ny!*" Skuli shouted, standing firm and holding up his hands. "I hear you and don't blame how you feel. But it's not that simple. Anyway, I'm on your side on this part. It's just that it's not up to me to say. The Thing will decide, and I'm sure they'll be fair. In the meantime, I'll assemble workers to return here and take care of the property and animals until determinations can be made. If you want to assign people to that group, it'll be fine with me."

Gyrth and his companions turned and headed back soon after that. Those up front, the neighbors, rode mostly in numbed silence. Not so in back, though, where the armed part of the group, riding two abreast, couldn't contain the thoughts that whirled.

They were young sons and hands about the age Ingvald had been, somewhat familiar with the arts of war because of training since early ages and subsequent gaming. But most hadn't been in actual combat, so the scene just witnessed had them abuzz, though respectfully in hushed tones.

"We've been told the Norns shape all of our destinies," one said. "But I don't see any sense to what's happened. All those people, even women and children whose fates should have varied in every way, slaughtered because of drunkenness and stupidity."

Another countered. "What's been said doesn't make sense. I've seen Gunnar drunk, but he wasn't a mean drunk; and Vilhjahn wouldn't ever turn and run. This is all so weird it's more like Loki's doing. You never know what's on his mind, or what wild scheme he's into."

A third ahead of the two looked back shaking his head, "I don't think this came from the clouds. Did you take a good look at Skuli? We've been hearing about him for years, but this is the first time I've seen him. He gave me chills."

"Me too."

"This could be work of the scum of the world."

"Ya."

"What do you think will happen at the Thing?"

"Who knows? They won't be able to get together until the ship that sailed away gets back."

"The ship. From what happened, those men don't seem like ordinary crew members. I wonder if that ship went a-viking?"

"Oh ya. That would be something. If so, Gyrth might be in for a lot of wergild."

"Or one hel of a blood feud."

"Ya . . ."

When they got past the cliffs to the lane leading to Gyrth's farm, Einer leaned close and asked, almost mouthing the words, "What do you plan to do?"

"For the moment, I'll just wait and see," Gyrth answered, also speaking softly to conceal his thoughts. "The truth will come out."

"You don't believe what Skuli said then?"

Gyrth forced a slit-eyed smile, then shook his head. "Did you notice how bare the rooms were? Hidden by the mess was the fact that anything of value was gone. Cabinets and storage areas were ransacked, and specific things were missing, like Gunnar's cart and its team of horses. I know because I'm just as familiar with his farm as my own. Ny, there's a lot rotten here, and it's not just the reeking ashes. The men who did this to Gunnar and his family weren't like us . . . good friends and farmhands. They were pirates . . . cruel, unconscionable pirates. And Skuli is a conniving, cheating, lying bastard."

Chapter 2
SIGURTH
982 - 985

Sigurth saw them coming and dodged out of view, grabbing Trulsi and dragging him along. Then he moved to a cluster of bushes where he'd often hidden, just one of the many places he'd used. The boys who passed were older and had been his nemeses since he'd been brought to this farm, or at least it seemed so in his mind. They rambled past the cookhouse nearby, jostling each other as they did, and disappeared into the barn across the yard.

"*Na na na na nyah na,*" Sigurth muttered, sticking out his tongue. He released his grip, and Trulsi, who'd obediently frozen as if understanding something important was about, shimmied, shook his tail and looked eagerly eye-to-eye for the next clue to what was happening. In response Sigurth ruffled his neck, squeezing him and rubbing noses. Actually, the boys had only been a nuisance. What *was* weighing on his mind was that it was that time of the year again. Temperatures had fallen with a dampness that chilled, and the chill meant several things. It meant clouds would blot out the sky and bring winds and snow—one of the reminders that bothered him.

The weather, by itself, would usually cause only a mild haunting, a haunting that could be shrugged and forgotten, but then there was the voice, another reminder—a loud, booming voice that shouted orders with an authority that always had people scrambling. He knew who it was from. It was from jarl Skuli Thorbergsson, the owner of the farm. Skuli was of average height, but otherwise large and powerfully built with a barrel chest and prominent black beard. Among his peers he was known as Skuli Blackbeard, but in the privacy of the craft-shop where he now lived, his foster-parents, Orm and Thora, referred to him in whispers as Skuli Blackheart.

Sigurth lifted a bit and parted the branches, ever so carefully, to see what goings on were about this time. The first thing to catch his eye was the longhouse, which he maintained a curiosity about because it was the largest building he'd ever seen. The others he'd known were only faint recollections, and were different in more ways than size. For one thing, the longhouse here stood by itself, having only a few jut-outs to complete its shape; while in his recollections, comparable but smaller longhouses were linked to an assortment of other buildings. Another difference was that here, the longhouse was near the center of a large yard, separated from but surrounded by many others, like a cookhouse, and storage buildings, bunkhouses, and byres, barns, pens and corrals, all of them likewise large. With all of these and their functions, there was considerable traffic at certain times of the day.

Most of the buildings were scattered along the eastern and southern sides of the complex. A few others, such as the craft-shop, were north of the longhouse along the edge of a forest. The forest extended in that direction to a cove in the fjord a half-hours walk away where a marina was located.

The bush Sigurth was in wasn't the best of his hiding places, being too close to the normal workings of the farm; but it was a good vantage point from which to see what was happening. And on this day, with more going on than normal and with frequent bellows from *that* voice, the day already had two reminders.

The reminders were parts of a memory that kept repeating. A memory of happenings that would wake him screaming in the night, causing Thora to take him in her arms and calm him down. During the day, however, these reminders were only shadows of that memory, parts of something that happened; and because they were, they portended that the awful could happen again. There were several of these—oncoming winter, parties and certain voices—which meant that the more that were at one time, the more it affected him.

As the afternoon dragged on and Sigurth watched, other people arrived, some on horseback, some in horse-drawn wagons, and some walking. With each arrival, Skuli was out to greet them; and with some of the groups, there were voices that made him wince.

With an obvious party now taking shape, there were more reminders than he'd ever sensed at one time before, and he was definitely uncomfortable.

Three years before it had been a day like this one, grey and cold, with gusting winds that indicated a winter was on its way. There was also a party, with drinking and singing and laughing and foolery. He'd fallen asleep as the party wore on, but had wakened to something else—shouting and cursing and screaming. He remembered a hiding place and Ma and his sisters, and a dreadful silence as the door opened. He was tied and masked, then subjected to a long, bumping, freezing ride, alongside Rogna and Solveig, who were no comfort to him as they were crying too.

When the ride was over, he was turned over to a couple on a strange farm, who took him in with a warmth and tenderness that contrasted completely with what had just happened. The new parents couldn't have been more different from the one he'd known. Whereas what he could remember of "Pa" was a large and gruff person who walked with a stomp that reflected strength, the new man in the new home was short and lean and walked with a slight limp, a limp that Sigurth heard years later was caused by a childhood disease. As for the person he'd clung to as "Ma," the new woman was taller but softer spoken. All of this was incomprehensible to him, made even more so when in time he realized neither his sisters nor any who had been his family were around any longer.

Then there was winter with snow that piled, temperatures that froze and winds that whirled, all of which, being so, was a sameness that seemed to soothe him from what had happened. Those conditions also kept the people living in the shop inside most of the day, which gave Sigurth as excuse to withdraw from seeing anybody other than those he'd gotten to know.

With all the activities there, the shop turned out to be a fascinating place, especially for a youngster who was not only curious, but also needful of something to take his mind off a horror he couldn't comprehend. Among the interests were weaving and sewing which his new foster-mother Thora directed.

For weaving, two looms were leaned against the wall in part of the work space. Each loom consisted of uprights holding a horizontal top beam from which weighted warps were hung; additional horizontal, movable heddle-rods fitted into brackets on the uprights. With this simple loom, a device almost ageless in its history, work was conducted, while standing, until a fabric panel was completed. The panels, in a variety of fabrics and patterns, were then used to sew an assortment of garments and furnishings.

Several young girls assisted Thora as apprentices. One of their chores was spinning, which was working wool or flax strands onto a distaff wheel, and forming threads that could be wound into skeins ready for weaving.

The work was busy, and in its way entertaining, but it was more the chatter that came to delight the quiet but attentive Sigurth. Having such an audience, the girls soon adopted him and used him in parts of their banter. One time when Thora was behind a partition in another area talking to Orm, the girls started a whispered chant, eyeing Sigurth and speaking with witchlike words and gestures, all the while pretending to work at one of the looms . . .

> *Blood runs*
> *From the cloudy web*
> *On the broad loom*
> *Of slaughter. (hisses)*
> *The web of man,*
> *Grey as armour,*
> *Is now being woven;*
> *The Valkyries*
> *Will cross it*
> *With a crimson weft. (hand gestures and evil faces)*
> *The warp is made*
> *Of human entrails;*
> *Human heads*
> *Are used as weights;*
> *The heddle-rods*
> *Are blood-red spears;*
> *The shafts are iron-bound,*
> *And arrows are the shuttle,*
> *With sword we will weave*
> *This web of battle.*

When the girls ended the song and cackled, Thora heard it and returned. She figured out what happened and gave the girls a head-full, but then they all laughed when they saw how Sigurth giggled and clapped his hands.

As entertaining as the work in the weaving area was, it was that in the other part of the building that Sigurth favored. Here Orm worked at woodcarving. With an assortment of axes, adzes, awls, chisels, scrapers, files, augers, saws and knives, he turned rough lumber into works of art.

Among them that first winter was a large dragon head. On a rough assembly of several pieces, he marked out design intents, then methodically carved, transforming the mass of little consequence into an ornately hideous design. While this work was in progress, Sigurth sat quietly, mesmerized by the magic he was watching. He focused on Orm and his features, the hair swept back and tied in a bun, the narrow face and oversized, sharp nose, the eyes that were fixed in concentration, and always the gentle explanations to a curious mind. Orm explained that the finished carving would be placed on the leading end of a keel on a ship being built, becoming the ship's identifying symbol.

Many other projects caught his interest, especially the toys Orm made for him, such as a short, blunt-edged sword, a small round shield and a small bow and arrow set, all of wood. These were the first toys he could remember, and they gave him mostly the ability to become a nuisance. However joyful these were, the most entertaining of all was watching Orm work and create his magic, which at times inspired Sigurth to chip away and create a mess.

Work each day started and ended at times that didn't relate to the light or darkness outside the walls. This was especially true in winter when only about a third of the so-called day was with daylight. Further, since there was only a main entrance door, a smoke hole in the roof over the central fire-pit, and a few vent panels but no real windows in the walls, interior lighting was in proportion to the number of candles in use, none of which related to what was outside. At some roughly defined point, however, work each day did stop, making time for eating and relaxing. During the latter there was story telling, which included fables of the Gods and legendary heroes, romantic tales and scary mysteries; there were also hnefatafl and kvatrutafl, games with boards and play pieces, with which to while away the hours.

Then there was spring and the first meaningful amount of time outside in months, and the first reminder. It was the deep, loud, commanding voice of the man who'd brought him here, and he'd recoiled when he heard it . . . and both Thora and Orm seemed to understand. This was also his first encounter with other boys on the farm. Like boys everywhere they were energized by warmer weather, melting snow and snowballs, which meant Sigurth was on the losing end whenever their paths crossed. Because of this he begged to tag along with Orm when in the spring he went to work at the cove, even though it meant a long walk along the edge of the forest.

The first assignment for Orm that spring was to help with the ships placed in winter storage. All of them needed to be moved from their sheds, serviced and launched, all efforts that required a number of men. And when men get together there was conversation and joking and fun, which created an atmosphere Sigurth loved. Watching the men and getting to know them brought him partly out of his shell, so much so that he tried to help, bringing praise and thanks from the men even though he was mostly in the way.

It wasn't long before all boats were in the water, docked and ready to move out, and it was also a time to go into hiding. This was because other groups arrived, seemingly out of nowhere, and began to load up and take their places on board. This would have been interesting, but unfortunately there were those voices, not only that loud voice of command, but also others among the sailors that were reminders . . . and so he hid.

The ships soon put to sea and took with them those voices, and with that came a new adventure—Orm and the men were starting to build a ship. This work was such that having a small boy around to look after wasn't good; so once it started, Sigurth was left to spend the summer at the shop.

At the shop most work was now outside, which everyone preferred after the long winter indoors. For Sigurth, being outside was unnerving, mainly because of the occasional reminders, so he drifted towards becoming invisible. That meant he stayed away from the busy side of the longhouse and instead ranged about in the woods on the quiet side, soon having every bush and hiding place fixed in mind.

It so happened that at the jut-out at the northeast corner of the longhouse, the side in view from the shop, that near the inner corner a small tree had sprouted. Being ignored because it was in the low traffic side, the tree had grown and attracted bushes and weeds. The corner also attracted a badger who picked this spot to dig a hole and start a family. This was a bad choice, because a few boys, the same ones Sigurth avoided, spotted the tailings extending from the weeds and went to war on the helpless animal. While Sigurth watched in hiding nearby, the boys, whooping all the while, brought a harpoon-like spear into play, snagging not only the badger, but also its little pups.

The incident would have been forgotten, except that there was a party. This was the first Sigurth was to witness; but from conversations he overheard between Orm and Thora, the party wasn't unusual because "Blackheart" loved them. On this occasion, two things came to mind. One was that among the voices that made him seek hiding was another that evoked pleasant memories. He couldn't make a definite connection to the voice, but it was a warm one, like from someone who'd held and squeezed him and made him laugh. The other was that where the badger hole was nestled was not only a perfect hiding place, it was also a place that might enable him to hear more of what happened in the longhouse, a curiosity that grew and grew.

The next day, when all was clear, he crept into the corner, at first only sitting against the wall behind the bushes. Then, feeling securely out of sight but bored, he mulled over what to do next. He eased his hand into the badger hole, inching down, down, until he'd reached the end, which was the length of his arm. What he learned was that the hole arched down, then back up to an expanded area. He shrugged and sat back against the corner.

By being in so close, he could touch and feel what he'd come to recognize, that construction of the longhouse was similar to impressions he had of others in memory, with tree-trunk timbers forming a network of framing for both walls and roof, and that between the wall posts, rough vertical boards completed the buildings enclosure. Not really knowing what to do, Sigurth started to dig at the wall at the first space between columns from the corner, dumping tailings into the badger hole. After excavating a sizable hole, he sat back. From the dig he could see that the trunks rested on a row of large, flat boulders; then at about ground level there was a horizontal spar to which the siding was anchored. There was a gap of dirt between them.

His eyes widened as possibilities came to mind.

He dug with such fervor that he had to force himself to stop and look up occasionally to make sure he wasn't attracting attention. He enlarged the initial hole, then tore at the gap, creating a tunnel into which his head, arms and body were able to penetrate beyond the siding, and therefore under the inside of the building. He was enlarging the space all around him when it happened—the soil above the tunnel collapsed.

It was terrifying. It felt like he was suffocating, but with a frantic effort he broke free, tearing his tunic and banging his head on the spar as he wiggled out. Sputtering dirt and clearing his eyes, he covered his face with his arms to keep from crying. He lay back, stifling tears until his hiccuping-like convulsions subsided. Then he sat up and thought *What now?*

What now turned into filling most of the pit, then covering it with sticks and leaves in a poor, hurried attempt to conceal what he'd done. Still shaking, he moved to get out of the corner, spreading the bushes first to make sure the way was clear. When safely in the woods, he dusted and cleaned as best he could, and didn't return to the shop until dark so his condition didn't draw attention.

And that was it for tunneling.

The second winter was much like the first. If there was a difference, it was that Sigurth became closer to Orm, who shared with him more of the work he was doing, allowing him to use his tools and guiding him along the way. When spring arrived, Sigurth was allowed to follow him to the cove again; but this time to stay, because there was another boat to build and now there might be ways he could really help.

As before there were over a dozen men, including Orm, in an operation that began on a flat section of ground near the waters edge. While Sigurth sat and watched, the group split into teams, and like bees on a honeycomb, scurried about in what appeared to be complete confusion.

It was far from it.

Some of the men took to a large stack of tree-trunks nearby, approximately fifteen of them if Sigurth had been able to count, and began to trim and debark individual members. Most logs were large and long, requiring a coordinated effort with levers and rollers and braces to move them about and work them. Another team concentrated on the assembly site, setting blocks at intervals from the water, then leveling and aligning them in preparation for the first of ship components—the keel.

These initial operations didn't seem to accomplish much, at least in Sigurth's mind. He didn't understand that in the beginning logs had to be reviewed and selected for special purposes. After this, workers began the more demanding work. One large, straight log, deemed best for the keel, was moved in position and braced. With axes, sledges and wedges the men sectioned the log, splitting it several times until a rough but suitable working timber was formed. With that timber secured and set in place, they switched to shaping tools, mainly axes and adzes, and the chips flew as they worked. Other teams selected logs and, with similar procedures, began to address the multitude of shapes required.

Finally, after a seeming endless and pointless busyness, they put the first member, the all important keel, on the blocks and secured it in place. Then they added other pieces—the first of the rib and crossbeam assemblies—and the visual evidence of progress accelerated. Day after day, men dropped members into place until a skeleton-like frame affirmed the extent and proportion of what the ship would be.

Long before this point, Sigurth felt he had to be involved. He saw that with all the workers doing their thing, chips and waste piled up around members being worked; then he remembered how during the winter, Thora swept and cleaned around Orm as he chipped away. So he did the same here, scampering about and at times getting in the way again, but in most cases being appreciated for what he was doing.

It happened there was another way he could help. The workmen needed sharp tools, so every now and then they'd stop and hone, an aggravating necessity that was also time consuming. Orm noticed how Sigurth seemed obsessed with everything going on, and had a thought regarding this part of it. At the end of the day he took a few tools home and started sharpening. As expected, Sigurth moved in to watch.

"Do you think you could do this?" Orm asked.

The boy's eyes sparkled.

After Sigurth's many tries and much coaching, Orm sat back and smiled.

The next day Orm held his adze up to one of the others and asked, "What do you think of the edge on this one?"

The man ran his fingers over it, then nodded. "Not bad. You do good work."

"Oh, I didn't do this. Sigurth did it for me last night. That kid just amazes me with what he can do once he sets his mind to it," he said as he walked away.

Before the day was over, and each day thereafter, Sigurth had all the sweeping and sharpening he could handle.

Coincident with the placement of the hull-shaping ribs was the work of forming and anchoring planks, or strakes as some called them, which were to comprise the sides of the ship. As with all other wood members, workers first split the plank from a log in phases until a double thickness of uniform width was reached. Then, with adzes and chisels, they reduced the thickness to only about that of a thumb so a cleat, an integral part of the double thickness, could be formed on the inside surface. These cleats were for tying to the hull-forming ribs. When properly shaped, which was a challenge requiring great skill, they set each plank over oakum, then riveted it to the plank below it, tying the cleats on the inner side to ribs at uniform intervals along the length of the ship.

After completing work on the basic hull, the men continued with the shaping and installation of cross beams, floor planks, the gunwale or meginhelfr, keelsons, knees and top rails. This led them to final operations, which included the mast block and mast, oars and stack frames, cleats and ties, ropes, and the sail.

Now ready for a test run, they removed stays and blocks and eased the ship into water. During the run they marked leaks and adjusted rigging, then returned the ship to the blocks for final tweaking.

Finally the work was over, a grand new vessel for a thousand oceangoing possibilities. What Sigurth didn't know was that this particular boat was a special order, and because it was so, it meant a ceremony.

For the ceremony a crowd gathered—a few from the farm Sigurth had seen before, a number he hadn't, another thirty or so who'd be recognized as the crew, and of course, "Blackheart." The key figure, however, was none of these. He was an ornately bedecked man who walked with a presence that shouted of importance, and an entourage around him confirming the impression. There were grand statements by the key figure, horn-filled drinks in abundance, prayers and thanks to the Gods, and stuff like that which Sigurth hardly heard because he moved into hiding with all the reminders bouncing around. When the ceremony was over, most of those who had gathered turned to walk back to the longhouse where a party would extend into the evening.

The builders of the boat chose not to join in with that party; instead they lingered about the marina with drinks and joking insults and praise about what had happened over the past few months. By this time Sigurth, who had to be dragged from behind a stack of trash, was a part of the group. He was given a sip of grog which resulted in a contorted face and "yuck."

Sigurth asked, "Who was that man with the fancy jacket?"

"Why that was our great King Hakon, boy," one of the men answered. "If you get yourself screwed up enough, someday you can be like him."

Everybody laughed, but Sigurth didn't understand. Nor did he with what another said, "We'd better break up and get home. We need to be hiding our women folk and maybe our sheep too. That bastard with the fancy jacket has as much of a roving eye as anyone that's ever been, and that's a lot."

Soon thereafter the group did break up, but not before the men presented Sigurth with a gift. They handed him a basket, and in it squirmed a newborn puppy.

The third winter was different in many ways. Now a little older, Sigurth was less content to be a shut-in even though goings-on with Thora and Orm, and also the girls who assisted, were rarely boring. But now he had an urge to play games in the snow and ski the slopes to the fjord, even if it meant mixing it up with the other boys. The biggest difference, however, was Trulsi, the puppy, who was always at the door to greet him with tail wagging, eyes flashing and body twisting in circles. They played together and slept together, and when Sigurth was busy, the dog lay by his side.

When summer came, the puppy, growing quickly, became a companion outside as well, following Sigurth to the cove when work resumed. This summer was much like the one before—a new ship was completed and tested and added to the fleet the district was building. During this time Sigurth was busier than ever, doing all he'd done before, and even getting involved in some of the painstaking shaping of wood members.

When the weather cooled, work at the cove was over.

Sigurth continued to survey the farmyard and the growing number of arrivals to the party. While doing this, however, there was a distraction because he kept looking at that damned corner. He'd been ignoring it for years because he was afraid of it—according to a vague memory, the tunnel there had almost killed him. Now he began to think of it in a different way.

What had collapsed? Why had it collapsed? Did the part that fell on him open the tunnel to the interior of the longhouse, from where he could hear what was happening?

With his work over the past two summers he'd also learned to curse.

He cursed.

Sigurth returned to the shop just after sunset, but only long enough to leave Trulsi. He headed back to the woods, eventually crossing to the corner when he could see the way was clear. It didn't take long to scramble the cover, re-dig the pit and remove what had caved in, the digging bringing the incident vividly back to life. Ever so carefully, he wiggled back in, reaching above as he did to see what more there might be to come crashing down.

Only there wasn't anything.

He gulped and took a deep breath, then scooched in a bit further. He turned and reached higher, and when he did, he hit wood planking. By feeling around and digging out more, he was able to determine there was open space all around where he now sat, at least to where other framing blocked the way.

In the dim vestiges of light, he at first didn't understand. Then he remembered. In the shop there were raised platforms along the walls, with a central floor at ground level in between. As that came to mind, there was an image of a place in memory something like that and he'd slept there.

Could he be below such a raised platform?

His thinking was interrupted by the sounds from above that were beginning to intensify . . . and that scared him. So he wiggled back out just to make sure he could. There being no problem in doing this, he looked around. Everything about him in the corner was also fine as he was well hidden by the bushes; but if he wanted to return to the woods, it wasn't a good time. It wasn't a good time because there was heavy traffic, mainly by servant girls, with things being carried back and forth under torchlight between the service door on the other side of the longhouse to the cookhouse, the closest building on the east side.

The smell from the food being carried hit him and he wished he'd stayed at the shop long enough to eat. He even thought of running into one of the girls, grabbing whatever she was carrying and bolting to the safety of the woods; but then there was a roar of laughter from within the longhouse and he forgot about it.

Back in the tunnel, the noise from above became an ebb and flow of continuous revelry. There was shouting and laughter, and though Sigurth could rarely put more than a few words together, he got the impression that some were toasts, and others were insults as part of a game he didn't understand. Most constant of all the sounds were those of drinking and feasting and moving around, with footfalls thumping on the planks a foot above where he sat. In one of those instances, a knot fell out of a plank and bopped him on the head. This brought sounds clearer than before; but when he stretched to see what he could, there was little to be gained.

He didn't know when, but at some point he fell asleep; and most likely would have slept the night except that someone fell with a loud crash almost directly above him, jolting him awake. The crash was followed by curses and laughter, which soon died back to murmurs, meaning to Sigurth that the party, like the one vaguely in memory, was coming to an end.

It was also long past a time to go home. With his fascination with what was happening, he'd forgotten that Orm and Thora might be concerned with his absence. So he slithered out again, dusted off, and even though it was now in the wee hours, he parted the bushes to see if the way was clear.

What he saw brought him to his knees.

The woods were moving, and at first he couldn't tell how or why. As he watched, eyes bugged, the movements coalesced and became men, men creeping out of the woods carrying things. Then the silence of what was happening was broken by shouts from the other side of the longhouse, the front and entry side, and while movements before him increased, so did sounds from that front—shouts and thuds and steel on steel and cries of pain.

It was if the horror foretold by the reminders had returned!

A fire was started at the edge of the woods drawing the men in about it. Before he could understand what was happening, the men separated, making waves of bouncing fires, fires that only lingered a moment, then flew through the air onto the thatched roof of the longhouse. While this dazzling show was unfolding, other ghost shapes carried bales of burning hay and stuffed them under the eaves.

Sigurth gasped as one of the shapes headed toward the corner where he hid. Squealing like a trapped animal, he jumped back into the pit and then the tunnel, just as men broke through the bushes to wedge a burning bale under the eave in the corner where he'd been.

Sigurth struggled to breath, but that was just nerves, because soon, when he realized he was really okay, he was able to relax. He tried to piece together what was happening. From the opening to where he sat, he saw flashes of light and heard shouts from the men he knew to be circling outside. From the planking above, he heard different kinds of sounds. There had been quiet, drunken mumbles moments before; now there were rising and strained sounds, as in that awful memory. Like before, the most prominent voice was that of Skuli Blackheart, who bellowed orders again. Only this time his orders had a different sound . . . they reflected fear and uncertainty. Other voices joined in what became a babble of curses and shrieks, and among them were others Sigurth recognized.

These sounds grew into a roar, which was worsened when something heavy crashed onto the platform near where Sigurth huddled, scattering shards of planking and smoldering debris. Sigurth also screamed—a reaction lost in the din. He curled into a heap of helplessness as there didn't appear to be any options. It got worse. He'd hardly noticed the fire while he huddled where he was, because a gush of cool air, like from a bellows, rushed through the gap to feed what was happening above him. But that was momentary, because soon he did feel it, the heat, and it grew.

Sometime before he'd felt he wasn't a child anymore. He was only five, but already he'd been able to work with men, not only to sweep and clean, but also to sharpen tools and use them, making cuts and shaping surfaces that were useful parts of intricate work. Now he could only wail.

A hand came through the opening and grabbed his leg. He shrieked and fought back, pounding with his little fists.

"Sigurth, stop! It's me, Orm . . . You've got to come out! Now!"

Sigurth relaxed enough to allow himself to be pulled through, and then he was in Orm's arms being carried through a gauntlet of smoke and fire and moving men.

Orm had stepped outside earlier, concerned by Sigurth's absence, but had held back when he realized something sinister was in the making. Then he'd seen the killings and guessed what it was. When he could wait no longer, he'd ventured out and passed without harm, initially because the attackers saw he was a small unarmed man, and then because he was rescuing a terrified, sobbing boy.

When they were away from the longhouse and almost to the woods, Sigurth wiped away his tears and turned to look at what was happening. His jaw dropped . . . The longhouse, the largest building he'd ever known, was aflame from one end to the other, with many fires on the roof, and others at the eaves growing to meet them.

They moved along the woods, staying far enough back to avoid any involvement. When they got to a point past the shop where they could see the entrance side of the building, they stopped, Orm dropping Sigurth to the ground but holding his hand. They saw that the entrance was blocked with logs wedged in place, and that bodies were stacked a short ways away. The bodies were of guards who'd been on duty while Skuli and his merrymakers had been celebrating.

While they watched, the fire grew, as did the sounds from within the longhouse; but those sounds were anything about making merry. The sounds were of people making efforts to break out any way they could, attempts that were hopeless because at the main entry, as well as along the perimeter, armed men stood by to stab and slash at any body part that appeared.

In time there were no more attempts, and the screams faded into the growing roar of the fire. Flames grew into a single, angry boil reaching high into the night sky, not only illuminating the area, but also driving everyone back. There they stayed, the attackers who were now spectators, as well as the farmhands and assorted laborers who were not targeted and who'd spilled out of the buildings along the far side of the yard. They watched as bit by bit, parts of the longhouse roof crumbled and fell into the central cauldron, with the last including sections of framing, some of which leaned into each other, leaving contorted remnants of what had been there. When the fire abated to a point where the ruins could be approached, men took to the bodies that had been piled. Working in teams, each body was picked up by its arms and legs, and in a series of swings to gain momentum, was hurled into the cauldron.

The spectacle was eventually over, with only the entry door, which projected outward enough to miss the most intense fire, and assorted bits of framing, still identifiable. The onlookers, transfixed through the burning, now began to move about, generally with an uncertainty as to what was going to happen next.

Orm didn't wait to find out. He took Sigurth by the hand and rounded what was left of the longhouse, threading his way back to the shop. Thora was outside waiting for them, holding on to Trulsi, who became hard to contain when Sigurth came into view.

She said, "We'll be having company tonight."

"Company?"

"Yes. A man was by earlier. His name was Gyrth Torkelsson. He said he and his men would be staying overnight on the farm and resting. Our shop was one of the places they'd be using. Shouldn't be for long though, the man said."

Orm shrugged, "I don't think we're in a position to argue. Let's get some rest ourselves. Looks to me that whoever they are accomplished what they set out to do, and that the fighting is over."

Orm, Thora, and Sigurth hadn't been inside long, certainly not long enough to shake off what had happened and get to sleep, when the door opened and a dozen men filed in. The men were dirty and tired, and a few were bandaged and in pain. For most of them, tired prevailed, and with little recognition to their hosts, picked a spot on the platform, circled like dogs getting comfortable in grass, and went to sleep. Two of them, however, even though thoroughly wrung, introduced themselves and sat back to talk.

"Are you the leader?" Orm asked.

Gyrth nodded.

"And Sven here is your nephew, you say?"

The question had hardly been asked when a sound turned them to where Sigurth had bundled, for he'd gotten to his feet and stood wide-eyed.

"And this is your son?" Gyrth asked, pointing at Sigurth.

Orm hesitated, then shook his head. "Sir, I know who you are now, and know why you're here. Let me explain. I'm a finish carpenter and boat builder, and Thora, my wife, is a weaver and seamstress. We've been here for several years, and have been mostly content with that. We *had* a son, about his age," he said, pointing to Sigurth, "But three years ago he got the ails and died. As you can imagine, we were devastated.

"Well, soon after that, Skuli went on one of his forays. We didn't know where or for what at the time, but as you know, the truth eventually works its way out. When Skuli returned, he had several youngsters covered and trussed. One was Sigurth here. You see, Thora had been a favorite of Skuli's ever since she'd made him a beautiful coat, and he rewarded her for doing so by replacing our loss."

Gyrth looked at Sven, who'd yawned and laid down, trying to get comfortable and out of the conversation. But he revived and looked at Orm, taking a moment to absorb what had been said. Then he sat up, sputtering, *"Sigurth? Did you say his name is Sigurth?"*

Sven stood and moved to where the boy was standing. "Could you be my brother? I thought my brother was dead. Let's have a good look at you, boy." He moved Sigurth to one of the candles and held him at arm's length. *"Ya, ya! I see Pa all over you! By the Gods, you are you!"* giving him a hug.

Sigurth remained standing, stiff as a board.

Gyrth noted the reaction and would have moved forward for a closer look, but then another thought came to mind. He said, "Orm, you said there were several people trussed, one of whom was the boy here. Who were the others?"

"Two young girls, maybe eight or ten years old."

Sven gasped. "They must have been Rogna and Solveig, my sisters. Were they spared too? What happened to them?"

Orm shook his head, "Don't know for sure. But Skuli had his hand in many pots besides farming. One was boat-building, which I'm involved with. One was piracy. He has sponsored several boats, which you probably knew. Another was trade—all kinds, particularly slave trade. Young, blond girls are always in demand far to the south. Agents from there, Moors I think, come through here every now and then. I'm sorry to say that's most likely where they ended."

Sven looked back at Gyrth, both of them openmouthed.

"That's all I know," Orm said. "While I can guess why you did what you did tonight, there's a lot I don't understand. For instance, the talk from one who'd been on that foray of Skuli's, was that everyone, except the three they'd brought back, had been killed so there'd be no witnesses. Now there's Sven here from that family and very much alive. There's more that doesn't fit. Gyrth, you were here a year or so ago at one of Skuli's parties, weren't you?"

The two looked at each other a while, then Gyrth smiled.

"Okay. But that meant you and Skuli were on good terms, which doesn't make sense with what happened tonight."

"I'm sure it doesn't," Gyrth said after a pause to collect his thoughts. Then he told about his brother Gunnar and the tax problem; about the plan to accompany him in to settle the debt; and about meeting Skuli at the farm the day after the massacre. "I was back home at Bird Mountain the day after the meeting, and was pacing the floor with a combination of grief and anger, when guess who walks in?"

"It was me," Sven said, still holding Sigurth. "For a reason I really didn't understand, Pa decided to have a party after work that awful day, and we did. During the party, I'd had more to drink than ever before, and it got to me. After trying to sleep it off, which didn't work, I went outside and puked somewhere in the corral. Then I walked out into the pasture to sober up, and that's where I was when all hel broke loose. I was so far away I didn't realize at first what was happening; but then with riders holding torches circling the compound, and screams and merciless killings of people I knew, including Ma, it got through to me.

"I stayed in hiding the rest of the night and all the next day, and got sick all over again with what else I witnessed, like one of the attackers laughing and holding Pa's head up on the tip of his spear. Then the day after, when Uncle Gyrth and his group came along, I almost came out to warn them and tell what happened. But Skuli and his cutthroats were still there, so I held back, being afraid that doing so might lead to more killing. Anyway, I stayed in hiding until dark, leaving by way of the back trail over the mountain."

"You can guess what happened after that," Gyrth said. "When he told me the truth, it verified what I'd said earlier about Skuli—that he was a dirty, rotten liar.

"The first thing I did was to send Sven out of the area to relatives way, way up north near Naumu Dale; because if Skuli knew he was alive and a witness, there'd be only one alternative, and that would be a war I'd lose. So I hid him and began planning, which wasn't easy because not only were there many to settle with, there was also the fact I was unprepared. It took time to do all that needed doing, and yes, I was here, acting like a contrite and obedient servant and even hugging the bastard, as part of the planning."

"But there were many people burned tonight," Orm said. "Not all were a part of what happened to your brother's family and farm. Horrible as that was, there were little over a dozen people involved. In contrast, there had to be four times that in the longhouse tonight."

"That's true. However, many of them were pirates with a history that'll curdle your imagination."

"Sure. But there were also important farmers. This end of the district will be a mess, meaning that many from those families, including Earl Hakon, who was a good friend of Skuli's, will be after your hide."

Gyrth nodded. "That's also true; but the mess is not for me to work out. It will be the Thing's, and they will certainly meet. With regards to that, I've got many friends, while Skuli, who was ruthless in his dealings, had many enemies. When all the evidence is in, I think we'll be able to settle with the families okay, and if I can assure the King he'll still get out of the district what he wants, he'll most likely let it slide too."

He turned to Sigurth. "Are you able to follow any of this?"

Sigurth only mumbled, his eyes first bouncing between Sven and Gyrth, then looking at his foster-parents for direction.

"Do you remember your cousin Sveyin, Sigurth?" Gyrth asked. "You and he loved to play together. He's going to be doing handsprings when he finds out you're alive and back home."

"Sveyin?" Sigurth mumbled. Then he smiled.

It was a special moment, and would have lingered; but there was a sound . . . Thora had retreated to the far corner and was weeping.

Gryth sat back, looked around and took a deep breath. "It's very late," not a particularly brilliant remark, but one giving him time to think. "Orm, the men that aren't on watch right now are billeted in buildings around the yard. Tomorrow, after everyone's rested and patched, all of us will need a good meal before returning. Can you help us with that?"

"Certainly. There should be a lot on hand in the cookhouse. If not, the pen's are full of animals, with at this point no-one owning them."

"Good.

"Oh . . . One thing more. Sven, of course, will be returning to his farm at Bird Mountain and taking over. I know he'll be shorthanded. Would you and Thora be interested in coming back with us and helping him out?"

Chapter 3

DANAVIRKI
988

"That's a ship!" Sveyin said, jumping to his feet. He pointed as the speck moving through the mist in the distance took shape. After focusing on it, he saw it was moving toward the fjord north of them.

Sigurth, who'd almost fallen asleep during the boring watch, jerked up and scrambled to where Sveyin was standing, sending a slough of pebbles cascading off the edge of the cliff. Skidding to a halt, he cupped his hands over his eyes and squinted, then said, "Ya sure . . . I see it too."

As they watched, the ship cleared the mists hanging offshore. Doing so, it took on more detail, although still in silhouette, of a distinctive leading edge and sail. This not only had the two of them hopping, but also had Trulsi spinning and trying to understand what this was about.

"They've *got* to be on this one," Sveyin said as he bounded over to the fire-pit on the crest. "Pa said after the last ship arrived there was only one yet to return." He bent over the small burn-pile, made quick strikes on a flint, and continued until sparks flew and the handful of tinder in the pyramid of sticks took the bait. A few puffs later and there was fire. When the fire was well along, the boys dumped green leaves and weeds over it, resulting in a white plume rising high in the afternoon sky before scattering with the wind.

They maintained the fire longer than 8-year old patience would normally manage, until Sigurth said, "Let's go."

"Ya . . . If anyone hasn't seen the smoke by this time, they're just not looking."

They scrambled over the rocks to the rough trail zigzagging by in a north-south direction across the top of Bird Mountain. There they split, each running home, with Sigurth yelling back, "Wait for me. I'll saddle up and be over as soon as I get down."

What this was about started the year before.

"Pa, *dammit!* I'm going this time."

Gyrth grumbled, got up and went outside. He was definitely in a pickle. Rumors had been flying about, and then they became official when war-arrows were received. The story along with them was that Earl Hakon had made an agreement with the Danes to assist them in a defense against Emperor Otto of Saxland, a large Duchy south of Denmark in the mainland. The Emperor, along with troops from Saxony, Franconia and Frisia, demanded that the Danish King, King Harald, be baptized and adopt the true faith, the one of the White Christ that had been making inroads north for some time, or he would attack and force him to submit.

In order to assist Harald and counter the formidable force Otto commanded, Hakon had to assemble a large fleet of fully complimented ships. This would require a contribution from all districts, a *leidang*, and so the war-arrows went out.

And Gyrth was more than obligated. The destruction of Skuli a few years before had been a shock to everyone in the district. At the Thing organized to review what had happened, the issue had been hotly discussed, with the outcome in doubt from the beginning. In the end, however, he'd won the gamble, sort of, with a generous wergild pledged to survivors of some of the families involved, and of course, an enhanced commitment made to the good King.

Neither of the farms that Gyrth represented had young women to share, which was a Hakon thing; but they did have men. So when the arrows arrived, he had to respond quickly and enthusiastically, and thereby set an example encouraging other farmers throughout the district who might naturally be reluctant to contribute to the leidang.

But he pondered ... *who should he send?*

Hrolf followed him about. "You wouldn't let me go to fight Ragnfroth."

"You were too young."

"Only a few years younger than cousin Ingvald . . . and he went."

"You were too young."

"I wasn't too young when you gathered a group to help Uncle Gunnar, and I wasn't too young when you raided Skuli Thorbergsson and burned him down. Everybody's been talking about that since it happened, and I wasn't there."

"Hrolf," Gyrth said, reluctant to go there because this was a matter ragged and worn-out by previous arguments; and he knew this time he'd lose. He couldn't help but think of Gunnar and how he felt losing Ingvald. Now his oldest son would be at risk.

He finally nodded, saying, "Hrolf, yes it's time. I held you back before because each time someone had to stay and tend the farm, and each time you were the logical person to do that. You were just too valuable. You're still too valuable; but I don't have many choices. It now looks best, that from this farm, you and two of the hands go; and from the other side of the mountain, Orm and another two hands."

Hrolf's face lit up at first, then he frowned. "Orm?"

"Oh yes, Orm. You'll probably be sailing in a boat he built. The trip you'll be making is short by comparison to others that've been made, but it's still in the open sea. Any time you're in the open sea, the most important consideration for all aboard is the ship. So what better person to have along to look after the condition of that ship than Orm?

"Now, the people going will be gathering and sailing out in a matter of days. Get your men together, decide on gear, and conduct as much training as you can in the time that's left. I know you're an excellent archer, and you're probably up on everything else regarding combat, but it wouldn't hurt.

"I'll head over to see Sven and let him know."

By the time they arrived at the landing, Sigurth and Sveyin on horses and Gyrth and family on a wagon, the ship had docked and was mostly unloaded. The group shuffling about on the pier was growing as those remaining on board worked their way down the planks, most glancing to see who were among those gathering on the banks to greet them.

Sveyin recognized Hrolf before he'd cleared the saddle, even though Hrolf's back was turned at the time. Without being able to control himself, he hit the ground running, reaching full speed and jumping, landing on Hrolf with a thud.

Hrolf shrieked and almost fell, buckling in Orm's direction, who was close enough to catch him and hold him up.

"*Ny o ny!*" Orm shouted. "Don't do that. Hrolf's still on the mend."

Sveyin let go at the cry and retreated to the side, his face turning red.

Hrolf straightened, groaning a little; then beamed when he saw who'd clobbered him. "Sveyin, you bugger . . . I might have known."

"You okay, son?' Gyrth said, coming up with the rest and putting a hand on his shoulder.

Hrolf nodded and winked.

"He's been hurt," Orm said. "Most everyone has been one way or the other, and some didn't make it back. But he's doing fine, just no more of that," rubbing Sveyin's head and making fun because he could see Sveyin was on the verge of tears. "Beside being banged up in general, he took an arrow in the side. Missed the vitals though . . . So he was lucky.

"Look, I've got to stay on and make sure the boat is tied-up and tented. Why don't all of you take our travelers home; they can sure use a warm meal and dry bed. Just leave me a horse and I'll follow as soon as I can."

The families didn't get together until two days later when all the men had rested and cleaned and settled back to life at home. For the occasion, Ingabjorg and Thora prepared what would be a feast when compared to the sparse, tasteless fare common during travel at sea. Gyrth also collected a supply of spirited drinks that would normally last a month.

The gathering wasn't intended as a celebration, but it took on the character of one as a battle had been won, sort of, and those who'd returned had returned as heroes with stories to tell. That being so, not only family, but also the hands that could be spared, ended up crowding into the longhouse of the northern farm.

Gyrth took the high-seat, as was appropriate for the host, and those who'd made the expedition were next around him; but other than that, formalities were ignored, and the rest settled in as comfortably as they could. There was a buzz of excitement in the air, assisted more than a little by the horn or two that had quickly been consumed. The buzz continued until Gyrth rapped for attention. "I know our travelers may already be tired of talking about it; but not everyone here has heard the same thing, so please bear with our interests a while longer.

"Orm . . . How about you starting things off."

Orm paused for a moment to collect his thoughts, then said, "The boat, our *Sea Eagle*, worked beautifully; and in all our travels, didn't burden us with problems we couldn't handle. But it wasn't easy. The wind, as you all know, is always a factor; then there are tides and currents, particularly around inlets along the coast that can be so bad they even cause maelstroms; and finally there are skerried shorelines you didn't want to go near. Along the way there were times we had to go to shore. The landings by themselves weren't usually bad, because after days at sea, everyone's ready to get off the ship, get a hot meal and enjoy a good night's sleep under cover. But there was rarely enough good shoreline to take in all the ships wanting to beach. So when all that was available was used up, the ships behind had to edge in and hawser-up, sometimes in multiple combinations, or drop anchor farther offshore. Once on shore it wasn't always what we'd hoped for either. At one place the sand fleas were so bad that most retreated back to their ships where sea-breezes gave some relief.

"Sounds like fun, doesn't it?" He said, then added. "Coordinating with the continuing addition of ships along the coast was also no simple matter. But by the time we left Lithandisness, the farthest point south on our coastline, and crossed to Denmark, we'd done it well enough that there was a truly impressive flotilla moving along. Here again, we had to enforce a discipline of sorts to keep from banging one another. In doing so, we ended with three well spaced lines."

A few more comments about the time aboard ships was about all some of the eager listeners could stand. "What about the battle?" Sigurth said from the far corner.

"*Ya da!*" Sveyin added, swinging a wooden sword in the air. "Tell about the Danathing."

Everyone laughed, because that topic was the one most were waiting for.

Orm sighed. "I guess you don't want to hear how the flotilla made its way down the east side of Jutland, then across the Limfjord all the way past Funan."

"What are you talking about? What's Funan?"

"What's Funan? It's one of the biggest islands in Denmark," Orm said. "Anyway, we went ashore shortly after that, and that's where we met King Harald and his Danish army.

"Now, I could tell all sorts of interesting things about that, and how we managed to survive among the sand dunes; but I guess you're more interested in what happened at the battle. "Hrolf? Ulf? Eirik? You were all in the thick of it. Tell us what happened."

Since all eyes had swung to him first, Hrolf started to speak, although by the look on his face, he wished he were anyplace else. He'd hardly started when he choked, eyes misting, and stopped. After a bit, he managed. "You know, of course, that Erling didn't make it."

"Yes, we know."

"Erling was a good man, a hard worker, my right arm for everything that's got to be done around here. He'd been in that mess with Ragnfroth, and then again at the Skulifarm, and from what's been said about him in those instances, he was a rock among men when things got rough."

"There's no doubt about that," Gyrth said. "No doubt at all."

"Absolutely none," added Sven. "In fact, he reminded me of Vilhjahn ... remember him, Pa's smithy? Well, Vilhjahn was slaughtered along with everybody else in that ambush at our farm, but we later found he'd been like Thor before going down. Erling was like that. He led the attack on the guards at Skulifarm, and those poor bastards never had a chance.

"So a toast to Erling, may he be looking down on us from Valhalla, with a beautiful Valkyrie on each knee, and receiving our salute with the sweetest sweet ever to fill a horn."

"Here, here . . . *skoll!*" And so it went until all horns were drained again.

When the room settled, Hrolf started over. "Hakon gathered all of us on the shore and presented us to King Harald, who spoke with generous compliments, praising and thanking us for stepping forward on such a worthy cause. Hakon said, "The Gods above will calm the waters of all your travels, and bring good fortune in the days ahead for what you do today."

"The speech was impressive and made us feel good in a way; but mostly, we thought it a bunch of bullshit. Regardless, when all the speeches were over, we marched off."

"To where?"

"To a defensive line the Danes had built. Evidently a threat from the south was nothing new, because sometime in the past an earthen wall had been built connecting two fjords, one extending inland from the east, and the other from the west. They called this wall, which was more of a long ridge, the Danavirki. With the recent threat, this line had been strengthened and raised with stone and turf and timbers. In addition, a broad and deep moat, bristling with spikes and impediments, had been dug in front of the wall.

"Hakon held us back behind the wall at first. Then when Emperor Otto assembled for his attack, he sent us in to support the Danes, by units, wherever the need appeared to be greatest. Each unit was essentially a boat load, so we were the *Sea Eagle* company with our own commander. Anyway, we were sent in, along with several other units, and it wasn't until we took positions along the top of the wall that we had a real understanding of what was happening. Believe me, it was scary.

"Behind us all the while, were men on horses riding back and forth shouting orders, and delivering further inspirational messages few could really hear or understand. There were also drums and flags lumped together in sort of a pageantry intended to remind us of the purpose for which we were gathered, and the courage we needed to display. And frankly, we needed all that.

"While this was happening, our eyes bugged because across the moat the damnedest sight we'd ever seen was assembling—a horde that filled the space before us with banners and noise-makers, riders back and forth, and knights in armor that shined with a thousand pulsating sparkles.

"It seemed like this horde moved about on and on forever, but finally the attack began, only it wasn't in a wild charge like a pack of dogs that we'd come to expect. Instead they marched to a point in range and stopped. Then the air was filled with missiles. There were stones from slingers and rock from catapults and lances from large cross-bows and arrows. We'd never seen the likes of the arrows; they filled the sky like locusts.

"When all this started, we went into our shield-wall stance, unable to keep from looking at first, but then closing up and ducking under as all that crap came in. Most of us fared through the slings and arrows pretty well, with only a few getting through. But the heavy stuff was bad, sending men and parts of men and shields and weapons flying in all directions; and hitting the men who rode back and forth behind the line hard as well, particularly the horses. Oh the horses . . . We take care of ours here on the farm and they become like family and are given names; so when you see one of them get hit, and it half comes apart making the most god-awful sounds and thrashing about, it tears you up."

Hrolf let that image sink in before continuing.

"Then we heard horns, and although missiles were still coming in, I couldn't resist peeking over the top to see what that meant. What I saw was that while the bombardment had been going on, light wooden bridges had been carried forward and slid into the moat, in some cases all the way across. Now men were moving forward and starting to cross.

"The command *"Archers"* was screamed all down our lines. And since I was among the archers grouped along the back of the formation, I dropped the shield, stood, and armed. A moment later we heard *"Fire,"* and from my bow and a thousand others, our own cloud rose and fell and did its work. In the next few minutes I emptied several sheaths, and was so busy with it all that I was barely aware of what else was happening around me.

"Then came *"Charge,"* at which time we, we meaning the archers, stopped firing, while the ranks in front exploded with a roar and moved forward with shields and lances set for close quarters.

"I really couldn't make out much of what was happening with all the movement and noise, which was a witches brew of thuds and metal on metal and grunts and shouts and screams. All I knew for sure was that as an archer, I now had to put the bow down, and ready my other weapons so I could be part of a reserve in the event the enemy broke through."

"Ulf, you and Erling were in the front ranks. Tell us what was happening there."

Eyes now turned to the old hand who happened to be finishing another horn, and almost choked when he realized he was now the center of attention. He coughed, wiped the last attempted swallow from his scraggly beard, and thought.

"What was happening?

"What was happening was that everyone around me was up and yelling . . . so I was up and yelling. We charged down the bank and crashed into the bastards like an avalanche of berserkers swinging swords and axes. They, Saxons I think, didn't have much of a chance, at least the first ones. The bridges they'd tried to push across didn't quite reach all the way, so the first ones to make it past our arrows stepped into water and muck to their asses, which meant they were helpless and cut to pieces. But they kept coming, the later ones using bodies of the first wave as the last part of the bridge.

"It's hard to describe. At first there's a semblance of trying to work together with the men on each side of you like we're taught to do. Then things go every which way, and you're hacking and slashing and stabbing and spinning and blocking, and not remembering much of any of it.

"Thinking back, they had the larger force, with knights in shiny armor and fancy colors prancing in the background and being pretty useless; but we had the wall, the high ground and the moat. We lost many good men, though, that's a fact. Their losses, however, were many times more, with only a few momentary breakthroughs to show for it. Eventually they gave up and backed off.

"My understanding is that they tried a few other points along the Danavirki with similar results. We can give credit here to Hakon for this; he stayed on top of what was happening, and shifted forces around to meet every threat. Anyway, before too long, their glorious army disappeared, and word was we'd won."

All of this was received with ear-to-ear grins and jostling as if they'd forgotten what they already knew; so it was a perfect time for passing pitchers and filling horns and clinking in celebration. But the questions continued.

"Hrolf, you were wounded. You haven't told us how that happened."

Hrolf was only halfway into his drink, but since there was no way to set it down without spilling, he look his time and drank the rest.

"*Aaaah.*

"Ulf mentioned breakthroughs. There were some and one was right in front of me. In all the confusion I didn't realize what had happened until suddenly there was a surge climbing my way, and I was in a fight. Like Ulf said, it's hard to describe. The man that got to me was in the colors of a Saxon. He was also muddy and bloody and heaving like a spent horse; but he still had fire in his eyes and was giving it his all. He stopped for a moment, I guess to size me up; then he charged, jabbing and swinging with a sword that was already bloodied. The force of his charge bounced me back a few steps as he was bigger than me; but I got back with a few good swings of my own. He'd just swung in a new charge, his sword crashing on my shield, and I was about to counter again, when I slipped. As I fell, it seemed time slowed as I remember it so well. Anyway, with my sword already in motion and me falling, I completed the swing, slicing into the side of his knee. Then I rolled, intending to get back up, only to hurt big time in my side. I didn't know it, but sometime before I'd been hit; and when I fell, I landed on the nock end of the arrow, which pushed the point through and out the other side. The last I saw of the Saxon, he'd crumbled, blood shooting from his knee, and was rolling back down the slope."

The buzz resumed, with many more questions about details of the battle. Then Orm broke back in. "The story is far from over, for what happened after Danavirki might be of just as much interest.

"I was back on the dunes with the bunch seeing to the ships, when riders arrived telling us what happened and to get ready. Then the companies returned, most straggling, but some strutting their stuff when they came into view. They were really a sorry lot, so much so that a week was spent feeding and cleaning and patching before we were ready to sail out.

"Some died during this time; and for them we built a large pyre. Then all were assembled and the fire started, with fine words and extolments to the Gods for what had been done. Earl Hakon had been grand in this regard, making everyone feel proud."

And skalds would later do their thing

> Not easy was't to enter
> into breastwork by him
> defended, fiercely though the
> foeman stormed against it,
> when with Franks and Frisians
> fared the battle-urger—
> had the roller-steed's rider
> raised a host—from southward.

> Fray most fierce arose, when
> foemen, shield 'gainst shield, clashed.
> Stalwart steerer-of-sea-nags
> stood his ground 'gainst Southrons,
> Promptly the prow-steed rider
> put to flight the Saxons.
> There it was he threw back
> throngs of the assailants.

"Then it was to the ships, where one by one we pushed off, first by oar, and as soon as a wind could be gathered, by sail. We moved, generally single file, as we retraced our way up the Jutland coast; but we got only as far the Limfjord, where conditions caused us to stop and tie up again.

"That's where the damndest thing happened . . . Emperor Otto struck again."

"Emperor Otto?"

"Yes."

"You said he was beaten."

"He was," Orm said. "At least by us at the Danavirki. But it seems he regrouped, crossed the western fjord to outflank the defenses, and marched up the coast. King Harald and his Danes tried to stop him, an effort that didn't work at all. Harald retreated to the island of Marsey in the western side of the Limfjord, where he holed up, sending messages to Hakon for help.

"Hakon, who was ashore with the rest of us, responded, and with several companies, hurried overland to Marsey. When he got there, however, he found that not only was the fight over, but that Harald and his army had surrendered and been baptized."

"Baptized? You mean we won the battle, but lost the war anyway?"

"Sorta."

"What do you mean sorta?"

"Well, Hakon was in a pickle. In order to save his skin, and that of those who'd accompanied him, all of them had to submit to baptism. Hakon also had to agree to convert his subjects, meaning all of Norway, to the new faith. Toward that end he was given a number of priests and learned men, who would accompany him back to insure that the converting was properly done."

A pin drop could have been heard in the next few moments.

Orm laughed. "Not to worry. When a breeze picked up, we all cast off again. But before getting underway, Hakon dumped the priests and clerics and learned men with their crosses and sacred books into the shallows and made them wade ashore."

The room went abuzz again, with a sigh of relief.

"There's a little more. All ships were back in the water and jockeying to move north, when Hakon peeled off to the east with most of the ships following. The word relayed to us was that Hakon was going a-viking in Scania. Well, the boats from around here wanted no part of this. Besides, we had crops to harvest and stock to tend, so we broke from the pack and headed home.

"And that's it. I don't know where Hakon is right now, but we wish him well. We're just glad to be home."

This had been so spellbinding to Sveyin, that until the story was over and another round of horns was being consumed, he hadn't turned to Sigurth, who most likely had been as transfixed as he had. When he finally did, however, Sigurth wasn't there.

He wasn't anywhere in the longhouse either as far as he could see; so he stepped outside, only to realize that time had flown and it was dark. It was also chilly, being so late in the year, and it was spooky because no one had thought to post lamps outside. It took a few moments for his eyes to adjust to whatever the night sky provided, which wasn't much as all he could see were outlines, most prominently of horses tied to wagons and patiently waiting for something to happen.

Then he heard a sound out on the main road west of the stead. He stopped and turned his head, hearing more, even though faintly, that convinced him it was a horse.

Who would be riding there this time of night?

He crept down the lane, at intervals stopping and listening before continuing until he'd gotten as far as he could go without moving into the main road. Finding a bush, he moved in behind it and waited.

Nothing happened for a time, although he thought he heard a horse snort somewhere out there, but that was it and the silence remained. He was about to start back when he saw a movement—a subtle but real movement. Bug-eyed and holding his breath, he watched as a horse and rider moved out of the gloom, slowly and quietly like a phantom. As they glided past he recognized the shape of a lance, and saw the metallic reflection of what could be a sword. But what seemed as strange as any was that the rider was small, no larger than he was, or that Sigurth would be.

He looked back in the direction of the longhouse, only a silhouette among the many others of the night. It was so innocent and vulnerable with occasional sounds of laughter still being heard . . .

. . . and he didn't understand.

Chapter 4
JOMSVIKINGS
994

"A little more," Sigurth said, easing up on the safety line. Sveyin, thirty feet above on the edge, responded by letting out a few more feet on the main line. The main line, taut over projecting chunks of the cliff wall, stretched to Sigurth, where it tied to a crude rope-chair passing on each side and around his butt. The new level he reached with the drop didn't quite get him where he wanted to go either; but by a combination of pulling on the safety, and kicking out from the cliff, he was able to swing to the ledge he was after. Steadying himself there, and swatting away a bird that dived in to challenge the invasion, he picked the downy feathers that had accumulated there in a messy pile, stuffing them into the bag hanging from his belt.

"Okay, done here . . . Give me another five feet."

And so the process continued, with Sigurth swinging from ledge to ledge along a drop whose reach widened the further down he went. All the while he was doing this, birds flew about and did what birds do, and now more so since they'd been interrupted; and the hatchlings in their nests, who didn't know any better, flopped and opened wide and squawked in anticipation.

When he'd gotten to a point where little more was to be gained, he shouted the fact. Then, working together, Sigurth climbed the safety while Sveyin pulled the main, the two heaving in unison to a cadence which brought him bouncing and scraping back to the top in an amazingly short time.

They'd been working for several hours by this time, and had a full bag to show for each of the descents. Sveyin took the bag Sigurth untied from his waist, and placed it where the others had been piled, then he helped

Sigurth out of his crude but effective harness, making preparations for the next drop, which was his turn to make.

"Let's take a break," Sigurth said as he stood and brushed off the dirt and feathers and birdshit that seemed to be everywhere. "A couple more drops and we should have most of what the mountain has to offer this time around."

Sveyin nodded, coiling up the ropes to make ready for when they'd move to another location. "Two more will be enough.

"Want some water?"

"Ya, sure," Sigurth said, taking a few long drafts from the leather water bag, some of which spilled down over his chin. He sighed, then wiping at the drippings, looked for a place to plunk.

"What do you think, Trulsi?" He said as he moved to what seemed like a good place, grabbing the dog's head in both hands and scuffling his ears. Trulsi yipped and spun away, tail sweeping about as he begged for more of whatever was to follow.

"Aaaaah!" The cousins grunted, almost in unison, as they eased in among the rocks.

Trulsi didn't follow them at first. Instead he padded to the edge, barking in a show of supposed authority at the birds, who didn't seem to be affected one way or the other. Then, evidently feeling he'd told them a thing or two, he moseyed over and joined them.

"We're getting a good haul this time," Sveyin said, looking at the bags. "This should make Thora happy."

"For sure.

"She's such a wonder," Sigurth added, thinking of the beautiful garments and accessories she'd fashioned during the dozen years he'd known her. His mind lapsed briefly to his real parents before Thora and Orm, who were more like shadows, then bounced back. "She'll make the most comfortable pillows you've ever put your head on with all of these feathers . . . maybe a quilt or two to boot. There's plenty of time for her to do this with the next festival over a month away."

"Ya . . . over a month. I can hardly wait."

"Wait for what? Oh, I know. There were a few cute girls from up north at the one last year. I'll bet you're looking to see them again."

Sveyin smiled and pitched a pebble, which Sigurth ducked. "Maybe so. It's better than just looking at cows and sheep all day long."

"Oh ya . . . although there's a ewe in our herd that's looking pretty good."

They both laughed at that, while Trulsi reacted with ears up and another confused look.

"Will you get into all the contests again this year?" Sveyin asked. "You sure were itching to get into as many as you could at Rauma Dale last fall."

Sigurth shrugged. "I'm not sure about that many this time. Last year I was stupid; the number of contests I lined up for were just too many, so I don't want to do that again.

"I think we can both compete in archery . . . I mean, you're better than I am, but we're both damned good at it. As for the other stuff, the javelin and sword-play and such," he said shaking his head, "and I'm not going to wrestle guys older than me anymore. I damn near got killed."

Sveyin pitched another pebble, this one bopping Sigurth on the head. "If that's the case, then I'll be one of those you'll tangle with."

"Maybe so . . . *Grrrrrrr!*"

"Oh, speaking of girls . . . have you heard the latest about Hakon?"

"I've heard a lot. Is there more?"

"Ya. Pa had been with Einer the other day, and Einer told him what recently happened. It seems a farmer in Orka Dale, you know, just south of Trondheimfjord, has a couple of good looking young daughters. Well, Hakon saw them, and soon after sent word to the farmer to send them to him. I didn't hear what the pretense was, but the farmer caved in and sent his daughters as was asked. Apparently Hakon kept them for a week, doing as you can imagine, then sent them back.

"Pa said the farmers in the area were really pissed. It's not the first time something like this has happened, because it seems Hakon's been inserting his interest far and wide. He also said most feel this kind of thing's gotten out of hand, and someday there'll be a reckoning."

A gust of wind streamed past the edge of the cliff, kicked dust and forced them to cover up, interrupting the discussion. With this quieting, both settled in with other thoughts, which didn't last long because when Sigurth looked up, he saw Sveyin gazing past the edge to the horizon. He turned in that direction, saw nothing of interest to him, and settled back. "What do you see?"

Sveyin didn't answer at first. Then he shook his head, as if clearing cobwebs, and repeated, "What am I seeing? I see England and Ireland and Scotland, and the Islands north of there, the Orkneys and the Hjaltlands."

"You see them?" Sigurth sat back up and squinted for a second look.

"I see them in my mind, because I know they're there."

"Oh ya, sure."

"Don't any of those places interest you?"

Sigurth shrugged. "I guess so; but out there only looks like a lot of cold water to me."

"*Hrummmf* . . . Do you ever think of where the end of it, the world, might be? I mean the edge of the water?"

"You mean the serpent?"

"Ya . . . Jormungand."

"Not much . . . but it *is* a scary thought. No one who's been there has lived to tell about it; and there's a good chance they didn't get all the way there because of other monsters." He paused and pointed west, saying, "Don't have a clue about going farther that way, but from what's been told from the trading and raiding that's been going on, a ship can sail way, way south, and still not run into that edge. My sisters, Rogna and Solveig, could be somewhere down there."

"There where? What's down there called?"

"Don't know, but you've heard the stories . . . Ships can sail south, then turn east and enter another ocean entirely. The people in the land that fills that corner are called Moors. Orm said they travel around as much as we do, and show up at some of our markets as traders. They're darker than we are, maybe because its hotter there, and have another religion, one different from that White Christ we keep hearing about."

"I've heard you speak of them before. How have you learned so much?"

"It's really because of Orm. You know he works a lot at the marina."

"Ya."

"You also know he often asks me to help him out. This goes way back to what we were doing at Skulifarm. Well, many interesting people pass through there—boat owners, traders, and even pirates. Sometimes they're all of them. Anyway, they talk, and some have pretty interesting stories to tell."

"About way down south?"

"Sometimes."

"Doesn't that get your curious up? I mean, wouldn't you like to travel and see some of those places?"

"Ya, It's hard not to think about doing that. There's got to be more to life than working on the farm. Right now I'm not in line to inherit it anyway."

"Then why don't you talk to the birds and hear what they have to say about what's out there."

"The birds?"

"Ya ... Aren't you able to do that? Like Odin who sends his ravins, Hugin and Munin, out each morning to find out what's happening. You could do the same thing with some of the critters hovering around here . . . like your namesake."

Sigurth snorted. "That would be fun if I could."

"What about going a-viking? Have you thought of that?"

"Be a pirate? *Oh wow!* Don't let Gyrth hear you talk like that. Orm either. They both think pirates are scum; and they killed Ma and Pa."

"Ya . . ."

They sat for a while just looking, then Sveyin added, "That edge might be farther out than we think. There's Iceland farther out, north and east of Ireland, and Pa said there's rumor of a place called Greenland beyond that."

"Really . . . and it's called Greenland? What a nice name."

On the last drop of the day, Sigurth was dangling as far down as he could go, when he heard horses approaching on the road twisting by over two hundred feet below. When the makers of the sounds came into view, he saw three men on horseback, with one carrying a banner. The banner meant they were on an official mission. One of them was Sven.

Sigurth normally would have watched them pass by, or maybe pitched a stone their way to see if he could bop one of them; but seeing his brother, he held back, shouting, *"Sven! Sven! Up here . . ."*

The three reined in, horses turning every which way as they came to a halt. Looking up, they scanned the cliff. Sven, who thought he'd recognized the voice, laughed when he saw the figure dangling at the end of a rope and waving. "Hey Sigurth, you guys still at it?"

"Ya . . . We're almost done though. What's happening?"

"War arrows. The runners here got to me first. Now we're on our way to tell Gyrth. If you're about to finish, come down and hear about it firsthand."

The riders didn't intend to wait for the boys to get off the mountain, it just happened to work out that way. When the three reached the farm, Sven found Hrolf, who'd stepped out of the barn when he heard horses approaching. He, in turn, sent a hand into the field to get Gyrth. By the time they were all together, which took a while, they saw Sveyin and Sigurth coming their way. They'd hustled off the mountain and now jogged their way, weaving like drunken fools as they struggled to balance the light but bulky sacks around their backs. So the men waited, gathering in front of the longhouse where a few crude benches gave them a place to squat.

"What's the problem?" Gyrth asked Byof Skoptason, a man he recognized as one of the many who'd been in Hakon's company.

"We're being invaded is the problem." Byof said. "A large force from the south sailed past Agthirs, you know, the southern tip, a while ago. Our people down there saw it sail by, a force they estimated as being as many as sixty ships. This force continued up the coast, landing in the Rogaland area, where their army disembarked and began to move northward, plundering along the way.

"Actually, Earl Eirik, Hakon's son, learned of plans being made to do this when he was in Raumariki north of the Vik. He'd assembled troops from his area and crossed overland to Nitharos and informed Hakon, so Hakon wasn't surprised when reports came from the south. Anyway, Hakon is sending arrows, not only around the Trondheim districts, but also south to Moers and Ruama Dale, and north to Nauma Dale and Halogaland. His summons are for a total conscription of men and ships."

"Just who is it that's invading?" Gyrth asked. "From the south could be anybody?"

"The Danes, for sure, are part of it. It seems they have more rulers than territories to rule; so they've decided that Hakon and our Norway were ripe for plucking. They've been joined by forces to the east from Scania, and also from Wendland to the south on the mainland—Jomsvikings they're called. Anyway their combined force is large."

"How's the conscription going?"

"Too early to tell for sure; but Hakon hopes to end up with over 150 ships. And he's certainly expecting help from around here."

Byof and his flagman left soon after that, heading north to the farms along the coast. When they were out of sight, Gyrth slumped where he sat on the bench, resting his elbows on his knees. His mind whirled . . .

Who was he going to send this time? At 51, he was getting too old for this crap. Or was he? It was certainly better to die in combat than to waste away in old age; anyway that's what he'd been told all his life. Hrolf and Sven were in their prime; but Hrolf had gone the last time and almost died from his wound. Besides, they're both too valuable on their farms to be considered. Orm could go again, but this time the engagement might be a battle at sea, with no place to hide. This meant everyone was in harm's way if something went wrong, either in battle or with the ship. And Sveyin and Sigurth were too young to have much chance if fighting got to close quarters.

But he couldn't send only hands . . .

Orm and Sigurth had been at the marina for days, making sure the *Sea Eagle* was fit for the journey. The ship had been out of the water in storage, where it had been most of the time in the six years since its great adventure to Denmark and the Danavirki. So it had to be checked and caulked where problems were obvious, and launched and checked again . . . a simple sounding task amounting to a thousand details. Now it lay tied at the landing, quietly swaying to the soft swells moving in from the fjord. Another ship of similar size was at a dock a stones throw away, also tied with its gangplank down and ready for boarding. While a few men scampered around on both boats making final preparations, the balance of the crews, which totaled near to forty in each, were beginning to collect on shore.

Einar Jonsson kicked pebbles about, occasionally looking up to take in the scene unfolding along the waterfront. "Damn, I wish I was going too."

Gyrth snorted. "You know, I think the Norns are playing a silly game with all of us. You say you'd like to go along, and I believe if you say it, old friend, you mean it. And here I am, looking at that ship and having to admit that climbing aboard is the last thing I want to do. But I've got to."

"You feel the Skulifarm mess still makes you beholden?"

"Ya, no doubt about it. Hakon let me off with many, many pledges, so I have to continue answering his call."

"For that matter, my neck's out too," Einer said, "I didn't go on the raid, but several of my people did."

"I'm well aware of that, and am forever indebted; but none of that matters. The simple fact is that I *have* to go, and since I do, you must stay. If things go wrong, this part of the district will need leaders to keep everything around here from being scrambled, and right now that's you."

The decision about who was to go wasn't an easy one, and in the end, Gyrth didn't follow his first inclinations. But then it was what it had to be. The first hurdle was regarding his son Hrolt, who'd been so offended when not chosen before. This time, as an obvious choice, his eyes sparkled when Byof made his announcement.

Gyrth didn't do anything at first, other than alert Orm and Sigurth to make the boat ready. Then he pondered, working the farm as he normally would as he thought of the options. There wouldn't be much time for this, unfortunately, as riders churned the roads daily with updates of the enemy, and of plans for the growing fleet.

He remembered Gunnar's words . . . *"Why should we have to go and fight someone we don't know, every time someone we don't care about says so."* Now he had to admit he felt the same way. But there was another side to the argument that riders were bringing this time. While the enemy ships followed offshore, the army had come ashore and was moving up country. This he'd generally known from the first announcement. With each day as more news was received, however, he heard of people, Norwegians like himself, being driven from their steads and fleeing, of efforts being made to hide families and valuables and stock in the forests, of those who didn't get away being tortured and raped or killed, of farms being burned while everything of value was taken back to ships. And so it went.

This collaborating force wasn't just an invading army or a political movement, they were also pirates; and therefore the situation was worse than with Ragnaforth and his invasion years ago.

Yes, once again everybody has to pitch in and help . . . And much as he hated to think on it, he had to go with the ship their area would send. Oh, Hrolf would protest and make a scene. But he was in his thirties now, not so young anymore, with a good wife and a couple kids who lighted up the place. And his protests wouldn't exactly ring with the conviction they once did. More than once he'd screamed out in the night and awakened, trembling and sweaty. There was no need to ask what that was about, because he'd experienced the same thing a time or two himself.

We're weaned on the Gods and their struggles from the earliest times we can remember, and are imbued with the glory of combat and heroic deeds and even dying, so that the concept of it all seems irrefutable. But then there's a wives embrace and the playful gurgle of innocence personified in a child, and even in the evidences of something to be considered in the birds that fly and the animals that roam, and with all of that, many, and it may be a majority, question.

So he couldn't proceed without a second objective, and that was to bring the Sea Eagle back, with all hands if at all possible . . . and so . . . there had to be a plan.

The eyes of both Sigurth and Sveyin were ablaze, and they really didn't need an explanation, but Gyrth gave them one anyway.

"Look you two," he said, "you're really too young, but you're both good archers, and that's what we need as much as anything."

"But neither Hrolf or Sven are going," Sigurth said. "They've earned the right, and would be towers of strength in any battle line. I don't understand."

"You're right about their being towers of strength. They're also the anchors for both our farms and families on each side of the mountain, so we can't put them in jeopardy if we can help it."

Sveyin laughed. "What you're saying is that *our* futures aren't exactly written in the stars."

"*O ny o ny o ny!* That's not what I meant. I don't have a vision of the future. Some of the sorcerers claim they know what the Norns are weaving for each of us, but I'm skeptical about that. All I know is that the two of you are each outstanding in your own right, and that it might well be that there will be great stories to be told before your days come to an end.

"Now both of you, get on with whatever you have to do to make ready. We're running late as it is."

After a series of delays mostly orchestrated by Orm, the last few boarded, the gangplank hauled aboard, and the *Sea Eagle* untied and pushed into the channel. Oars were extended, orders were barked, and in jerking efforts that slowly segued to orchestration, the ship moved down the fjord and into the ocean to join the parade moving south.

Days later, the flotilla, an extended line of ships, moved down the coast, eventually coming together and settling into a place called Hallkels Inlet, where they lay at anchor while feelers were sent out. They found the invaders nearby at Hjorungarfjord, also at anchor and aware of their presence as well.

The next day the battle began. It started with a series of jockeying movements, with ships in the lead being tied together to form battle platforms. Earl Hakon and two of his sons, Earl Eirik and Earl Svein, each led one of those platforms, which were sized to counter corresponding combinations of the Jomsviking fleet.

In doing so, it was obvious that Hakon had more ships; but his ships were generally smaller and lower than those of the invaders, which gave the invaders an advantage—It made the boarding of their decks difficult, and allowed them to shoot down from more protected positions. Fighting was nonetheless carried to the invaders, who Hakon intended to either destroy or drive back to where they'd come. The encounters were intense, particularly within the areas of direct contact, with ship platforms dropping back and moving forward again as momentums ebbed and flowed.

Gyrth and the *Sea Eagle* were among over half the ships in the armada just outside the conflict area, jockeying to stay clear of each other while at the same time looking for opportunities to thrust into the fray and make a contribution.

In the beginning, the battle was confined to exchanges of missiles because of the height differences; but even so, casualties mounted on both sides, with many ending up in the water. It was at this point, early in the fight and nowhere near to any conclusion, when it seemed the Gods intervened . . . which ones, no one could say for sure, for even the skalds would later disagree. The intervention was in the form of a storm, which hit with high winds that churned the waters and confounded all the ships, particularly those not hawsered together. Without a moment to prepare, ships scrambled every which way, at times tangling oars or colliding with one another and even grounding. In addition, the boiling black clouds that accompanied the winds brought hail that fell with such a fury of large stones that the battle was momentarily lost from view to those outside the platforms.

For Orm and the *Sea Eagle,* the storm had its own unique impact. The crew fought for control, avoiding other ships trying to do the same thing, and tried to preserve oars while doing so. Because of the hail, shields were raised as if in battle, and part of what could be damaging was avoided; but most men were hammered one way or another and definitely removed from awareness to what was happening around them.

The storm, which seemed to last an eternity because of its intensity, passed by as quickly as it had moved in; and when the residual mists of it cleared, it could be seen that the battle continued on as if nothing had happened. As for the ships treading water in the rear, it was different. The *Sea Eagle* among them was in good shape, with all hands breathing a sigh, even laughing, at what had been no more than a scare.

That wasn't the case for everyone.

Sigurth, who along with Sveyin and the other archers assigned to the stern near Orm and the steerman, saw it first. "Orm, look! They're in trouble!" He yelled, pointing to a sister ship that had been driven near shore. "They're not moving and everyone seems to be bailing!"

All heads turned to a situation about a hundred yards away.

After a quick look, Orm turned to get Gyrth's attention, who was up front focussing on the battle. It was difficult to communicate because winds and waves hadn't completely abated, so hand signals, together with a few words getting through, called attention to the fact that a boat nearby needed help. Upon his understanding, Gyrth nodded and signaled in a way that could be taken as "Let's do it."

Orm barked orders, and in a series of movements, the *Sea Eagle* turned and moved towards the floundering vessel. When they approached, they could see that the situation wasn't much different from the impression from a distance—no-one was at the oars, instead everyone was bailing, and it wasn't working.

A good guess, which would later be verified, was that during the worst of the storm, with high swells and deep troughs, the ship had been dumped atop a rock that normally wasn't a problem. The result was a crushed hull and an amount of leaking that made bailing a losing battle.

When the *Sea Eagle* reached a critical point of closeness, Orm ordered a raising of oars on the near side, then had lines thrown to draw the boats together. This seemed simple enough, but in the confusion aboard the floundering boat, oars hadn't been retracted, and so they were forced every which way, with many of the oars shattering.

There wasn't much time. The ship had risen with a swell after being punctured, and had drifted clear of the rocks into open water where it was slowly settling. As with most ships in the armada, this one was loaded with the provisions needed for a sustained operation. These were now doomed, and it was only the crew that hopefully could be saved.

A reasonable discipline was maintained at first, but now, with water coming over the deck, the urgency was having its effect. Some panicked, diving in and swimming to a shore that seemed reasonably close, and a few stepped aboard the skiff that was available; but most remained to concentrate on the *Sea Eagle* as it crunched in and tied up. As soon as this was done and the gangplank extended across, the transfers began.

"Easy now, don't panic!" Orm barked as the closest ones scrambled to get onto it. "There's plenty of time. We'll get you out even if your ship goes down."

He was wrong about that. A number of men were armored, with chain-metal brynies and helmets and fine swords on baldrics, treasured implements of war that may have taken a lifetime of achievement to acquire. For these men, trying to save their treasures was a life or death decision, and there *wasn't* much time.

Gyrth, like Orm, gave whatever direction could be given, but mostly matters took a natural course. The oarsmen stayed where they were, knowing they would need to respond, and quickly, when the time came. Others extended hands and aided those scrambling across, not only on the gangplank, but also directly over the nearly adjoining rails. Sigurth was one of them. When he saw the oarsmen couldn't move, he gave Sveyin his weapons and moved to where he could help.

"Easy now! Easy!" Gyrth shouted, adding to a din that hinted of things not going as well as hoped. "No, No! Leave the baggage . . . We don't have room!" He looked across at Orm and their eyes met with the same questions—*Were they putting Sea Eagle in jeopardy by taking everybody aboard? How do we draw the line if we have to?*

Gyrth looked about the fjord to the closest ships to see if they were responding, and saw that they weren't. So he waved and yelled, hoping for a response. Finally the closest one showed life, with oars moving and the craft turning in their direction. He heard Orm, so returned his attention to him, and although the words weren't clear, the meaning was. Orm was motioning with a quick series of cutting-like strokes across his neck. All about the side abutting the *Sea Eagle*, men were piling on top of one another and the ship was settling, not too gracefully, to a depth that when combined with the shifting mass of cargo, could be their undoing as well.

"Cut the lines!" Gyrth shouted. *"Cast off!"* Orm shouting the same from his end. With that, the oarsmen on the abutting side, who later stated they were waiting for the order, quickly reacted, pushing away with whatever means they could, until they could put their oars to work and complete the separation. During these actions, a full-blown panic did occur, with an explosion of sound and a mad scramble from those still in the sinking ship.

A few made it, but most didn't. One with more armor than made sense now, dived and didn't quite reach the rail or the outstretched hands, and hit the water like a lead sinker. He would have hit bottom a few moments later, but a hand from Sigurth, who super-extended over the rail to a point of almost going in himself, caught his wrist, and with others assisting, pulled him back up over the side.

Once the *Sea Eagle* was clear, Orm directed the oars until the ship was safely in open water, then both he and Gyrth worked to stabilize all that now settled within the rails. Looking back, they were surprised to see the last of the doomed ship, its leading and trailing towers disappearing beneath the waves. Since the ship was of wood, it had been thought it would linger near the surface along with the flotsam and jetsam that now bobbed, and provide something to hang on to. But not so; it sank out of sight except for the mast and its lines, which would soon also disappear, leaving the gangplank as the largest floating object where the ship had been. As for people, they were splashing about amongst it all, and now giving attention to the other boat moving in to help.

Gyrth couldn't help but wonder about the armored warriors, as he didn't see any among those crammed about the *Sea Eagle* deck other than the one miraculously rescued. That meant that anyone who hadn't shed his armor in time was now on the bottom. As disturbing a thought that was, he didn't have long to think on it as noises from the other direction turned him to witness what was happening there.

When the storm hit, the battle was in a seesaw with neither side able to sustain momentum. Fighting had somehow continued through the worst of it, however, with heavy casualties on both sides, as evidenced by the many splashing about in the water.

But now as they watched, men surged over the rails onto the higher decks of the foremost Jomsviking ship. This surge continued until the enemy was boxed into the high stern and trapped. Rather than being slaughtered or captured, the Captain of the ship, later identified as Bui the Stout of Borgundarholm, took his treasure chests and jumped overboard, as did many of his men. With the surges momentum now unstoppable, one after another of the invading ships tied together in the battle platform were cleared, with few prisoners being taken. The cheering with each triumph turned into a roar as it became evident the rest of the invading fleet, those not yet involved in the fighting, were straining at oars in hasty retreat.

> Wounds the warrior dealt to
> Wendish host with bloody
> sword—with savage bite it
> sundered bones—in battle,
> ere of their crews could clear the
> combat-urger—was it
> fraught with fearful danger—
> five and twenty longships.

Sveyin was among those jumping and cheering, elated that in an experience with many opportunities for storytelling that would be talked of for years, he'd survived on the winning side. Then he noticed Sigurth beside him.

"What's wrong?"

Sigurth looked back and shrugged, not saying anything.

Orm, who was nearby and watching, laughed. "Sveyin," he said, "your cousin's just plain pissed. He'd raised his bow several times, even before the storm, hoping to get a shot off; but there was never a time when he was either in range or with a decent target."

Sigurth smiled at that and nodded in agreement, saying, "Even if there'd been one, it would have been impossible to get off a shot with all of us being crammed in as we were." With that he unstrung his bow and added a faint "Whoopee."

At first opportunity, the *Sea Eagle* threaded through the throng of ships and beached. Everyone unloaded, including those rescued, who were to fend for themselves and find sister ships that could provide them return passage. This turned out to be anything but a problem, because after all the clearing and patching that needed doing after the battle, there were over two dozen ships captured and added to the fleet.

For those onboard the *Sea Eagle*, as it was for those on ship after ship anchoring in, it was a time to set tents and cook meals and relax. It was also a time to walk about and hear stories, particularly from those who'd been a part of the battle they'd witnessed. While doing this, Sigurth and Sveyin came upon a crowd gathered around a group of prisoners. The prisoners were tied together by their feet, lined up on top of a log where they sat while being subjected to judgement.

Some of them were beheaded on the spot. As grizzly and gut wrenching as that was, especially for the boys, the part more impactful was the nonchalance of those about to die. One man asked for a knife because he wanted to see if he could continue to hold it after his head was off. He couldn't. Another, a handsome, strapping man with a head of lengthy blond curls, seemed more concerned about blood messing up his hair. Eventually most of the prisoners ended up being granted quarter.

Few of the actions the boys witnessed were understood at the time. But they did gain an appreciation for Hakon and his sons, who had been up front in the thick of battle, and had weathered, not only the storm, but also difficult battle conditions to accomplish the outstanding victory.

"So that's the great Earl Hakon," Sveyin said as he watched the King and the group around him, bantering in obvious good humor.

"Ya," Sigurth replied, "I saw him first years ago; but I remember him more by his voice than anything else. Besides, he wasn't in armor then, and he wasn't bedraggled and bloody."

"Hrolf said that at the Danavirke, he been a brave and effective leader. I guess he was here too."

"Ya."

Walking in another direction, they watched as a large group gathered at the shore, and by means of ropes, pulled one of the captured ships out of the water onto rollers on the bank. While this was underway, others collected bodies from the water and kindling from the shore.

"What do you suppose this is all about?" Sigurth asked. Then he realized what this had to be for. "There'll be a funeral pyre and ceremony, won't there?"

"Ya."

Returning in a roundabout way to where the *Sea Eagle* was tied, they saw Gyrth and Orm in conversation. They seemed in good spirits, and it was almost as if they were congratulating each other.

What about? Sigurth thought. *They'd been late joining the armada; hadn't tied into the combat platforms; and didn't have a single exploit in battle to brag about.*

Whatever he thought, however, it didn't matter. At a gathering of the crew beside a campfire early that evening, Gyrth spoke of how proud he was of everyone. "Even though the Norns hadn't chosen to send them directly into battle, they'd performed well in the other challenges thrown there way. The obligation of the war arrows has now been satisfied, so eat hearty, rest well and make ready."

At first light the next morning, the *Sea Eagle* cast off, joining the scattering of ships sailing home.

Chapter 5

OLAF TRYGGVASON

995

Orm tugged on the reins and the horses turned into the lane leading to Gyrthafarm, the small flatbed carrying him and Sigurth groaning at the change in direction. Three men on horseback followed, hooves digging into the soft dirt along the way and leaving a plume hanging in the air where they'd passed.

The procession stopped at the longhouse, the horsemen dismounting and tying up. They didn't have to wait as Gyrth, who'd been outside near the corral, heard them approaching before they'd come into view and was ready.

"How are things with you, then," Gyrth said, knocking workings of the farm from his clothes and greeting them in mass. "The fact you're coming like this means you've got something important to tell. Let me make a guess . . . It has to do with Earl Hakon."

Sigurth didn't wait for an answer, or for any of the conversation he knew was going to take place as he'd already heard it. Instead he jumped from the seat and said, "Where's Sveyin?"

"He's high in the north patch helping Bjorn repair the shelter."

Sigurth took off jogging, first past Ingibjorg at the garden where she and Jorum, Hrolf's wife, were working while at the same time trying to manage two tots.

"Sigurth, what's happening?" Ingibjorg said, standing to ask as the sound of running feet hinted of something. "Anything urgent?"

"Ny," he said, slowing to a sideways step as he passed. "Ny, but I think you'll find the news interesting."

"What about?" Jorum added.

Sigurth was beyond them by now and didn't answer. Instead he pointed back to where the men were gathered and resumed speed.

He also waved at Hrolf in a nearby field, who must have heard the noise at the longhouse as he was putting an end to what he was doing. Without stopping, Sigurth continued past the fields into the rolling hills that served as pastureland. It seemed like forever before he spotted Sveyin, who was with two others at some crude workings that clearly weren't finished. As he headed in that direction, a few sheep scattered, but most only looked up. The dog that had been lying in watch with ears perked long before Sigurth came into view, jumped to his feet and took a few steps forward in attack mode until it heard the tone of Sveyin's voice.

"Well, look who's here," Sveyin said as Sigurth slowed down. "Why didn't you take a horse?"

Sigurth came to a stop and plopped on the nearest object that could serve as a seat, gasping and speechless as his lungs heaved to catch up.

Sveyin dropped what he was doing and walked over, saying, "What's so important that you have to run like a fool to get all the way up here?"

Sigurth forced a faint laugh, then gasped, "That's the sorriest excuse for a wall I've ever seen. I don't know what you expect to either keep in or hold out with that bunch of crap."

"Rave on, rave on . . . Is that all you came here to tell me?"

Sigurth shook his head and waved a hand as if to say *hold on a second.*

"What then?"

"I'll tell you . . ."

"So?"

"Hakon's dead."

"Ny o ny!" Sveyin said, taking a few steps going nowhere, all the while looking at Sigurth; then he picked a spot the sheep hadn't gotten to first and sat close by. "The last I heard, in fact you told me, was that Hakon was in the Trondheim area, and was pissing off farmers again because he was continuing to mess with their women."

Sigurth nodded, almost breathing normally now.

"So tell me," Sveyin said, swatting away a grasshopper that landed on his leg. Then he turned to the scraggly, almost toothless, old man who'd stopped working with the interruption and was just standing alongside a younger hand by the wall and listening. "Bjorn, you guys take a break too if you want, or keep at it on the wall. I'm going to be here for a while.

"So what happened," he said, turning back to Sigurth. "How'd he die, and how'd you find out?"

Sigurth slid off the rock and onto the ground, leaning back to get comfortable.

"Okay, it happened this way. A few hours ago, Orm and I were at the marina, working on a shed to house one of the Jomsviking boats Hakon confiscated at Hjorungafjord. You're aware that they were considered too valuable to destroy, so he had them sailed to different districts along the coast for safe keeping."

"Oh ya."

"Well, we're sawing and nailing when these two traders rode up. Ashjorn Rausmason and Halldor Eisli were their names. They'd ridden from Viggja with a story so amazing, that Orm said they had to repeat it to the most prominent farmers in the area. When they agreed to do that, we got on our wagon and accompanied them, picking up Einer Jonsson along the way and continuing here. They're now telling Einer and Gyrth and Hrolf the same thing I'm going to tell you."

Sveyin squirmed.

"It gets complicated."

"How so?"

"Have you heard of Olaf Tryggvason?"

"Ny."

"Me either. Like Gyrth has said many times before, there are blood lines all over the place that are or claim to be of royal lineage; and this "Olaf" is another one of them. Apparently he's the son of King Tryggvi who used to rule somewhere in the Vik. Anyway, a ways back the King was ambushed and killed. His wife, Queen Astrith, who was pregnant at the time, was forced to flee east to her relatives, and that's where Olaf was born. Olaf grew up in that area, spending time in places like Estonia and Garthariki and Wendland, usually in one royal court or the other."

"When Hrolf was with Hakon at the Danavirki, this Olaf led a contingent on the other side."

"Nyman!"

"Ya, weird isn't it? By that time he'd turned into a pirate like so many others in Wendland, and had been raiding all about in the Baltic. He subsequently went on to do the same along the east coast of England and Scotland, and then around the islands to Ireland. To make a long story short, and without knowing how or when or why, along the way he became converted to the White Christ, and began to take it upon himself to convert others. He also began thinking about Norway, and since he had a bloodline, about how nice it would be to be its King. Recently he and a small band, only five ships worth, secretly landed on our coast. When he heard that King Hakon was in the Trondheim area and having trouble with the farmers, he headed there.

"His timing was perfect.

"Just before, and true to form, Hakon requested that the wife of a prominent farmer be sent to him. Well, the farmer rebelled and didn't send his wife; instead he sent war-arrows to other farmers, organizing a small army to go after Hakon with every intent of killing him. Hakon wasn't exactly caught with his pants down by this, but he was cut off from his main forces, which were with his son Erland and the ships at anchor at Viggja. He still had a small group of men accompanying him like he always did; but he didn't see any sense of going to battle if he could help it. So he sent his escort back to base, thinking they could travel safely if he wasn't with them. He also thought that he and his thrall, a man named Kark, being only two, could easily sneak through the woods, scoot around the farmers and manage their return.

"Then Olaf came on the scene.

"Olaf heard what had happened, so he first chased after Erland and killed him; then he and his men joined the army of farmers and went after Hakon. The combined forces were directed to a farm of one of Hakon's mistresses, where in fact, Hakon was hiding at the time. But Hakon had gotten word of the pursuers coming his way, so had a pit dug in the pigsty and had it covered with boards, and then you know, crap. Anyway, he and his thrall hid in the pit, thinking they were now safe and secure.

"The forces arrived soon after that and searched every nook and cranny, but were unable to find any trace of Hakon. Unfortunately, before the farmers left to look somewhere else, Olaf stood on a rock near the pigsty and spoke to them, telling of the reward he would give to the man who would kill Hakon."

"And Hakon and Kark heard him?"

"Ya. We can only guess what it was like in the pit after that; but we do know that in the night the thrall killed Hakon. Then he cut off Hakon's head, taking it to Olaf at an estate in Hlathir where he was staying."

"And what was his reward?"

"Olaf immediately had *his* head cut off on the premise that a thrall didn't have the right to kill a King. He then had both heads taken to Nitharholm, an island nearby used as a gallows for thieves and evildoers, and put on display. It seems that as we speak, people from all around the Trondheimfjord are stopping by the island to throw stones at the heads . . .

". . . and Olaf Tryggvason is claiming to be King of Norway."

Unlike Sigurth, Sveyin did use a horse. So after exhausting what they could say about the news, they both mounted to amble down the twisting trail back to the stead. The messengers, Ashjorn and Halldor, were still there, as were everyone who'd gathered, preferring to stay outside for fresh air while there was daylight. The conversation continued, the group only looking up and nodding as the two dismounted and tied the horse.

The boys may have been only a distraction to the visitors, but not the other way around, especially to Sveyin. It seems Sigurth, in his hurry to describe the story, had neglected to say anything about the storytellers. This was an oversight because the two would have stood out in any group, particularly of farmers in their drab, undyed, coarse homespun.

Both men were of average height, with Ashjorn probably the older because his hair, thinning in front, was swept back to a mass that gathered at the shoulders. His eyes, almost hidden under his bushy eyebrows, seemed kind, however, and his voice had a complementing softness, a combination that if someone analyzed, might say belonged to someone in sales or diplomatic services.

Halldor was younger with fuller cheeks. His face, although partly obscured by short, ruddy and curly face hair, combined with alert eye movements which seemed to be on the verge of being humorous.

These impressions were dwarfed by what the men wore, however. Although the two weren't matching, they both wore hip-length tunics of weaves that were of obvious quality, subtly trimmed at all edges.

Returning attention to the topic, which was Olaf Tryggvason, Ashjorn said, "The one thing I want everyone to realize, that even though what's happened appears to be a fluke, you don't want to underestimate this man Olaf. We've met him and can say he's not only obviously in charge, he's also disarming, being most personable and full of fun. As for the men accompanying him, they're not a large contingent, but they admire him greatly and are very dedicated. They had this to say about him—He was stronger and more agile than anyone had ever seen; he could balance and walk outside the oars while his men rowed; he could juggle three daggers with one in the air at all times; he could wield a sword just as well with either hand; he could hurl two spears at the same time; and when in battle, he was the bravest and most ferocious of men. They also added that when angered, he was exceedingly cruel."

Throats cleared and glances went from one to another.

"What should we be doing?" Hrolf asked.

"Absolutely nothing," Orm answered. "We're just farmers, and in my case a carpenter. We'd like to be left alone and live our lives in peace. Most of the time doing that and leaving our fates to the Norns works out fine. So standing aside and letting these bastards flex their ambitions is usually best."

"You might be right," Halldor said, "but then again, maybe not. Things may not work out in a way that allows everyone to stay out of what's happening. From what we understand, when Olaf sets his mind to something, he's hard to change. Right now he's trying to take over all of what Hakon ruled, and while he's at it, converting everyone to a new religion. That intent, to be successful, must eventually end up involving all of us.

Orm shook his head, saying softly, "Damn."

"Damn what?"

"Oh . . . Hakon."

"Hakon's dead and gone."

"And that may be a pity. Hakon had his faults, no doubt about that. There's no excuse for some of the things he did . . . unfortunately it seems that when some men get to power, they can't resist taking advantage of it. At least he's not as bad as a certain Vladimir in Garthariki a ways back. He reportedly had a number of wives and 800 concubines . . . and was written about by one as *fornicater immensus at crudelis.* which you can guess what that means. Anyway in more ways Hakon was a good king. And his sons, Earl Erik and Earl Svein, heroes at Hjorungafjord where we were all spared from coming under Danish rule, have been put in an awkward position. Their best choice may be to collect their followers and go to Sweden."

Orm sighed. "Well, we're not going to solve anything tonight. And speaking of the night, it's here; which means, Sigurth, that our families must be wondering where we are. Let's climb aboard and get going. There's not much light, but the horses know the way."

Chapter 6
THE CRANE
998

"Well look who's here," Orm said, looking up from the wood panel he'd been carving.

Traffic wasn't unusual about the marina, because being the first cove in from the fjord inlet, it became a minor crossroad for trade as well as news from around the area. In this case, the men who rode up immediately caught his attention, not only because they'd stand out anywhere in these parts, but also because he'd seen them before three years ago.

"Ashjorn, Halldor . . . It's good to see you again," he said, laying down his tools and sitting back.

The two dismounted, tied up and walked over to where Orm waited. "We thought we'd find you here," Ashjorn said. "How are things with you then?"

"I'm mainly getting older, that's for sure. What about you two?"

Halldor smiled. "We're still wearing our skins."

"I noticed that right off, and that's a good sign. Let's see now . . . the last time you came by, you had some mind-boggling news. I take it by the looks of you that it's not as startling this time."

"No, nothing like that; but we *are* here for a reason."

"I guessed that much, because this place is too far out of your way to be a case of just passing by. Do you see that circle of stumps and logs over there? It's the only place around here where we can sit and relax. You can tell me what's happening there."

Orm turned as an afterthought and yelled to a group working a ways away from his work shelter. "Hey Sigurth! Look who just dropped by. Come over."

Sigurth had already stopped and looked at the visitors, thinking there was something familiar about them. So when he heard the call, he didn't hesitate. He walked over bare-chested, dirty and sweaty, and with a spring in his step that revealed how glad he was to be interrupted.

"Now, who is this?" Halldor said. "Is he the same youngster working with you last time?"

"Yes, he's my foster-son Sigurth."

"Of course . . . Sigurth." Halldor said, turning to greet him, "I should have known, but the fact is you've changed. Look at you; you've grown taller and filled in. My guess is that no one fools with you these days."

Orm nodded, "You've got that right. There were games in the valley last week, and Sigurth pretty much had his way."

"Well almost," Sigurth said with a shrug. "You remember Sveyin, Gyrth's son; well. He's bigger too, and is still beating my ass with the bow.

"What brings you here this time? No more invasions, I hope."

"No, nothing like that."

Orm sat on a stump, and gestured for the others to do the same. "So, how *have* things been going. This Olaf has been King since we saw you last, but we haven't heard a lot, and haven't been affected one way or the other. I mean, things have been about the same and no one has sent war-arrows."

"I'm surprised to hear you haven't been affected," Halldor said.

"How so?"

"The new religion. Olaf isn't going to rest until everyone's been converted, and he's already traveled far and wide doing so."

"Oh ya, we're aware of that," Sigurth said. "People have been around, but we've managed to stay clear when they do. It's all a bunch of bullshit as far as we're concerned. The Gods have served us well, so we don't see the sense in changing."

"I didn't hear you say that."

"Oh, come on," Orm said, slapping his knees. "You come from Trondheimfjord, where everybody knows Olaf's having trouble. From what we hear, farmers around there, right in Olaf's backyard, are maintaining their Gods as much as anyone. They're of a common mind on other things, too. Didn't they organize and go after Earl Hakon?"

Ashjorn and Halldor looked at each other.

"Okay, you have a point. It doesn't matter, however, because that's not why we're here."

"That's good. So what is it this time?"

"A boat," Ashjorn answered.

"A boat?"

"Ya, a boat. I know . . . Olaf already has a number of them, and he gained a bunch more when he took over for Hakon; but for some reason he wants a special new one."

Orm thought about that for a moment, then said, "Okay . . . So why *are* you here?"

"When the King said he wanted a "special" boat, I thought it would do well to assemble the best artisans and boat-builders available."

Orm cocked his head. "I still don't understand. You're from Viggja, right? There's a large marina there, and several more along the Trondheimsfjord. You shouldn't have to come all the way here to find good people."

"That's true. There are good people there. Do you happen to know any of them by name?"

"Ny."

"Well, people up there have heard about you."

Orm blinked and almost blushed, but was saved when Sigurth jumped up, clapped, and slapped him on the back. "This guy's amazing. His booth has been one of the most popular at fairs for years, and his carving always sell out. I'm not surprised that word's gotten around."

The two nodded, waiting for exuberance to settle, then turned back to Orm, "Will you come and join the team? I think it'll be a rewarding experience, and it will be a great help to us."

Sigurth, still on his feet, said, "Of course he will; but only on one condition, and that's that I go along too."

Orm laughed. "That's true. I can't get along without my right hand man."

"And Sveyin too," Sigurth added.

"Sveyin?"

"Yes. He's as anxious to get away from the farm as I am."

The ship was finished that winter at a landing by the Nith River, near the new city of Nitharos that the King had recently established. It wasn't a particularly large ship, but it had subtle differences: it was designed for swift sailing with thirty rower's benches; and it had higher platforms in both bow and stern. Most noteworthy, however, was its craftsmanship, which included artful details and carvings that made it sparkle in comparison to others.

The King called his new ship the *Crane.*

"Here they come," Sveyin whispered.

Orm, Sigurth and he were a part of the crew of workmen standing to the side of a crowd from the area, mostly Nitharos, gathered for the formal "Christening," as it was being called, of the new ship. Necks stretched and whispers combined into a low buzz that slowly dwindled to almost nothing as they sensed great words were about to be spoken.

And they were. Leading the procession of dignitaries who would do the talking was the Bishop of the recently created new "White Christ" district. He was festooned in white—a stiff white, heavily embroidered and jeweled robe-like garment and a conical cap of the same material. In one hand he carried a staff that was equally impressive, with an ornate, gilded carving of something meaningful on its top. In the other hand, which was extended, he waved a smoking pot, whose aroma eventually worked its way through the crowd and back to where the three were standing.

Several others from the church accompanied the Bishop, but their coverings were much less distinctive, and they were generally ignored as they didn't seem to do anything except to be on hand to take the staff and pot when he was through with them.

Then the Bishop spoke, and it was grand. At least the three thought it must have been because they didn't understand a word. Whatever the message, it was spoken in Latin, which they were somehow led to believe was a language of spirits way up there who had great influence over them.

Finally King Olaf took to the front, and he was not to be outdone, either in regalia, decorum or oratory. He was a sight to behold, with not only a bejeweled crown, but also a fur-trimmed, hip-length jacket, with a studded belt and a cross-body sash holding a sparkling scabbard and sword. What he wore wasn't a surprise as he'd been by the site many times during the summer months of construction, and was always dressed to impress. He spoke in lofty terms in a language they understood, being complimentary to the construction team, and even mentioning Orm for his exceptional talent. In Sigurth's mind, however, his words wafted away in much the same manner that Hrolf had described of Earl Hakon at Danavirki, where Hrolf didn't remember any of them.

When the formalities were over, there was the inevitable celebration with lots of good food and, of course, drink. This could have gone on for all hours where they'd assembled, but it was late in the year, and not only did darkness descend, but chilly, sleety wind gusts also swirled in from the northwest, scattering the crowd to wherever shelter could be found.

Ashjorn found the three in a shed used for storing tools and supplies during construction. Others had also crammed in at first; but since the ceremonies were over, bit by bit they drifted away. By the time he came by, the three were by themselves.

"So there you are," he said. "I've been looking all over for you. Why aren't you at the King's Lodge? That's where most have gone."

"And most not able to get inside, I expect, and freezing," Orm answered.

"That's true, that's very true," Ashjorn said laughing. "This weather's a shame, but then it happens all the time."

"This is nothing compared to the hail at Hjorungarfjord," Sigurth said.

"So I've heard," Ashjorn said. "I wasn't there.

"Is there anything I can get any of you?"

"No," Orm said. "We managed to grab enough food to suit us before the weather turned, and of course, a bit of this," holding up a bulging goat-skin bag.

"Care to join us?" He added, handing Ashjorn a horn.

"Ya sure."

"Our work is done here, it seems," Orm continued. "So we were discussing heading out in the morning. It's time to go home."

Ashjorn shook his head. "That wouldn't be wise. I thought you might be thinking that way, and that's one of the reasons I was trying to find all of you."

"One of the reasons?"

"Ya. I'd hoped to see you at the Lodge. I mean, the King is really excited about his new ship, and knows all of you played an important part."

"Especially me," Sveyin said, lifting his horn high and taking a bow.

"Can you believe him?" Sigurth said, "All he did was tell jokes while the rest of us chipped away."

When the nonsense this started ran its course, Orm repeated, "One of the reasons?"

"Well, you know about the Kings main obsession."

"Of course, to convert all of us . . . to this so called Christianity."

"Exactly, and beware. I don't want any of you to be hard-headed about this issue, because if you are, you're going to lose."

"Whoopee!" Sveyin said, screwing up his face while Sigurth remained stone-faced.

"No kidding, I mean it," Ashjorn added.

Orm said, "They can't help themselves, so please ignore them. The fact is that all summer long we're been hearing about what the King's doing. There's not much that isn't discussed while work's going on. We've heard about Olaf's continuing efforts around Trondheimsfjord; and we're aware it still isn't going smoothly. People here are, if nothing else, steadfast. They feel the Gods have served them well and don't see why they have to change."

Ashjorn nodded. "That's true. But don't get carried away with what you hear. The King wants a change, and from what I've seen he's going to make it happen. In fact, you're among many who are expected to be at an assembly being planned."

"Why don't we just load up and sail out in the morning. I doubt we'll be missed."

"Oh *ny o ny*, don't even think about it?"

"All of you have been very visible because of the good work you've done. That makes you special, and at the top of the list of those Olaf wants to be baptized and at his side. If you've been talking about him, you know how resolute he can be."

"You mean plans have already been made for us?"

"That's right. As soon as the weather clears, there'll be a meeting to make sure everyone around here has accepted the new faith and been baptized."

"Why should we, though?" Sigurth blurted. "I know I'm repeating myself, but from the time we're kids, we've been told about how the world was formed. During long winters we've heard all kinds of stories . . . of Odin with Sleipnir, his horse, and Thor with his mighty hammer Mjollnir. And every sound that surprises us is interpreted as one God or the other doing his thing. Now, you say we must change. But people all over are saying ny; particularly here around Trondheimsfjord, where resistance to change has continued from the beginning."

"I'm not here to argue," Ashjorn said. "I only came to inform you what to expect. There'll be a meeting that all of you, along with several other groups, will be required to attend. At that meeting, after the speeches, everyone will be expected to accept Christianity and be baptized."

"Required?" Sigurth said. "Expected?"

"Ya."

The meeting didn't take place immediately, at least the one in which the three of them were to attend. King Olaf was busy with other affairs along the fjord, at times aboard his new ship which he loved to show off. Orm, Sigurth and Sveyin, therefore, had to busy themselves in the Nitharos community, spending most of the time around the marina, where there was work enough to make use of the days while waiting. At one point they boarded a skiff and rowed to Nitharholm Island to see if Hakon's and Kark's heads were still on display; but that was no longer the case.

Ashjorn and Halldor were frequent visitors, not only keeping them informed, but also providing them entertainments when they could.

Finally, they brought news that Olaf was back in town, and that the meeting they were all awaiting was finally scheduled.

By this time it was late in the year with the spirit of the Yule Season in full swing. This being so, the gathering and christening of a number of people seemed at odds with what was happening, but nonetheless the word went out.

"There's not much in the way of daylight this time of year," Ashjorn said, "so everybody will assemble at noon by the church. This will give those in outlying areas time to arrive and depart with good visibility both ways. The combined group won't be overly large because of the short daylight hours, so the ceremony shouldn't take much time."

"I assume from what you've told us the matter isn't debatable," Orm said.

"Not much," Halldor answered. "Oh there'll be some pomp and ceremony and short speeches to the glory of it all."

"To warm up our spiritual beings, I guess."

"Yes, while we're freezing our asses," Sigurth added.

Ashjorn laughed. "That's true too. And maybe it's a good thing, as it may discourage any arguments."

"What if we don't show, or if we show, but refuse to cooperate?' Sveyin asked.

"As we've told you before, don't do that. In some places farmers have organized and armed themselves with such large numbers that Olaf backed down. But tomorrow won't be one of those times. I can't stress enough how hard and cruel he can get if he doesn't get his way.

"Did you hear what happened last spring at Ogvaldness on the island of Kormt?"

They shook their heads.

"Well, Olaf had stopped there with a large force, and was in the process of celebrating the Lenten season. It so happened that a ship, fully manned with warlocks and sorcerers, docked nearby on the same island, with passengers and crew disembarking to do their rituals. To make the story short, Olaf heard of it and had the whole bunch captured. After only a brief trial, which was a farce, Olaf had all of them taken to the skerries offshore at low tide and tied down.

"They drowned a few hours later."

As had been ordered, several groups of men from northern reaches of the Trondheimsfjord arrived late the next morning, mostly by boat, to join another number from Nitharos which included Orm, Sigurth and Sveyin.

Waiting to greet and assemble them was a large contingent of Olaf's guard, similarly garbed and heavily armed. When it seemed all were there who would be there, horns were blown. Then the Bishop and his group came from the church, while King Olaf and his aides came from his residence nearby.

The program proceeded as had been expected, which was in a format similar to the Christening of the ship, finally ending with words from Olaf. Speaking softly and plainly like a friend, he told of the wonderful spiritual revelations that had come to him, as it had to so many around the world. He emphasized that for the good of the country and all its people, he was on a mission to bring the glories of Christianity to all corners of the land.

"And that's it my friends. So now, if there are no objections, please line up and make your way into the church, where each will make a pledge and be baptized."

Olaf probably saw what happened next coming. There hadn't been anything said to that point; but there had been a general show of agitation as he spoke, especially on the grizzled faces of one of the groups, along with mumbles that unmistakably revealed an undercurrent.

The mumbles grew until one man burst when Olaf finished with *"Ny Ny Ny!"*

Olaf said nothing.

After a pause, the man added, "I speak for many here today. We don't see why we should have to change. We're happy with the way things have been. Our lives have been guided by the Norns and have been good and abundant. There's no telling what will happen if we turn our backs on the Gods now."

A good part of the crowd burst with their support. Following which the man shouted, "We just don't see it! We don't want to change! We want to be left alone to worship as we please!"

Olaf remained silent until the outburst waned, then said, eyeing the speaker. "Come forward, please, so we can discuss this further and understand each other."

The man did, the crowd parting, with many patting him as he moved through. While waiting, Olaf whispered a few words to his assistants.

"Would you repeat what you just said?" Olaf asked as the man came to him.

"Yes . . . We just don't see it."

"You just don't see it?" Olaf repeated, as if to completely understand.

"No, I don't."

At a subtle nod, the assistants, moving quickly, grabbed the man, who's name was Skeggi Lyra of Frusta, and held him as if in a vice.

"What are you doing?"

Olaf moved forward and put both hands on the man's face.

"Ny o ny! Stop that! **Nyyyyy!***"*

Olaf crushed with his thumbs ...

"Ny Ny Aaaaeeeeeoooooeeeeee!"

Olaf stepped back, as did his assistants, as Skeggi slumped to the floor, blubbering and moaning pitiful, ghastly, tell-tale sounds that stilled the crowd.

"Now, I hope the rest of you can see better," Olaf said. "If so, please line up as I requested earlier, and move into the church.

"So now we're Christians," Sveyin said as he rubbed his hands over the fire. The three had exited the church as soon as their part in the ceremony was over. Without seeking or wanting to talk to anyone, they'd returned to the marina and back to the storage shed, where they'd build a fire.

The three stood immersed in their individual thoughts for a good while, not caring to say what was on their minds. But when Sveyin took the little wooden cross from his tunic and prepared to toss it in the fire, Orm said, "Don't do that."

"Why? Right now, I'd like to burn not only this, but also the whole damn Church we just came from."

"Of course you do . . . and so do I. But these little tokens of our pledges have our names inscribed on them. We may have to account for them later as evidence that we're keeping the faith."

Sigurth grumbled, while Sveyin shook his head, both still in a bit of shock.

Orm threw more scraps on the fire, and jostled them around with a stick until they were properly placed, all of which was a delay to collect his thoughts. "Look . . . at this time we've got to go with what he wants. We've been warned about Olaf and how cruel he can be if he doesn't get his way. Today was just a sample of that. He's also chopped hands, burned feet, stabbed, hung and drowned to get his point across; so be mindful of the facts. Our only choice at the moment is to play his game, and grin and bear it."

"Grin and bear it?" Sigurth said. "I don't feel much like grinning right now."

"Me neither," Sveyin added. "Let's go home. We can go now, can't we?"

"I think so," Orm said. "But it's late in the year and a bad time to be in the water."

"Could we trade our skiff for a wagon and take the road?"

"Oh no, that would be worse. The uppers will be deep in snow." He stirred the fire some more. "I'm as sick of this place as you two are, and there's only one way to get out of here. So let's get back to the barracks and make our plans. If there's any chance on the water, I'm willing to give it a try."

"Shhhh . . . someone's coming," Sveyin said.

The door swung open, the rush of cold air scattering smoke and bits and pieces of the fire.

"Well, here you are again." It was Ashjorn and Halldor, with Ashjorn speaking. "All of you left the church so fast, we missed you."

Orm nodded, then said, "We're done here . . . right? So we had some planning to do."

"Planning?"

"Yes, it's time to go home."

"This time of the year?"

"We know it's not a good time. But we have farms and families and things to do there. And the weather is still at least sixty days from improving."

"We thought you might be thinking that way," Halldor said, "so we had to find you. The fact is that all of you *aren't* through yet."

"All of us?"

"At least one of you, I'm afraid."

"Afraid, heh." Orm said, breaking the stick he'd been using and throwing it in the fire. You know, since we've met, you've both seemed like friends; but with what's been happening around here, we've come to wonder who's side you're on."

Ashjorn thought on it, rubbing his hands over the fire as if he needed to, then said, "In a way, we're on both sides. Yes, we've cozied up to the King to help him out. But we've also talked to the likes of you, in hopes of the sides working together with a semblance of coexistence."

"You didn't help poor Skeggi . . ."

Ashjorn and Halldor looked at each other, with Halldor turning back to speak. "Look, we tried. All we can say is it could have been worse."

"How worse? You say we're not done here. Is that part of worse?"

"Not really. But I know you're not going to be happy with what I'm going to tell you. The King is well aware that what he's doing isn't pleasing to many of you, maybe most of you; but he's determined, despite that, to succeed in converting the country. He's doing what he feels he has to do to make sure all of you stand by your pledges. As part of that, he's requiring that the sons of certain leaders be hosted here at Nitharos for a reasonable time."

"Hosted! You mean kept as hostages?"

"Olaf prefers to call them guests."

"Oh bullshit. If the leader doesn't . . ." Orm stopped, eyes widening.

Halldor looked down while Ashjorn turned away.

"You want either Sigurth or Sveyin to stay . . . and be subject to the actions of those of us who leave?"

They nodded.

"Look, it's not as bad as it sounds," Halldor said. "Whoever stays will be treated as guests, that I can assure you. And life here in Nitharos should be a lot more interesting than back on the farm in the dead of winter. I say that because since all of you have been here, it's been hard not to notice the fun the boys have been having with the local female population."

"How long?"

"We don't know for sure . . . Maybe a year."

After a few moments while everyone looked at one other, Sveyin said, "I'll stay."

"No, I'll stay," Sigurth said. "Gyrth needs you."

"That's not true. I'm just another hand on the farm, while you and Orm are a team, really. So it's got to be me."

"Whatever you decide will be fine," Ashjorn said. "Right now, let's all return to the Lodge. It's a lot warmer there, and Olaf is making sure there's plenty of food and drink for everyone. Besides, it'll give you a chance to meet some of the others who'll be staying.

"Do we know any of them?" Sveyin asked.

Ashjorn shrugged. "I don't know all the names, but there's Thorkel Arfindson from Skaun, Harvath Othyrmirason from Agthaness, Bjorn Bersinian from Austraut, and Arnljut Vikarson from Vrjer. Oh, there's another who just sailed in from Greenland, and Olaf invited him to stay over as well. His name is Leif Eiriksson."

Chapter 7

LONG SERPENT
999

It was harvest time, and Sigurth had been wielding a long-handled sickle with both hands since dawn. Now, hours later, he was still at it, making sweeping cuts with a sweep-step-step-sweep cadence, leaving neat rows of grain along the length of the field.

Sven was doing some of the same when he wasn't directing the actions of the many others, including Orm on the wagon, his children, and Gudrun and several hands, in a sequence that included shocking the rows, carting the shocks, threshing the grain and stacking the hay. The work was hot and dirty, with dust and chaff and bugs all about . . . not the kinds of circumstance that kept anyone in good humor. But it was one of the most important operations in the year.

Sigurth was bare-chested, wearing only long, open-bottom trousers tied at the ankle, and a loose head-cover tied across his forehead. He was dirty and pumped, with bulging muscles glistening from sweat that oozed and ran in rivulets. He was so into what he'd been doing he didn't hear the horse hooves noisily churning the dirt the length of the lane, past the stead and into the fields until the horse was almost upon him. He didn't take notice even then until the sounds that were building ended. Then as if awakened, he stopped and looked up . . . "What?"

"Now that's a fine greeting if I've ever heard one."

Sigurth blinked. "What? Who? Sveyin? *Sveyin!* What are *you* doing here?"

Sveyin slid off the horse. "Well, I just happened to be riding by . . ."

Sigurth dropped the sickle, and still breathing heavy from the last few swings, stepped forward, grabbing his best friend by the shoulders. At first speechless, then saying, "You . . . are . . . one . . . miserable looking . . . son of a bitch."

Sveyin burst out laughing, grinning from ear to ear. "This is about the welcome I expected."

Sigurth couldn't think. He had so many questions. It had been almost a year since they'd parted in Nitharos, and although there'd been a few bits of information filtering down through the marina, there hadn't been much in the way of detail. So now he didn't know where to start.

Before he could, however, Sven shouted from down the line, "Hey . . . What's going on?"

"Sven . . . Sveyin's back. He just rode up!"

"Well, Sveyin . . . that's nice, real nice . . . good to see you. But you've come at a bad time. We're behind with the work we've got to do, and we need to catch up. Sigurth, this isn't a time to be goofing off!"

Sigurth inhaled, his face turning red and his eyes about to pop. But Sveyin, not quite as rattled, shouted back, "Uncle Sven, sorry to barge in this way. I see you're all hard at it; how can I help?"

With that he pitched in and worked any way needed, he and Sigurth trading looks and shaking heads from time to time as they went along. Sigurth continued to seethe about the put-down; but he sucked it in, letting off steam by working even harder than before. When the time finally came to stop, after sunset when light was fading, he did so with a flair, casting the sickle aside and grabbing Sveyin, who was now as much of a mess as he was. After a quick scuffle, they rounded up the horse and jumped on. Ignoring Sven and everyone else, they waved to Orm, signaling to head for the craft-shop.

When they pulled up, Thora, who was standing by waiting, wasn't surprised to see Sveyin as she'd seen him ride by earlier. But when he and Sigurth dismounted, with Orm close behind, she first gave him a big hug, then, pinching her nose and shaking her head, said to all of them, "Get yourselves cleaned up . . . None of you are coming in dirty as you are. There are basins filled and soap on hand on the counter over there, so on with it. I'll dig out some clean clothes and toss them out."

Then there was stripping down and dusting off and soaping and splashing and snapping towels and enough foolery that even Sven and the men across the yard at the longhouse had to laugh. Finally done, they slipped into what Thora had provided and entered the shop, plunking on the platform around the fire. Thora had anticipated a spirited reunion the moment Sveyin rode by, so in addition to setting up for cleaning, she had horns on hand and mead ready to go.

"Okay, let's have it," Sigurth said to Sveyin, holding out his horn as Thora began to pour. "The only word we've received was back in mid-summer, when Ashjorn came by. We didn't expect to see you until Yule."

"Not a word," Sveyin said, "until I've had at least one horn. I came here in peace and had to work my ass off to keep it. What's going on?"

"Oh you mean Sven?

"Ya . . . That wasn't a particularly warm welcome I got from a supposedly favorite older cousin."

"That's for sure," Sigurth agreed. "And in case you didn't notice, he didn't speak too kindly to me either."

"Oh I noticed, all right. Is there bad blood between the two of you?" Sveyin asked. "I can't imagine anyone working harder than I saw you doing."

Sigurth grunted, shrugging his shoulders.

"Let me comment on that," Orm said, taking a good swallow before speaking. "Sven's behavior had nothing to do with what was happening today. There may be a little jealousy festering because little brother here is bigger and stronger and better in just about everything than he is, or it may be a bit of defending his territory. If what's happened in other families is an indication, it's not always good to have a number of brothers hanging around if there's an inheritance to consider. It's about the same as those with an ounce of nobility in their blood who feel they have rights to the same throne. We've seen a mess of that."

"It hardly makes sense here though," Sigurth said. "In my mind this farm *is* my home, and I work here. And although I've felt kinda like a partner, I haven't challenged Sven about who owns what. To me, since he's the oldest, he's in charge. But I'd like to think I have an interest."

"From what I've seen, you haven't done anything to indicate otherwise," Orm said. "But Sven's been acting like he doesn't see it that way. In fact, I see him treating both of us, more and more, as hands rather than as family. Who knows why? Possibly it's to make sure his kids are next in line. Remember, there are many examples of family members killing one another in situations like this."

"Well Damn! Now that's a pleasant thought," Sigurth said. "When I think about it, though," he added, "this bullshit shouldn't come as a surprise. When we got back from the raid at Skulifarm, the three of us moved into the old longhouse. That worked out well enough for a while; but then it got complicated. First, Thora and her weaving, and then you Orm with your carving, kept taking more and more space. Then Sven marries Olver and we're crowded, with more privacy in the back of the barn.

"So the shop is built, and although we still assist on the farm, and act about the same to each other, at least at first, there's a clear separation forming. I never thought much about it, but it's apparent now that others sure did. And Olvor's no help in this either; she's very territorial with her space and protective of her kids. It wasn't long after she moved in that I began to feel like tits on a boar."

Thora, who was shuffling around getting the meal prepared, but listening to every word, said, "Oh don't worry about the kids. They think "Unca Sigur" is next thing to Thor. Maybe that's eating on Sven, too."

Sigurth didn't respond to that other than snorting. Instead he changed the subject, saying, "How has it been on your end, Sveyin? Has Hrolf been acting like Sven?"

Sveyin shook his head. "Ny . . . at least I haven't picked up on it. But our situations are different." He added, laughing, "Gyrth is still alive, and though he's getting creaky, we're sure not hinting about a family cliff. He's still the head man, which brings stability, I guess."

"No doubt about that," Sigurth said. "He's really the man both sides of the mountain still look up to."

"Ya . . . There have been a few things that have happened, though, that might be in a similar vein."

"Like what?"

"Well, all of them, I mean Gyrth and Ingibjorg, and even Hrolf and Jorum, have been talking. As you know there are farmers about who have daughters but not sons. So they've been suggesting about certain matches I should be thinking about."

Sigurth laughed. "And how's that working?"

"Make fun if you want, asshole, I've heard the same about you."

"That doesn't answer the question."

Sveyin threw up his hands and let them drop. "If I really wanted my own farm . . . I mean real bad, then I guess any amount of ugly wouldn't matter. But the fact is a farm isn't tops on my list, and as for the hints . . . well," with that he screwed up his face. "What's more, there are a few cuties in Nitharos that are more interesting."

"Some or someone?"

Sveyin smiled. "You of all people should know about that. Look, we've gotten off track. Isn't anybody interested in what I'm doing here?"

"I've been waiting for that part," Orm said. "Have you been released as a guest of Olaf's, or are you on assignment?"

"The answers are ny and yada. Ashjorn is with me, but he wanted to stop at the marina first, then go see Gyrth. I didn't care to wait, so I rode ahead to collect you guys and bring you over. Let me explain what it's all about before we do that."

"Don't tell me it's another boat," Orm said. When Sveyin hesitated, he added, "Oh shit."

Sveyin settled back, poured another drink all around, and took a healthy swallow. Then he said, "It's all so complicated.

"You know King Olaf is a man of action, and that if he has an objective, he goes after it."

They nodded.

"Well, he went after it, the religion thing, I mean up north this time."

"Sounds like he gave up on the Trondheimsfjord," Orm said. "That whole area seems to be firm with the Gods they have."

"That's true . . . Anyway, as soon as the weather allowed, he assembled his fleet, and leading in the *Crane*, sailed up the coast with the intent of converting everyone he could find. The fleet didn't return until recently, so it wasn't until then that people around Nitharos knew what happened.

"Here's the story I've been able to piece together.

"Things went smoothly enough until they got offshore of Halogaland, where they were met by an opposing fleet. It seems a couple of powerful chieftains around those parts, Rauth the Strong and Thorir Hart, heard Olaf was coming. Since they and the Norwegians and Finns in the area wanted nothing to do with the new religion, they gathered troops and ships and sailed out to confront him.

"That didn't prove to be a good idea. They got involved in a fight, and soon found themselves on the losing side with several of their ships being cleared. Rauth fled into the Salptifjord to his home in the Gothey Islands; while Hart beached his ship at the nearest shore and fled on foot. Olaf went after Hart first, beaching the *Crane* and chasing him. According to what's being told, which between you and me sounds a little fetched, Olaf personally ran him down and killed him with a spear.

"Back aboard their ships, they found that winds and tides weren't favorable for entering the Salptifjord at the time, so they continued north to Omth, baptizing along the way."

"Wow. Omth is almost as far north as you can go," Orm said.

"For sure. Anyway, they reversed course after that, making a second attempt at the fjord leading to Rauth. This time they were successful, easily overcoming the forces that remained and capturing him.

"Here the story gets really grim. We've seen Olaf in action, so know what he can do if he doesn't get his way. Well, there at Gothey, Rauth and many of his followers refused to be baptized, crying out against Christianity. Olaf didn't stand for that. Some he tortured, some he killed, with ways like letting wild dogs tear them apart or casting them off cliffs. For Rauth he gave special treatment. He tied him to a post and forced his mouth open, putting a wedge in to keep it that way. Then he put the hollow stem of angelica-stalk in his mouth, inserting a snake into the stalk and applying a torch to the end of the snake to encourage it to work its way through."

Faces contorted as each person visualized what that must have been like.

"And that killed him?" Sigurth asked, almost choking.

"Oh ya . . . The snake eventually chewed its way in and down and out."

"Well, that's very interesting," Orm said, "But . . ."

"You mean disgusting," Sigurth said.

Sveyin shivered, "The man who told a few of us about it, went into more detail than we wanted to hear; so I won't repeat all of it now, but you can imagine."

"Okay, disgusting," Orm said. "What has this got to do with a new ship?"

"I was about to get to that. Rauth was a wealthy man with a big farm and many workers. When he was killed, Olaf confiscated all of it, including gold and silver and precious goods and weapons, and the biggest ship he'd ever seen."

"A ship?"

"Yes, a ship. It's larger than the *Crane*, with a dragon's head on the stem and a crook shaped like a tail on the stern. Both sides of the neck and all of the stern are gilded. The ship is called the *Serpent*, because when the sail is hoisted, it looks like the wing of a dragon."

"Wait a minute," Orm said. "I got the impression you were going to ask us to go back to Nitharos to help build another boat for Olaf. But now he *has* a new one, the finest in Norway."

Sveyin nodded. "If you're confused, I can understand, because I am as well. Maybe it's just the nature of Kings, or men of great wealth, to be obsessed with more or larger. Anyway, he does want a new ship, one even bigger than the Serpent, which is, believe me, pretty damn big. I was in the crowd on the banks overlooking Trondheimsfjord when the fleet sailed in, and we were all in awe. Even so, stocks on which the new ship is to be built are being set in place as we speak, below the Hlathir Cliffs, just across the Nith River from Nitharos.

"Oh . . . Maybe he's doing this to impress his new queen. You probably hadn't heard, but also as we speak, preparations are being made for a wedding celebration. Olaf is marrying a certain Queen Thyri, who recently escaped from an arranged marriage to King Burizlaf in Wendland. That's another long story, but it really doesn't relate to why I'm here. Anyway, it's getting late. Let's grab a quick bite of what Thora's been fixing, and then go over and meet Ashjorn."

Orm and Sigurth once more traveled to Nitharos, this time escorted by Ashjorn and Sveyin. In the months that followed, they were heavily involved as the new ship was built. It was constructed as a dragon ship much like the *Serpent*, only it was larger and more carefully fashioned in all its details. The head and tail were gilt, and the gunwales were as high as those on a seagoing vessel. Olaf called this new ship the *Long Serpent*, and the one he had commandeered at Salptifjord the *Short Serpent*. The new ship was the largest and best ever built in Norway, and correspondingly the most costly.

Chapter 8
SVOLTH
1000

Sigurth and Orm were on the *Sea Eagle*. The ship had only recently been taken out of its winter shed, and although there weren't problems they could see, they felt a test run should be made. They gathered as many crew as necessary and rowed out into the fjord, then turned toward the inlet. Since a light breeze was blowing out of the south, they unfurled the sail and tied the lines, and soon the ship was slicing water in fine fashion into the Norwegian Sea. After making a few moves in open water, they turned the ship about before losing sight of land and headed back. Everything was in order. Floor plates had been lifted while the run was being made to inspect the tightness of plank siding; here things checked out as well, with only a few damp areas to be seen. These were marked, so when back on the blocks they could be reviewed, with either recaulking or the fitting and riveting-in of closure spars.

They'd been so busy rowing and steering they didn't see the two men riding down the trail to the marina. But as they eased the ship into place by the blocks and tossed the hawsers, there they were. Neither Sigurth or Orm recognized the men by name, but they were ones seen previously in Nitharos, and were dressed in colors identifying them as Olaf's men. The most disturbing thing about them was that one was carrying a banner on a long staff.

"Oh shit," Sigurth muttered as he and Orm worked their way down the gangplank. "Any idea what this is about?"

"None at all."

Any hopes that the two weren't looking for them were dashed when as soon as they stepped off, the men straightened, waving for them to come over.

"Can we help you?" Orm said, aptly concealing the fact it was the last thing he wanted to do.

"Ya. You're Orm and you're Sigurth Gunnarson, right?" One of the men said, leaning forward in the saddle.

Orm nodded. "And you're from Nitharos."

The man laughed. "I guess that's obvious. I'm Vagn Akason, aide to King Olaf, and this is Markus. We know you two because we've seen both of you before in Nitharos, working on those ships for the King. You're well known because of what you did there; so you just can't hide anywhere.

"You've probably guessed why I'm here because of this banner, and if you guessed it represents a war-arrow, you're right. The King is sending riders in all directions to assemble a fleet for a special mission."

"Are we at war?"

"Not really . . . and we don't want to be. As you know, King Olaf recently was married. That's working well enough, but there's a concern about considerable holdings the Queen owns in Wendland. In order to remove any doubt about them, the King intends to gather a fleet and make such an impressive show that a certain King Burizlaf won't challenge possession of the holdings in question."

Orm looked at Vagn, then at Sigurth, his face bland; but Sigurth could tell his mind was whirling.

"Let me get this straight," Orm finally said. "The King is assembling a fleet to sail around Norway and past Denmark and its damned Oresund, all the way to Wendland, a land full of Jomsviking pirates, the same ones whose invasion we had to fight off six years ago, just to make sure the Queen's dowry, which she got when she agreed to a marriage she subsequently jilted, is in good hands?"

Vagn shuffled in the saddle and glanced a Markus, then looked back. "I haven't heard it expressed that way before, but that is what it is."

He changed the subject. "Now, the ship being pulled out of the water, is it yours?"

"Oh ny o ny," Orm said. "It belongs to a number of farmers about here in joint ownership."

"Is Gyrth Torkelsson one of them? He's on a list of men I'm supposed to see."

"Ya. He's only a short distance away. We can take you to him."

"Good.

"Now the other ships docked here . . . Who do they belong to?"

"Well, the smaller ones and the skiffs are for fishing and local traffic; which means none of them will do for what you want. I don't know who owns the two larger ones. We get traffic from time to time of boats with people either wanting to trade or needing to repair. They come and go."

"Any of them pirates?"

Orm shrugged. "You ask them."

Vagn snorted. "Well maybe not." Then he looked at Sigurth, who'd been standing by but out of the conversation. "Sigurth, how old are you?"

Caught by surprise, Sigurth hesitated, then said, "Nineteen . . . Why?"

"Close enough," Vagn said. "Close enough . . . Let me explain. Both of you know Ashjorn, right?"

"Oh ya."

"Okay. He's helping the king assemble the crew for the *Long Serpent*, and the King wants it be composed of the best fighting men available, men no younger than twenty or older than sixty. Sigurth, your name came up, not only because you helped build the ship, which could be helpful if there were troubles along the way, but also because you're recognized as a champion in games and martial arts. Ashjorn spoke very highly of you.

"As did a certain Sveyin Gyrtheson . . . Of course you know him."

"Well, ya! He's my cousin. What's the word with him? Is he being selected for the crew too. He should be . . . He's the best archer I've ever seen."

"Really," Vagn said. "I didn't know. It doesn't matter because he may be involved in something else.

"But enough here. I need to get moving, first to see Gyrth, then to be on my way. As usual, assembling a fleet isn't a simple matter, especially when the schedule is tight. I'll be back this way in a few days, though. So Sigurth, if you can get your things together, you can follow along with me back to Nitharos."

Later, after Vagn and Markus left, there was a meeting. Gyrth, Hrolf, Orm, and Sigurth, who'd been there initially, and Sven and Einer, who'd been summoned, were now all together.

"Another mission . . . damn!" Gyrth said, shaking his head. "And for the shallowest of reasons."

"It sounded like there wasn't much danger, though," Sven said. "I mean, being just an escort and all."

"Oh don't let that fool you," Orm said. "Any time you go to sea, you've got to be aware anything can happen. In the times we've been out, we've been lucky. We haven't been involved in a battle at sea, the fighting part that is. At Hjorungafjord we were little more that spectators; and we haven't been hit by weather we couldn't handle. Either of those can be disastrous, particularly the latter, as ships and even fleets of ships have disappeared in storms; and once in the water, we all know we'll have only minutes to live if we're not pulled out."

"Being an escort sounds too cushy to me," Gyrth said, shaking his head. "Too cushy. I know Olaf is familiar with Wendland; he spent a lot of time there growing up; but . . ."

"Seems like he started with pirating when he was there too," added Einer.

"And remember," Hrolf said. "He was in one of the groups against us at the Danavirki."

"Ya. All of that adds up to something that bothers me," Gyrth said. "How can you trust people around Wendland when they switch sides as easily as the wind switches direction. On the other hand, Sigurth, I like the part about you being selected to be on the *Long Serpent*. That's some ship with its size and height. It should be the safest ship around if things do come to fighting."

"That may be, but I'd still rather be on the *Sea Eagle*," Sigurth said. "The *Sea Eagle's* our ship and holds our people, and I feel it's where I belong."

"Nonsense," Orm said. "Being a part of the group that's going to be on the *Long Serpent* is quite an honor. You're going to be rubbing elbows with folks that will be good to know, as well as the King himself. As Vagn explained, the backbone of the crew will be the King's bodyguard, which had previously been picked for their strength and prowess; so all in all, it should be a great experience. By the way, Gyrth, any ideas on assignments for the *Sea Eagle*?"

"Would you like to go?"

"Sure. The boats in good shape, but you'll still need someone who knows it real well, and that's me."

"Well, Hrolf and Sven won't be going for the same reason as before," Gyrth said, "and I've been told Sveyin may not be available; all of which makes the first choices from around here quite limited. So I'll go again too." He laughed. "It was good to hear that Olaf would consider men under sixty for his crew. I guess I'm not as old as I thought."

"I'll go too," said Einer, standing up and taking the stance of a warrior in combat. "I missed the other trips and all the fun you've had, and I'm tired of it."

When Vagn stopped by a few days later, Sigurth left with him; but he wasn't alone because Gyrth and Orm hitched the wagon and followed along. There had been something about what had been said that had them wondering, with the words "something else" in the description of an assignment for Sveyin having too many meanings. Could there be a possibility they might never see him again? That thought was far-fetched, Gyrth admitted; but he couldn't help thinking it for someone whose energy and spirit delighted him so much.

They drove into Nitharos with the intent of heading to the barracks where Sveyin had been staying during the building of the *Long Serpent* the year before; but they didn't get there.

The main reason was that the whole area was hopping. When they rounded the last turn, the panorama that was the town and harbor and all the surroundings, as usual, came into view. Normally expansive but quiet, it was now more active than they'd ever seen before. Docked along the shore were a number of large ships, including the *Long Serpent*, the *Short Serpent*, the *Crane*, and others they couldn't identify. In addition, there were many ships the size of the *Sea Eagle*, one just arriving and jockeying to find a space to dock; while in the surrounding waters of the fjord, smaller craft moved about like water-bugs.

The crews from all those ships had come ashore and were moving about, as sailers do, looking for anything of interest. This was a problem since Nitharos was a new town with not much yet built, certainly not large enough to accommodate the numbers now roaming about. This led to a city of tents being formed in random fashion offshore beside the docks.

As they passed the church, one of the few buildings in place, a shout came from someone in the group exiting the front door. They immediately recognized the voice, as no one else they knew could be as idiotically spirited. It was Sveyin. Before the wagon could be brought to a halt, Sigurth was out and jumping, with the two meeting and tussling and making enough noise to bring everyone in the vicinity to a standstill.

When that settled, Sveyin turned, bouncing and smiling, to greet the others. During this time, the group he'd been with had patiently stood by and smiled at the antics. One finally said, "Sveyin . . . Have fun, we'll be on our way. Catch up with you later."

"Whoops," Sveyin said. "Hold on . . . I'd like you to meet my family."

As the introductions were being made, both Gyrth and Orm had questions, as in most cases they were familiar with the families, or at least the areas, they were from. All except one of them, that is.

"You came from Greenland?" Orm said.

"That's right," said the young man called Leif.

"We get a lot of traffic at our little marina south of here, and hear of many places; but of Greenland almost nothing, as if it's more of a rumor."

"Oh, it's real all right," Leif said with a chuckle. "Sveyin will soon have a lot to say about it."

With that the group nodded their good-byes and turned away.

As things quieted, Gyrth said, "Son, direct us to a place where we can relax and talk. Things have been hinted at in ways we have no way of understanding. And while we have to get back, and quickly because we have the *Sea Eagle* to sail, we didn't want to do so without coming here first and talking to you."

"Pa, Orm," Sveyin said. "You have no idea of how happy I am to see all of you. I really wanted to get home and visit; but things weren't going to work out for me to go. And it's not because of this mission of the King's . . . that's something else entirely.

"But first things first . . . a place to go park."

Sveyin thought on it, looking about. "The barracks are loaded up, and even double bunked. The same for the barns and almost every other building. As you can see, the town's nowhere near big enough to handle what's happening right now. I'd suggest finding a spot away from traffic and setting up a tent, much like what you can see already happening down by the ships."

This they did, tipping the emptied wagon and using it, not only to buffer the wind, but also to give a bit of enclosure to the area they selected. They set up the tent and stocked their goods, and were in the process of settling in and getting comfortable, when Sveyin noticed what was left in the way of provisions. He grabbed Sigurth and snapped his head as if to say *follow me*, and with that they were gone, last seen threading their way in the direction of the Lodge.

Not choosing to wait, Orm and Gyrth started a fire, set up the tripod, hung the cook-pot and made preparations for a meal that could be made from what was left. They didn't need to go further, however, for they soon heard familiar voices long before the people appeared. They were from the boys making their way back, laden with loaves of bread, slabs of meat, a pot of stew and a keg, that altogether were almost too much for the two strapping men to carry.

Setting them down, the first item given attention was the keg, from which a quick round of horns were poured. As the last was filled, Sigurth raised his and said, "Here's to Sveyin, who I hope will tell us what he's been doing since we saw him last, because it's got to be interesting. When we went into the back of the lodge where food was being prepared, the girls . . . well . . . they couldn't stop giggling. And when "Lover-boy" asked for food to take to his family who'd just gotten into town, they fell all over him."

"Oh, listen to him," Sveyin said. "They were agog over the hunk I brought along. Let's drink to him."

The older men looked at each other, shaking their heads as the nonsense continued, until Orm raised his horn and said, "Whatever . . . *Skoll!*" With that they finally sat down.

"Okay, let's get serious," Gyrth said. "Son, what's going on. When Vagn brought the war arrow, he said you wouldn't be a part of the armada King Olaf is assembling because Olaf had another assignment for you. Then this Leif fellow said something about you soon knowing a lot about a place we weren't sure existed."

Sveyin settled back, looked into the fire for a moment, then scanned the three. "It's obvious the armada to Wendland isn't the only thing on Olaf's mind. Before that there was the Christianizing of all lands under his control. We know about that first hand from last year. Well, that mission is still ongoing. A few weeks ago, two ships left for Iceland. Aboard were several ordained men. Their assignment was to proclaim and establish the new religion there. As a part of that plan, Olaf is retaining hostages from some of the noblest Icelanders currently in Nitharos. Their names mean little to you, but I've been in their company since being detained.

"In a few days, two more ships will leave, this time for Greenland. The ships will be knorrs, and will be loaded with supplies needed for the new colonies there, including as many cattle and sheep as can be carried. Also going, in addition to the crew, will be Leif Eiriksson, who you just met, a priest and a few clerics, whose mission will be like those going to Iceland . . . to establish Christianity.

"I am to accompany him and be his assistant."

Gyrth's fear had been correct.

For a good while the only sounds were those from the city. Somebody yelled; a horse whinnied; a girl laughed; all blended by the sounds of movement. Then Sigurth got up and poured another round.

"You're going to Greenland," Gyrth said, more as a question.

"Ya."

"Tell me about it . . . Who discovered it? When was it settled? What's it like?"

Sveyin shuffled a bit, "I've spent a lot of time with Leif this past year, so all I can pretend to know is what I've heard from him.

"The fact you've heard little about Greenland isn't surprising, because any awareness to it at all is fairly recent. I'm not sure who discovered it or when, but the impression I got was that it was by accident, someone getting lost going to Iceland and finding it instead. Then fifteen or twenty years ago, Leif's father, a man called Eirik the Red because of his flame red hair, went there, spending two years exploring its coasts."

He didn't mention that Eirik left Iceland because he was banished.

"Satisfied that it would be ideal for colonization, he returned to Iceland and extolled the land's qualities, giving it its pleasant sounding name. The result was that he was able to interest a large group, over 500 people, to return with him. Leif had to admit, however, that it wasn't an easy trip; because of the 25 ships that left, only18 made it."

"You mean seven ships sunk? That would mean over a hundred people . . .'"

"Leif said the others turned back. He didn't say whether any of them sunk.

"Anyway, that's basically it. More people have moved there since the first group, and the settlements are growing. As for what it's like, apparently it's much like the north country here, and also like Iceland, with fjords along the coasts and glaciers in the mountains."

"If it's beyond Iceland," Gyrth asked, "just how much farther is it?"

"From what I gather, Greenland's as far from Iceland, as Iceland is from here."

"By the Gods," Gyrth said, shaking his head. "That's a long way."

"Ya sure, it is. But Leif said that in coming here last year, he felt he could have made the trip from Greenland without stopping along the way."

"Is this Greenland getting near to the edge," Sigurth asked. "It must be getting close."

"I asked Leif the same question, and he laughed. He said that Asia going east is a long, long way; and Africa going south is too. So there's no telling how far west that edge can be expected. What's been settled so far may not be close, because there's a man living in Greenland, a Bjarni Herjolfsson, who got lost trying to find Greenland soon after Eirik established the colonies, and sighted lands even farther away. Leif's very interested in what Bjarni had to say about that, and wants to go there."

Gyrth rocked in place as he tried to absorb all of this. Finally he said, "Sveyin . . . a trip so far . . . when will you return? Will we ever see you again?"

"Oh, I certainly hope so. Ya, It's quite a trip, one that I'm getting excited about; but it's not a forever thing, at least not in my mind. There's no telling, though, what will happen once we get there."

"But the farm . . . your life here?"

"Pa . . . We've discussed that already. The farm, my home, which I love, will not be *my* farm; and I won't fight Hrolf for it because he's not only my brother, he's a good man."

"Ya," Gyrth nodded. "But it will always be your home if you want it. Another thing," he added. "You said you were going to help Leif bring

Christianity to Greenland. Have you become a Christian? Do you no longer believe in *our* Gods?"

"That's difficult to answer. Here in Nitharos there's much more traffic than we experience around Bird Mountain. So we hear more about what's happening in other parts of the world. To the east for instance, ships have been traveling the rivers across Garthariki to places way south of it, like Byzantium. Men who've been there have seen parts of the world we've hardly heard of, like Greece and Rome and Spain and Egypt. And they've said each of those lands has at one time or another had unique religions, with gods and goddesses and stories and ceremonies that go back in time as far as ours and more."

"So what makes any of these superior to our own . . . including the latest one, this Christianity?"

Sveyin went silent, not knowing what to say.

"Oh, I know a little about it," Gryth said, "and so does Orm. So tell me this . . . does this "White Christ" tell us how the world was formed? Does his religion have anything to compare to our World Tree Yggdrasil; or have an explanation of the heavens and all that's in it; or of Midgard; or of the seas and the Midgard Serpent that's at the edge?"

"Ny . . . You know it doesn't. His bible only says that God, the Father, created the heavens and the earth."

"Ya right."

"Well, it's difficult to prove most aspects of most religions," Svenin said. "But there are some things about what's in the bible that I like. They make sense."

"Like what?"

"The Ten Commandments for one. They include things like "Thou shalt not kill" and "Thou shalt not steal." Things we know are right, yet we tend to ignore them if they get in the way."

"You're talking about pirates now, not most of us."

"That's partly true; but there's also revenge and blood feuds that are fairly common, and not just with the pirates. And might I mention Skulifarm?"

Sigurth just sat, his eyes sifting from one speaker to another, but the words from his cousin were penetrating deeply.

Gyrth snorted, then after a bit said, "All those words of reason sound so good. But look who's pushing everyone to change . . . our holy and good King Olaf, who was a pirate for years before he became "enlightened." He raided and destroyed peoples dreams like pirates do, killing and raping and stealing and plundering. Even now, supposedly a holy man, he continues to torture and maim and kill and steal to get his way."

"Shhh!" Orm said, taking hold of Gyrth to calm him down as he sensed that people walking by had stopped. He waited until it was obvious traffic had resumed, then said, with little more than a whisper, "There are things we don't want to discus in public. I'd prefer to leave town with the skin I came in with. Besides that I'm getting hungry. Let's take a break and eat some of the free food the boys scrounged."

Two days later, Gyrth, Orm and Sigurth stood on a high point on the bank, as clear of the large crowd of well-wishers as they could and still get a good view. The boats bound for Greenland were leaving from the docks at Viggja rather than Nitharos because of the tangle of ships there making other preparations. At Viggja, with room to spare, all was going well. As they watched, anchors were raised, ropes untied, and the ships eased out until oars could be dropped.

Sveyin was in the second ship to pull away. He stayed on the afterdeck opposite the man working the steering-oar, and remained there until the three on the high point had almost disappeared. Then there were lusty waves from both ends, and they were parted.

The night before they'd eaten well and partied hard. There'd been a camaraderie with Leif and a number of the crew that lifted the weight of what was on everyone's minds. And the King also joined at one point, with grand words that were listened to with flashing eyes, mainly because they gave reason for having more toasts. But there was no further conversation of a serious nature among the family, as all that could be said had already been expressed.

Now, as the ships faded into the mists of Trondheimsfjord, Gyrth and Orm snapped the reins to get the wagon moving, leaving Sigurth to go to where the crew of the *Long Serpent* were assembling.

The *Long Serpent* was the last of the ships to leave Nitharos. In a process that was intended to impress, the smaller ships, which were the larger part of the armada, led the way; then followed, in generally an increasingly sized manner, the others.

Sigurth was as aware of the Kings's concern for appearances, as he was about most else that was occurring, because once underway, and particularly after clearing the fjord, unfurling the sail and retracting the oars, there was time to walk about and chat. Most of the others did the same thing from time to time, so eventually every rumor and speculation, as well as each bit of real information, was universally shared.

Riding on the largest and most impressive ship ever seen in this part of the world was less of a thrill to Sigurth than to most others. Since he'd worked on its construction from the beginning, and had been aboard for its trial runs, it was, in a way, more of the same. But then again, when he walked by the rails, and stroked the shapes and carvings and intricate workings, he couldn't help but swell.

The ship notwithstanding, he was more in awe of its crew. King Olaf was most resplendent, as usual, with his cloak of colors trimmed with furs and sparkling embroidery. If his clothing and adornments weren't enough, when the ship left the harbor, he stationed himself high on the afterdeck, and while still within view, manned the steering-oar. Among others with him were Ulf the Red, who carried the King's standard, and Kolbjorn the Marshall. It seemed to Sigurth that each member of the crew was of some renown from where they'd come, with names like Bersi the Strong, An the Marksman, Thrand the Strong, Olaf the Manly and Grjotgarth the Brave. It wasn't long, however, before the great names and initial bravado segued into real people, all of which came naturally for him because he was not only outgoing and considered handsome, he was also known for his skill with a bow as well as recognized for his part in building the ship. The latter gave him a bit of prominence because also aboard was Thorberg Skathogg, who'd been in charge of the ship building, and who now looked to Sigurth for assistance at every need.

As large and impressive as the ship was, it was like any of the others in that it wasn't crafted to provide comfort and pleasure. It was crowded, with a complement of men sized more for battle than for travel. As such it had stacks of spears and bundles of arrows and lockers of individual armor, in addition to provisions for lengthy stretches at sea.

When the *Long Serpent* left Nitharos, it was the last of the thirty-one ships that started. Along the way, other ships fell into line from almost every fjord and inlet, including the *Sea Eagle* in its turn. In anticipation of this, Sigurth moved up to the high point on the prow hoping to spot the linkup; but it occurred too far in front to be seen. The line of ships, which continued to grow in number, sailed on without a break until it rounded the southern tip of Norway and stopped at East Aghir. There the leading ships made landfall, waited on shore and organized provisions for the rest coming in. Being the last to leave Nitharos, the *Long Serpent* was also the last to anchor. This could have been a problem, because it wasn't unusual for satisfactory shoreline to be limited, causing ships to stack up and be tied. But this wasn't the case here because the choicest frontages were reserved for the final grouping.

Like everyone else on board, Sigurth was anxious to go ashore, and did so as soon as he could, first having to assist Thorberg in making an inspection of the hull. Once free, however, he did, but didn't join the men from his ship who were raising tents, starting fires and settling in. Instead he walked down the line of camps springing up, soon finding what he was after.

"How are things with you then," he said with a swagger as he approached, his cloak in King's colors flapping in the breeze.

"Well, look whose here," Gyrth said. "We were just wondering if you would stoop to coming our way."

Orm, who'd been at the fire and stirring a pot, jumped up, and after a quick hug, said, "Damn, I'm really surprised to see you. I didn't think that ship we built would actually float."

"Oh it floats all right . . . and it sails like the wind. You might find this hard to believe, but we had to drag oars to keep from running over the ships like yours in front of us."

"Would you listen to him," Einer said, walking up. "You must have started drinking before you came ashore."

"Ny ya . . . Not so, but," he said, pulling a horn out of his belt. "I *was* hoping to find someone who would fill this for me."

And so it went, with food being prepared and the *Sea Eagle* crew lining up for the first hot meal in days. Then, as light faded, most gathered around separate fires to relax and chat before retiring for the night.

"What's the word?" Orm said as he and Gyrth settled down beside what was left of the cooking fire. "You've been elbow to elbow with the King for days now. You must know something we don't."

"I can't think of a thing," Sigurth said. Then holding up his horn. "But maybe one more round would help me remember."

Gyrth shook his head. "Orm, I continue to be amazed at the poor job you did raising him. Give him a drink before he pitches some kind of fit."

"Okay, okay," Sigurth said, taking a big swallow. "There's really not much to tell. There was a day when the wind kicked up, so we had to wrestle with the sail a bit, and it's damn big as you know."

"Did you tent up the deck?"

"Ya . . . Didn't you?"

"Ya . . . We had the same trouble."

"Other than that, everything went smoothly."

"Did the King behave?"

"I guess so. Anyway, nothing bad happened. I spend most of the time in the center section close to Thorberg. It's lower than the other decks, and since we check the hull from time to time, it only makes sense."

"Any leaks?"

"We had a few during the rough weather. But not serious enough to need bailing. Everything worked out fine. "Oh," Sigurth added, "I was given a chain metal byrnie."

"Ny o ny . . . A byrnie, an armored chain-link tunic?"

"Ya . . . I couldn't believe it. Those things are expensive. I never expected one, but a few of us who weren't as equipped as the King wanted us to be were furnished with one."

"I don't know if that's a *good* sign." Gyrth said. "It seems like the King is thinking that this mission isn't such a peaceful one after all."

"Well, I haven't heard anything to the contrary. And you know how rumors are; they'd be around the ship in a heartbeat. I think it's just the King's way with appearances. He wants everyone around him to look like a seasoned warrior with proper weapons and proper colors."

"Let's hope that's all there is to it."

"Ya let's. In a way the armor's a pain. It's heavy so we haven't worn any of it since leaving the fjord. And the salt air's a problem . . . We spend time almost every day cleaning and coating to keep all the metal from rusting."

A few days later when they put to sea again, the armada comprised sixty ships. The second half of the trip was much like the first, with neither weather nor hostility causing a problem. The most exciting part of it was running the gauntlet at the Oresund, where Denmark's shores rise seemingly close enough to touch on both sides. A number of boats from there did sail out; but they were hardly a threat because they stopped at a respectable distance and waved as if watching a passing parade.

Finally there was Wendland. Sigurth didn't see how it all worked, but he heard later how well their arrival had been orchestrated. The *Crane*, commanded by Thorkel Dyrthil and Justein, maternal uncles of the King, had started out first from East Agthir, leading a long, double line of smaller ships. When they came within a mile of land, the smaller ships peeled-off to either side, setting the stage for the large ships to make their approaches, the *Long Serpent* being the last.

As for the voyage, matters with regard to the purpose of the visit were successful, at least for the King. Word filtered back to the tent city crews had formed on the beach, that the meetings with King Burizlaf had been amiable, with the claims uncontested. It went so well, with parties and renewals of old friendships, that the King and his entourage were content to stay longer than originally intended.

For the crews it was different. At first there were the essentials of setting up camp—organizing defenses and assigning duties. Then, along with the routine of living, there were games and contests and contrived entertainments. The people of Jomsborg and the surrounding area were also surprisingly peaceful, considering that a few years before they'd invaded Norway and had been trounced. There were interchanges with them that were interesting enough, but with all that together, the conditions still drifted to boredom and eventual discontent.

Gyrth, as Captain of the *Sea Eagle*, was invited to some of the affairs by the King, so there was some diversion for him. Orm adjusted better than most. He'd brought carving tools, and set about crafting deigns that not only filled the time with what he loved to do, but also proved to be of interest in local markets.

Sigurth, besides being on guard duty on occasion, took part in the games, with the usual good result; but it wasn't long before those things lost their appeal. Eventually he gravitated to doing what Orm was doing, which wasn't unusual for the two of them had been working together for years, most recently on the rich carvings that made the *Long Serpent* outstanding. So parroting Orm in part, and adding his own creations as well, he joined in carving designs for sale. In time, the two had an impressive bag of silver coin to show for their efforts.

"Not bad, not bad," Sigurth said as he patted the bag and heard the metallic jingle. They were seated around the evening fire, had eaten and were biding time before moving to bed rolls.

Orm grunted, his mind somewhere else.

"What's wrong? You're not pleased?"

Orm straightened. "Oh, the carving part's worked well enough," pointing to the bag, "but I'm beginning to wonder if we'll ever get it home. I'm beginning to feel uneasy about this place."

"You're not the only one," Einer added. "The men have been grumbling for a good while already."

Gyrth didn't say anything, which seemed strange.

"Do you know something we don't?" Orm asked. "It's not like you to be so quiet."

"Oh," Gyrth said, hesitating.

"What?"

Gyrth looked around, as if to make sure no one was near to hear what he might say. "I don't like it either, our staying here so long, I mean."

"Gyrth," Orm said, "I know you well enough to know there's more to it than you're letting on. I think it's more than a feeling."

"Well, for one thing, there are rumors cropping up?"

"You mean about the Danes assembling a fleet and coming after us? We've all heard about that, but most aren't much afraid of what the Danes can do. But you said for one thing . . . What else?"

"Okay . . . The King's been aware that the troops want to leave, and has been on the verge of doing so several times; but each time Olaf's been about to give the order, he's been encouraged to stay a little longer by a certain Earl Sigvaldi, who I wouldn't trust as far as I could throw him."

"Who's he?"

"He's the husband of the sister of Olaf's former wife. They all appear to be good friends and all, but I just don't like it. Something smells."

Shortly thereafter, word was finally sent to make preparations to leave, which everyone scurried to do. Then in quick order the trumpets sounded, the cables were cast-off, and ships pushed out. As before at East Agthir, the small ships rowed out first until they were clear; then they unfurled sails and were on their way, the *Sea Eagle* among them.

The large ships took much longer to get moving, so by the time they were into water and under sail, the small ships had left them behind. This seemed odd to many who noticed the separation, because it hadn't happened on the way down. Another thing was noticed. The ships in the remaining group were eleven in number, all of whom stayed in close order as they had before. But there were also eleven other ships, smaller ships from Wendland, that seemed to be providing escort.

Sigurth had been at the rail watching lands to the south disappear, and hadn't really focussed on much else, when he heard a conversation nearby.

"What's going on here? We seem to be following *their* lead. Why?"

"Word is they're more familiar with deeper channels."

"Nobody worried about that coming down."

This went nowhere and was soon forgotten as the crew, after hours of growing monotony, began to settle in with preparations for a long journey. In some cases, board games broke out, and in others, assorted hobbies. Sigurth brought out a block of wood. At the camp at Wendland, the carving he'd made that brought the most coin wasn't one of Norwegian swirls; it was a figurine raised on a flat panel. In his mind the depiction was of Thor; but the person who bought it thought it represented a forceful God, to which he never said otherwise.

Now he thought he would try that figurine again, with improvements in mind to make it even more impressive. He was in the process of lining out the general design and preparing for the first cuts when his concentration was interrupted.

"What's happening now?" He heard from the group at the rail.

At about the same time others manning the ropes began to lower the sail.

Sigurth put the block and tools back in his locker, then joined those crowding along the rail. He could see their other ships, the *Short Serpent* and the *Crane* among them, now dead in the water.

"We're just drifting!"

Then there was a sound . . . not a sigh, more of a moan . . . growing from across the length of the ship, as men looking to the north saw and understood. Out of a bay on the island in that direction, there appeared a ship, then two, then four, then in ever increasing numbers soon too many to count.

Sigurth heard, as everyone else did, the arguments taking place on the afterdeck. Officers were begging the King "to hoist sail and run past the ships assembling in their way while there was still a chance." They were only eleven ships against a multitude, their own smaller ships and the bulk of their army having disappeared. If this wasn't enough, the friendly escort was surprisingly paddling away. To everyone aboard, and most likely to the crews of the other ships who were drifting, they were being trapped.

But the King stood tall, and all within hearing gasped as they heard him shout, *"Lower the sail? Let not **my** men think of fleeing! I have **never** fled in battle! May God dispose of my life, but I shall never flee!"*

The Marksman, the Strong, the Manly, the Brave . . . all gulped as they realized they were part of an impressive but small in number flotilla, facing an armada whose sails were spreading across the horizon directly in their path. They were silent as all ears turned to the discussion on the afterdeck.

"Who are they?" One man asked.

The men atop were looking at the banners carried by the ships, with answers finally surfacing. It was a coalition—there of Danes; there of Swedes; and there, the largest part and most shocking, *of Norwegians.*

Trumpets blew as a signal to prepare for battle; and with that the ten other ships moved in to form a platform. In doing so, the *Short Serpent* rowed to one side of the *Long Serpent,* and the *Crane* to the other to form the core; others then moved in and were lashed in place.

Sigurth, who watched, somewhat in sickened fascination as all this unfolded, didn't really know where he was supposed to be. He slipped on his byrnie and helmet and then looked to Thorberg for direction; but Thorberg had gone into shock and had nothing to say. Then he heard his name being called from up front where archers were being assembled, so he scurried over the rail and reported, joining a group of two dozen men taking up most of the triangular deck once weapons and supplies for battle had been set in place. The deck, being high and forward, was one of the best places for seeing everything, particularly the enemy vessels, which approached like a menacing wave. The wave was so long and wide, that when it was near enough to contact the forward ships in the defensive platform, it was also able to swing around to surround and cover all sides.

Sigurth was ready, with his left arm through the shield strap to hold the bow, his quiver in place and his first arrow nestled and ready for drawing; but at this initial stage of battle, there was little to shoot at effectively. "Hold your fire" . . . "hold your fire" was shouted from time to time as some found it hard to stay out of the action. It was difficult to hold back because the battle, once started, quickly rose in pitch; and they could see clouds of arrows going both ways along the contact points. Occasionally some would come their way, at least enough for them to keep shields up, a need emphasized when arrows thudded and vibrated, one catching a man in the shoulder.

They watched, hoping otherwise, as the inevitable unfolded. At abutting rails, where clashing shields and slashing swords and stabbing javelins were everywhere, there was the growl of combat and its redness as men fell along he line. But on the enemies side replacements streamed forward; while on their own the ranks thinned. Then, like a dam bursting, the line collapsed, and except for those who retreated to the next ship behind, the deck of one of the outer ships was cleared.

This brought the battle closer and it became possible for those in the larger ships to become involved. Sigurth and the archers, who'd been standing by, were now able to fire effectively. With a shout they dropped shields and raised bows, sending volley after volley into the ranks flowing across the abandoned decks. At the same time, men from the large ships surrounding the *Long Serpent* combined with the survivors of the initial battle. They hurdled the adjoining rails and drove the attackers back across, with the surge continuing past the decks in the outer platform to clear some of the enemy decks.

It was a momentary victory. For the Danes and Swedes, who'd led the first attack, the defeat was so shocking they cut the grappling hooks that bound ships together and drifted away out of range.

By this time the casualties had been high on both sides, with a number of enemy ships floating free with only bloody remnants of what had happened. Still, there was a roar from the men along the rails, and a shaking of swords and banging of shields from the flotilla that was damaged but very much intact. Sigurth, high on the foredeck, was one of those celebrating. But then the cheering slowly subsided to an eerie silence as it became obvious a second phase of the battle was unfolding. The larger part of the enemy force were on the move, soon jockeying for position and moving in, led by a large, menacing ship with plated sides.

"That's the *Barthi*," someone whispered. "That's Earl Eirik's ship." *Earl Eirik, Earl Eirik,* Sigurth thought. *He was the son of Earl Hakon who had led the victory at Horundarfjord 6 years before.*

The battle began again, with the attackers having a fresh supply of men and arms. It followed the same as before with heavy casualties on both sides, which with the relentless pressure being exerted, led to another sickening inevitable. One by one, remaining parts of the defensive assembly were cleared of men, including the *Short Serpent* and the *Crane*, meaning that the *Long Serpent* was finally alone, hemmed-in on all sides.

There had been a lull as preparations were being made for the final assault. On the *Long Serpent*, survivors from other ships were now combined with the regular crew to form a formidable looking wall along the rails looking down on the ships surrounding them. On the foredeck, however, appearances weren't quite as impressive, as there there was an almost frantic search for arrows. Sigurth had used up all but a few of his, as had everyone else. And while they'd received a number in return, most enemy volleys had been directed to where the lines were in contact. So now he had to scramble about, wrenching arrows from wherever they'd stuck, even those porcupined in bodies.

Then the assault began, with the din rising to a cacophony of horrible sounds eclipsing what it had been before. As it raged, Sigurth emptied his supply of arrows a second time, taking aim with each shot and knowing there were hits; but in the frenzy knowing there wasn't time to count. Nor was there time to think of safety. Arrows passed like angry bees and screams sounded around him. He felt tugs more than once as incomings snagged folds of his byrnie; but he wasn't seriously hit and didn't move from his station until his arrows were gone and he'd hurled his last javelin.

Then he scrambled again to find more arrows.

He was scampering about collecting what he could when he turned to a roar even louder than the din . . . The lower rail of the center section on the side abutted by the *Barthi*, which provided a lesser height difference, had been breached and men were streaming over. He put down his bow, grabbed his sword and shield and hurdled the rail to land on the lower deck. Then as part of a human wall, he pushed and stabbed and clubbed, stepping over bodies and slipping on the gore that had become the deck. At the rail the last invader was toppled back for a brief reprieve, only to have the surgers regroup and press forward again. A man next to him jumped on the rail to better slash at the ranks below, but a javelin caught him in the chest and flung him back. Sigurth, whose blood was at a boil, wrenched the javelin free, and jumped back on the rail to take his place. Only he didn't stop there; he dropped to the deck of the *Barthi* below, and screaming like a berserker, stabbed and slashed until he'd cleared a space before the bewildered men that had been there. Then picking out the largest man in the ring now formed, he hurled the javelin with all his strength. Following the momentum of the throw, he spun, and jump-stepping, vaulted back up and over onto the *Long Serpent.*

There was a roar from one end of the ship to the other for another momentary triumph.

Sigurth didn't look back until he'd returned to the foredeck and his position; then he took stock. He was bleeding about his shoulder, as he was on his hip where there was a stab wound, and he could feel blood running down his cheek. He only remembered a sword that crashed into his helmet and stunned him; but he felt no pain and the battle was still at full, so once more he sought arrows.

Time and awareness became a blur where detail was lost, but then there was another explosion of sound announcing that the lower rail had been breached again, this time by more men against fewer defenders. Sigurth and the men on the foredeck switched to swords and shields and braced for the onslaught, but it didn't come in their direction. They could only watch as the breakthrough cleared the center section and then turned away from them to the afterdeck. The afterdeck was where King Olaf and the rest of those in the command center were stationed . . . along with the standard that fluttered bravely with the breeze.

There was a brief, futile struggle, and then the unthinkable—King Olaf, Kolbjorn the Marshal and others of high rank jumped over the side.

> Yester-year at Svolth, as
> ye have heard, pressed sorely—
> smote keen wands-of-wounds there—
> was the king's Long Serpent,
> broadside when his Barthi,
> boarded high, Earl Eirik—
> loot won the lord in battle—
> laid 'gainst Fafnir's bulwarks.

There was unrestrained Jubilation.

The attackers roared, with cheers resounding from deck to deck across the armada, and men jumping and screaming and banging shields. The celebration lasted and lasted, until eventually and slowly, it died down. It was then that the men who'd scaled the rails and conquered the

Long Serpent turned, and like lions in the den, looked at the sixteen men, bloodied but still standing on the foredeck. Shouts built up again and blended into insults and threats and shaking weapons, until one of the attackers stepped down from the afterdeck and threaded his way through the center section.

It was Earl Eirik.

As he approached, someone in the group on the foredeck had the sense to whisper "drop your weapons," and they did.

Earl Eirik laughed when he got to the rail, *"Oh ho!* It looks to me like you're all giving up. For a moment there I thought you were Norwegians."

The men around him howled, shouting threats and making gestures.

Earl Eirik held up his hand to quiet them down, then turned back to face this last remnant. Holding his chin, he said, "Now what in the world am I going to do with all of you?"

Sigurth didn't know what the other men were thinking, but his mind went back to Hjorundarfjord. After the battle he and Sveyin had walked about, and at one point had seen prisoners tied and sitting on a log. He remembered the beheadings; he remembered the brave indifference of the men about to die.

He didn't feel indifferent.

His thoughts were broken by a man, obviously a leader, who was climbing over the rail from the ship alongside. The man was angry and growled. "Sire, I know what you can do with that bastard standing on the end. *I want his head!* He threw a javelin so hard he killed one of my best men and wounded another."

Voices raised again all around the ship, and Sigurth had a sinking feeling. He wondered if the Gods of his fathers were real, and if this was to be his fate, would he be awakened in this place called Valhalla where beautiful Valkyries would welcome him into a life of continual carousing. There would be solace in that, and suddenly he was very thirsty. But he also thought of Orm and Thora. He hadn't thought much about their life together; he'd taken it all for granted. But now as his mind raced, he realized he'd been truly blessed to have grown up in their care. He'd never expressed it, but the feeling of love came to him, with the possibility along with that that maybe they loved him as well. And then there was Sveyin, that fool, going off to Greenland. He wanted to be with him and make sure the only trouble he got into was what he caused.

"Oh my," Earl Eirik said. "So you're a great warrior are you? I saw the javelin throw . . . it was awesome."

Sigurth didn't know what to say.

"Where are you from, son?"

"A farm along Bird Mountain, a few days south of Tronheimsfjord."

"A farmer?"

"Ya . . . I'm also a carpenter and a shipbuilder, like my foster-father."

"A shipbuilder. What ships have you built?

"The *Crane* . . . and this one.

"Really! You fought well for a shipbuilder. You must have been in other battles."

"Only Hjorundafjord."

"You fought with me at Hjorundafjord?"

Sigurth looked down, shook his head. "The only thing we were able to do was rescue some men on a sinking ship."

Earl Eirik laughed and clapped his hands; then he turned to the man who'd wanted revenge. "Sverri, you want this man's head, and he may be the one who pulled your fat ass out of the water."

"It wasn't him, that's for sure; it was some skinny kid."

Sigurth winced. He remembered the incident, but clearly didn't recognize the mans face which he'd hardly seen. He blurted, "I was only thirteen at the time."

Earl Eirik shook his head at how this was unraveling. He'd originally thought executions would be a fitting start to the victory celebrations they were going to have. He reconsidered.

"Young man, what's your name?"

Sigurth Gunnarson."

"Well, Sigurth Gunnarson, would you have quarter and honor me as your King?"

"Only if it's offered to all of us Sire."

Chapter 9

AFTERMATH

1001

Orm was on the steering oar, and Gyrth up front guiding the rowers, as the *Sea Eagle* slowed on its approach to shore at East Agthir.

"Oars up left," Gyrth said, "easy now right," as he coaxed the ship to a soft grinding stop in the sand. After raising oars, soft bumpers were laid across the rails, the bumpers extending to the gunwales and positioned to cushion contact with the ship already berthed. Lines were thrown and tied, oars were stacked and unloading began.

"Ooooh, this feels so good," was invariably heard as men splashed ashore. It wasn't that movements on the water were bad, they were hardly noticed because as the ship flexed with the pulsating surface of the sea, the crew adjusted without thinking or knowing about it. Back on land, there was an absence of those movements and it felt different.

Gyrth went to the spot on shore they'd used on the way down, and with the help of others in the crew, set up camp. By the time Orm, who was responsible for tying up the ship, was able to join them, tents were up, fires were going and preparations were underway for cooking.

Arrangements for provisions at both the initial stop and this one had been made with the local community, so when the first line of ships appeared, word went out. By the time the lead ship inched up on shore, rigs were pulling up loaded with stacks of wood, tanks of water, bins of grain and bundles of meats and vegetables. "Where have you guys been?" One of the drivers asked. "We expected to see you weeks ago. Everything okay?"

"Everything's fine, except that we're so hungry we could eat the ass end of a bear," one answered as eager hands helped unload the rations. In most cases, the first items reached for were kegs, and as soon as camps were set up, horns were out and spirits on their way.

Since the arrival was late in the day, by the time the last of the small ships like the *Sea Eagle* were in, it was getting dark. Had the sky been clear, the stars, along with the many fires dotting the beach, would have been enough to go by for the remaining big ships, which everyone knew were lagging behind. But it wasn't, it was overcast, with a light rain falling intermittently. With visibility so compromised, a signal fire as a beacon was lit at the opening reserved for those ships.

Orm paced about. He made his way to the top of the dune several times, then circled back to the fire.

"Sit down, Orm," Gyrth said. "You've hardly eaten."

"Oh, I had a bite a while ago. I'm not hungry."

"Bull shit to that. Here, have some more; this is the last bit we've cooked, and we're saving it for you."

Orm sat and reluctantly picked at it. "The big ships should have been here by now."

"They'll be here . . . they'll be here," Gyrth said. "No telling what's held them back. Everything was fine when we left."

"In fact," Einer added, walking over from his tent on hearing the conversation. "I heard from someone on one of the last ships to beach, that the last bunch had an escort of eleven Jomsborg ships to help clear the hazards."

"What hazards?"

Einer shrugged, "I didn't ask about that; but the escort was led by a good friend of the King."

"Who?"

"Earl Sigvaldi."

Gyrth stirred the fire, but didn't look up.

"There's a ship!"

It was late, and most were in bed rolls when the cry was heard.

Orm and Gyrth, who were still up in a self-imposed vigil, jumped and ran as soon as they heard it, joining the crowd that quickly formed around the signal fire. From there eyes strained at the faint outline of something being there. First seen as a torch that had been lit and waved while far out, the ship moved from the east and turned towards shore. Now, as it approached, it took on enough detail to be recognized.

"That's the *Pelican*," someone said. "That's Hrot Starason's ship."

Orm watched, stone-faced, as a ship about the size of the *Sea Eagle* eased to shore, throwing off its lines to hands eager to assist. Most of the crew immediately began to disembark, leaping over the rail into the shallows and by their manner obviously glad to have arrived. A few, however, stayed in the water, and despite the poor light it could be seen they were helping others who appeared to be injured.

An ominous quietness along the shore replaced what would normally have been cheers and welcoming hurrahs. This didn't make sense. Why the injuries? Why only one boat? From the conversations around the fires in the hours before this ship was sighted, it had been established that there were eleven ships in the final group, and all of them had been identified. The *Pelican* was one of them.

Hrot was one of the last to come ashore. When he did, he stopped when he saw the crowd that had moved forward of the fire and now looked at him in ghostly silhouette.

"I'm very tired," he said. "I told my crew to get something to eat and rest as best they could; but I also told them that by first light, I want them and the boat back in the water. I'd advise all of you to do the same."

"Hold on now Hrot," said someone who knew him. "Where are the others? What's happened?"

"Let's find a place where we can sit," he said. "I sure could use a drink."

A quick scurry later, and Hrot sat on a dune on the land side of the fire, with everyone else scrambling to remaining sides so they could hear what was said. Orm and Gyrth stood together on one of them in sick anticipation of what was to come.

"Where are the others?" was blurted by so many voices it was almost a chorus.

Hrot shrugged. "Don't know for sure." Then he told about the slow departure from Wendland, the strange redirections by the escort, and then, somewhere off the cost of Svolth Island, the appearance of a large fleet spreading out before them.

"We were confused. We were dead in the water for reasons we didn't understand, until we realized this was a trap."

"By whom?"

"Danes and Swedes for sure . . . It was hard to tell at first.

"Everyone looked for direction. Then we got word that King Olaf wanted to stay and fight rather than make a run for it. Trumpets sounded and we were told to form a defensive platform around the *Long Serpent*. Our ship was the last to move into position, which happened to be in a second line behind the King's ship. We were in the process of doing so when the enemy appeared on both sides of us. Thorkel Dyrfhil on the *Crane* nearby trying to guide us in, saw what was happening and threw our lines back, yelling for us to make a break for it and try catch up with the rest of the fleet.

"Well, we left, and it was a mess. Our men paddled balls to the wall to get away, passing between enemy ships as they came around to complete the encirclement. We even mingled with a few of Sigvaldi's ships before reaching open sea."

"Weren't you chased?"

"We were for a while. We were even shot at, with a few aboard taking hits; but we weren't the prize and that may have been what saved us. We'd just cleared a tangle of ships and gotten under sail when we saw others trying to cut us off; but they only made a brief try before turning back. Anyway, we went wide to the east and then, when we felt safe, turned north. The first land we spotted was identified as the coast of Scania. We followed the shore going west, but didn't know for sure if we were back on course until we passed the Oresund."

"What about the other ships? Was there a battle?"

"Ya da, for sure. We heard a roar when it started, and saw a little of it . . . clouds of arrows in the air and the sounds of ships and warriors crunching together; but we were busy and soon lost contact with what was happening."

For a time, the only sound was the crackling of the fire, then someone said, "Oh, they'll show up. That *Long Serpent's* so large and high, there's no way anyone's going to come aboard."

"That's true," Hrot said, "and her crew is as mighty a force as ever put together. But then again, they were seriously outnumbered."

"We all should have been there," someone said.

Another answered, "We had no way of knowing."

Orm and Gyrth went back to camp.

At dawn the next day a large crowd lined the shore extending both sides of the now smoldering fire. When the horizon cleared and revealed its emptiness, the crowd broke up. By mid-morning most ships were back in the water with sails unfurled and heading home.

A few, including the *Sea Eagle*, stayed two days more, then followed.

"Where are you going?" Thora asked.

Orm didn't answer. He'd been listlessly carving on a project that was taking far too long, when for no apparent reason, he threw his tools aside and headed for the door.

Outside the springtime air was still chilly, even though snow was melting and water was pudding in places around the farm. But it felt good . . . the sting of cold and the brightness of the day being a relief from the dark dreariness the shop had come to be.

It had been a difficult time since returning.

After the *Sea Eagle* docked at the marina, the ride home had never been longer. He knew there was no way he could color the news to Thora in a way that would make it easy to swallow. He'd played the scene over in his mind a hundred times until he knew exactly what she would ask and how he would answer.

> *What do you mean Sigurth won't be home for a while?*
> *The ship he was on, and a few others, were ambushed.*
> *You mean they were in a battle at sea?*
> *Ya.*
> *With who?*
> *We're not sure . . . Danes, Swedes. Then he'd shrug.*
> *Well, who won?*
> *We don't know.*
> *Where is he now?*
> *We don't know.*
> *Is he dead?*
> *At that point he wouldn't know what to say.*

Only it didn't go anything like that.

When he walked through the door, she was at the loom, so intent at what she was doing she didn't hear him at first. In fact she didn't hear him at all; but the glare from the open door startled her and she turned. Her face lit up when she saw and recognized the silhouette, and dropping threads and tools, rushed forward to greet him.

Then she stopped. Maybe it was the way he smiled; but whatever it was, she read something he tried hard not to show. She looked past him, where usually Sigurth would be standing with that stupid smile of his . . . and he wasn't there. Then came another telepathic look that she could read and her face dissolved.

It had been awful. He tried to explain that at the time there was no way of knowing what happened, and that until they found out, there was still hope. But she didn't get much comfort from what he said, and he didn't either by telling it.

Then there'd been a trip to the market which only made matters worse. As usual there was the social aspect of it, with the meeting with other women from around the district usually enjoyable. Instead of uplifting, this time it was the opposite, as a few of them had loved ones on the

Crane, another one of the missing ships, all of which restirred the agony and sorrow.

Had it not been for the children, Sven and Olvor's children—Thurith, Sverri and Thyra—they might not have made it. The children were a godsend, a second family, who'd been a delight from the time they were born. As they grew older, the bonds became stronger because they spent most of their time in the shop when the weather was poor. From the time they were tots, the shop had been their favorite place because of the crafts Thora would teach and the toys Orm would make. These were entertainments far better than what was in the longhouse.

Orm walked over to the corral, jump-stepping in an attempt to stay on dry ground. At the corral, he leaned on the top rail, gazing without absorbing, at the horses that had wandered out the open gate to the fields but had gotten no further than what was left of the haystacks nearby.

"Hi Orm, what are you doing?"

It was Sven, stepping out of the barn door while pushing a load of manure on a wooden, one-wheeled contraption. Orm also saw Sverri and one of the hands in the shadows behind him, all apparently at work cleaning the barn.

"Oh," Orm said, grasping for a reason to be where he was because he really didn't want to talk to anybody right now. "Oh . . . I've been wondering if the ice has melted enough for boats to be on the water. Thought I might hitch up the wagon and take a run by the marina."

"Can I go, Pa?" Sverri said, jumping through the door. "Can I go? We're almost done here, and I can finish up when I get back if it isn't."

Damn, thought Orm. He wasn't looking for company right now. Especially Sverri, who resembled Olvor more than the line that had spawned Sven and Sigurth, which really didn't matter as it was only because he was in a bad mood that he even thought of it. Besides, Sverri had a spirit similar to what Sigurth had had at that age, which meant he *was* a likable kid.

"Oh, let him go, I'd love to have company," Orm said, lying. "Especially if it's someone like Sverri."

Sven nodded okay, acting like he'd given away the farm; but then he swatted the boy's backside and everybody laughed. With that they rounded up the horses and hitched the wagon and soon were on their way, Sverri beaming and Orm more pleased than he thought he'd be.

The lane was wet and crusty, but the ground below the surface was still frozen so they were able to move along well enough. Orm shuddered to think at what it would be like in a few more weeks when the road thawed and turned to mud.

"Can we go collecting down feathers for Gammy soon?" Sverri said as they passed beneath the cliffs.

"Who . . . you mean you and Hjalmar?"

"Ya."

"Oh, I'm not sure about that. Hjalmar's a little young, and the collecting is dangerous work."

"How old were Sigurth and Sveyin when they started?"

"I don't remember. Let me see now . . . I'll check on that. I know Thora . . . Gammy," he corrected himself, "could sure use some more right now."

And so it went.

When they made the last turn, they gazed down on a marina that was empty and forlorn, with snow still gathered in places and rivulets meandering all about. They went into the shed to look at the *Sea Eagle*, but there was nothing to see other than the same ship that had been put on blocks late last fall. There wasn't much to see anywhere else either, or anything to do. So Sverri skipped rocks while Orm went by each dock and into every shed, mainly to be able to say he had.

Back on the wagon, he took a last look at the cove. Ice still extended from the west side about a third of the way across. That being so, he estimated it would take at least another week before it would be clear. He turned and snapped the reins.

"Papa! Papa!" Sverri yelled, poking him on the arm.

Orm held back, the horses stopping, but stomping a bit at the confusion.

"What?"

"Papa, look!"

Orm turned, seeing nothing at first; then he made out a barely visible masthead moving along the bank rising on the west side of the opening to the cove. As it moved, it revealed more and more until the profile of a mid-sized fishing boat came into view. His heart skipped and he stretched almost off the bench trying to see better; but then his hopes deflated as the boat continued across the opening without turning. It seemed to be slowing, or was he imagining things? Anyway, it kept moving and disappeared behind the eastern bank.

Orm sat for a minute, his eyes misting.

"You okay, Papa?"

"Ya, ya," he said, putting his hand to his nose, turning his head away and blowing. "I'm okay."

He picked up the reins again and was about to snap, when Sverri poked him again. Turning, he scanned for whatever it was this time, until he saw what Sverri had seen—something, a head. As he watched, the head became a body—a person climbing the bank the boat had disappeared behind. Then the person cleared the top, carrying a large duffle, walking down the trail that came from the bank towards the marina. It was too far away to make out the man's features, other than size and stature, *but there was no mistaking the walk.*

"*It's Uncle Sigurth!*" Sverri screamed as he jumped off the wagon and started running.

Orm wanted to jump and run too, but the horses were too excited by all of this, so he had to stay and hold them back or they'd all be in for a long walk. Besides, he was losing it.

At the farm, the largest and fattest sheep was slaughtered in sacrifice to Thor, the great God of the common people, with stirring exaltations by Gyrth, who thanked the Gods for their good fortune, and especially for returning Sigurth from the dead.

Then as light was dimming and the chill turning to cold, everyone, the farmers and family members who'd been aboard the *Sea Eagle* to Wendland, worked their way into the longhouse where kegs were waiting.

Horns were filled and raised and toasts were made, and time and again the process was repeated until there was a glow about the room that had everyone in comfort. It was Gyrth who finally got the celebration into what everyone wanted to hear.

"Sigurth, Sigurth," he said. "I know you've been asked questions too many times already, but it's been at different times for all of us. So now that we're together, please tell us . . . What happened?"

Sigurth, who was as relaxed as he could ever remember, burped, and then forced himself to sit as if he were under control. That worked for awhile, until he burped again and extended his horn to be filled. That being done, he took another drink while others did the same. Then he took from his tunic a wooden cross. He held it up, and without saying why, threw it in the fire.

"I left Nitharos," he said, "on the largest and most beautiful ship ever built, with the grandest and bravest crew ever assembled, for the shallowest reason ever contrived, all of it directed by a man whose self importance felt it necessary for all of us to support his whim. As a result, several hundred of those fine men were slaughtered. I wish I had the wisdom of Odin, who hung by a tree for nine nights in order to get the ultimate wisdom that would guide him, but I don't. But I do want to search for what makes sense. There are too many people about, this room is full of them, who deserve the conditions that will allow the fulfillment of their dreams."

This wasn't what anybody was expecting, and the room sent silent.

Orm came to the rescue. "Son, that's all well and good, and we'd like to discus this some more as there are some deep meanings expressed that you've probably been thinking about for some time. But there are things we'd like to know about that would be easier to understand. Like what happened in the battle? Who were you fighting? How did you manage to survive? How many others did?

"You've said King Olaf jumped off the deck and drowned. That means we no longer have a King, or rather means we will be having a *new* King. Who is he?"

Sigurth slouched, eyes flashing, seeming to be battling some internal fury. Then he sat back up and took a deep breath. "Okay, but one thing at a time.

"I found out after the battle, that while you and me, Pa, were filling the weeks and weeks of boredom with carvings at Wendland, the kings of Denmark and Sweden, along with a bunch of Norwegians who'd left when Olaf took over, were assembling forces for a trap; and while our King partied with all his former friends, they were very aptly setting the spring. How *any* of our leaders came to trust the Jomsvikings, who invaded us only a few years before, is hard to understand. Anyway, as a result of the battle, we'll have a new King. Norway is being divided into three sections, each to be ruled by participants in the victory. Our King will be the person most responsible for our victory at Hjorundafjord; he is the son of Earl Hakon, whose head many threw stones at when it was spiked on Nitharholm Island. He plans to sail into Trondheimsfjord aboard the *Long Serpent* in another month or so and to set about what needs to be done. I'm speaking of Earl Eirik."

"Earl Eirik?"

"Ya."

"Do you have any idea what he intends to do when he gets here?"

"Not much. Eirik had an intense hatred for Olaf Tryggvason, which he has now satisfied; but I'm not aware of anything specific. And I didn't hear him preaching Christianity. Hopefully, he feels we can worship whoever we want."

Sigurth then retold what he could remember of the battle, generally repeating himself, but adding details he hadn't mentioned before as they came to mind.

"Did any ships sink?"

"Only one that I know of. Sometime the boats sides were rammed together pretty hard; not only during the assault, but also when the defensive platform was being assembled. It was the *Beaver,* a ship of average size out of Maerin at the north end of Tronheimsfjord. Anyway, no one knows exactly what happened, but after being swept off into the next boat, the crew counterattacked and fought back across it. By then water was over the floor boards. The ship went down in a matter of minutes after that, much like that one at Hjorundafjord."

"How many survived the fight? You said there were sixteen on the foredeck of the *Long Serpent.*"

Sigurth looked down, reached for his horn which was quickly filled. He downed that, wiped his chin, and thought. Then he said, "We were lucky. I know Eirik intended to carve us up because I saw the look in his eyes. But then things happened, his mood changed and he yelled for all to hear . . . "We've won! Stop the killing! Quarter for all!"

"Maybe it was because we were Norwegians, but that about ended it. Up until then, during the fighting, those wounded and helpless were tossed over the rails to make room. Those with armor sank, and many of those who swam were axed. But it varied. Not everyone was a killer, so some were pulled out of the water. A few groups like ours who were trapped, also dropped weapons. That didn't always work, however; but most often it did, particularly after Eirik said what he did.

"Of those who jumped from the afterdeck of the *Long Serpent*, the only ones the men in the ships below were able to pull out were Kolbjorn the Marshal and Einar Thambarskelfir. This made Eirik furious because he wanted to capture all of them, for reasons you can imagine as well as me, particularly Olaf Tryggvason.

"Anyway, in all only forty-seven survived. That's a pitifully small number of happy homecomings from all those in the ships that had been ambushed."

There were more questions and more attempts at answering when, because of the late hour and the many horns, the party came to an end. Gyrth slapped his knee and said, "Okay, that's enough. This could go on forever if we let it; but it would be better to save something for another time.

"Hrolf, Hjallmer, wake up . . . it's time to go home.

And it was over.

Einer who'd gotten groggy, snapped back, and after mentally fumbling with what was happening, staggered to his feet, yawned and stretched, as did other neighbors and the sons they'd brought along. Sigurth didn't waste time either. As soon as the wagonloads from the neighboring farms were moving, he was on his way to the shop. Only he didn't go in.

Orm and Thora had gone through the door first, and were halfway into the darkness of the room where only a feeble candle was still burning, when they realized Sigurth hadn't followed. Orm backtracked and found him standing by the hitching post.

"Are you okay?"

Sigurth didn't answer. The evening was cold but the heavens were putting on a show. Without a cloud to mar the view, stars shone with all their glory, even adding the streak of an occasional meteor. If this wasn't enough, to the west above the blackness of the mountain, the "lights" snaked an eerie pattern.

"It's beautiful, isn't it?" Sigurth said, more as a statement.

Orm looked about, silently agreeing but wondering what this was about.

"Which of the Gods do you think is doing this?" Sigurth asked softly, as if trying not to disturb what they were watching.

Orm shook his head, then realizing that wasn't a response, said, "Oh, I don't know; the Gods are much of a mystery to me."

They stood a few more minutes, then Orm put his hand on Sigurth's shoulder, asking again, "Are you all right, son?"

"I'm fine, Pa. It's so good to be home. I just wanted to savor the moment. You have no idea how long this whole stupid affair has seemed to me. When I saw that wagon by the marina today, I thought I was going to fly."

Orm nodded, then remembering again to put his thoughts to words said, "The time was long for us too . . . very long. But now you're back. You said forty-seven survived. Have all of them been returned?"

"A few died where we wintered in Sweden; but the rest, including me, were on three ships that sailed up the coast, stopping along the way to let men off. Most of the men were from the Trondheimsfjord area; that's why they let me off there. As I told you before, I was lucky to hitch a ride on that fishing boat to get here."

Orm nodded again, deciding he'd already heard part of this, so didn't have to respond; but then he said, "Well it's good to see you're not on guard duty."

Sigurth laughed as he didn't realize anyone had ever caught on to what he had been doing. "No, there aren't any of the reminders here tonight."

"Reminders?"

"Never mind."

Orm didn't know where that was going, so he changed the subject.

"Well, you're home again, safe and sound, and for the moment, that's all that matters. It's going to be good to have you back in the routines around here, as my guess is that you've had a snoot full of travel."

Sigurth didn't comment.

"You are planning to stay, aren't you?"

"Maybe . . . Maybe not."

"Whoops. What's on your mind? Not Greenland, I hope."

"Maybe . . . Maybe not."

"Oh please. Don't toy with me, with us; I mean Thora was devastated when you didn't return. I'd hate to see her go through that again. So what are you thinking?"

"Pa . . . maybe I will settle down. I don't know myself. Without a doubt this last mess, the ridiculous trip to Wendland and all, has me on edge. I'm tired of all the people who want to be King so they can treat us like puppets, puppets on a string. I don't remember Gunnar, but I understand he felt the same way, and railed against the things that happened to him. From the time we're tots we've been told the Norns decide our fates. That's a little hard to imagine, because it seems so many others are trying to do the same thing. And I'm tired of it."

"So what do you plan to do?"

"I don't know. Staying home, as much as I love it, doesn't seem to be the answer."

Orm didn't know what to say, then, "I hope you're not thinking of following Sveyin to Greenland. That's so far away it's like another world."

Sigurth didn't answer at first, which wasn't a good sign. "To tell you the truth, that has crossed my mind."

"Any other thoughts?'

"Ya . . . Another idea was to sail south."

"South?" Where south?"

"Not sure. The whole trip we made, plus having to be in Sweden for months afterwards doing nothing, gave all of us more time to talk than we wanted. We were in limbo. Most were as frustrated as I was and wanted to do something that would keep them from having to go through this again. The most common idea expressed for becoming independent was to become a trader."

"A trader?"

"Ya."

"What do you have to trade?"

"Nothing at this point. I haven't figured out that part."

"You know, of course, that many traders start by being pirates. They plunder and steal and amass goods and slaves in the process; then trade them off for other things of value, usually gold or silver. Are you ready to go a-viking to do that?"

Sigurth shuddered at the thought. "There's plenty of opportunity for that. Every year, of the ships that stop by the marina, we know some are pirate ships. And almost every one of their Captains tries to tempt us workers to join their crew. Since I've come to full size, there's been a lot of that.

"But that can't be the only way . . . I could build my own ship."

"Ya sure you could," Orm said, "and I would help you. You could also carve decorations and figurines, like you did at Wendland . . . and Thora could weave her magic with luxurious, ornamental jackets and belts and handbags and scarves."

Chapter 10
NARVESUND
1002

Sigurth didn't build a ship. A number of trees for that purpose were felled from the nearby forest and trimmed and stacked beside the marina, but then they were left as Sigurth's attention shifted to amassing trade goods. With that in mind he, Thora and and Orm went to work.

For Thora, the effort was particularly enjoyable because she was excited about the challenge. Weaving and sewing were what she did every day; but with too much of it, the work was a drudge, producing woolen or linen products for everyday use or repairing the same. Even when she attempted works of higher quality, it was for local markets with limited ability for high end products. With what was intended for distant markets, however, the full range of her skill could be exercised, with special weaves and furs and leathers and braids and buttons and multi-colors coming into play. So she went at it with an enthusiasm she hadn't felt in years.

The possibilities were a rejuvenation for Orm, too. At Wendland, the satisfaction he'd received with the success of his carving had been short lived, because what happened to Sigurth had cast such a pall. Now there was nothing to hold him back, so with Thora's spirit adding to his, he reached deeper into his ability, progressing to complex threadings of serpents and animals and reflections of Norse Mythology.

The same for Sigurth. He'd never thought seriously about his experiences with carving, because his focus in life from as far back as he could recall were of things manly. Farming had been a chore, and carpentry had been a diversion, but the things that excited him were the bow and arrow, the javelin, the sword and shield, and all the training and events that were built around skill and strength and courage. In these he had been so skilled that most other matters, in his mind, were of little consequence.

The fact was, however, that he'd developed well in other regards. At a young age at the Skulifarm, he'd become not only introduced to, but also skilled in, the use of tools and their care, progressing surprisingly far. Then at the marina near Bird Mountain, this skill had steadily been enhanced, because whenever farming chores were over, he'd be at work beside Orm. During long winters in the shop, woodworking would segue from the nuts and bolts of basic carpentry to the art forms of carving and sculpturing. So when challenges were given to be involved in shipbuilding for King Olaf, Sigurth was more qualified than he realized, which even the accolades that followed didn't seem to dent.

Wendland changed that. When he went to market with his work, saw looks of appreciation for what he'd done and felt the jingle of coin, he was awakened. So he dived into the new challenge and joined Orm and Thora with an enthusiasm that made the days fly by. The problem was with interruptions. When the snow melted, the farm came alive like buds on a branch. There was land to till and crops to plant and animals to calve and on and on. And it wasn't that Sven glowered or cajoled or shamed him into doing his share; because he expected to do what he'd done since coming of muscle, and that was to be the hardest working and most productive person on the farm.

There was also the marina, which became a busy place soon after the cove was clear of ice. Both Sigurth and Orm were regulars there, not only enjoying the work as a source of income, but also being depended upon by the whole fishing and boating community. The *Sea Eagle*, for instance, wasn't just on hand for the whims of demanding royalty; it was an asset of the district which was used mostly for trade purposes at distances greater than what smaller boats dared to undertake, particularly those trips across the Norwegian Sea to the Hjaltland and Orkney Islands.

With all of these involvements, the amount they'd hoped to assemble didn't come together until late in the summer after harvesting, which was a poor time to begin building a boat. They started anyway, laying out blocks, then starting with work on the keel.

Coincident with this a longship turned from the fjord into the cove and docked. From the way the ship was unloaded, run up on shore and tented, it seemed obvious that whatever its owner did, he was through for the year. This was not unusual.

Nor was it unusual when the owner walked over and talked to Orm about certain maintenance and repair his ship needed.

His name was Audn Barkarsson, and he was far from being a stranger. He'd wintered ships in the cove before; but the history with him went back years earlier when as a young man he'd docked ships at the marina near Skulifarm. He was no longer the stocky youngster Orm remembered back then, because now his scuffy beard was streaked and his round face was weathered. His demeanor, however, seemed more mannered than his appearance; and the fact that he was still alive and active in a questionable and hazardous businesses made Orm pause.

"Looks like you're building quite a ship," Audn said as he saw the extent of the blocks and the length of the first member being shaped.

"Yes," Orm answered. "But we're getting a late start, and we're also shorthanded with what we can do until harvests are in."

Audn nodded and turned away to leave, but then turned back. "It's none of my business, but I see a perfectly good ship about the size of what you're starting. Why can't you use it for whatever it is you intend to do?"

"We might for a short time," Orm said, "but for long trips, like last year's to Wendland, the user needs to represent more of the district."

"Oh . . . So you intend to go far," Audn said.

"Maybe, we haven't worked that out."

"Where is maybe?"

Orm shrugged.

"What are you going to do when you get there?"

"We've got some merchandise and artwork to sell," Orm said.

Audn nodded, "I see . . . but you'll have a full crew on hand for when the ship is ready."

Orm looked at Sigurth, who had to bite down to keep from laughing; but it didn't work as Audn read the looks and howled. Beginning with sheepish grins, they did too.

"Looks to me that you haven't worked out all the details for what you want to do," he said, looking down, shaking his head and continuing to chuckle.

He stayed that way for more than a few moments, then looking up, said, "Tell you what . . . I'll be here tomorrow as I'm expecting another ship. Can you bring some of that "fine merchandise" for me to see? I may have suggestions for you to consider."

Orm and Sigurth brought samples of each of their works, and they also brought Thora. Actually, they didn't just bring her, she insisted on coming. It turned out to be a long day, because while there was a little activity around yesterday's arrival, a second ship, which Audn had expected, didn't turn into the cove until late afternoon.

Then Audn rode in. He waved, but went straight to the ship where he stayed a good while longer. Only then did he stop by.

"I've got some more repair work you can help us with," he said. "You'll see what I mean when we get her up on blocks; but the crew was heavy into bailing to get here."

Orm said, "We'll take a look first thing tomorrow. It's pretty late, and we're about to wind down for the day."

"That'll be fine," Audn said. "Sorry I couldn't get here earlier, but I had a lot to do today. By the way, did you bring a few samples of what trade goods you mentioned?"

"Yes . . . They're in the wagon over there where my wife is waiting. Give us a minute to wrap up and we'll meet you there."

At the wagon, introductions were made and then the samples were uncovered, Orm and Sigurth first taking out their carvings and holding them out for Audn to see. Orm's was an intricate decorative panel, while Sigurth's was more sculptural in nature.

Audn looked them over, taking them in hand and turning them around a few times. The two didn't know how a Sea Captain, of ships of questionable purpose, was a person qualified to evaluate their work; but they eagerly awaited his comments anyway, looking at each other and back to Audn several times.

"Very well done," Audn said, mouth and chin crunching unconsciously as he nodded. "My compliments. I didn't expect to see this level of quality."

Orm remained composed, while Sigurth was more readable. "We did carvings at Wendland last year," Orm said, "and even though they were done quickly under conditions at camp, they sold well. These and others like them were worked on in our studio and are much better."

Audn examined the samples a second time then looked up, "Are you the two that helped build the ships for Olaf Tryggvason?"

When they nodded, he smiled.

"How did you come to know about that?" Orm asked.

I make it a point to know as much as I can," he answered. "It's helped me get this far.

"And you, Sigurth Gunnarson, you're an odd one. You don't look like an artist. I see freshly healed scars in several places. You were in that battle at Svolth, weren't you?"

Siggurth fidgeted. This was something he'd rather put behind him.

"Are you the one who almost singe-handedly cleared Eirik's deck?"

Orm jumped in. "Hold it right there. We're here to show what we're able to do; we're not interested in going to war or reliving an old one."

Audn eyed them both, then smiled. "You're right, sorry. I'm just fascinated by what I've been able to find out. Now, what does the lady have to show? I've assumed that's why she's here."

Thora was waiting, and saying nothing to elaborate, unwrapped a package, unfolded its contents and held it up. It was an armless jacket that would extend past the hip, with a dazzling combination of fabrics, furs and sequins adorning each of its features.

Audn liked to keep a straight face at times like this, but his jaw dropped. He took it from her, and like with the carvings, turned it over, examining the inside lining as well.

"Do you have many of this quality?"

"Yes," Thora said, "Each a little different in color and material. There are also a number of accessory items that can be matched to the jackets . . . Women love them."

Audn nodded, looked at each of the samples again, then looked at Orm, "You said you'd be back in the morning to look at the boat that came in."

"Yes."

"Good," he said, then turned and started walking away, saying over his shoulder, "I may have some ideas for you to consider at the same time."

All of them returned in the morning, Orm and Sigurth going to examine the second ship, while Thora did what she had done the day before. She found a comfortable place out of the wind in the open work shelter, plunked down with a shawl over her shoulders, gathered materials and needles from a large wicker-basket, and went to work.

Audn arrived about mid-morning, tied his horse and started straight for the docks at the end of the quay where his boats had been pulled out. When he spotted Thora in the other direction, however, he stopped, doffed his cap and bowed with a broad smile.

Thora sat back, almost flustered; but then she smiled back, and still sitting with work in hand, acknowledge him with a wide, sweeping imitation curtsy.

You old fox she thought as she watched him walk away.

An hour or so later, upon looking up as she'd been doing from time to time, she saw that the three were leaving the boats where they'd been scrambling about, and were heading her way.

"They tell me you're the boss," Audn said as they arrived.

"Phooey to that," she answered. "If I were, there'd sure be some changes around here. You men have been yakking away for sometime now, so I hope some of it's been about those ideas you were going to share.

Whatever they are, please share them with me . . . You have no idea how curious I can get."

"Just start from the beginning, Audn," Orm said. "She'll have you back there with questions in any case."

Audn massaged his beard for a moment, then, "I was a little harsh with the men, but there are some realities that need to be expressed, so forgive me if you find my words demeaning."

"What you're going to tell me is that we don't know what we're doing," Thora said.

Audn nodded, with a hint of a smile, "Something like that.

"Look, you're all talented people with beautiful products for sale. My first thought doesn't involve me at all, and that is for all of you to move to Nitharos. You could set up shop there and take advantage of all the trade that's going to happen in a growing community where Earl Eirik, our new King, will spend most of his time. People are more aware of you than you think, and I have friends who could help you get started."

"That's a good idea," Orm said, "and is one we've already discussed. But the reason we've been doing what we've been doing this year, is that Sigurth wants to get away."

"From Norway? Where do you want to go?"

"It's not Norway," Sigurth said. "I love my family and home. It's just that we get pulled this way and that way from time to time, by people and issues we have no control over, nor interest in. So I thought, or rather hoped, that by reaching out and trying something else, we might find something better somewhere else."

"And you think somewhere else will be better?"

"I know what you're going to say about that," Orm said. "We love farming, but we get so wrapped up in the day to day of it, we end up subject to, and at the mercy of others. The King sends his arrows, and we go to war and fight and often die; and if we survive, we return and milk the cows and gain nothing by it. Sigurth's thoughts of getting involved in trade might give us better control of our lives. We can't fight the Norns, but maybe we can buffer the parade of other peoples blood lines and egos."

Audn laughed. "It's not the first time I've heard words like that. I guess I do what I do for much the same reason. I intentionally stay clear of Kings, and settle as far from their influence and ambition as I can."

"What *do* you do?" Thora asked. "Do you go a-viking?"

Audn hesitated, then looking her in the eyes, said,"Look, we're not here to talk about me. I don't have a problem, other than a few boats that leak. You, all of you, do have one. You want to do something; but if you start out without the proper help, you're almost guaranteed to fail."

"You said you had ideas," Thora said. "You've suggested Nitharos. What are some of the others?"

"Okay, but first, an overview. Since you were moving, in my estimation, blindly into something you know little about, I thought a little of what I've learned might be helpful. My education has not only been by a lot of doing, but also by a lot of listening at a thousand campfires on long voyages, and at many lodges on long winter nights. Many of these stories have been pure imagination, or contortions of stories told over and over through generation after generation. The gist of it all is that things keep repeating, and yet there are subtle changes. For instance, raiding or a-viking: it's been going on and on and is continuing today wherever there's an opportunity. But a number of changes are having an effect. It's been affected in England, where raiders stopped raiding and settled down, marrying local heart-stoppers and reverting to farming; and the same in Ireland and Frisia and farther in that direction for much the same reason. Our kin, the Swedes and Rus, have been doing likewise in Gartharika.

"So now, anyone on shore, almost anywhere we go, knows who we are when they spot our ships, and knows what they have to do if we get out of line."

"You mean it's getting harder and harder for an honest pirate to get ahead," Thora said.

Audn stopped, looked at her, then continued as if he hadn't heard it. "Our third ship is in a cove a ways down the coast. It's a knorr, and it's loaded with furs and tusks and goods from Finland, including a number of slaves. My plan for the new year hasn't yet been set; but I usually get going before the ice is clear, so I can get an early start at wherever I decide to go."

"And where are the ideas that concern us?"

"I'm not sure. I had in mind to take your goods, and offer to share half of what I could sell them for; but that didn't seem right, even to me."

"Did you think we didn't want to go along?"

"I assumed Sigurth did. He could not only verify the sales, but also bolster our strength if ever things get . . . shall we say, combative."

"And you said share . . . you mean half and half?"

"Of course."

"What about a quarter for you, the rest for us, and both Orm and I go along?"

Audn blinked.

"Look, don't tell me that an open ship is no place for a lady; your typical longhouse isn't long on privacy either. And look what you'll get in return. Orm can see to ship maintenance along the way; Sigurth can add muscle if needed; and I can help in keeping crews fed and in good repair.

But the biggest thing we three can provide for you is credibility. Wherever you come ashore, you're going to be looked at with suspicion, if not alarm. When we disembark, set up booths, and present honest, desirable goods for sale, that picture will give all else you plan to do a sense of business as usual."

Audn stared at her for a while after she finished. Then he said, "Damn!" and burst out laughing.

"Let me think on it," he finally said, then "damn!" again. He walked a ways as if returning to his ships; then he stopped . . . for more than a moment. He turned and came back. "Okay, we've got a long winter ahead of us, and time for planning. When the ice starts to break, we're going to be out of here. I'm not thinking of England at all, it's a mess. Maybe Normandy or places south . . . We'll see."

The start wasn't as smooth as hoped. In accord with Audn's direction, after the ice began to break and the winds became favorable, the cove came to life with two heavily laden ships rowing out. In a short line only a hundred yards apart, they turned towards the fjord inlet and were soon in open sea under sail.

The first thing that happened was Thora. She'd scoffed at the fact that her only experience on water had been short jaunts along the coat, and had assured anyone who questioned her to save their concern. For some strange reason, however, she was hanging over the rail and chumming fish before the first hour was over.

This minor problem was only a distraction for most, and most likely would have resolved itself, but winds picked up to such a degree that the two ships only made it to the cove where the third ship was waiting. When they turned in, sails went down and oars were manned, Sigurth taking one of the stations. If rowing and steering were difficult, beaching was worse, with oars and hawsers and anchors all being used to bring the ships in without the flexible but fragile plank siding being damaged. This done to sighs of relief, the ships were tented, some of the crew staying on board, but most wading ashore to set up shelter and wait it out.

Three days later, winds and seas finally calmed, and the flotilla of now three set out again, having hardly made a start. For Sigurth, Orm and Thora, the three days were a total waste; but that was true for everyone and was the nature of sailing where progress is at the mercy of the elements. The tent they'd stayed in on the shore was cramped and snapped about so violently as the winds gusted, that they spent most of their time bundled outside. They relieved the boredom that resulted in that by walks about the area. Doing that they got a good look at the *Goose*, which is what the knorr was called; and, if there was such a thing, took a little pleasure, or at least some acceptance, in the fact that everyone else was as uncomfortable as they were.

The only ones of these noted who seemed more miserable were the slaves. They were young people, eight in number, of which six were girls. They were cloaked as much as needed to survive; but they were also tied, so about all they could do was bundle together. That being so was more than Thora could let go by without taking some action. She'd seen slaves before, the traffic around marinas usually having a few, but this was beyond the norm. So she returned to the tent and took from provisions, then fed them food and drinks, not bothering to ask if anyone on the *Goose* had done the same.

Aside from the storm, everything around the cove had been peaceful and quiet. Then came the news that conditions were good and it was time to leave. Ships were boarded, lines were untied, anchors pulled and oars put to work again. The first ship, which the three and Audn were on, cleared and left; then the second. But the last, the *Goose*, started, but stopped in the shallows while a small party jumped overboard, raced into a thicket offshore and slaughtered some cattle they'd been eyeing since they'd been in the cove.

The next few days were smooth and uneventful, almost joyful for Thora as she'd finally developed her sea legs. The ships made a final stop for one night at the southern tip of Norway, Lithandisness. There they refreshed water and provisions, and enjoyed a hot meal on the beach highlighted by fresh beef.

Then it was back into the water and the North Sea, with intents to pass Denmark and Frisia and England to somewhere points south. Points south became a question, and not only to Sigurth and Orm and Thora, because when stops were made, Audn declared that it was only to rest and refurbish. So outside of nights on the beach and hot meals, there weren't attempts to set up booths and mingle with the population.

When on occasion they sat with Audn to understand what he had in mind, his answers would usually be the same. "These lands have been visited so many times, generation after generation, that I don't see much purpose in stopping." At other times he was more expressive, as when once when we sailed by the mouth of a sizable river, he said, "It's my understanding that the raiders in the past plied way into rivers like that, going hundreds of miles to seek out unsuspecting targets. They even set up stations near the mouthes of some from which to operate. Many of the raiders stayed, eventually blending in with the locals, the result being that now much of the population here about are ancestors, at least of the Danes. When they see us sail by, even though generations have passed, they remember what happened back then and are wary, looking at us like sheep eying wolves in the distance. If we had three-hundred ships, or even thirty, we might be in a position of strength or impressiveness to do whatever we might want. We are only three, so we must be careful."

They traveled generally southwest, always in sight of land, for days. Then they rounded what must have been a peninsula, because they turned south, then almost southeast for another good while. As before their stops were only for refurbishing; then with the next sunrise, they'd be on their way.

They turned west again for several days, only to turn south another time.

"What are these lands we're passing?" Orm asked.

"I'm not sure," was the unsettling answer. "I've never been this far south before. But a number of traders from around here have been to our land. For years I've wanted to repay a visit and see what their world is like. Possibly it will also be a land of opportunity for us."

"The slaves you have," Orm asked. "You've made no effort to sell them so far. Why is that? They require a great deal of attention and supply."

"That's true," Audn said. "I could be wrong on this, but for years, as I've mentioned, I've seen traders from somewhere down here, "Moors" is the word we've often heard, who put great stock in northern slaves, particularly young women. I've wanted for some to time to visit and see what I can about *their* culture. We won't be the first to do that; but then I'm guessing there hasn't been enough traffic to keep us from being unique."

Sigurth listened to the conversation with little to add; but the word "Moors" caught his attention and he didn't remember why.

At all the stops to that point, there was always a hope that something of special interest would be in store, like a meaningful exchange with the local population, but it never happened. After days moving south again, with increased boat traffic on the water and more settlements visible on shore, Audn gave the word that we were near a critical stop. The flotilla continued past a river with more activity than they'd seen since passing a place called Rouen near Normandy, when the signal was given to drop sail and set oars. Then they drifted.

"What's happening?" Orm asked.

"I'm trying to determine where we are in the cycle of tides. We don't want to go in at high tide; that could open us up to getting stranded."

Orm didn't ask how that mattered; but he did notice people beginning to gather on shore, and that was a good thing.

In time, Audn got the answer he wanted, that the shore was at low tide, so he directed the men to row. The beach was wide and clean, and soon all ships were in the shallows securely tied.

Another nod then directed the crew what to do next. Orm and Sigurth, with help from some of them, carried bundles of components to a place along the high dune, and in a short time completed nicely framed and festooned sales booths. Then merchandise was brought out and put on display.

The response was immediate. The ships had been watched from the moment they'd appeared on the horizon. Then as they beached and set up the booths, an initial trickle of the curious worked its way to them. When these first arrivals were treated with smiling faces and displays of products that amazed them, they spread the word and soon a crowd from the nearby community, that had gathered a short distance away, moved in.

They weren't just the curious, they were customers. Before long all displays were doing business with furs and tusks initially being most popular. These went to weavers and artisans who valued them to enhance their products.

Slaves were also in demand. They'd been cleaned and preened as could be done under the circumstances; and being young, and in most cases blond, they came off as unusually attractive.

The thought of selling these young people, even though they were from northern Finland and spoke a different language, had been hard for Thora to stomach. She knew slavery was part of the world, and that by this time, after months in captivity under grim circumstances of confinement and fear and hunger and discomfort, that they'd cried all the tears they could manage, and were most likely welcoming any kind of change.

On the good side, all products were getting attention; and the fact the buyers and sellers couldn't understand one another wasn't much of a problem. There was the language of value and money, and that, along with hand gestures and head movements and sounds of either pleasure or disdain, moved things along very nicely. But there *was* hard bargaining taking place. Neither Thora nor Orm nor Sigurth were selling their wares cheaply, so there were the inevitable looks of astonishment when prices were expressed. Eventually, however, the uniqueness and quality prevailed, and customers, usually well-dressed with the air of prosperity in their manner, stepped forward with the gold and silver required.

Unfortunately, good things can come to an end, and they did. A dozen riders approached, scattering the crowd and stopping short of the booths.

The men were in uniform, armed, with a few holding banners that could only be interpreted as being official and important.

Audn had spoken about something like this being a problem, especially if where they stopped to do business was near a well developed city, which this appeared to be. Cities had governments and governments had regulations and taxes; and cities also had merchants, and merchants had shops and guilds and protective covenants. To those groups, the foreigners who came from the three ships on the beach were no more than gypsies who were avoiding the regulations the community lived by.

So he was prepared. He met them with a broad smile, and made his efforts at communication in the most diplomatic of ways. This was to no avail, however, as the leader, in a resplendent plumed helmet, braids and medals, raved and pointed accusingly at what was happening. On his orders, most of the riders dismounted and moved towards the booth, by their manner indicating they intended to demolish them.

Then Audn responded, barking *his* orders, and on cue, many of the smiling, simply clad merchants, stiffened, produced shields and swords, and stepped forward to face them. With things now at a standstill, Audn returned to a diplomatic mode; he smiled, spoke softly and became embarrassingly humble. While this was happening, others not involved in the confrontation dismantled the booths, bagged the remaining goods, and carried all of it back to shore where the ships were now afloat in the rising tide.

With clockwork precision, the goods were carried back on board, then anchors and hawsers were drawn and the ships pushed clear. When the last boarded—those with shields and swords—oars were extended and slowly but deliberately the ships backed out to sea.

Orm and Thora were aft with Audn next to the steering-oar. "Just look at that," Orm said. He was watching the scene on the slowly receding beach. The crowd, many of them who'd been customers, had moved in mass to higher ground where they now stood as spectators. The horsemen, who'd tried to raise havoc, were in place, looking almost forlorn as they watched the ships, and possibly their reputations, moving away. But it was the long double line of cavalry snaking from the city and now reaching the beach that had his attention.

"The bastards sent for reinforcements."

Audn nodded, then pointed to the opening that was the river, where two ships were moving under oar. "They even sent word to hem us in from the sea."

"Can they catch us?" Thora asked.

Audn was busy and didn't answer as the ships were turned south with sails being raised. As the sails began to catch the wind, he ordered the oars up and out and stacked, with a corresponding business until this was done and everyone settled.

Looking back at the river, he laughed, finally answering. "Our knorr isn't the fastest ship afloat, but the men rowing in those boats don't really want to catch us; they're only trying to be manly and save face. Did you see the expressions of that first group of riders when our men picked up shields? I think there are more than a few turds lying on the beach."

"But that *was* close," Orm said.

Audn gave a soft whistle. "Too damn close. I was afraid something like this would happen; but was hoping it wouldn't. At least we found out there is a solid market for our goods. We were all doing fine until that prissy bastard showed up."

"Both Sigurth and I sold a number of carvings," Orm said.

"And I moved almost half of what I had," Thora added, "at good prices, too."

"Great . . . just great!" Audn said. "But I'm glad you didn't sell everything. If I have it right, in a day or so we'll turn east again. From what I've been told, the largest cities are in that direction."

Late in the afternoon on the second day they did turn. Audn was up front at the time, hanging on the prow to get as good a look as was possible. When everything appeared to his satisfaction, he instructed that the sail be furled and the oars be manned.

"We're going in for the night," he said to Orm as he returned aft. "We may be half way to where we want to be from where we last were, so this will be a good place to refresh."

"Are we coming to another city?" Thora asked when she heard.

"Not at this stop . . . But hopefully we will a few days later and need to plan for it."

"Will we be doing the same thing there as before?"

"No . . . That might not be wise. We got by the skin of our teeth last time, so I don't want to take such a chance again."

"But you have a plan of course," she said almost teasing.

"As a matter of fact, I do have something in mind," he said with a catbird eating grin . . . Let me tell you about it."

There were no problems, and soon all ships were in the shallows offshore. After the usual analysis of tides, a time was picked so that leaving at a convenient time the next day would be possible. That done, gangplanks were set even though they didn't reach shore, meaning all were knee-deep going in, which being of little inconvenience, didn't stop anyone from doing so.

Tents were set up, fires were lit and soon the aroma of warm food was in the air. A light breeze blew in from the ocean, masking the that it had been a very warm day, which was expected for being this far south. The fact of this was verified by those who went inland for firewood, where they could feel heat still radiating from the ground. But along the shore it was balmy, and the clear sky with its stars aglow, another result of the heat and dryness, made the scene very pleasant.

When they landed and made the usual inspection of the vicinity, they saw on a knoll in the distance about a mile away, a small village, but could make out little of its detail. Now as they sat relaxing around the fire, they could see more of its extent by the lights, although dim, of what had to be windows. The view from there to the beach, however, possibly because of trees, must have been blocked because no-one from there ventured to see what or who had landed. They were left alone, which was a good thing after the last experience.

"So what's this plan of Audn's again?" Orm asked.

"It's basically the use of a diplomatic party," Thora said. "He wants all ships to anchor offshore at a respectable distance. Then a few of us will go ashore in the skiff. He expects officials will be there to greet us."

"Us being only you and me and Audn?"

"Ya."

"Why not Sigurth or any one of the other Captains?"

"Audn says that our role is purely diplomatic; and although Sigurth is an artist, he still looks like a war god, which he also happens to be. Anyway, Audn says it's important to keep it simple and non-threatening."

"How does he intend to communicate and negotiate with them?"

"He doesn't have a clue."

The cool breezes from the sea, together with the serenity about them, did their work, and before long there was a sleep as peaceful as any they'd had since leaving. It just wasn't as long as it could have been.

An hour or so before dawn there were noises, noises from the quiet village at the knoll. The noises grew, and when listened to carefully, could be considered as coming from a battle, because they included the unmistakable sounds of terror and pain and suffering. There were also fires that turned the quiet scene of window glows into conflagrations.

Orm and Sigurth were outside the tent when Thora crawled out.

"What's happening up there?" She asked.

"I don't know," Sigurth said, as confused about it as she was.

But Orm didn't say anything, the fire from a mile away taking on a meaning. Then he whispered "damn," not intending for any to hear.

"What is it?" Thora asked again.

"Well," Orm answered, hesitating.

"Well, my foot." Thora prodded. "What's going on up there.?"

"I don't know for sure," he said, "but I've been aware that our crews were mad about what happened at that city a few days ago where we'd set up our booths. That smart ass with the plumed hat would have died in a heartbeat if Audn hadn't had his way. But no . . . the men had to hold back and walk away as if it were a simple social."

"You mean to tell me the men are now taking it out on *that* village? Those people there had nothing to do with it."

There was little more to be said. They continued to watch as the sky began to lighten in the east, then they heard sounds of people returning through the weeds and thickets that filled the area between where they camped and the village. The sounds were from several dozen men, singly and in groups, with most carrying something. When they reached the campsites, the increasing light of day was such that the fears they speculated was verified. The men were torn and spattered, but mostly intact; and they were carrying booty.

"In case you're wondering, I didn't order them to do that." Said Audn who'd walked up while they were watching the men return.

Thora turned, her face pinched. "But did you try to stop them?"

Audn sighed, then said, "If I'd tried, there might have been a mutiny. We depend on these men to get us through each day. Sometimes the only reward they see is what they can get by hassling."

"But you're trading furs and ivory and slaves . . . Isn't there reward enough in that?"

Audn didn't answer, only to say, "Get a quick bite and break camp. We need to be aboard and moving as quickly as we can." With that he left to speak to the next nearest group.

Back under sail, things settled back to a normal that seemed to deny that anything of consequence had happened. As always there were conversations to relieve the long hours of inactivity; but when voices were lowered to almost a whisper, or when someone laughed in a certain way, it drew suspicion that something awful was being recalled.

Sigurth and Orm couldn't drive what had happened from their minds, but they were able to consider it as part of the world they were in. Thora, however, had a problem. In the weeks and weeks of close confinement aboard the ship, she'd gotten to know everyone there, and become familiar with their human characteristics of strengths and weaknesses and personalities and dreams. She had exchanged jokes and fashioned hair and mended clothes and prepared food, and had, with them, gotten to feel the boatload was as much of a family as a crew. Now things were different, particularly for her. Now when she spoke to them it was different, and when she mended a piece of clothing, she could read into a tear or a bloodstain something of a more appalling nature . . . She could see the horror it concealed.

Fortunately, there was a third day, and as dawn broke the flotilla was dead in the water. The night before they'd sailed under starlight until they saw the telltale lights of a city. Furling sail, they waited offshore until shortly after daybreak when there were signs they'd been sighted. Then the skiff was deployed, and Audn, Orm, Thora, an oarsman and a few items of merchandise were loaded.

Events unfolded almost exactly as Audn anticipated. As the skiff reached shore, three riders came down from the city, scattering the small crowd of the curious who'd gathered. Then, also as anticipated, confusion began when one of the horsemen, speaking with authoritative bravado, asked who they were and for what purpose were they at their shore. In response, Audn, with gestures and expressions, all in humble tones, conveyed that they were merchants with desirable items for sale, asking what they had to do to get permission to set up booths and conduct business.

By the looks on faces, not all said was properly deciphered, although it was surprisingly close. After this initial conversation, the three on horseback jabbered among themselves for a bit. Then the leader nodded, which must have meant something, because one of them turned and rode back into the city. More communication of sorts followed, with the meaning, finally conveyed . . . that they were to follow the remaining two into the city.

So they did, on streets that were more cobbled than comfortable, on inclines that were steeper than expected, and for distances greater than legs that had spent too much time on a ship with nothing to do were prepared for. Both Orm and Thora had to stop a few times, which at first irritated the horsemen. But then they softened, possibly because they realized the two were not a threat; they were old in their eyes, and Orm, who had a slight limp under normal conditions, was now struggling with a good ways still to go. The leader, almost with tenderness, offered his canteen to give them a drink and then reached to take their bundles and lighten their loads.

As they continued on, the city became more and more impressive. Unlike the rock and wood and thatch that characterized the northern world, here were sculptured masonry, brick and stone in soaring archways and towers, mingled with plant boxes and gay colors and banners and fountains. There was also a busyness as people, men in sweeping silks and women in muting black, moved about with an unusual vibrance, rarely stopping to view the strangers passing through.

Then there was the heat. At the beach that morning the air had been pleasant, but as they climbed into the city, they became aware of an increasingly dry hotness unlike anything they'd previously experienced. There were more stops.

Finally they arrived at a building that by its appearance had to be of importance, like a city hall or a magistrates official office. The third horseman was waiting for them, along with others, at the top of a broad series of steps serving the building's entranceway.

After a brief exchange, whose meaning was somehow grasped, they were led inside, then down a hallway to a chamber where several more people were waiting. The scene was intimidating. At the center was the Main-man, whatever his title might be, with several more on each side. All of them were dressed in a splendor rarely if ever seen in the north, and were sitting on ornate high-backed chairs that fitted with the importance of the individual. If this wasn't enough to cement an impression, there were also servants behind each of the chairs, gently moving large fans for reasons that had everyone in envy. Orm thought that Earl Hakon, with his flair for clothing and pomp, would have been very much at home among these people.

The leader of the horsemen started the conversation, which could be interpreted as a report of what this was all about. While he was talking, a group of women were ushered in to stand to the side. They were all in black and heavily veiled in the same manner seen on the streets, with only their eyes visible.

The Main-man then spoke, directing his comments to Audn in a manner that could be interpreted as a diplomatic welcome, with a request to tell what he and his ships were doing here.

When he finished, Audn answered, being careful to say the same thing he'd told the three who'd greeted them on the shore.

The Main-man, or Magistrate, then turned to the women in black and spoke, almost in a whisper, which wasn't loud enough for Audn or Orm or Thora to attempt an interpretation.

The women shuffled a bit, with most shaking their heads. One, however, said something, to which the Magistrate responded sharply.

The one who'd spoken, did so again, it seemed, in an apologetic manner. With this the Main-man, acting like his patience was being tested, spoke to her as if giving instructions, at the same time flicking his hand as a signal for the other women to leave.

"Aha," Orm said softly to Audn. "Now we're getting somewhere. My guess is that the women are slaves or concubines, and that they were bought and brought from different northern countries. They were singled out and brought here in hopes that at least one of them were from our part of the world and could serve as an interpreter."

Audn nodded.

The theory was confirmed when the girl moved closer, then with halting words, as if struggling to find the right ones said, "Master asks where are you from?"

"We are from Norway, which is north of England and Frisia and Denmark."

Then began a process of the interpreter translating to the august group assembled up front, their reacting to it, and then another question being relayed.

"Why are you here, so far from home?"

Now Audn was in his element. He had much to say and knew how to say it; but he also knew that if he unloaded with one lengthy explanation and appeal, that most of its effectiveness would be lost. So he chopped what he had to say into short phrases, and let the interpreter pass each of them on before continuing.

"Sirs, we are traders . . .

"Traders from here have been to our land with good result . . .

"So we wanted to come here in return, to learn more about your nation . . .

"We have merchandise to sell, that we believe your people will value . . .

"We have slaves, healthy young people from even farther north than our nation . . .

"We have leathers and furs, winter coated, that your artisans will love . . .

"We have wood carvings . . ." and with that he passed the sample Orm had carried, to one of the soldiers who took it up front to be examined.

"We have items of clothing, as well as accessories . . ." passing the jacket Thora had carried.

"Sirs, we ask permission to bring our ships to shore . . .

"So we can set up our booths and sell our merchandise, like those you've seen . . .

"We have only three ships . . .

"And what we have is all we have left . . .

"So we shouldn't be here a long time . . .

A discussion then ensued among those in the chairs, with the samples being passed about again and examined every which way. There were attempts at being blasé as they viewed them, but signs slipped through that they were impressed.

Then the Main-man spoke, "You said our traders were at your shore. What tax did you impose for them to sell their goods?"

"Sir, you know the answer to that question . . .

"The merchandise they brought to us . . .

"Like the quality of goods we bring to you . . .

"Was so much welcomed by our people . . .

"There was no tax."

By noon the ships were in the shallows, the tides again being considered, the booths were set up, and a brisk business was underway. While the discussions in the city center had been conducted, a crowd had gathered, so when the three returned with the blessings that were needed, things moved quickly.

The three horsemen who met them in the early morning accompanied them back and stood by on the slopes above where the booths were located, evidently on guard to see that everything was in order. The woman who'd been the translator was also brought along in case of need; but she was confined, as if by some invisible tether, to sit beside where the men gathered.

The trading response was almost identical to what had been experienced four days before. There was initial shock at the prices being quoted, but then the more serious buyers took over. The slaves went first; then all the leathers and furs. When the last of what Sigurth and Orm and Thora sold, there were such broad smiles and lofty spirits that everyone was having trouble containing their excitement.

Audn anticipated this and moved about as if in restraint. When some suggested they go into the city and find a place to celebrate, he shook his head.

"Look," he said. "We're not going anywhere to drink. I don't know much about these "Moors," but you can see by the men on guard that they're a no nonsense group. Did you see the swords they're carrying? They're curved and shiny and look like they could slice any one of us into tiny bits. You may not have noticed but several groups of others, some soldiers with swords like that, also came down during the day just to make sure there were no problems.

"And that woman over there dressed in black, she may be a slave, but all the women we've seen are dressed the same way.

"And finally, about drinking . . . I think their religion forbids it."

"Forbids drinking?" One commented, finding it hard to believe.

"That's right," Audn said. "These people are real serious about their religion . . . they pray several times a day. Although there are beautiful sights to see in the city, I'm more than a little uneasy because of the other things I see. Let's break down the booths and get everything loaded up. Then we can decide what we're going to do in the way of celebrating. Believe me, I'm as thirsty as you are."

Thora listened and silently agreed. Being in a strange place with a culture as defined and as strict as this one appeared to be gave her chills too. Four days ago was still fresh in mind, when as things deteriorated on the shore, organized armed forces seemed to appear out of nowhere like hornets from a disturbed nest.

But she had something she felt she had to do. Thinking of the forlorn girl who'd been so helpful to their success, she'd saved a small purse with a long looped woven strap. While others did as Audn directed, she went over to where the girl was sitting. The guards stiffened as she approached, but she did so anyway.

"How are you doing?" Thora asked.

The leader quickly sputtered words that had to mean that any conversation with her was forbidden.

"Oh please." Thora said, turning to the men. Then with soft words and swaying gestures she hoped would convey the thought that she was a mother who had held a baby that had grown to someone like the girl. She continued . . .

"Please!"

The leader glowered at her, said some things under his breath that were probably bad, and looked at the others, who were no help as they were trying not to laugh.

"Please!"

He threw up his hands, turned and stepped back.

Thora looked at the woman, whose eyes, which was all she could see, seemed to be talking. She had the strangest feeling, but she pressed on. "My name is Thora. What's your name?"

The woman answered, mumbling something Thora could hardly grasp.

"Ny," Thora said. "What was your name when you were born?"

The woman hesitated, seeming to struggle piecing that together, then mumbled again, something like "Rogna," but said it so low Thora wasn't sure what she heard.

"Well, look," Thora said, "you've been a great help to us today, and we really appreciate it. As a token of that, we'd like you to have this little purse." She turned to leave.

As she did the woman grabbed her hand. Thora was torn because Sigurth was yelling for her to come, saying, "Audn has decided we should get on board."

Thora turned back to eyes that were wide and intense. The woman asked, "Who is that man? He's the image of . . ."

Thora said hurriedly, "That's my foster-son. He carved the figurines. His name is Sigurth Gunnarson." Then she broke away as the guards were moving forward to stop the conversation, and voices from the ship were toned with urgency.

Audn was barking orders, but while doing so, trying to keep a sense of calm control at the same time.

"What's the problem?" Orm asked. "The day has been perfect, beyond our hopes. At a time when everyone wants to celebrate, you seem about to explode."

"Ya, perfect." Audn said, ignoring the question as he bounded from one end of the ship to the other. He directed the *Goose* to back out first, row a couple miles and wait. Since daylight was fading, he added for them to light a lantern so there wouldn't be trouble rendezvousing.

As soon as the *Goose* was clear, the second ship pulled in lines and dropped oars. While he was watching this, he turned to Orm, "You asked what's the problem."

"Ya."

"I have no answer," Audn said. "Sometimes things are just too perfect, that's all I can say. I'll breath easier when we're away from here."

Then he gave orders to follow, and oars that had been on ready began to drop, when Thora jumped up and shouted *"Look!"*

As they did they saw a lone black figure emerging, running out of the shadows on the cobblestone—the same ones they'd walked up early in the day—down the slopes towards them. The figure reached the beach and kept running, even into the water. By this time they could see it was a woman in the traditional garb. When she had waded as far as she could, she yelled something they couldn't understand, but there was urgency in her voice. Without stopping she began to swim, her head piece coming off revealing hair a shade of blond.

When she got to the prow, still sputtering, men up front pulled her aboard. As soon as she hit the deck, she yelled. *"Thora, Sigurth, get the ship out of here. A rider came in and reported a pirates raid to a town west of here. They're gathering forces to attack right now!"*

Audn said, "Damn, that's what I was feeling!" Then he barked orders and the oars dug in.

Sigurth, who was straining at the last oar aft, was confused. He'd heard what the girl said, which included his name and therefore didn't make sense.

"Who *is* that?" he asked Thora who was nearby but starting forward.

"That son, is your sister."

A large force of heavily armed cavalry thundered down the cobblestones, scattering everything to the side as they passed. When they got to the beach they spread out and stopped, putting all bows into ready position.

But there was nothing to shoot at; the beach and ocean behind it were empty as far as the eye could see . . . in the darkness that had descended.

The flotilla sailed east, keeping as far from shore as they could while still seeing lights from shore. They continued on that course all the next day, making good time as they were running with the wind. As the sky lightened on the second day, they saw it . . . a huge pointed mountain dominating the horizon, as if to guard the seas before it. Audn gave orders to turn south then, but before the day was over, he saw land again.

"Okay," Audn said, "that's enough. I know exactly where we are. We're looking at Africa."

"Where are we going?"

"We're turning around," he answered. "We don't want to go south, and going east would take us into a world we're not prepared for.

"We're going home."

All the while this was happening, Orm and Thora and Sigurth and Rogna, talked and talked and talked.

Chapter 11
THE MULE
1003

"There it is," Orm said, pointing to a dark object that rose on the horizon. "That's Bird Mountain."

"Ya, sure," Sigurth said nodding. It had been more than half a year since they'd stood together and watched the same shape disappear. They knew it well. There'd been a number of voyages now—to Denmark and the Danavirki; to Horundarfjord; to Wendland; and to lesser distances for trade—in the total of which a number of landmarks had been memorized, this one the most meaningful.

They looked over at Audn, and saw him rolling his sketches and putting them in a leather case. The sketches had been new for both of them. On previous trips, they'd sailed in a line of ships, basically following the leader who it was always assumed knew where he was going. On this trip Audn was the leader, and although like most with extensive travel had memorized routes and used simple instruments, he'd also conveyed his findings to rudimentary, dog-eared drawings.

Even Orm, who knew a lot about many things, was intrigued by the sketches. So whenever Audn unrolled them, he and Sigurth looked over his shoulder and tried to understand the concept of identifying where they were in relation to what was on the parchments. In the beginning, there'd been squiggled masses drawn for Norway and Sweden and Denmark and the Baltic areas, and England and Ireland to the left of that, with a line from Denmark extending past Frisia and Flanders below England. There'd also been small circles for the Islands north of Scotland and a blob for Iceland. But the line below England, which they were paralleling, had been as far as the lines went.

As the trip passed that point, Audn added extensions, so it took directions and lengths approximately corresponding to the turns and distances they experienced as they'd continued south, ending with the spear-headed rock and the shoreline called Africa, at which point they'd turned back.

Even in the rough form that they were in, the sketches were still a wonder, and that wasn't just because of the way squiggles represented countries. Since Audn, ever so mindful, still had only a rudimentary knowledge of letters, key points along the squiggles featured symbols, some pictorial, that had specific meanings, like the spear-headed rock at the end of the line, inked in as "Narvesund."

It seemed to those who'd been aboard from the start, that the return took much longer than the way south. In the beginning, each shore and each stop was a new adventure, a stepping stone for a mysterious something that had no form. The last stop, which was an extremely close call, had been the culmination of the adventure, and from that point the only thing to look forward to each day was surviving.

So the trip north had been long, with days without wind, or days with the wrong wind when they bobbed and waited, and days with gales when they held on with sails furled and oars out until they could find safe harbor. And there were times when they had to anchor and spend days ashore to replenish or make repairs. All of this would have been tedious and boring, except that Rogna was now aboard, and what the family could glean from her never failed to entertain.

It was miraculous, either a manipulation of the Norns, or something they didn't yet understand by one of the Gods, that she and Sigurth were back together. Their last recollections were as could be expected. To Sigurth, Rogna had been a faint memory of an older sister who'd been bossy and always right; and other than the trauma of their last hours together, there was little to tie him to the woman in his midst. To Rogna, Sigurth had been a young imp who was into everything, and a real pest when she was trying to concentrate. Now he was a man, so much in appearance like Pa Gunnar that she kept marveling at it.

Rogna's memory of Ma Gurtha was distinct and loving. It was shadowed, however, by the horror of that awful night when it seems her world ended. She hadn't seen the fighting because she'd been asleep, but was awakened by the awful sounds of battle that initially numbed her. Then she'd been hustled into hiding, and an experience that would awaken her screaming years afterwards. She remembers Gurtha's desperate efforts to protect everyone she could, and the unthinkable when all failed. She didn't see what happened to her mother after being dragged away; but she heard her screams, and that, like other bits of that night such as Papa's head on a spear, couldn't be forgotten. Now it was as if, unexpectedly, there'd started a healing to a wound that had never closed. All the things that happened since, twenty years of it, had occurred to a mind that was almost numb to further feeling, with anything pleasant or joyful or hurtful or unkind receiving little more than zombielike responses.

Somehow on the beach, there'd been an awakening of those senses by an inadvertent combination—a genuinely caring voice, a kindness, the sight of someone from the past, and a name. It had prompted her to do something that would have resulted in a cruel death if she'd failed.

Then, safely aboard ship in the shield of nightfall, the feeling of being free, that had been absent for so long, came to her while she shivered in the loving arms of Thora. And there was more, that neither were aware of, for as Rogna was bonding to the closest thing to a "mother" in all those years, Thora was somehow feeling she'd found the daughter she never had. In the morning with the dawn, both sensed a pleasing new chapter in their lives, or at least the hope of one.

"When we first saw you," Thora said, "you were with several other girls. Did you live with them?"

"Ya . . . We were all, I don't know what you call it, not exactly slaves, but we worked very hard. We were part of a harem."

"Oh.

"So you weren't married?"

"Well ya . . . in a way."

"In a way?"

"Ya . . . the masters would call us when they'd want."

"Masters?"

"Ya."

"Do you have children?"

"Ya . . . Two, a girl and a boy."

Thora was at a loss, as were Orm and Sigurth who were listening. How could a mother leave a family without a sign of remorse?

"Tell me about them," Thora finally managed.

Rogna shrugged, her eyes misting momentarily, but then clearing. "The first was a girl, a healthy baby; but she was taken away after only a few days so I don't know what happened to her. Sometimes babies are given away as favors."

Thora nodded. "And the boy?"

"I got to keep him for a while, well after weaning. But then he was taken too. Boys are put into special training from the time they're young. I was forbidden to talk to him whenever I saw him; and trying to do so wouldn't do anything but bring punishment. Besides, as he grew older, he had no idea who I was and probably didn't care."

Thora shuddered, changed the subject. "Tell us about Solveig . . . Did they keep the two of you together?"

"Ny. We were separated as soon as we got to there," she said, pointing to where they'd been. "I never saw her again. I only heard that she tried to run away, and ended up jumping off a cliff."

Thora and Rogna joined the men at the rail, with the sighting having more of an impact to them. Rogna couldn't hold back and cried softly, leaning into Thora's arms.

The mountain got bigger and bigger, then they were opposite it and gliding by, still too far away because of the skerries offshore to make out any detail. Finally a point was reached at which the ship could turn into the fjord. Furling the sail and setting the oars isn't usually a process that's eagerly anticipated; but this time it was. Each man at oar set himself with a particular concentration as if contending in some well attended competition, and waited for Audn's command. That given they responded, making their equivalent of a victory lap, down the channel and into the cove, coasting to a stop at the end of the quay from which they'd left a summer of adventure before.

All of this would have been anticlimactic, with only the quiet of a small out-of-the way marina this late in the year; but this time there was a surprise. There were several wagons just above the landings, with people standing and waving, while on the ground children jumped and screamed and played the fool.

They would later learn that Gyrth had talked to Hrolf and Sven a few days before, with the conversation turning to the family members who'd sailed away, and the fact that the ships should have returned by this time. Hoping for the best, that the ships *would* return, they had Sverri and Hjalmar meet on top of the mountain at the favorite vantage point to see what they could. They'd done so for several hours a day since then, and were there when blips were first seen on the horizon. They had the sense to wait until there were at least two in line, but no more than three. When that became the fact, they split, and riding hard, raced home screaming the news. Groups from both farms, and a few neighbors as well, had just pulled to a stop at the marina when the mast head from the first boat was seen moving above the bank.

Sverri jumped and yelled, "I see Sigurth!" Then he and Hjalmar raced down the landing to where the ship had docked, magnetically drawing every other youngster along.

"There's Thora! There's Orm!" others yelled, everyone grinning from ear to ear and waving like crazy.

But then *"Who's that?"* was whispered as they watched Sigurth step up on the gangplank, turn and help someone who hadn't been aboard before, a woman wrapped in a nondescript shawl, beneath which was showing something full-length in black.

The adults waited by the wagons while the passengers disembarked and threaded their way through the youngsters who were too excited to be contained. Seeing that everyone coming ashore was overburdened with carry, Gyrth led men forward to scatter the kids, give bear-hugs of welcome and help with the loads.

There was an awkward moment, however, when they came eye-to-eye with the stranger who'd been standing back, eyes flashing with restrained emotion. Sigurth broke away from the manly hugs, turned, and gently taking Rogna's arm and moving her forward, said to his brother, "Sven, say hello to our sister."

Sven stood wide-eyed, mouth agape.

Gyrth reacted the same way, but managed to say, "Who?"

"Uncle . . . This lady is your niece, Rogna Gunnersdottir, surely you remember her."

There had to be a party, and there was. Gyrth, as the patriarch of the families, led the way, directing everyone to the south farm as that made the most sense. A steer was slaughtered, and in accordance with ancient custom, words of praise and thanks were expressed with the utmost of sincerity and emotion. To everyone there, it was as if three of the most loved and admired members of the family had returned from the bowels of the earth, the very underworld of creation. And if that wasn't enough, there was the miracle of Rogna. Actually, it was too much, and the amazement in good fortune was difficult to contain.

They crowded into the longhouse, which wasn't roomy enough for all who were along to fit into comfortably; but it was fun, anyway. Sven gave Gyrth the high seat, with he and Sigurth on either side, and before everyone had settled in it began, with a round of toasts and horns and then more of the same over and over.

Along with this came the questions, and an unraveling of the stories, bit by bit, with all travelers contributing to the telling, of which there never seemed to be enough detail. The party could have gone on until dawn; but at a point Gyrth turned to Sigurth to get his version of a particular incident, only to find that Sigurth wasn't there.

He looked at Orm, pointing at the empty space and hunching shoulders as if to ask where he was. But Orm only looked back, and then as if making a point, yawned.

Gyrth stepped outside on a pretext to pee, which really wasn't a pretext, because he added his marks to all the others along the side of the house. Looking about, he shivered. He noticed that the horses in harness, stood as closely together as they could, patiently waiting, their only movements being an occasional swish or puff of breath. The sky was dark and brooding, with slow moving clouds covering all but a few stars and allowing the moon only a faint glow to indicate where it was. In the poor light he felt it before he could see it, that snow crystals were drifting. Looking at the shop across the yard, he thought Sigurth had done the smart thing by going to bed; because inside the longhouse, half the people were dozing. The only thing still going strong were the women, who were so focused on Rogna and the twenty years that they could talk all night.

Going back in, he looked about. He saw a party that wouldn't stop of its own accord; so he drummed on one of the columns and said, "Attention everybody, we're so excited about what's happened that we've forgotten a few important things. First and foremost is that our travelers haven't had a chance to get settled and rest. Sigurth, who loves to party as much as anyone, has already gone to bed in the shop. Another thing is that the weather, if you haven't noticed, is doing what it does this time of year, with flakes in the air. And finally, our poor horses are freezing their asses while we talk on.

"All of us want to hear every detail of the trip and drink toast after toast to honor each bit of good fortune. But what has been told is enough for tonight. With thanks to our hosts, Sven and Olver, let's adjourn and go home. There'll be time in the days ahead, with the Yule season soon to be celebrated, to hear all there is to hear."

With that the group disbanded, or rather unraveled, and the wagons brought up and loaded. It was only then that most realized a sobering chill had descended, a fact helping to spur everyone on their way.

A short time later and past the cliffs of Bird Mountain, when Gyrth tugged the reins and turned down the lane to home, little Ingstad, who was bundled next to Hjalmar but facing backwards, burst out with "Papa! Papa!"

"What is it?"

"A man on horseback . . . standing by the trees."

All heads turned, but the brief opening in the clouds exposing the moon passed; and if there was anything to see, it had disappeared.

Sigurth watched them go, then turned towards the marina. He carried a bow with a full quiver slung on his back, a sword in its scabbard and hung by a baldric, and a long javelin strapped in place. He stopped there and stayed for a long time until he was convinced there were no sounds or movements to be concerned about.

There'd been a lot to consider.

The two ships that docked earlier in the day had almost sixty men aboard. They were now somewhere in the vicinity, in a place way back in the woods from where Audn secretly maintained his headquarters, and they were either resting or celebrating, just like his family had been doing back at the farm. He'd spent most of the year with these men and had gotten to know them well, sharing laughs, experiences and triumphs. He had to admit he liked most of them, and under different circumstances would be good friends.

But he had been walking a fine line, much more so with this trip than on any of the others. Beginning with the first one, both Gyrth and Orm had schooled him carefully with regard to his conduct. Being handsome, a recognized champion and also spirited, he was in danger of being targeted by almost anyone whose ego needed a boost. Therefore he needed to thread his way through the relationships without being drawn into a holagang, or duel. He succeeded, but the stern hand of Augn may have helped. And since it had, there may be brooding emotions still looking for an excuse to act, like on the innocent villagers on the hill who suffered every horror because of the unfriendly treatment by others a few days before. Another reason for concern was the fact that he and Orm and Thora carried back impressive amounts of gold . . . and all the likable, smiling men he'd gotten to know, were pirates.

"That's not your normal longship, is it?" Asked Audn, who'd ridden up and was leaning on the saddle horn.

Orm stood and dusted himself off, the only one working at the time. "No . . . Very observant of you; and it's your fault."

"My fault?' Audn said, tilting his head.

"Ya . . . The trip last year cured Sigurth of wanting to go to sea in a regular longship."

"Is that so?

"Speaking of Sigurth, where is he, and where are the other workers? You can't get much done by yourself."

"They're still tied up with spring planting; but they'll be along."

Audn acknowledged, then said, "I thought the trip was something else, the best part of which was coming back alive."

Orm laughed. "You're right. Things were scary, but couldn't have gone much better. All that doesn't matter, however. Sigurth wants to travel differently next time, and he wants a different direction. He wants to see his cousin Sveyin."

"And that requires a new ship? Where *is* this cousin anyway?"

"In Greenland . . . Sveyin left three years ago."

Audn sat up in the saddle as if to collect his thoughts. "Greenland? That's a long ways."

Orm snorted. "What did you call where we went last year . . . Andalusia?"

"Andalusia, Hispania . . . something like that."

"Do you think Greenland's farther?"

Audn shrugged. "All I know is the water's colder. But why is the kind of ship my fault?"

"Because you have a knorr. Sigurth saw how much more could be stored on it."

"Well, mine is not the first time he's seen one of them. They're all over, especially around Nitharos."

"That's true. But it's the first time he's traveled with one; and where he's going, he wants to take a lot along, including animals."

"Will you be going too?"

"No. I'm getting a little old for that. This last trip was about as much as I can stand. And Thora's really against it. She wants to do what you suggested earlier, and that is to go to Nitharos and set up shop."

"Still a good idea," Audn said.

"So what are *your* plans?" Orm asked. "And what are you still doing here? You're usually gone by this time."

Audn had to shift as his horse moved to reach a patch. "I'm not sure. I'm getting older too. All of us did real well on that trip, and I'm in better shape than I ever thought I'd be; so I keep asking myself if I want to do it again. We had close calls on several occasions, which really isn't that unusual. But it made me think; because no matter how smart I try to be, I know it won't always go my way."

"And another thing . . . everything's getting more complicated."

"For trading or going a-viking?"

"For both." Then he added, "Well, I just can't sit around. The boys are getting restless, so if I don't lead them somewhere, they'll take off on their own. Therefore we're going to load up in a day or two, and head back into the Baltics. The furs and materials we can load up from there are easy to sell farther south.

Orm picked up a chisel and hammer. "Looks like we've both got things to do."

Audn sighed and nodded in agreement, then spurred his horse and sauntered away.

The ship, which Sigurth jokingly called the "Mule," because it wasn't as sleek as the *Sea Eagle*, wasn't completed until late summer. It took longer than expected even though it wasn't the first of this kind they'd assembled. It was because every feature that could be incorporated had been included. During the summer, visits were made to Nitharos with Orm and Thora, who were following up with their plans. While there, he was able to meet people who'd been to Greenland and get their advice, such as ship features to incorporate, trade items to include and animals to bring.

He was also able to interview a number of people who wanted to go along, mostly men who could serve as crew, but also wives and children who were looking for new lands and opportunity, which they had been led to believe Greenland provided.

He saw Audn a few times during the winter after he'd returned, which gave him a chance to glean more from the seasoned sailor. Of special importance were the travel sketches, which Sigurth copied, with special interest to parts of Norway and points west, leaving space on the parchment for additional information further in that direction.

"Do you know of any of your men who might be interested? Orm told me you might be cutting back, which means you may have more than you need. I'm not going to go behind your back and recruit anyone; but I thought I'd ask as I still have a few oars to fill."

"Hmmm," Audn said. "I may have a few . . . and thanks for asking. I haven't decided where to take what we got out of the Baltics, but the thought of cutting back *is* real. And I know I'm going to miss the three of you when it comes to trading. Thora was absolutely right; all of you gave us credibility and made our goods easier to move.

"Do you think she'll have some of her work on hand for us to take along? They're so beautiful that just the products might be of help."

"Don't know," Sigurth said. "She's trying to accumulate as much product as she can for an opening in Nitharos; but you can ask her.

"In a different vein, I have a question."

"Ya . . ."

"Audn, you've been far in all directions. I've never heard you speak of the edge . . . or the Midguard Serpent. Have you ever been close to it, or know of anyone who has?"

"Ny . . . that's such a mystery that few people ever bring it up. I've been to Garthariki, in fact I crossed it along a river with incredible waterfalls all the way to Mickligard, which I thought was the end of the world. But it isn't. What I heard when I was there is that there's land way, way farther to the east, distances we find hard to imagine, and land routes that take months to travel. A lot of the trade goods we barter for come from there, like silks and spices and gold and silver and fine jewelry. I've never heard of the travelers from there mentioning anything about an edge.

"Then there's west and the ocean. Most feel the edge is out there somewhere, but no one's seen it. We try to stay within sight of land, though, just to make sure we don't come to it and get into something we can't handle. It's a good question, though. When you speak of Greenland, about all anybody knows is that it's far away, as far as we used to think the edge might be. I'm almost curious enough to want to tag along; but only almost. I'm too old for that crap too."

The *Mule* left a week after Audn set sail in early spring. It sailed first up the coast and into Trondheimsfjord, where it stopped at Viggja. At Viggja it took on the last of passengers and crew, and all the livestock and remaining baggage the ship would carry. Among the things Sigurth took were a full set of woodworking tools and blacksmithing implements, anticipating that they would be of use, not only for carving, but more importantly for boat building and repair. In addition, he included sacks of other supplies, such as ropes and canvas and trenails and pulleys and assorted metal devices, enough for a complete new ship, as well as quantities of metal rivets and caulking required for assembling the hull planking.

Another ship of like size and character was coincidentally making the trip.

On an early morning in late March, when the boats rowed out into the main channel, a small crowd lined the heights above the docks. Orm and Thora were among them.

"What's new in Greenland?" Orm asked as he looked over the goods piled in the booth. They were mostly furs from seals and walruses, with a few large white bundles, which Bolli Thorklesson had explained were from arctic "polar" bears.

"Well, just about everything's new there," Bolli answered.

"I meant, is everything going all right?"

"Ya, I guess so; but it sure is a rugged place, even more so than Halagoland. I'd hate to spend the winter there. Even in summer glaciers are in view, with ice usually floating somewhere off shore."

Orm nodded. This was the kind of conversation he'd been having with men who'd arrived from Greenland for over seven years now. There'd been a fair amount of traffic, ships coming and going in groups, leaving in the spring and returning in late fall. Sometimes, groups would make more than one round trip in a summer, but that was rare.

Outgoing ships usually carried the same things—settlers and animals and badly needed supplies; with returning trips carrying what Orm was looking at now, with walrus tusks sometimes among the goods.

The questions Orm asked were also about the same.

"Did you happen to meet a man by the name of Sigurth Gunnersson?" Bolli shook his head.

"He's a woodworker, among other things, and often gets involved at marinas in boat-building and repair. If you had any work done on your ship while you were there, you probably saw him."

"I did have some work done; but I don't remember the name," Bolli said. "What's he look like?"

"He's almost a head taller than me, broad-shouldered . . . a handsome man; has a scar on the left side of his head that his hair doesn't always cover. If he was around, you'd know it as he's on the outgoing side. He's my foster-son."

"How'd that happen?"

"What? Being my foster-son?"

"Ny . . . The scar."

"Oh," Orm said. Then he looked past to a landing a couple hundred yards away to the dock under Hlathir Cliffs. "Do you see that ship over there?"

"You mean the *Long Serpent*?"

"Sigurth was on that ship ten years ago when it was captured by Earl Eirik."

Bolli looked at him in that 'are you kidding' kind of way.

"It's true," Orm said, deciding not to say that he and Sigurth also helped build the boat.

"Okay, if you say so," Bolli said. "But to answer your question, I didn't see anyone who fit the description you've given. There seemed to be a lot of talk about lands farther west of Greenland, with a boatload of timbers coming in while we were there; and that's about all I can tell you."

The year Sigurth sailed away, Orm and Thora stayed in Nitharos, using the earnings from the trip south to build a shop for their new venture. It was larger than either of the ones at the Skulifarm or Bird Mountain; and it was also better constructed, with timber framing and walls formed in a manner more fitting to the city. Business had been a success from the start, particularly for Thora, whose impressive works brought a steady stream to the door. Besides the work she did herself, she had several looms in operation, with apprentices as well as customers making the shop a busy place.

When Orm returned from the docks, the sun was low in the horizon, with the workers and customers already gone.

"You don't have any news to share, do you? Thora said as she saw him enter.

"Do you have something warm to drink?" Orm said. "Maybe tea or ale."

"Ya . . . which do you want?"

"Ale if you have it."

She filled two cups and sat beside him. "So the ship that came in today didn't have anything you wanted to hear?"

Orm shook his head, then took a drink.

Thora settled back. "I don't know what to make of it. During the first year, people told us they'd seen both Sveyin *and* Sigurth, but at different times, and only once. Then it's like they've vanished."

"Ya . . . they sure did," Orm said. "My understanding is that there was traffic to some islands further west, like to places called Helluland and Markland and Vinland, and they may have gone to any or all of those places."

"They were seen together at Vinland, and then on a couple trips, but after that nothing."

Orm nodded. "Strange . . . Maybe they've fallen off the edge."

Thora looked at him like he was nuts.

He laughed, "I'm kidding; but Sigurth found the edge to be a mystery to be solved. Didn't you pick up on it?"

"Ya, I guess. All of those who stick to the old Gods feel the edge is out there somewhere."

"And you don't?"

"I find it best not to think about it. There are many religions people around the world believe in. Who's to say who's got it right, and how can you tell? Our dear Rogna sure doesn't think much about the Moors and the way they worship."

"Well, I don't either," Orm said, "from what I've seen. But I will say this about them . . . there's no doubt in what they believe. Here in Nitharos, as in most of Norway, that's not true. Olaf Tryggvason tried to convert all of us to the White Christ, and built a church right here in the town he started. He tortured and maimed to make sure everyone believed as he did, none of which seemed to connect with the Prince of Peace part that went with it. But he's long gone feeding the fishes somewhere in the Baltics, and Earl Eirik has taken his place. Eirik doesn't seem to care what we believe, which makes the people around Trondheimsfjord very happy."

"So where are you going with this?"

"I don't know . . . I just wish I knew the answer."

"Well, I don't know about that either; but I do know I'm homesick."

"Homesick!" Orm laughed. "You mean for Bird Mountain?"

"Yes. Nitharos is fine and business is good and we've made many new friends. But home is home and Rogna is there and the kids are growing and I want to see them all. The Yule season will be on us in a couple months, and I'd like to plan on being there with the family."

Orm stood in the doorway. "We're ready, let's get moving."

Thora, who'd been going in circles inside the shop trying to make sure something wasn't forgotten, adjusted her fur-lined shawl and stepped out where the wagon and drivers were waiting. She turned back to give instructions to the interns who'd followed her out, who only laughed before she could speak.

"Yes, Thora, you're going to be gone through Yule and maybe the winter. You may not return until spring. Not to worry, we'll look after everything."

Orm helped her up into the wagon and onto a cushioned space, then joined her among the bundle of bags. The driver, who with his assistant sat on the only seating up front, snapped the reins and the rig jolted forward.

It was a pleasant day, a surprise for being so late in the year, and because of it there was more activity outside than was normal, particularly among the children who seemed to be everywhere.

"Wouldn't you know it," Orm said, "we haven't seen a day like this for some time. It better be as nice back home."

Orm saw the look on her face, saying, "Oh ny o ny, no second thoughts. Think of all the reasons you wanted to make this trip. You've got jackets and boots for all the kids, shawls for the women and overcoats for the men. They're some of the best work you've done. Their eyes are going to pop . . . just picture that."

Thora looked at him with a weak smile, then sighed.

They lumbered over the hill, then wound down towards the water, turning left and snaking along the shoreline to Viggja where a coastal boat waited. They'd considered traveling by wagon all the way; but wagon travel was a lurching, bumping process that continued to follow the shore, except at the shortcuts that switchbacked over the mountains. But the shortcuts were treacherous under normal conditions, and impossible after the first good snow, which could be expected any day. Traveling overland was also slower, usually taking at least a day longer. So they headed to the docks at Viggja, arriving by late morning. Here again the children they passed were outside enjoying what could be the last good day in months. This time Orm didn't comment on it.

The crew on the coastal boat were waiting and by the looks on their faces were anxious to get going, probably for the same reason the kids were having fun. Another reason was that a larger ship had just docked and was beginning to unload, complicating the scene on the docks that had been clear only minutes before.

"Where'd you guys come from?" Orm asked a man who'd finished tying the larger ship in. It was the first question he'd ask the first of the crew off of any boat coming in.

"We're just in from the Hjaltlands."

"Anything of interest?' Orm said as he carried another bundle from the wagon.

Just then there was a wail from the back of the ship. The man he was talking to swung his head in the direction of the sound and said, "Well, I suppose if you call that interesting."

"You mean the trip was uneventful. That's a good thing anytime on the open sea."

The man stopped. "Actually, they're not ordinary travelers."

"Who?"

"The three of them—a man and two boys who are aboard. One's a tot, the one making all the noise right now. And the man . . . He's a shipwreck survivor, so I've heard, wanting to get back to Norway. But he's a mess and dumb as a board."

"You mean stupid?"

The man shrugged. "Could be that too. What I really meant is that he can't talk."

"Orm?" Thora called from the wagon, "What are you doing? Solvi and the crew are anxious to leave, and we haven't finished loading."

He turned and headed back to the wagon to pick up the last parcel. On the return, he stopped as he could see the three passengers the man had been talking about making their way down the gangplank.

He tapped Thora. "Look, that's the bunch with the kid that's been crying."

One was a boy, maybe two years old, in rags. The second was an infant bundled in pitiful wrappings. The man was the worst of the lot, bent and emaciated and stumbling along as if about to collapse. But when the man saw the two of them staring at him, he straightened to full height.

Orm had to grab Thora as she sagged to her knees.

The man was Sigurth.

Solvi stomped back and forth on the landing, cursing, while the four other crew members sat in the boat, trying not to see any humor in it.

"We're missing perfect conditions, you know that. And you know that it can change at any time. If we don't go now, we may not *get* another chance . . . and in case you haven't figured it out, you're not the only reason for going."

Thora didn't move, but stood with hands on hips, repeating what had gotten all this started. "Well, we'll just have to take the chance. The three that got off the ship are going too, but they're not in shape to travel right now."

"That's another thing," Solvi said. "Three more makes us near to being overloaded, and I don't like that. You know what the currents are like . . . *damn!*" With that taking another short walk and stomping back."

Thora still hadn't moved, but she knew it was time. "Look, I understand, believe me I do. But you *must* understand how important this is to me. As I said before, the man is my son. Orm has taken him and the children to an inn where we can get them attended to and make them ready for travel."

"*Ready!* How long is that going to take?" Solvi snorted. "He looks like he's ready for the bone yard right now."

"Watch what you say!" Thora snapped. "If I told you all he's done in his life, you probably wouldn't believe me. But you better believe you don't want to offend any of us, and have him coming after you."

Solvi cursed under his breath, turning in a circle with a few more steps, considering but not kicking a dog that slunk past.

"How long?" He asked. "We've got the boat loaded so we'll have to put a tent over the goods and have a guard aboard until we go."

Thora shook her head and crunched her shoulders. "I can't tell you. He's a strong man, but I have no idea what he's been through."

"The man from that ship said he'd been in a shipwreck," Solvi said.

"Well, that could mean anything, and by the look of him, it was awful. Right now I need to go now and see to them. I don't think we can work miracles in a short time; but we'll try."

Then she held out her hand. "Solvi, if you're here first thing in the morning, this will be yours in addition to what I've already agreed to pay."

She opened her hand to reveal two shiny gold coins.

"How's it going," Thora said as she rejoined Orm at the Inn. "We've only got until tomorrow morning."

Orm whistled. "Well, take a look."

The baby had been bathed, fed and was fast asleep rolled up in a clean blanket. The boy was the same, except he was sitting in his wrap with eyes darting from one to another around the room. Sigurth, however, hadn't made it past the bath and a drink of mead, and was fast asleep in the loose folds of a blanket, which didn't cover as much as it should have, also showing ribs and stringy remnants of once bulging muscles.

"Has he eaten?" Thora asked.

"Only a few bites. I tried to talk to him, but that went nowhere. He made an effort to speak; but whatever he tried to say came out as a gravelly whisper that pained him even to try. There's a nasty scar on his neck which might be a clue to what happened."

Thora looked over the three, then said, "Let's let them rest for now. I'll go out and see if I can find some decent clothes for them to wear. What they had on can be thrown away. When Sigurth wakes up, he's got to eat. That and a good nights sleep will hopefully be all he needs to be ready in the morning."

She was about to leave when she looked back and saw the boy staring at her.

"What's your name, son?" She said.

The boy froze, then looked down.

"Son . . . Do you have a name?"

He nodded.

"What is it? My name is Thora."

He mumbled. "Garth."

"Did you say Garth?"

The boy nodded.

"Who's your papa, Garth?"

"Papa."

"Aah," Thora said, looking at Orm, "At least *he* can talk."

"Where's your papa?"

The boy's eyes welled up and he began to cry, while pointing away.

"Oh my," Thora said, "no more of that."

Seeing a problem she couldn't solve, she looked at Orm, waved goodbye, and left.

With the door closing and the absence of vitality only a woman can give, the room became quiet, with the only sound a perceptible bubbling from the pot over the fire. Orm raised the pot so it would only simmer, then sat back, a little uncomfortable with the boy's eyes watching his every move. He wished he had a toy or two to give him something to play with, but he didn't and it probably didn't matter.

"Let's see what's happening outside," Orm said, going over and picking up Garth and heading for the door. The boy was bundled well enough, except for his head; so before stepping out, Orm took off his cap and plopped it on him with an emphatic *"There!"* that miraculously prompted a figment of a smile.

Outside was as it had been, a beautiful day, with the sky clear and sunny and the slight cool of winter hardly perceptible. Kids in an open area nearby were playing a version of knattleitr, with crude wooden bats and the remnant of a ball; but as elemental as it was, they were hopping and shrieking and having a good time.

They'd only been watching a minute or two when Garth started to squirm, his bare feet making their way out.

"Oh no you don't," Orm said laughing. "If I were to let you down to get all muddy, I'd be in trouble big time." With that he turned away to see what was happening elsewhere. But then he remembered there was a baby in their room, so scolding himself for being careless, he hustled back. Everything was fine and he let out a sigh.

Garth squirmed again and pointed to the door, saying, "Outside."

"Ya sure; you want to play don't you?"

"Ya . . . outside."

"Well, I tell you, Garth, we can't do that right now." Orm said, taking his cap off. "Everyone else is taking a nap; so that's what you're going to do too."

With that he lay down on the bench, the boy wrapped and securely cradled in his arms. Garth thrashed and babbled, with words with meaning starting to flow, but Orm didn't move, pretending to sleep, and slowly Garth's actions ebbed to quiet breathing.

When Thora returned with her arms full, all four were asleep.

It was only a little past daybreak when they walked down to the docks and Solvi, who was standing beside his boat. Solvi couldn't believe what he now saw. Orm and Thora were the same, but the others wouldn't have been recognized as the same miserable group that had stepped off from the Hjaltlands less than a day ago. The baby being carried by Thora was wrapped in a clean blanket, his head poking out with rosy cheeks and a colorful, knitted beanie on top; the boy was neatly dressed from head to toe, and had a look of embarrassment as if he'd never been appointed as well before. But it was with Sigurth where the change was most astounding.

When Thora returned from shopping, she'd awakened Sigurth even though he'd been in a deep sleep. She forced him to eat as many bowls as he could, bowls of a rich stew laced with potatoes and meats and vegetables, and bread on the side. When he'd eaten as much as he could at that sitting, she trimmed his beard and cut his hair, only then directing him to crawl back to his pad and blanket to resume the sleep she'd interrupted. He obeyed, but with a sly grin that was the first show that there was still something burning.

Another meal had been forced down early in the morning, after probably the longest sleep he'd had since that first night with Orm and

Thora twenty-eight years before. The result wasn't the old Sigurth; but the one that started the day was rejuvenated well past where he'd been.

They were all almost aboard, with Orm and Sigurth and Solvi still standing by, when two riders thundered down, one of them holding a pole with a banner atop that fluttered as they rode, as usual calling attention to their importance if nothing else did. They came to a stop just short of the docks, with the elegantly dressed one of them dismounting.

"Ashjorn, what a surprise," Orm said. "What brings you this far from home?"

"Didn't Solvi tell you?"

Solvi shuffled a bit and lied. "I didn't forget, but they just got here and we've been busy."

"Okay, well," Ashjorn said. "Yesterday was such a pleasant day, I decided to make the rounds and see what was happening, with the intent of reporting anything of interest to Earl Eirik. Solvi told me about yesterday, and about Sigurth coming in on the ship.

"Sigurth, how are you doing? It's been a long time."

"Aah, we have a little problem," Orm said. "Did Solvi tell you Sigurth has lost his voice?"

"Oh, that's right." Then he didn't know what to say.

"We hadn't seen him in seven years," Orm said, "and we haven't had much of a chance to glean from him what's happened. And that's as much as we know."

"Wasn't he in Greenland?"

"Ya . . . or thereabouts. Rumor has it he was shipwrecked coming back; but we don't know the details of it."

"Well, I'm very interested. Eirik is also very interested. He's hearing all sorts of things from that part of the world, most of it conflicting; so he doesn't know what to believe."

"I'd like to tell you more, but we're on our way home for Yule," Orm added, "and maybe for the winter."

"Okay. Well . . . I'm glad I caught up with you anyway. In case you don't know, Sigurth and Einar Thambarskelfir, both of whom he quartered at Svolth, are two people Earl Eirik admires as much as anybody. I know all of you are anxious to go, so I won't hold you up; but I did want to say hello. Have a *great* Yule, I'll see you in the spring and we can catch up then."

Chapter 13

GRIM
1012

Gyrth stopped by again, which wasn't unusual because he was a frequent visitor ever since the return of Orm and Thora. This was significant in itself after so long an absence, but having Sigurth and two tots along, one being his grandson, made for one of the greatest winters in memory.

The winter was all but over now, a time when temperatures warmed enough during the day to indicate that spring was almost here.

"So how's it going?" Gyrth asked, glancing away from Garth who was bouncing on his knee.

Thora shrugged. "It's about the same."

"You mean you don't know any more?"

"Not really. He rarely tries to speak anymore. From the look on his face, when he does, it hurts. But I think it goes beyond that. I see considerable frustration with the situation, especially the parts, I mean, about trying to tell us what happened in Greenland, or why he was coming home. When you think of seven years, I'm sure there's a lot to tell. Day to day he does fine by pointing and grunting and gesturing; but as for the past, he hasn't been able to convey what he wants."

"Is there a mental problem?"

"Ny, it's not that. At first he unrolled a number of sketches and put them on the wall, being careful to do so in just the right way. You know the ones . . . you've seen them."

"Ya."

"He's tried to tell us stories using the sketches as a reference, and that's where we hit a snag. First of all, we were familiar with some of them, because they were copies of what Audn had representing his travels. One was made during our trip together to Narvesund. The others Sigurth must have drawn; but without the words to describe the shapes, neither Orm or I got a grasp of what he was trying to tell us. Surely the sketches represent places he'd been; but we were confused by other drawings relating to them because they were composed of lines and dots and disconnected squiggles and images.

"Not getting to an understanding was very disturbing, especially to Sigurth, who at first seemed to have an urgency with it all. One time, after seeing he wasn't getting anywhere, he went outside and grabbed the rail on the hitching post and hung his head, almost in tears. Then he exploded, picking stones and throwing them with all his might until he was vented. His rage was so violent that birds scattered and animals in the pens bolted away.

"He tried again later after calming down, altering his approach with more hand gestures to create images; but once more I'm afraid we didn't get it. Some of the story seemed to do with ships, which we thought was a link to the work he and Orm had done for the King; but that didn't prove to be it. He finally stopped, and with as sad a look as I've ever seen, walked out. I mean, really walked out . . . probably to the top of Bird Mountain because he didn't return until the next morning."

"Oh there's more," Orm broke in to say. He'd been in the corner carving, but had stopped to listen. "The business about ships did lead somewhere."

"Ya?"

"Ya . . . It turns out the ship that wrecked wasn't the *Mule*, which we had all assumed. We don't know who it belonged to, but it wasn't the *Mule*, which means the crew, including Arni, Jon, Frothi, Thor and Ondur, may still be alive."

"That's good to know."

"And there's more good news," Thora said. "We've learned a few things by asking ya and ny type questions, to which all he had to do was nod or shake his head if he didn't want to mouth the words. That's how we found out that Garth is Sveyin's son; that little Gunnar is his son; that Sveyin and his wife *may* be alive, but he isn't sure; and that *his* wife is not, a fact that obviously and understandably pains him. When I try to get more detail on any part that requires words, however, the effort at communicating breaks down."

"I haven't been much help," Gyrth said. "I've asked questions to everyone who passed by the marina, and have only learned that Sigurth and the boys were rescued at sea by a fishing boat from the Hjaltlands. When found they were bobbing on the water with a few others in a little skiff. Once ashore, Sigurth worked and begged his way across the island until he managed to get aboard the ship you saw him disembarking from."

Gyrth shook his head. "It *is* frustrating. I don't even know my daughter-in-law's name. Whenever I ask Garth that question, he says "Mama." And you say you don't know much about Sigurth's wife either."

"Ny, not yet anyway," Thora said. "But I think in time we'll find a way to get answers. We just haven't focused on some things because his concerns have been so much more important. But speaking of that, have you had a good look at the baby?"

"Well, ya . . . cute little tyke."

"Ya, for sure—black hair, black eyes, dark . . ."

"What are you getting at?"

"Don't repeat this to anyone, but I think the mother is from that 'Vinland' place."

"A screecher . . . a skraelingar?"

"Well, if so, it doesn't matter. Babies are babies and they're all precious. It just seems the coloring on this one isn't all Norwegian. Time will tell on a number of things."

"That's true. There is another issue, though."

"An issue?"

"Ya . . . Well, it might not be an issue, and then again it might. You know, of course, that Audn retired several years ago."

"I guessed as much. He disappeared as if he fell off the edge."

"That's because he tends to be secretive. He'd heard about you and Orm returning to Bird Mountain for the winter, and he'd also heard about Sigurth; and because of that he stopped by yesterday."

"Why did he see you and not us?"

"I wondered about that too at first. But then he said he was in a hurry, and since I should be told as well, he left it for me to pass the word on. The reason he came by wasn't to say hello, it was to give a warning."

"And that's the issue?"

Gyrth nodded. "When Audn called it quits, he turned most of his ships over to his crews and wished them well. Since then he's been out of touch. But when he heard all of you were coming here, it rang a bell, and he wanted to do something to protect people that meant a lot to him."

"You're not making sense so far."

"It's simply this—once a pirate, you always think like a pirate. Putting two and two together, he reasoned you two had been in Nitharos a number of years and had been successful. With your return and stay for the winter, he doubted you left your gold behind. Therefore he's afraid some of his former crew would come to the same conclusion. If that's the case, then sometime before they sail out for the year, which isn't far off, they might plan a raid.

"That's a pretty wild speculation."

"It is, and I probably would have ignored the warning, except that it reminded me of something. You didn't know my brother Gunnar, Sigurth's father; but the day of his murder, he'd had a premonition."

"He did? This is the first I've heard of that."

"Well, it's something I've just figured out. During the afternoon before the ambush, Gunnar rode over the mountain pass to see me. He was armed to the hilt with about everything he could carry. He gave some lame excuse for doing so; but I think now he had a feeling of impending doom, like a raid."

"That may be what Audn had in regards to you two; but whatever . . . I needed to pass it on."

"Did you tell Sigurth?"

"Ya . . . just before coming in to see you and the kids, one of whom is now my grandson."

"What did he say?"

Gyrth looked at her.

"I mean," Thora said, "how did he react?"

"With little in the way of expression. But when we parted, he did more . . . a lot more. Hjalmor came with me today, you know, and went scampering after Sverri as soon as we got here. The two of them are a lot like Sveyin and Sigurth were at that age. Anyway, they were horsing around as if in battle."

"Gyrth, they're not kids anymore, they're grown men."

"I know. And I'm ashamed to say that when I saw them having fun, I realized we hadn't done as much to train them as we should have. Well, Sigurth saw it too; so when I finished telling him what Audn said, he headed over to where they were. Right now he's putting them through the paces. He can't turn them into champions in a few hours time, but he can sure make them better than they were."

The kids had been fed, and it was the grown-ups turn as they sat around the central fire, Thora ladling and passing out the food.

"What an unusual day this was," Orm said, "I mean, the weather was unseasonably pleasant. I'm sure winter isn't over."

"And that's not necessarily a good thing right now," Thora said.

"You mean because of what Gyrth said today . . . about Audn's warning?"

"Well, I would think an attack would be more likely in good weather than in bad. Wouldn't you agree, Sigurth?"

Sigurth shook his head.

"You don't think a raid is more likely in good weather?"

He made an expression that indicated he felt the weather didn't matter that much. What he couldn't easily tell was that what really mattered was the element of surprise, with skill in combat being next in importance, and weather being the least of considerations.

Rogna was over in the corner getting the baby ready for bed, and while doing so had been listening to the conversation.

"Is that what made Gyrth come over to tell us today . . . to be on the lookout for pirates?" she said, walking over while patting the bundled-up baby.

"Just a caution," Thora said.

"But we spent months with them, the pirates . . . and we became friends."

"Rogna," Orm said, "first of all, that was years ago and half of the crew we knew then are gone by now; and secondly, they're pirates, and with pirates, friendship may not mean anything where money is concerned."

"Well, I guess I'm being naive about the possibility. But everything's been so peaceful and quiet since coming here. I just love it—the farm, the family, the animals—everything about it. It's hard to believe what happened years ago actually did, or could happen again."

"Ya," Thora said. "Peace can be deceiving, and we've had a long run of it, at least here. We can't ignore what Gyrth said, though. You never know. Sigurth, I wish you could tell us *your* story. You thrash around and make sounds in the night, so I know there are experiences that will make us shudder. As it is, all we can do is guess at what they might be."

Sigurth gave half a smile, but that was all.

"Sigurth," Rogna said, "I don't mean to put you on the spot, but could you teach me how to defend myself . . . how to fight? I'm a big strong girl and have been through a lot. I don't mind the work here on the farm, in fact, I love it because I'm free and it's a choice. In all those years with the Moors, there were no choices. I was no more than a thrall, subject to whatever the men who were my masters wanted. What I'm getting to is why can't you teach me the things you're showing the men? I've already been shooting arrows, but more in the way of kid games. If it ever comes to a fight, I'd much rather be able to do something other than cowering in a closet and praying. I've already tried that and it didn't work."

Sigurth smiled, then cocked his head as if to say, "sounds good to me." Then he stood, reached over and messed her hair like a brother should, grabbed a coat off the rack and stepped outside.

The balmy day's warmth had dropped enough to remind everyone outside that it was really still winter. He crunched along over ground that had melted earlier, and then, as temperature dropped, sent tendrils of ice out to link it all back together into a frozen oneness. When he opened the barn door, another world hit him, a warm, moist cloud of earthy mixtures which jarred his senses, while the opposite in cold, dry whiteness exchanged and swirled inside until he could get the door closed.

He gingerly stepped his way to the third stall, which he entered, petting the animal along it's length until he embraced its large, majestic head.

"How are you doing," he whispered.

The horse shook his head a slight bit and snorted; but otherwise stayed in place.

Sigurth continued to whisper, or at least to move his lips, because very little sound managed it's way.

"They can't hear me, which can make things very difficult. But at least I have you and you seem to understand every word, and that's what friends are for.

"Did you notice that it's been a really nice day? It was so warm that I got to work with some of my younger kin and show them the basics of combat. They're full of vinegar, and puff out their chests and flex their muscles, but for the most part they don't have a clue. I'll keep working with them though, and maybe they'll learn enough to live another day.

"And guess what? Rogna wants to learn, too. And why not? She's strong and quick and brave. You should have seen what she did when we were near the end of the world in Spain. She may have saved all of our lives. So if I can teach her what I'm trying to teach the others, anyone who's fool enough to come a-viking to Bird Mountain may be lucky to carry his balls back.

"Rogna's such a jewel, and men are such fools; they think that because of what's happened to her that she's ruined. But that's wrong and so unfair, because she'd make anyone a wonderful wife, even as old as she is. Well, we'll see.

"Did you see who visited us today? Uncle Gyrth came by to tell us to be on the lookout and why. Can you believe that, that it's taken somebody this long to figure out what was as obvious as the nose on your face. When we got here, Orm and Thora gave me a load of gold and silver coin, and a few pieces of jewelry to boot, and asked me to hide them in a secure spot. I guess they knew that I knew the area, and certainly the mountains, better than anyone. So anyway, I hid their treasure in a good spot, but far from where what's left of mine is hidden, and showed them where in case something happened to me.

"From the moment of hiding the treasures, I've had the feeling that someone, most likely a pirate, would think about the possibility of substantial booty and give a raid a try. And if they did and we weren't on our toes, it would be bad, possibly as bad as what happened thirty years ago, or what happened to those poor villagers in Spain, because pirates have no mercy. They make their fortunes by being the scum of the earth. What's really surprising is that men can be as good and friendly as we'd ever want in one circumstance, and then be a pirate in another. There are farmers about who plant crops in the spring, then jump on a boat and go a-viking to do the most awful of things to gain somebody else's treasure, then return as if they been on vacation to peacefully harvest.

"The Kings we've had have been some of the worst. Earl Erik, who was kind enough to let me keep my head, seems to be one of the better ones, so I've heard. Anyway, we don't see much of him and I don't know that he's done anyone any harm. He's certainly a far cry from that Olaf who was so proud.

"But Sveyin liked Olaf, and liked the religion he was cramming down peoples throats.

"Oh my . . . Sveyin. Horse, if you can hear my whispers and understand, maybe you can hear what he's saying as well, even though he may be a ways away. If so, give me a sign as I'd like to talk to him. I can't do what I came here to do, which leaves him and a bunch of friends on their own, and I'm so sorry. Maybe you could talk to the Gods too and get them to release me . . . anyway just try.

"Well, got to run. Nobody knows we've been making our little rides early in the morning, but that's okay. Maybe there's nothing to be concerned about and that's better yet. In any regards have a good rest. I'll see you in a few hours."

A few days later, Orm and Sigurth pulled up to the marina in the wagon, came to a stop near the work shelter and tied up.

They were surprised to find the amount of activity at the far end of the pier where both boats that used to belong to Audn were now in the water. In addition, several carts were drawn up and a number of men, almost enough to outfit both ships, were busy carrying stores from the wagons and setting them aboard, along with doing all the other details of getting ready.

A man called Hauk, who'd replaced Audn as the leader, turned from what he was supervising and walked over. He'd been one of the boat captains as far back as the Spanish trip, so everyone was well acquainted.

"Orm, Sigurth, good to see you. What brings you here?"

"Just checking on the ice," Orm said. "Last week this cove was still frozen over."

"Ya, you're right," Hauk said. "But we saw it melting away a few days ago, so decided to take advantage of the situation and get away early."

"How's the throat, Sigurth? I heard about your problem and was hoping it would clear up by this time."

Sigurth mouthed "thanks," then shrugged to indicate no change.

"It looks like you're in good shape," Orm said. "Does that mean you'll be leaving soon?"

"Ya, in fact we're shooting for tomorrow."

Orm nodded. "Then we'll hope to see you in the fall." This was said friendly enough; but he didn't add words like "good luck" or "have a good year" because he knew any good fortune would come at the expense of innocent, hard-working people . . . like those around Bird Mountain.

He flicked the reins, the horses responded, and they slowly moved forward, turning to get on the pathway leading home.

"Well, this should relieve a few anxieties," Orm said as they put the marina behind them. "By this time tomorrow our number one threat will be out and gone."

It was several hours before daybreak, and there were enough puffy clouds moving overhead to shift visibility from starlit to imperceptible. With this being so, Sigurth heard them before he saw them. Then they came into view, first as dark blobs moving towards the marina, taking form as they got closer to reveal two wagons being led by another two men on horseback. A little closer and it could be seen that the wagons were filled with men, which meant over a dozen were in the party.

They approached a point past the work shelter where Sigurth reasoned, if they continued around to the ships, they'd probably be a work party getting an early start in preparing to leave. But if they turned up the pathway like he and Orm had done yesterday, then there'd be a problem. They turned. When he recognized the voice of one of the men on horseback, even though hushed and only a fragment, he knew for sure. With that he kneed gently and rode back towards Bird Mountain.

"Did you see that?" Asked the driver of the lead wagon, almost in a whisper.

"See what?" Grim asked.

"Something up ahead . . . It moved."

Grim leaned in the saddle and took a long look. "You see anything?" He said to the other rider."

"What did you say?"

"Did you see anything?" Grim repeated a little louder.

"Ny . . . Who asked?"

"Uli."

"Damn . . . You tell Uli to shut up. That's the third time he's seen something since we started out. He's spooked and he's beginning to spook me."

Grim did, and the group moved on, only an occasional whisper being heard above the soft sounds of wheels turning and harnesses rattling and horses plodding.

The raid wasn't Grim's idea, but when Ola came to him with it to confidentially enlist his support, he jumped on it with such enthusiasm he had to be scolded to keep it under wraps. The thought of loot, and especially treasure, were always the fabric of his primitive ambition; but if it could be combined with a score to settle, it would be so much better.

There really wasn't a score to settle, because nothing had ever happened. It was just that something should have happened, and in Grim's mind that was enough. Ten years ago he'd been part of the crew aboard a ship that went all the way to Spain. Also aboard were a couple who specialized in crafts and were there as part of a trading strategy, and their son. All went well enough with most of the crew; but the fact that they were even there had grated on him, partly because Audn, his boss at the time, was so protective of them. Most aggravating was the son, Sigurth, who was regarded as someone special. It was said that in games, including contests with weapons, he'd been a champion. And then in a sea battle that had been recent history at the time, he'd distinguished himself in some way, adding to his renown.

So he'd been on the same ship, in close quarters, with a particular person, a handsome young man, who was much more highly regarded than he was, and it got to him. It became his objective to find cause to insult him, or to be insulted by him, or anything that could lead to a holmganga. Holmganga, or island going, which is where the duals were usually conducted, is one of the things the crew talked about a lot, because it was not only a way to preserve honor, it was also a way to embezzle or ransom tidy amounts. By insulting someone, particularly someone old or rich or both, who then must challenge you, seasoned warriors, like fearless berserkers, could make a good living, among other things. This tactic had grown in his mind until he could clearly see it happen, them getting together at one of the many stops, setting up in accordance with the rules for that sort of thing and having at it. He'd show that pretty bastard a thing or two and cut him down to size.

Yes, he'd do that, and he tried to make it happen. But each time he made a move, like saying something sarcastic or insulting or challenging, either Sigurth would laugh it off like they were funning as in the game of flyting, or Audn would come by with that look in his eyes that said his ass would be in a sling if he didn't shape up.

So nothing ever happened, and although Sigurth disappeared for years soon after that trip, he never forgot. Now Sigurth was back and there was gold on a remote farm, and they were sailing out in the morning and it was perfect.

The group came to a stop a short ways before the dark mass of the mountain rose to blot out what could be seen of the sky. It was also near the lane that branched out to the Gyrthafarm.

Ola whispered to Grim, "We've still got to pass by that whole line of cliffs before we get to where we turn off. We need to speed up once we're past this farm, so ride ahead to make sure the way is clear. Return and let me know."

With that Grim rode off while Ola led the wagons on, speeding up once they came under the wall of cliffs. They hadn't gotten far when they heard Grim returning. Only a strange thing happened . . . Grim galloped past, making Ola ride after him to find out what this behavior was all about.

He found out, and ordered the wagons to turn around. Grim was in the saddle all right, which was the impression they'd gotten when he'd ridden by. But he was tied down to be that way, and his head was gone.

Chapter 14

OLAF THE STOUT

1015

"Now what?" Orm said as he watched the riders approaching, a tell-tale flag waving on a long staff causing the question.

Sigurth, who was inside the hull of a fishing boat with a few helpers about, heard Orm's comment and raised his head over the rail. Seeing the riders, he ducked down to finish what he was doing. By the time he did and stood up, the riders were on their way. He'd heard most of what was said, but he climbed down anyway and went to the shelter where Orm was, already returned to carving on a decorative panel. Orm raised his eyebrows.

"We've got to see Gyrth," Orm said, looking down again to focus on a few more cuts. Then. "There, that's enough for now." Sitting back, he said, "Can you believe it, another war-arrow. We're being asked to get the *Sea Eagle* manned and ready."

Sigurth got the horses back in harness, while Orm went over to the other workers, giving instructions to keep them busy; then they climbed onto the wagon and were on their way.

"Where's Gyrth?" Orm asked the first person they saw after arriving and hitching up, a young girl whose name he couldn't remember.

She giggled and pointed to the barn.

Not understanding what was so funny about the question, they walked to the barn door and entered, only to find a few more kids grinning about something, like in a trick they'd pulled.

They found Gyrth asleep on a pile of hay in one of the stalls, snoring softly in a scene made idyllic with wild flowers set in around him. He awoke with a start when the men burst out laughing.

"You lazy bastard," Orm said. "It's not even noon yet, and there you are napping already."

"What?" Gyrth said, bolting up sitting and rubbing his eyes. "What is it?

And what are all these flowers doing here?"

The kids screamed and ran out the door.

"War-arrows, Gyrth, war-arrows. Thought you might like to know."

"War-arrows . . . *damn!*" Gyrth said, standing up and dusting off. "I've been up most of the night . . . One of the mares was birthing."

"Everything okay?"

"Oh ya. After we'd sent the mare and her foal out and cleaned up the place, I saw no sense in disturbing everyone in the house, so I plunked here."

They walked outside and over to the longhouse where they settled on the benches.

"Tell me about it . . . the war-arrow."

Do you remember a man by the name of Einar Thambarskelfir?"

Looking at Sigurth, Gyrth said, "Wasn't he one of those who was quartered with you at Svolth years ago?"

Sigurth nodded.

"That's the one," Orm said. "Anyways, he's risen to prominence since then, and has been quite the ally to Earl Svein ever since Earl Eirik died.

"And of course you know about Olaf Haraldson . . . Olaf the Stout."

"Oh ya . . . another pirate who's decided he should be king because he's got a bloodline. Earl Eirik didn't do us a favor when he went to England to help King Knut, and got himself killed instead. He was stronger than Earl Svein. His dying left the door open, enabling this new Olaf to move in and take over part of the country.

"So what's the war-arrow about?"

"Earl Svein doesn't want to give up the throne, so to speak, and a bunch around the country don't want him to. Things have been nice and quiet for a long time now and most don't want to change. Particularly if it means this Christianity thing is going to raise it's ugly head again."

"And?"

"Well Einar is helping to see that Olaf doesn't take over."

"What's he like?"

"Einar?"

"Ya."

"He's quite a guy, so I understand. I've seen him, mostly on that trip to Wendlands, but I've never spoken to him. He's something like Olaf Tryggvason in that he's a superb athlete. He's a skilled runner on skis, with enormous strength and great courage, so they say; and he's supposedly the greatest archer that ever lived in Norway."

"Really . . . You mean to tell me he's better than Sveyin?"

Orm laughed. "Oh not *that* good, or Sigurth here for that matter."

Sigurth shook his head and snorted. He loved these two.

Orm continued. "Einar's been such a close friend of the Earls that they gave their sister to him in marriage; so they're kin. Since Wendland and Svolth, he's become the most powerful and influential man in the Trondheim district, and obviously a strong supporter of the Earls. So he and Earl Svein sent out the war-arrows."

"To do what?"

"Well, as you know, the two raised an army in the region northeast of the Trondheimsfjord. They chased Olaf out of Nitharos, who then retreated overland and is now probably at his main support around the Vik. Earl Svein wants it back . . . all of Norway, not just the districts around here. He wants to mobilize an armada to go along with this army; then sail around Norway to the Vik and do battle."

"So here we go again, eh? Putting up ships and bodies and fortunes to advance the ambitions of someone who wants to be King, with our only reward being that we might survive if we're lucky."

"Ya."

"Is the *Sea Eagle* still sea worthy? It's over thirty years old, and the last time I saw it up close it was showing wear and tear."

"Good question," Orm said. "We're asking ourselves the same thing. We'll take it out of the shed tomorrow and give it a good look. I know on the last trip the ship made to the Hjaltlands, the crew did some bailing."

Gyrth sat back, *"Damn, damn, damn!"*

"Oh, I think she'll be okay," Orm said. "If not we'll just have to borrow another one. The main question I have right now is who would you include from Bird Mountain to be part of the crew?"

"That's easy," Gyrth said. "At least for starters, because Hjalmar and Sverri will jump at the chance.

"Sigurth, you've been working with them for years, and I take it they're about as good as they're going to get. I know Hjalmar's a little frustrated. He feels life and its adventures are passing him by. He trains and goes to the contests, and during the long winter hours hears about the things that have happened over and over. It all sounds wonderful and exciting when compared to day-to-day on the farm. Most men who show weaponry skills and seem eager, get invited to go a-viking; and I know both of them have. It's been all I could do to hold them back."

Orm nodded, then said, "Anybody else?"

Before Gyrth could answer, they heard Sigurth clear his throat, and when they turned they saw him pointing to himself.

"Yes, you too," Gyrth said. "I was hoping you'd volunteer. You have no idea how much you're respected. The fact you've lost your voice hasn't changed that one bit." He paused. "And then to round out the crew from here, I'll go again."

"You! Gyrth, you must be in your seventies."

"Somewhere in there."

"But you've done your part. This isn't necessary. I'd offer to go but I'd be a liability now."

"Ny, you've done your part too; and Sven and Hrolf are both not expendable, so it's back to me. Besides, I really want to go."

"You do? These trips have never been a joy ride. And they're aways dangerous, even without combat."

Gyrth nodded. "Ya, ya . . . You know, of course, that my closest neighbors and friends, Einar, Bergthor Bristil and Erling Skjalson, are all dead."

"Ya . . . So what?"

"They died in bed."

"Gyrth . . . don't tell me you want to die in battle so you'll get into Valhalla."

"Well, you never know," Gyrth said, then he laughed. "No, it's not that. In fact, if you really want to know, I want to be along to make sure we don't get into battle, like we succeeded in doing at Horundarfjord. The point is, when I die, I'd like to be doing something."

"Okay." Orm said, standing up. "Hopefully all will go well. I'm not anxious to see you go one way or the other, Valhalla be damned. You get with the usual neighbors and assemble the rest of the crew; while Sigurth and I make sure *Sea Eagle* is ready."

Before Orm got up in the wagon, Gyrth called him back, saying, "Sit back down a minute. I'd like to ask you about something weird."

This was awkward because Sigurth had gone ahead, untied the horses and was now up in the seat waiting.

"What is it? And hurry."

Gyrth nodded, then in almost a whisper, said, "There are some strange things going on around here. Erling's grandson has been with those pirates that used to be led by Audn. Anyway, they're spooked. He told my grandson about it recently, and he told me."

"Told you what?"

"About three years ago, their ship had gone to sea even though one of their crew was missing. Apparently, no-one knew why the man wasn't there, at least nobody said anything about it; but then they saw blood spatters about his footlocker, so they opened it up . . . and there was his head."

"His head?"

"Ya . . . You can imagine the effect that had. Anyway, whatever happened had been a topic of whispers ever since. Then just last week a couple of them decided to ride out in the early hours, just to see if there was anyone about."

"You mean like a guard?"

"Or like a phantom. They had circled around the area and were on that road not far from here, when one of them thought he saw something. So he shot an arrow."

"Hit anything?"

"They thought so because they heard a noise, like a horse's whinny."

"And?"

"That scared them, so they turned tail and headed back. They slowed when they got to the road through the woods leading to their compound, when one of them fell off his horse. The other dismounted to see what happened, only to find his companion dead, an arrow right through him."

"Really!"

"Ya. And as it turned out, the arrow was the same one he'd fired."

Orm didn't know what to say.

"I bring this up because years ago, maybe ten or twelve, we were returning from your farm when my granddaughter swore she saw a man on horseback in the shadows. Does any of this make sense to you?"

Orm shook his head. "Ny, it's weird all right. Sounds more like the workings of Loki than anything a person could do."

On the ride back, Orm said, "I noticed a scab on the rump of that horse you like to ride. What do you suppose caused that?"

Sigurth looked at him without an expression, except to shrug.

Gyrth held the *Sea Eagle* at the mouth of the fjord, letting as many ships pass as he thought he could get away with, before giving the order for the oarsmen to dig in. He maintained this position day after day as they sailed down the coast, other ships joining the flotilla along the way. When they turned the point at Lithandisness, they were joined by many other ships, bringing their numbers to a large and impressive force. Another day along they made a final landing at a place called Nesjar, giving the leaders a chance to review the situation and make battle plans.

As they sat on the beach beside the cooking fire, Gyrth asked, "Well, how do you two like it so far?"

Sverri, who'd been bouncing about ever since they'd left, still had a sparkle in his eyes. "Are we close to Olaf and his ships? Will we make contact tomorrow? If so, will we fight on land or stay in our ships?"

"Don't know, nephew. The men who brought us together are trying to figure that out right now. When you hear a horn blow, it will mean for all captains to assemble for instructions."

Sverri drummed his knee and looked about, "Well, I'm as ready as I'll ever get. Sigurth has grilled us thoroughly on how to form a shield wall against the rail, and positioned each of us somewhere on the deck. I'm to be in the back with the archers, but am also on reserve for the wall."

"How are you doing Hjalmar? Am I wrong, or do I see some color creeping back in your face."

"I'm going to be fine," Hjalmar grumbled, looking down and continuing to sample the fixings in his bowl.

Eat as much as you can," Gyrth said. "We don't know what will happen or when it will, so you need to beef up every chance you get. As for getting sea sick, get over it, it happens. The man who says it's never hit him is a liar."

Just then the horn blew.

Gyrth was back in less than an hour, and his arrival was foretold as other captains down the line to the east could be heard barking orders. The same orders were repeated after the first, with each one being closer and sounding like an approaching wave. Then there was Gyrth.

"Olaf is within sight," Gyrth said, his voice gasping and his legs shaking because of his long run in the loose sand. "From what we can see, he's moving his ships out into the channel and heading our way.

"To counter this, Einar and Earl Svein, who have the biggest ships, are going to go out first and tie together to start a platform. Then the rest, in an order already determined, are going to tie together each side of them to form wings, and then behind in layers . . . pretty much like expected. We're near the tail end, but we want to be positioned so we can move forward if and when we're needed. Let's break camp and make ready. We want to be in the water, oars out in a controlled drift until we get a sign to do differently."

The directions sounded like what Gyrth wanted it to be. He therefore delivered orders with such confidence that most relaxed with what they had to do; after all, it seemed like they were preparing to watch an event in the equivalent of a front row seat.

Only it didn't work out that way; and for most it would be years before anyone could gather enough information to determine how a perfect, simple plan ended up going so awry.

Sigurth, who was at last oar in the stern, saw as much as anyone. Down the line, a few ships had rushed into the water, too fast, and then had tried to turn and align for their place in the formation too soon. The result was a collision of oars with the ships beside them. Then others did the same until there was a tangle with some of the best ships not moving into position, and with Olaf's relentlessly approaching force turning urgency into panic.

Instructions to correct the mess didn't help, with screams for a quick solution doing more harm than good. A number of ships did manage a way out and joined the battle array in an improvised way; but for many others, it took too long with some never making it. One of the captains near the end of the tangle, spotted the *Sea Eagle* cruising along, seeming to be a ship that could be easily brought in. So with shouts that couldn't be understood, but with gestures that could, he ordered Gyrth to come forward, move past them, and take a prime position in the platform.

Gyrth had to comply.

He directed the *Sea Eagle* into place perfectly, with oars retracted and stacked, and lines thrown to tie into the opening awaiting. Then all aboard moved to their practiced positions. With that, they were ready.

They didn't have to wait long. They would hardly see it; but they could hear it and feel it. It was the sound of ship-boarded armies coming together with men beating shields, metal striking metal, and the deep wooden thud of ships butting ships. The scene segued into something unimaginable—a growl of sounds including cheers and curses and groans in a mixture few aboard the *Sea Eagle* had ever heard.

> Need there was none to urge to
> noise-of-swords the Earl's men,
> nor to egg on Olaf,
> eager ever for battle;
> for either host was apt to
> undergo—nor were they
> ever—the loss of life or
> limb—worse instead in combat.

For an initial part of the battle, the *Sea Eagle* was hardly engaged, the ship to the right near Einar's ship doing fine. But then the one on the left, the *Vera Dale*, began to have a problem. They were losing the battle at the rails and were in danger of being boarded. Its Captain, wide-eyed and sputtering, came to the rail to which the *Sea Eagle* was attached and begged for men to come over and bolster their numbers. The men of the *Sea Eagle* started to respond, but then, like a giant wedge, one of the ships the *Vera Dale* was contesting, sliced through, parted the front line and forced the *Vera Dale* to the side, putting *Sea Eagle* in a direct line of combat.

Now everyone was in the fight. Hjalmar stood at the rail as part of the shield wall; Sverri joined the group behind the mast, firing salvos of arrows; and Sigurth, with several other seasoned warriors, ranged from one end to another. They looked for weaknesses to bolster while also searching for targets, which when found, received javelins expertly thrown.

For Gyrth back by the steering oar, there was no way to tell how the battle was going down the line, but on the *Sea Eagle* there was an inevitable looming. The ship it was fighting was bigger and higher with more men on board, and although it was engaged with three ships, it had penetrated Earl Svein's front. The ship was also solidly backed by other ships whose crews were coming over the rails in mass to lend support; and, it was now concentrating on the weakest link.

Against these conditions Gyrth saw his ranks thinning. He looked behind for a support ship that could move into place and provide reinforcements, but here was none in position to do so.

Where had all our large ships gone?

Then at the bow, the rail was breached, which put Sigurth and his group into individual combat. Gyrth gritted, picked up his shield and sword and started forward. But his help wasn't needed; the men who'd made it over were quickly cut down. Then Sigurth, on his own initiative, cut the ties to the ship on the right . . . our ship; then he went to the other side and their ship and moved down the rail to cut those lines too, the shield wall stepping back to make room for him as he did. He would have been chopped to pieces, but Sverri and the archers sent volley after volley with such precision that the men on the other side hunkered down behind their shields while this was happening. The last tie was the most difficult and it almost cost Sigurth his life. He had to reach past an obstruction to get at it, and while he was slashing, he slipped on the bloodied rail, his momentum throwing him over the side. If he'd fallen in the water, his armor would have taken him down; but by dropping his sword after the last cut, he managed to grab the rail with a frantic stretch and pull himself back over.

Back aboard, Sigurth and others grabbed oars from the racks, and using them as prods, pushed against the abutting ships on both sides until they were floating free and drifting away.

Gyrth knew what to do next. He called out names and instructed them to set oars. As soon as that was done, the ship was moved out of the fighting, except for the war of arrows that continued until they were out of range.

Now the ship were little more than drifting with oars on hold. As it did, the crew became spectators to a battle still raging. But the battle was in its last throes, and it was obvious that the large coalition put together by Einar and Earl Svein was losing.

Besides the confusion at the beginning which had messed up grand strategies, another reason for what was happening now was that Olaf had more of the larger ships, and had a higher number of crews with professional soldiers rather than farmers called to duty. Bit by bit, the platforms assembled for the battle broke apart, then disintegrated, with only one, which was that of Olaf, still intact.

Other ships began to drift just as the *Sea Eagle* was doing; but there was no pursuit or battle between individual ships as would usually have been the case.

Maybe it was because the fight was Norwegian against Norwegian, Gyrth thought, which gave little cause to draw the fight out. Regardless, there was a victor, and the spoil was the Crown, and whether he liked it or not, Olaf was his King. So now for him the only thing that mattered was getting home. He called Sigurth and other leaders of the groups comprising the crew.

"The fight's over; let's get the ship ready to sail. That means cleaning up our messes and getting on with it. Quickly now, we know what we know; we want to be clear of the area before Olaf decides to make more of all this."

This was said with a calmness as if outlining objectives on a busy day on the farm; but it was anything but. During the fight, over two dozen men several layers deep had been grouped to form the shield wall at the rail. Where the rails abutted, lives were only minutes long on both sides, with replacements moving in almost automatically to the meat grinding that occurred. Many had nothing to contribute beyond their ultimate sacrifice, which included heart and limb and gore and gristle, and were cast aside to make room when made. Now with the battle over, the grim work of another kind got underway. Bodies of the enemy were dumped overboard; those of the crew were stacked at each end, whichever end was closer. The wounded were a different matter.

Gyrth's first impulse was to find a good shore before dark, then attend to the dead by creating a funeral pyre. This would grant to each of those dead that they take to Valhalla the weapons and goods placed beside him. But then as the *Sea Eagle* turned and moved farther away, it became apparent a favorable wind was about; so he called the crew leaders over again to discuss the options. They decided to take advantage of the wind and get in as much distance as they could before making a stop. So while the treatment of the wounded started, oars were retracted and the sail unfurled. It quickly billowed, pitching the ship forward in a manner that made even the men engaged in dreadful duty look up and smile.

Gyrth clenched his teeth at what he saw on the deck, but then he swelled with pride. There could have been thrashing about and screaming and begging for mercy and all kinds of justifiable reaction to the agonies. But there wasn't any of that; instead there was a bravado or fatalistic indifference to what had and was continuing to happen. He'd seen it several times before. At the height of the furies, for instance, the Arneson brothers, Kalf and Ketil, had been side-by-side against the rail. The fighting was at its most intense, and Kalf had made a thrust with his lance, extending himself and momentarily becoming vulnerable on the thrusting side. That action coincided with another from across the rail who made a sweeping chop with a long-handled, broad-faced axe. The blade caught Kalf between the neck and shoulder and cleaved muscle and bone and organ over a foot down, so far that when the axe was pulled away, the arm and side to which it was attached, slowly began to fall away, arteries spurting from a heart at maximum effort.

Kalf slumped, not at first realizing what had happened; then when he did, his eyes popped and he made a horrified sound adding to the growl. When Ketil saw and was likewise horrified, their eyes locked, then their faces calmed, surely forced but calmed, and they talked, knowing these were last words. Whatever Ketil said, it was the right thing as Kalf remained calm, even wincing a smile. When the spurting stopped, his eyes glazed and his head slumped. Ketil carried the body away, ducking under protecting shields as reserves moved in to keep the line complete; but he returned to the line a few moments later.

Gyrth was proud of them all. They were like family, and not just those around Bird Mountain, for there were six other farms to the north and east that had been neighbors and friends for all his years, and who had at every time of need responded.

And Sigurth . . . Everyone who had survived was alive because of what he'd done. They'd already lost heavily and were about to be breached a final time, in which case, without reinforcements they would have been swept clear to enjoy the afterlife with the Sea God Aegir. That might not be the same as Valhalla, but then again may not have been too bad. Fortunately, they'll never know because Sigurth prevented it from happening.

Gyrth leaned against the rail, winced but caught himself while maintaining the shield in front. He reviewed, not only the scene on deck, but also that about in the water, to question whether they were doing the right thing. The sun was still high in the sky and the ship was moving faster than usual under ideal sailing conditions. As he looked about he could see that they were already the farthest west of what was left of the armada; and, that work was progressing with the treatment of injuries . . . except that it wasn't progressing well . . . and there was the flaw.

Battle injuries are rarely simple and are better managed by experienced women with soft hands, as the saying goes, than by gruff, calloused hands of tired men. Furthermore, as bad as the talents were at treatments, conditions made it worse. Fire was needed to heat to red-hot the instruments used for cauterizing, and also to prepare strong-smelling leek or onion broths to test internal damages. But fire can't be started on board; and the work of sewing wounds and setting broken bones can't be done well either, even with the boat slicing water as gently as it was.

He called the leaders together a third time.

"This isn't right," he began. "We need to take care of our men the best way we can, and this isn't it. We need to be on shore to do that. If we maintain this speed for another hour or so, we should have all the distance we need to feel secure; besides Olaf has bigger fish to concern himself with, and my guess is that's what he is concentrating on right now.

"Agreed?"

Everyone nodded.

"Okay. Let the men know . . . I think that the thought of a hot meal will perk them up."

That said, with the men returning to what they'd been doing, Gyrth leaned back against the rising rail at the stern, trying to control another wince. He was now satisfied with what they were going to do; but he still had a problem. As his eyes turned to the boat scene, they locked into a stare from Sigurth, who'd initially turned away. Sigurth was standing bare-chested, having taken off his byrnie and padded jacket, and not yet slipped into his regular tunic. The armor had done its job well, but there were obvious welts with broken skin, draining punctures and slices about his arms and body, not to mention the torn legging and sizable blood stain.

"You seem to be looking after everyone," Gyrth said, "but you're a mess yourself. Who's looking out after you?"

Sigurth ignored him; instead he stepped forward and moved the shield away from Gyrth to see what it was hiding. An arrow, whose fletched end had been broken off, disappeared into Gyrth's left side near the base of the rib cage. Sigurth lifted Gyrth's tunic to feel around his back in hopes it had come through, but it hadn't. Then he looked about the floor for the broken end, also to no avail. He whistled at Sverri, who was over checking on Hjalmar, and motioned for him to come over.

As this was going on, Gyrth began to babble, as if needing to explain. "Don't ask me when it happened, because I didn't feel it at first. I'm normally back at this end close to the steering oar, moving about very little as I try to keep a handle on what's going on; and I've been careful to keep the shield up, to keep something like this from getting through. And I did . . . Just look, the shield was splintered four times. Beats me when this one got through. Didn't even know it until it snagged on the shield one time. Sorry about breaking off the end, or at least of throwing it overboard. I guess having it would be a good thing right now."

"What do you want?" Sverri said walking over. Then his eyes bugged, blurting "Papa" as he saw the stub.

Sigurth mouthed, "Arrows . . . do you have arrows . . . arrows they have shot?" He used hand gestures to clarify what he meant, a practice Sverri was well accustomed to.

"Arrows . . . sure, in fact all the ones I now have are ones I've picked up. Mine are long gone." He spun back to where he'd stacked his weapons, returning with several samples.

Sigurth looked at them, not being surprised by the heads as they were much like his own and of common use. He could only hope the one in Gyrth was shaped like the one he held for penetration rather than barbed for difficult removal. Lengths were also consistent enough to assume the one in Gyrth was similar; so Sigurth made comparisons, looking for markings that might indicate the depth of penetration. From that he concluded that it would be better to pull it out rather than cut in back in line with the arrow, break the rib in the way, and push it through.

He motioned for Sverri to stand behind and hold Gyrth up, then he looked at Gyrth . . . who nodded . . . and the pull began. Sigurth was as gentle as he could be, but this wasn't a gentle business, and he had to twist a bit as he pulled in order to ease it out. While in the doing Gyrth vomited and fainted; but other than that it went well with little in the way of flesh or else coming out in the final pull.

They laid him down then and comforted him with cushions, but there was little else that could be done at the moment. The nature of arrow wounds to the body is that they either hit vital organs, or they don't. If they hit an organ, sometimes the damage heals; however most of the time it doesn't. It's better to leave the wound open to drain, so cauterization isn't needed and a loose bandage will do. On shore, a leaks brew would be prepared and given to drink; if the strong smell were to emanate from the wound soon after, that would be a near fatal sign, among others. And it may be only a matter of days in any case.

Not long after this a fine stretch of sand beach was sighted with wooded hills behind the beach, so Sigurth pointed to Hilli Skreya, who worked with Gyrth in the stern and was usually on the steering oar. Hilli nodded and turned that way. As they got closer, the location continued to look good, so oars were set and the sail furled and the ship eased in.

As soon as the ship was anchored, the able-bodied swarmed over the rails and went about doing what was needed. Wood was collected, for not only the pyre, but also for cooking fires; tents were set up, as were cooking pots; excursions were started into the area to see what game was available or whether livestock was about.

Bodies were brought ashore and prepared for the pyre. The wounded were also given attention, as required, and soon the work of cleaning and sewing and bandaging was renewed, but under more favorable conditions.

There was much to do, and there was good reason for going about it quickly. Gyrth revived before they'd reached landfall, and managed to get to his feet with Sverri getting under his arm on the good side for support. Other than give out a few suggestions to the crew scurrying about, however, his only function was to be in charge of worrying, and to try to think of things that could go wrong so they could take action before it happened.

"Hilli," Gyrth said, overlooking the bustle of activity. "What do you think . . . is the tide coming in, going out or what?"

Hilli stepped over to the rail where Gyrth was leaning, which was only a few steps away, and looked at the quiet waves slowly extending and retreating. "Hard to say. It's near to high tide, but I can't tell which side of high."

"Well keep watching. I'd like to know if it's possible."

Hilli scratched his head and looked at Gyrth, "Why? Am I missing something?"

"I don't want to be left high and dry if the tide goes out."

"Are we in a hurry to get out?"

"Maybe . . . I just don't want to take the chance. We haven't met the people who may lay claim to this stretch of beach yet."

"But they're Norwegian."

"Yes, but you never know. If an ornery bunch came along and wanted to be difficult, in our weakened condition our best option might be to back out and set sail. If we're locked in by low tide, things could be difficult."

Just then a group of riders came out of the woods to the east and rode the beach to where the ship was tied.

"How are you feeling?" Hilli asked. "You strong enough to go ashore and talk with them? We should be able to find out if there's a problem."

"I'll give you a hand," Sverri said.

There was no problem. The farmers were helpful, and sold beef, grains, vegetables and other foodstuffs at a reasonable price. They were able to do all they hoped to do on this stop, were back on the water the next day, and were one of the first ships to return home.

Chapter 15

GYRTH

1016

Gyrth watched as the noise cleared the edge of the cliff and took the form of a horse drawn wagon. It turned down the lane, coming to a stop near where he was sitting at his favorite bench outside the longhouse. Aboard on the seat were Orm and Thora, with Garth in back bouncing around doing something, the something being directed at Sigurth who was following on horseback, cradling little Gunnar in front above the horn of the saddle.

Gyrth laughed when the something was Garth throwing pebbles at Gunnar, which wasn't surprising as there was always something going on with those two.

"You old fool," Orm said as they pulled to a stop. "It's colder than a witch's tit today, and here you are sitting outside."

Gyrth shook his head, "You have no idea how good kind words from old friends makes one feel. Did you come here for a reason other than running out of people to insult?"

Sigurth got out of the saddle while the nonsense was going on, hitched up the horses, and stepped over to help Orm and Thora down. The kids, of course, were already gone. They'd jumped down and spun by Gyrth long enough for a quick hug, then ran off to the barn, where if there was anything to do, it was there.

"We just thought we'd ride over and see how you were doing," Thora said. "Did we come at a bad time?"

"Ny o ny," Gyrth said, groaning as he struggled to his feet. "It's always a good time to see all of you. And you're right, you little fart, it *is* cold outside. It's just that it was so gloomy in the longhouse I had to come out for a bit of fresh air.

"Come on in . . . Maybe we can get Jorum to hustle us something warm to drink."

Jorum had been busy in a sewing circle with a few younger girls, mostly daughters, and jumped to her feet in surprise when the door opened and relatives marched in. This was a welcome interruption, and after greetings and hugs, the groups parted, with the girls adjourning to another room, the men settling in around the central fire.

"So what brings you here, really?" Gyrth said. "Not that you need to have a reason."

"We hadn't seen you in a while," Orm said, "and wanted to make sure you're still okay. Actually, we think it's amazing you're alive. Not many take an arrow in the guts and live. Isn't that right, Sigurth?"

Sigurth nodded.

"So how goes it? You look like death warmed over, but I still see a sparkle."

"Well, I'm still here. I guess that's something."

"But how do you feel?"

"About as good as I look. There's something churning inside that doesn't want to go away."

"Oh, you'll make it," Orm said. "Since you've lasted this long, you should have it licked."

"Hopefully so. Right now, I'm more concerned about Hjalmar."

"We thought he healed up just fine."

"Yes, the cuts and bruises did," Gyrth said. "But he's slow coming back otherwise."

Orm nodded. "Sverri said something about that."

"We thank the Gods for Sverri," Gyrth said. "He's been a friend and a great help in all this. You know, being in the shield wall must have been awful. Only half survived and all of them were wounded."

"From what I've heard, none of you would be here if Sigurth hadn't . . ."

Sigurth shuffled and waved Orm off, not wanting to hear of it.

"Well, Hjalmar *was* in the worst part of the fight," Gyrth continued, "and his wounds weren't the part that bothers him most. Evidently he did a lot of damage too, mostly with his lance. He remembers spearing one man in the eye; but instead of getting a berserker high from it, he said he almost threw up. Anyway, that's the part of healing that's taking more time. But I'm glad you're here and thanks for asking."

"There *is* another reason, though, for our coming here," Orm said.

"Another?"

"Ya. You're closer to the other farmers in this area, and all of you talk about things we're not party to. That mountain," Orm said, snapping his head to the south, "is enough of a separation to keep us out of the loop, particularly during the winter when we don't go to the marina. So what's happening?"

"Not a great deal, at least that I know of. Olaf has reclaimed all of Norway, but you already know that. In fact, I think he's spending the winter in Nitharos where he'd been chased from last year."

"And how's he treating everyone? He can't be feeling good towards an area that rose against him like they did."

"Surprisingly, about the same as before. My understanding is that he'll be continuing with his "White Christ" movement, and that makes me worry. I just have a hard time understanding how a religion that's supposedly based on peace and brotherhood and forgiveness, and all the other fine thoughts, can be so ruthlessly promoted. Those who have held firm to the old ways and refused to be baptized have been horribly punished. Can you imagine having your hands cut off, or your feet?"

"Yes," Orm said, only I don't have to imagine it. Several of us were in Nitharos years ago when the first Olaf gouged out a man's eyes. It really hits you in the stomach, I tell you."

Gyrth sighed. "I know I'm sounding like a crotchety old man, but then I've lived too long . . . and I *am* a crotchety old man. There are so many things I should be thankful for, and I am. But there are things that really bother me. One is the war-arrows. How many have there been in our lifetime? And how many lives have been lost because of them? And why? Because somebody wanted to be King!

"And then there's taxes . . . Why? What do they go for? I'll tell you what they go for. They go to support enough of a hird to make the King stronger than any other group in the country. With this hird, or private army, he travels about and does as he pleases, being entertained wherever he stops. And what do we get for what we pay . . . the protection against someone else becoming King and doing the same thing.

"The only ones around who might be worse for us are the pirates. We're sure not oblivious to them, because we have a bunch practically in our midst. They use our marina and have winter quarters tucked in the woods not far from here. I'd like to say we get along with them just fine; but that's not exactly true. They killed my brother, your Pa Sigurth, and most of your family years ago; and just last week a bunch of them raided Folasonfarm, which is only a dozen miles away,"

"Raided Folasonfarm?" Orm said. "I never heard about that."

"Ya . . . I just heard about it yesterday," Gyrth said. "They tortured Tosli and Signi until they told where they'd hidden their stash; then they raped their daughters anyway."

"Do they think it was the pirates who winter near here?"

"They have no idea. It was late at night and the men were hooded . . . They're just numb about what happened."

"When Audn was in control, things were different because he ruled with an iron hand, and had enough sense to know not to mess around in his own neighborhood. It may be that the new leadership isn't as strong, or as smart, and can't control the energy of a bunch who don't have qualms about anything."

"Because of that," Gyrth said, "I worry about you on the other side of the mountain. Audn gave a warning a few years ago, and although nothing came of it, there's still reason to be on guard."

Sigurth strained to keep from having a reaction to those last words. Sometimes not being able to speak wasn't all bad.

"Well, enough about pirates," Gyrth said continuing. "What really bothers me are war-arrows and the fighting for someone else's ambition. All of which leads me to the *Sea Eagle*. That ship has taken us almost as far as there is to go."

"Not quite true," Orm said. "With Audn we sailed to Narvesund, which if we'd continued past, would have taken us into the Middle Sea and places like Rome and Greece and even Miklagard. Anyway, we went twice as far as the *Sea Eagle* has ever gone."

Gyrth nodded to concede the point, then said, "What held you back from going into the Middle Sea?"

"Audn knew better than to try. He told us that many years before, maybe 140 years ago at the time, an armada of sixty ships went through and sailed around to those other places; but in the end, only twenty made it out."

"What happened?"

"Pirates . . . Moorish pirates who worked both sides of the narrows. With only three ships, we wouldn't have had a chance."

"Okay, so there was farther to go; but that doesn't change the way I feel. Continuing to send crews that consist mainly of farmers around here just isn't right. The *Sea Eagle* is old and creaky, like me, and one day it's just going to crumble when the wrong wave hits it. When that happens, there'll be a whole crew gone, which is far worse then what happened recently. We've all heard about ships making simple crossing to the Hjaltlands disappearing without a trace . . . And wasn't the ship Sigurth was on wrecked in that vicinity?"

Orm nodded. "So what are you suggesting . . . that we strip parts off the ship that are salvageable, and burn it up?"

"Actually, something like that."

"But that wouldn't solve the war-arrow problem. We'd just have to build or buy another boat to meet our obligations the next time we got the summons."

Gyrth growled and threw up his hands. "I hoped to find a way to be free of that kind of thing. But we're too small. Some areas, like the Tronders, are enough in number that they can come close to doing their own thing . . . like chasing the King away as they did last year. Well, maybe in time."

"Don't have an answer about that," Orm said. "There is another matter, though."

"Ya? Sill another? You really had a bunch of reasons for coming here, didn't you?"

"I suppose; but this isn't about anything urgent. It's about Greenland. Sigurth may not like my bringing this up, but all of us have been curious about what happened there. There were seven long years with family members and marriages and two boys and all, and none of us has but a faint idea of what happened. Some day people will learn to speak with their hands, but that someday isn't today. Thora and I have spoken to Sigurth about learning to write, because if he could do that, he could give us all the details we long to hear. We've been working with runes for some time now in both carving and weaving. The runes, however, are only useful for identifying ownership or expressing simple thoughts; but they're not much good for lengthy, detailed stories."

"Couldn't he be taught by the clergy of the "White Christ?" Gyrth said. "They have their bible and read from it and other documents all the time."

"We thought of that, but found they guard this ability, reserving it for only those who have convincingly converted and are dedicated to supporting them. Right now Sigurth isn't close to being that, either in their eyes or in his mind."

Gyrth sat back. "That's a great idea, though. I've heard of tutors going around and giving instruction. It's for children mostly, however, as they seem to learn much faster. But why wouldn't it work for anyone?

"Sigurth, what do you think?"

Sigurth mouthed a few words, making raspy sounds in the process; then he shrugged as he could tell by their expressions that little of the meaning was getting through. What he'd tried to say was there *was* a great story to be told, an almost unbelievable adventure, parts of which he relived with every breath he took, especially since there was an important reason why he was on that ship and coming home. What they also didn't know was that every time a sail appeared on the horizon, his heart skipped a beat, hoping it was the *Mule* with his crew and Sveyin coming to do what he had failed. He wasn't being secretive or reluctant to share any or all of it; the truth was that he was far more frustrated about the situation than they could ever know.

So there'd been a raid. Sigurth was as surprised as Orm had been on hearing that; and he really didn't know what to do about it other than what he'd already been doing. Orm's passing the news to those at the farm had been a help, because it meant he had no trouble getting the renewed attention of those he'd been training.

Assessing what he had in the way of a defensive force, even under the best of conditions, didn't give him much reason to relax. Sven, his older brother, could hardly walk on his tortured bow-legs, or do much of anything with his gnarled, twisted hands, so hadn't participated in training since Skulifarm, which was a long time ago. Sverri, Sven's oldest son, was his champion, the best by far of the three brothers. Rogna was a jewel in every regard, and couldn't be more supportive of the farm and the people in it. She understood better than anyone the dark side of what men could be, and would give everything she had in defense of home and family. Orm was useless a fighter; but he was still important because he was able to communicate clearly as well as assist in other ways. The smithy, Erlynd, was nothing like the legendary Vilhjahn Gyrth had told about. Erlynd was short and muscle-bound, so much so that he jerked when he walked, and was comical in anything that required agility or coordination; but he had a wit and sparkle that made even the most difficult task somehow enjoyable. He didn't take to the training until the recent announcements, after which he gave it his attention, which was something else. With muscle fighting muscle, the best that could be expected from him was that in time his arrows would take a general direction. Then there were a few hands, most of whom were extra sons of farmer friends, who had the moral fiber to be workers rather than drifters or highwaymen or pirates, all of which were in their world. Some were also eager assistants at the marina.

Altogether the group at the farm weren't much, but they were what they were and nothing would change that. What Sigurth was concerned about, besides the eight or ten he could put to a defense, was the element of surprise. If they were caught sleeping, then double the number wouldn't matter. Still there had to be a plan to cope with a raid. What he devised for that was a series of firing points, four of them, near the doorways of the buildings around the yard. At each point bales of hay were arranged in chest high semicircles, the idea being that the combination, with at least two defenders at each point, would result in a storm of arrows at any attacking force. If the force was large and determined, it might not matter; but Sigurth felt the typical pirate wasn't interested in a fair fight, except possibly the berserkers, and that they'd turn tail if they found themselves in danger.

That was the plan.

This particular night was much like the rest, except that temperatures were rising and snow was disappearing, all signs that spring was on its way. It was also a sign that the pirates would soon be leaving, which meant all the more reason to be watchful. Those things didn't change anything, however, as Sigurth had been on the road every night since the news of the raid. He had long before established vantage points during his rides, and would stay in one for a while, then move to another, always holding movements to a minimum and relying on cloud cover to mask whatever those movements.

So as usual, he quietly started out from the barn, the horse hardly needing direction as they usually circled the corral, passed the gardens, then angled around the nob and copse that marked its ending, down to the roadway that skirted north past the cliffs. On some impulse this time, he reined in just past the gardens and sat. Then he turned and headed past the nob towards the expanses that made up the bulk of the farm. It was an area he'd traveled countless times before, but not for what he was doing tonight, and somehow it reminded him of another time.

He went past where the cattle normally grazed, now only a lonely expanse, eventually stopping near the boundary of the farm at its southeastern extremity. From there, the end of a gentle ridge they'd climbed, the land dropped to a convoluted valley before rising again in the distance. Here, if there was light to see by, he would have a panoramic view of not only the topography, but also the winding trail which was the shared roadway for most of the area.

Sigurth sat staring at the vague details the dim and shifting smatterings of light allowed him to see. With that and the quiet that lay over the land, he soon had to ask himself why he had come to this place. The roadway meandered southward, away from the farms that made up their portion of the district. It was the roadway that led eventually to what was once Skulifarm, and was the roadway pirates used that day years ago when his family was slaughtered. But it extended in the opposite direction from the neighboring pirates on the other side of the mountain who were his concern.

Unless . . . his mind was racing through every option . . . unless a group of pirates from areas to the south heard of Orm and Thora and their successes . . . or . . . the neighborhood pirates decided to take the long way around the mountains.

And what if he was wrong about their coming this way; but they did come the normal way and he wasn't there. Would his other actions work?

Besides the training and the firing stations, he'd built two small dog houses, placed them on the main road near the lane, and tied a dog to each as sentinels in the night. They were habitual barkers at anything that moved, which was a good thing; but would they be heard by a slumbering household a few hundred yards away?

Sigurth didn't like where he was on the ridge. It was boring with little in the way of interest to occupy his mind. At least on the road he had different stations to move to, and that was something. Here, the sameness caused his mind to drift.

What was it Orm and Gyrth discussed earlier? That if he could learn to read and write, he could write a story about all that happened . . . happened from the time he and the *Mule* eased out of the dock at Viggja, to when he returned seven years later. All of it would be easy to relate, in words that is, because it seemed each moment and each day was etched in his mind so thoroughly, that in every quiet moment, parts of it came flooding back.

Let's see now. In the beginning . . .

Building the ships turned out to be the easy part, it's what he and Orm and the workmen at the marina did. It just took time.

The bigger problem, it seemed at first, was the assembly of the crew. He was starting from scratch. But then as word spread of his intentions—to sail to Greenland—more stepped forward. The first were fellow workers at the marina, Arni Snara, Jon Oddsson, and Frothi Eysteinsson, who said count them in. And then hands at the farm, Thor Hausakljut and Ondur Visbkursson, asked if they could go along. In each case the story was about the same . . . They were hard working, disciplined young men, living in a world with limited opportunity. They had grown up on farms in this somewhat remote corner of the world with good families, but older brothers, which meant they had little to look forward to under normal circumstances. Yet each winter as they were growing, they listened to stories of their heroes, real and imagined, who lived exciting lives with wondrous deeds in faraway places like Garthariki and Miklagard. In Garthariki, for instance, longships plied the rivers across expanses of land hard to imagine in the limited useable farming areas that characterized their world. At one point, one of the main rivers being used came to a series of thunderous rapids, with each so notable they were given names like the Gulpa, the Sleepless, the Impassable, the High-cliff, the

Seether, and the Courser. Yet ships passed all of them by being pulled overland on rollers until calmer waters could be reached. In this way, hundreds of ships moved south into a large sea leading to exotic lands and further adventure.

Then more recently, stories of Iceland and Greenland and even farther places reached ears on long winter hours, and there came with them thoughts of adventure more readily available.

As the ship neared completion, Orm traveled with him to Trondheimsfjord to continue with the details that needed attention. Here they had many acquaintances because of the work they'd done on the Crane and the Long Serpent, and soon the crew was complete. Most important of the additions was Odd Snorrason, a seasoned navigator who'd been to Greenland and would share the responsibility of managing the ship and manning the steering oar.

The easiest part was filling up the capacity of the ship, which by the time they rowed out from the pier, consisted of fifteen crewmen and ten passengers— six adults and four children—chickens in racks, sheep, goats, mules, and lots of everything needed in supply.

With all that was being loaded, he was worried the ship would be too low in the water; but when they were launched and underway, it glided with ease and seemed to be stabilized by all it contained.

Another ship, the Skaun, piloted by Visbur Arneson, an entirely different venture, was leaving for Greenland about the same time, so it made sense to adjust schedules in order to travel together.

Before leaving, He and Odd met with Visbur and his main man to discus a general strategy and direction. For this, he rolled out his sketches showing the blobs representing key known areas of the world. Visbur looked at the drawings, his hand stroking his short whiskers, then said, "Where'd you get these?"

"I sailed to Spain u few years ago," Sigurth said. "The Captain of the ship I was on had a drawings based on his experiences. I just copied them."

"Is that so?" Visbur said. "It's the first I've ever seen. All I know is that we'll be traveling straight west to start out, with the intents of stopping by the Faroes in a few days. After that, we'll steer slightly southwesterly to Iceland."

Sigurth didn't know what comfort they and the Mule were to the other ship; but the other ship was a great comfort to him. This was the first time he'd sailed when they went straightaway from land until the land disappeared and there was the endless sea to the horizon in all directions. Having another ship cruising along within one hundred yards made quite a difference.

Then there was the night. Fortunately the first one came with a clear sky, with the heavens in all their glory giving plenty of light to continue monitoring relations with their companion ship. A novelty on this night was that waves being splashed sometimes sparkled with an iridescence, giving a magical quality to the scene. In contrast to this was the next night. Before the sun had set they entered *a fog bank that not only reduced visibility to about fifty feet, but also blotted out any sense of direction. All they could do was assume that wind and directions were constant and continue on, at the same time blowing horns intermittently to maintain a connection.*

The Faroes appeared on the horizon as expected, which caused Odd to laugh. Sigurth, who'd been at the rail straining to see, didn't understand.

"This has been too easy," Odd explained, "Don't assume it's going to go this well every time. There's many a tale of ships that wander for days in search of a destination; and when you hear of one disappearing, there's no telling where they went or what happened."

Both ships made port and docked without incident, then spent a day disembarking and going through all they would have done had they been at sea for weeks. They brought out the animals and cleaned the pens, putting down fresh hay and restocking the feed bins. Then after a general cleaning, supplies were replenished and the ship made ready. A day later, with everyone having enjoyed a hot meal and good nights sleep on dry land, they set sail again, this time aiming for Iceland.

"How long would you expect," Sigurth asked.

"My last trip took seven days after the Faroes," Visbur said. "But that's a good question. We shouldn't have trouble finding Iceland, because there is debris in the sea and birds in the air to give clues as to when we're nearby. But if we don't find what we're looking for in a reasonable time, it may be better to continue on to Greenland. It's larger and will be harder to miss."

Sigurth whistled at that possibility . . .

He didn't get a chance to continue the recollection.

There was a sound. Actually, the first sound went unnoticed. Sigurth had dismounted and sat bundled, using the horses front legs as a backstop as his mind wandered. So the first sounds, which traveled clearly in the stillness of the night, grew louder and mingled into a clutter of hoof clumps and harness rattlings before he jolted back into the world.

He cursed. Whoever they were were now too close to the corner of the woods and the clearing for him to move. Then whoever they were were past the corner, with only vague movements forcing their way through the darkness for him to see.

His next thought was to mount up, race back and sound the alarm.

But he didn't. Instead he strung his bow, picked up his lance and crept down the slope until he was point blank beside the roadway as the forms coalesced and moved past. Unbelievably, what he saw was almost the same combination he'd seen a few years before—two wagons filled with men, being led by others on horseback, except that this time there were three horsemen.

Sigurth waited until the second wagon was almost by, at which time he took a stance and began firing as quickly as he could into the huddled forms, first into those on the bench, then those below. His firing was so rapid the first hits didn't draw a response. Then someone aboard realized something awful was happening, probably because of pain, and screamed. This led to other disorganized and undefinable reactions, except that the sound of galloping meant a rider or riders were doubling back. Sigurth waited, lance in hand, until a rider took form; at which time he stepped forward and threw.

Then he ran. He raced back up the rise, only to find the movements and sounds, all of which carried messages of urgency and danger, had spooked his horse, and it was bolting away in the direction they'd come.

Sigurth couldn't whistle, a signal that usually got his horse's attention, as this would give his position away. He had to hope he was still obscured by darkness as well as the confusion on the roadway; so counting on those things he ran. For the first fleeting moments, he knew he was in a pickle— he had two arrows, a sword and a throwing axe; but he didn't have either the legs or the lungs he'd had in his prime, and the horse he was chasing was winning. He stopped at one point, taking in huge gulps of air, and turned to hear if he was being chased.

There were sounds of things happening back at the road; but they didn't seem to be coming his way; so he kept going, this time at a lesser pace. Finally the shape of his horse came into view. It had stopped; and when he closed in to grab the reins, he could see the big head turned to him with eyes seeming to ask where he'd been.

Back at the stead, Sigurth went straight to the large iron triangle outside the longhouse and rang it with loud, rapid rings that didn't stop until everyone, mostly bleary-eyed, half-dressed and poorly armed, were outside.

Orm had the foresight to set a torch before slipping out, which gave a ghostly character to everything; but at least they weren't groping in the dark.

"What's happening?" he asked.

Sigurth mouthed and gestured and pointed in every way he could think of while the others crowded in around the light.

"Pirates," Orm said.

Sigurth nodded with more emphasis than a simple yes.

"How many?"

Sigurth flashed both hands twice.

"Twenty or more pirates! What do you want us to do?"

Sigurth went through another series of gestures, including some directed at the horse, who looked back with a blank look.

Orm translated. "Sigurth wants all of you to arm yourselves and take to your assigned stations. I don't get the impression he really expects an attack, but he wants us to be ready."

"I don't get it," Erlynd the smithy said. "If they're out there, why wouldn't they attack?"

"Because," Orm answered, "if you look a little closer, you'll see Sigurth and his horse have already had a workout. In addition, Sigurth's lance is missing, and he's down to two arrows. There's a chance he's ruined their little surprise and chased them away.

"Oh Sverri, Sigurth wants you to mount up and follow him. He wants to make sure they're gone."

An hour later, as the sky in the east was beginning to lighten, a wagon thundered down the lane to Gyrthafarm. At the longhouse, Sverri jumped out and rang the iron, while Sigurth helped Orm down.

"Damn, what's this about?" said a bleary-eyed Hjalmar as he opened the door and stepped out. He was soon followed by Hrolf and Gyrth, still in their night clothes.

"Come in, come in," Gyrth said. "You're all half crazy most of the time; but you wouldn't be here like this if you didn't have good reason. So come in . . .

Hjalmar, get the torches lit . . . Hrolf get the women up.

They settled in around the central fire, quickly drawing a crowd as the whole household had been awakened.

"So what's this about?" Gyrth repeated as he sat down, groaning with the effort.

Orm was about to speak, but Sigurth put a hand on his shoulder and shook his head.

"What's wrong?" Orm said.

Sigurth looked at all those who were crowding into the room, then looked back at Orm.

"Oops," Orm said. "Sigurth doesn't want me to start talking with everybody looking on."

"That's ridiculous," Gyrth said. "Do you have any idea how difficult it is to keep a secret around here?"

"I understand. It's the same our way. But it may be best to keep this under wraps for the moment."

"Okay," Gyrth said. Struggling to his feet, he turned to the household. "Look, I'm sorry, but our guests would like to talk in private for the moment. I don't understand what the problem is, but please forgive our rudeness."

When the room had cleared except for the few at the fire, Gyrth said softly, "All right, what's so damned important that we have to whisper?"

"We were almost attacked by pirates an hour ago," Orm said.

"Almost?"

"Yes . . . But Sigurth intercepted them at the southmost property line and fired a bunch of arrows."

"He also threw a lance," Sverri added.

With that, Sigurth reached to the side and extended two sticks he'd been carrying.

"What's this?" Gyrth asked. Then he saw what it was—two pieces of a lance. "And what's all this crap all over the point?" After looking at it more closely, he added, "I see what you're getting at . . . It's blood."

Orm nodded.

"So Sigurth intercepted a raiding party coming in from the south. I still don't understand why all the secrecy," Gyrth said.

"Just bear with us on this," Orm said, looking at the far end of the longhouse to make sure no one was listening. "We don't know for sure where they came from, but we have a feeling that they came from here. They could do that by taking the long road around the high country. If so, it's important that they don't find out we suspect them."

"I see . . . You feel the fewer that know, the better the chance they won't find out we know."

"Something like that."

"So how do you propose to prove it's them?"

"Isn't there a back road to their property, and doesn't that road pass by the property of one of your friends?"

"The farm owned by Gunni Erlingesson would be the one. The road's a rarely used one, but scoots by one of his corners."

"If they're the ones who were going to raid us, and if they used that road, then they'd be returning by way of it sometime in the next few hours. We should be there."

"Let's go," Sverri said.

The small group was hiding in the heights overlooking where the roadway, more of a rough clearing through the brush, came by at its closest. They had been there a few hours and were beginning to feel they might have guessed wrong, when they heard sounds. Not long afterwards, a sad procession, the same makeup as described by Orm earlier, plodded by.

They were in view for only a few minutes, then disappeared into the tangle that in reasonable likelihood would be a back way to the pirates property.

"What did you notice about them?" Orm asked when the procession had been gone long enough for them to relax.

"In the one wagon," Sverri said, "not everyone was sitting up."

"I thought I saw red . . . Could have been blood," added Hrolf.

"And one of the horses had a body tied over the saddle."

"There's no doubt about it," Sverri said. "Those are the bastards that tried to get us. There's no telling what they'd have done if they'd caught us asleep. Look what they did at Folasonfarm. Let's round up the farmers around here and wipe them out."

"Right away?" Orm asked.

"Sure . . . Okay, it might take a while to get organized; but we should be able to attack by tomorrow."

Gyrth didn't say anything while the thoughts with all their exuberance were being expressed; then he held up his hand, "Now just hold on . . . not so fast. Yes, I agree with all of you on what to do; but not on how to do it. First, the pirates have been hurt; second, they may be wary that their clever trip around the mountain has been noticed. If that's so, they'll be more on the alert in the next few days than ever."

"You have a plan?" Orm asked.

Gyrth nodded.

Gyrth sent out a war-arrow of sorts to the six farms that formed the western end of the district with simple instructions—to quietly assemble six to eight of their best men, and bring them, fully armed, to a meeting of extreme importance two days hence, at Thor Bergthorson's farm, which was near the center of all the farms. It was stressed that the element of secrecy was important, if at all possible.

By the time all of them assembled, Gyrth had learned that the pirate compound, or at least the targeted portion, wasn't a single building as had been the case at Skulifarm. Over the years previous to this, youngsters from the nearest farms had on occasion been hunting or just plain snooping around and had crept up to it. Those that had been there told that the compound was actually a working farm with barns, pens and gardens as well as a number of other buildings, the most prominent of which were two bunkhouses and a large longhouse. All of this made sense as there had to be something significant to house and entertain two or three dozen men for the winter.

The plan was simple. They would all move into position along a line on one side of the compound a few hours before daybreak. Then a select group would move forward and take out any sentries; followed immediately by other groups who would seal and burn the buildings.

The initial assembly went fine and the groups, trying to stay in contact with one another, moved into the trees. It wasn't as easy as they had imagined, however, as the forest was not only a tangle, there were also rises and drops and gullies and outcrops and fallen logs, and it was dark.

Sigurth led the group from Bird Mountain, approaching from the western end along the path that tied the compound to the marina. It was an area he was somewhat familiar with, but in the darkness, which at times was absolute as only forests at night can be, he was as confused as everyone else.

They reached a point where he felt that if all the other groups were in a similar position, they were close enough to start the attack.

It never happened.

Dogs on both sides of the compound barked, shattering the stealthy stillness. Then there was a ringing of irons and the sound of movements, of doors slamming and people moving . . . moving in an orderly fashion.

To Sigurth's amazement, which he saw from the edge of the pathway, a fire was started, which didn't make sense as that was part of *their* plan. Why would the pirates be starting a fire?"

Then he saw why. Men dipped hooded arrows into the fire, and when lit, moved to different points in the compound to shoot into the woods. They were doing this to illuminate the woods where attackers might be gathered so they could see and take the initiative.

He watched, sickened, realizing his fear was realized . . . that the pirates knew exactly what was planned and were prepared for it. Then came flaming arrows his way, some sticking in trees, but most flying past, and altogether doing what was intended . . . exposing them.

Sigurth signalled for his group to fall back beyond the fires and form a shield wall; but then he left them, moving forward and disappearing into the darkness.

All along the perimeter of the compound, pirates began to attack. From where he'd stopped to hide, Sigurth couldn't see much in detail from the muddled movements the splotches of light provided, but there were sounds—animal-like yips and growls and swords on shields and the silent swoosh of arrows, and in his case, approaching sounds.

They passed him, six or eight howling men, possibly berserkers. Then they stopped and loosed a barrage of arrows, some of them aflame, in the direction the initial volleys indicated his men were.

Sigurth moved. Leaving his sword and bow behind and using only his axe, he came to the last person in the group, striking down diagonally and hitting at the base of the neck. He hit two more before any of them, all of whom were concentrating on what they could see of the shield wall, had any inkling. A fourth was cut down as he turned, then Sigurth ducked behind a tree and whistled—a rapid *tweet, tweet, tweet* . . . which was the signal to charge.

With that his team, including Sverri and Hjalmar, who'd been hunkered down and listening to arrows swish by, some hitting shields, rose with a growl and moved forward, lances and swords ready for action. There wasn't anyone to fight, however. They moved across an area that had bodies on the ground but no one standing; so by the time they received another signal from Sigurth to stop and form up again, they had a good idea of what had happened. Like Sigurth, who joined them, they changed to bows, and sent volleys in the direction that vague movements told them their surviving attackers were taking. Upon another signal, they stopped and returned to a defensive position.

There were sounds ahead and occasional movements to be seen, but nothing that gave a clear picture, except to give the impression that whatever the action taking place elsewhere, that fighting had stopped with nothing seeming to be gained by either side.

After about an hour of waiting, the sky slowly lightened, and then what was there to see clarified what imaginations had pictured in the darkness. They were in a standstill with the pirates, who could be seen gathered behind the main buildings, now in their own defensive positions. And when they turned to look back, they could see that the carnage they suspected as they advanced in the dark was real.

There was an impasse, and it seemed like it was going to go on for an unnerving amount of time, but then two pirates came out from one of the buildings, one holding a pennant on a staff. They proceeded to a point near the center of the grounds and stopped.

"They want to talk," said Gyrth who was just coming out of the forest and moving slowly to make his way to the shield wall.

"You okay, uncle?' Sverri asked.

"Oh ya," Gyrth said, "but trying to keep up with all of you in this forest is more easily said than done for me.

"So they want to talk, do they? Okay, let's talk." With that he started out, at the same time waving to the woods for others to join in the parley. Soon there was a small group assembled near the pirates.

Hauk, the pirate leader, who was familiar to most of them, spoke first.

"What's happened that you should attack us in this way? We've been on peaceful terms for years. We don't understand."

"Bullshit!" Tolsi said, growling. "Your men ravaged our farm not long ago, tortured Signi and me until they got what they wanted . . . all that we'd saved. Then they raped my daughters. They're still in shock and may never be the same. There's no amount of wergil that will pay for our damages. I'm here to see you burn, one way or the other."

"Now hold on there," Hauk said holding up his hands. "I heard about what happened to you, and I'm very sorry. But that wasn't by any of us. I don't know who it was, and wish I did because we'd join you in going after them. They're making us look guilty for things we didn't do."

Gyrth burst out laughing at that, so much so he started coughing and had to be held as he seemed ready to collapse.

"Are you all right?" Hauk said.

"Oh, just a little cough."

"Good . . . So what was so funny?"

"You," Gyrth said. "You act like the good neighbor, but then go a-viking to farms that really are. Just a matter of days ago you or your men tried another raid, but were caught along the way."

"That's ridiculous!"

"Not exactly," Gyrth said with a grim smile. "We followed the wagons back, and back was to this farm."

Hauk nodded, "Yes I've heard about that too . . . and it *was* our men."

"Aha!" Tosli exploded. "You admit it, which means you raided me too!"

"Now wait a minute; that's not what I said. You must understand that for as many men as I have, to stay cooped-up for the winter puts a strain on everyone. Those days ago that were mentioned, the men were getting to aggravate one another, so I ordered them to take a long ride that included the high country, in a loop that would circle by Bird Mountain and the marina before getting back home. I figured this would take some of the energy out of them.

"But they were viciously attacked for no reason along the way and had to turn back. Now who's going to make amends for that? I've got four recent graves to prove the damage that's been done. And there's more. I've been told several more were killed this morning while defending our property. Who's going to make amends for them?"

Gyrth hesitated, blinked, then turned to the others—Tosli, Gunni Erlingesson and Thor Bergthorson. They whispered.

"It looks like you may be coming to your senses," Hauk said. "But if there's a slight chance you're not, you might want to look at our men. Yes, you do have a larger force than we do; but our men are all seasoned fighters. And do you see the ones biting their shields? You know who they are. So if you do continue this foolishness, you'll probably lose. Either way there'll be many a grave to dig and many a tear to shed.

"Instead of all that, consider this. We'll meet with you before a District Thing assembled for the purpose. I'm confident, that under the circumstances, the wergil they'll require will be reasonable."

There was a momentary hesitation as the four stood, hardly able to blink. Then Gyrth burst out laughing again. "Hauk, you are one very clever son-of-a-bitch. The only thing you said that made sense was about the graves we'd have to dig, because we don't like that. But make no mistake, we know you're guilty, and therefore, if you don't agree to our terms, we *will* attack, and there *will* be no quarter . . . *so fuck your berserkers!*"

Now Hauk stood stone-faced.

"And what are your terms," he finally said.

"We want all of you out of here. We'll give you safe passage to your ships, and allow you to sail away without hindrance. But you are niding in our eyes, you are skoggangur. That means that none of you may ever return, for if any does, he will be killed on sight. As for your property, it will all be turned over to Tosli as payment for the damages he's suffered.

"Oh, one final thing. You'd better take with you the bastard you've had as a spy, because if we ever find out who it is, we'll hang him by his balls."

Hauk stood, his face going through several shades and his eyes seeming to dance, until his whole being settled.

"If I went to my men with this," he said, "they'd want to attack, even if it meant getting killed. But the fact is they hate this place. It's spooked. We've never heard of any of the rest of you having a problem, but it seems every time one of our men strays away at night, he meets with a ghost who sees in the dark and strikes fast and never misses. There are more graves because of him than just the recent ones."

Gyrth and the others looked at each other and shrugged, most not having the slightest idea what he was talking about.

The pirates sailed away the next day, and so did Gyrth.

He'd been with the throng that lined the banks to watch what was quite a moment for the community; but he was tired and shaky and had sought a place to sit while all of the doings were going on. When the last boat disappeared, the crowd began to break up, many turning to see Gyrth and offer thanks for what he'd done.

They couldn't. His eyes, that had seen it all, were now glazed.

But there was a smile on his face . . . And because of that, all were sure that his spirit, so steadfast and true in life, was now with the Valkyries and fellow heroes in Valhalla. Valhalla, whose halls shine with gold, with great spears for rafters and roofed with shields and mail coats, so large there are 540 doors, each wide enough for 800 warriors to pass through abreast.

Chapter 16

SEA EAGLE

1028

Twelve more years passed, and there had been peace.

"That's enough," Sigurth mouthed, wiping sweat from his brow and brushing off, then walking away from the grounds that still had dust in the air from the dozen men still milling about. Garth and Gunnar, along with friends and hands of similar ages, had been at it for several hours. They were shirtless like Sigurth, and dirty, sweaty and glowing from what they'd been doing, which was vigorous gaming as well as martial arts training under Sigurth's direction.

Sigurth looked back at them, but only briefly, trying not to give his sons too much attention, which for him was a constant struggle. When they'd survived the disaster at sea years ago and been brought to the farm, there'd been a ready made family to welcome them and love them and give them direction. This was fortunate because he had to fight with himself to keep from being overbearing or overprotective, and Orm and Thora and Rogna kept it from happening. At this point in their lives, whatever happened seems to have worked. They'd both grown to be sturdy young men, full of spirit, but serious minded enough, not only to evolve with the work ethic needed, but also to develop skills in line with what Orm and he had been doing.

The two were a few years apart in age, and never seemed to be the same height until this last year when Gunnar put on a spurt; and they didn't resemble one another either, but they'd been so inseparable that in all other regards they could as well have been twins. Garth was much like Sveyin, not only in appearance and walk, but also in mannerisms—like speaking and humor—that if he came upon Sigurth when he was deep in thought, Sigurth's first reaction was usually to wonder which world he was in. In contrast to this, Gunnar had few features directly reflecting Sigurth. His skin and hair were both darker, as were his eyes. It was only in his frame with his wide shoulders and certain mannerisms, that hinted of a connection.

The day wasn't without purpose. The farming chores of spring were about at an end, with a lull that fitted perfectly with the festival that was being held a short travel away in a few days. It was the first meaningful event of the year drawing together a good part of the district. It would be festive, with rows of decorated, flagged and festooned booths exhibiting a wide variety of artwork and crafts. There would be many booths with food, along with jugglers and unique entertainments. And not surprisingly, for young men, it was not only a chance for honors and medals, it was also a chance to meet girls.

For this event, in addition to what the men were preparing for, were the results, mostly by women, of the long winter hours. These results included a few foodstuffs, although that was more the case in the fall after harvest, but mostly artwork and crafts, such as woodworking, pottery, metalworks, sewing and weaving. Rogna and the crew at the shop were at it from dawn until late after dark getting ready, assembling and finishing their work, which as it was turning out, even Thora at her best would have been proud to show.

Sigurth wasn't involved in any of it, not anymore. He remained busy with ship-building and repair, and in woodcarving and stone etching and works of that nature; but he wasn't interested in public events and didn't plan to display any of his works, which were mainly for his own use and pleasure anyway.

An explosion of sound caused him to look back to see that something funny had happened, with men reeling at whatever it was, with a few punches and jabs working their way in. He snorted . . . *so much energy.* He was curious, but then he was over twice their ages and couldn't talk, so he preferred to stay apart and let them do their thing.

Instead of getting further involved, he grabbed his tunic and headed to the barn, finding his favorite horse seemingly waiting for him beside the corral. The horse sidled up to him as he fumbled with the harness, so he took the big head in his hands and head-butted, whispering *"Hello horse . . . it sure is good to have someone to talk to. It's a beautiful day today, don't you think? Such a good day for a ride. And while we're at it, how would you like to take me to visit some old friends? I haven't seen them in years, and miss them terribly. It will be good to have a chat."*

It was an easy ride, breaking into a trot for only a few stretches, as Sigurth let the horse set the pace most of the way. They went past the fields and through the pastures on the high ground so quietly the cattle hardly looked up as they ambled by. When they reached the forests where a rivulet gouged a meandering, rocky gully, he stopped for a few moments by one of the small pools it had created. He never wondered why this place had such appeal to him, but it did; and like he always did, he eventually heeled the horse and moved on.

The horse knew where they were going. Without further direction, it picked its way up the figment of a trail, then over its crest and down the north side until the other farm could be seen in the distance. At this point they turned west onto another faint pathway paralleling the slope of Bird Mountain, following it almost to the cliffs. Sigurth reined in and dismounted beside a lengthy oblong mound from which sprouted an unusual array of wild flowers. He reached into the bag he was carrying, a bag filled with seeds of more flowers, and emptied it, casting the contents randomly along the length of the mound.

While standing beside the mound, it was difficult to make out its shape because boulders and bushes and flowers tended to obscure its outline; but higher above and looking down, as if being one of the birds that circled, it could be seen that the shape was regular, coming to a point at each end, with raised protrusions there as if being extended ends of the keel of a ship.

They *were* extended ends of the keel of a ship.

The ship was the *Sea Eagle*.

When Gyrth died, there were strong emotions about a proper burial. He was much loved and respected, and living as long as he had and doing as much as he did, he touched the lives of many generations. Sigurth remembered what Gyrth said about the *Sea Eagle* a matter of days before his death, and then thought of a certain ravine along the side of the mountain. The ravine was just one of the many features that made up the plateau, but he remembered this feature because as a youngster climbing over it all he'd noticed, along with Sveyin, that it was of such a shape that a ship could fit into it.

Sigurth brought Orm to the site, and with gestures and signs as had become his custom, explained a concept of moving the *Sea Eagle* to it, and then using it as a crypt. Orm took it from there. When he explained the idea to both households who were gathered at Gyrthafarm in memoriam, the thought was first met with silence.

Finally Hrolf ventured to say, "Isn't a ship burial more a matter for royalty?" Then he was sorry he'd said it.

Orm laughed. "I don't know about any rules regarding that, but what you're saying is that a ship burial, or a burial at sea in a burning ship, is as high an honor that can be conveyed, and should therefore be only be used for someone exalted. Well, in my mind, Gyrth is as honorable a person who's ever walked this earth, so I'm all for it. As for royalty, in our lifetime, we've seen that the very royal Earl Hakon, who even sheep ran from, was beheaded in a pig sty, with his head put on display for his subjects to ridicule . . . and Olaf Tryggvason, the scourging pirate who was reminded of his bloodline and got religious, went for a swim with all his armor to celebrate his passing. Need I say more?"

"But is it possible?" another asked.

Orm answered, "At the marina, we hear all sorts of stories. Some travelers passing through have told of what has happened in Garthariki, in fact its been going on for over a hundred years. Merchants traveling there, mostly Swedes but also Danes and Norwegians, have been staying on the waterways for most of their travels; but at times they've had to portage, to move across land to get from one river or body of water to another. They've been doing this through forests and over every kind of terrain for distances as long as one hundred miles. If they've been able to do that, we can move the distance needed to set the ship in place on the mountain."

When word got out about the idea, everyone in the neighboring farms thought it great and wanted to help. Working quickly, as there was an obvious urgency, the volunteers were split into groups, with some cleaning the ravine and making a pathway to it workable, while others moved the ship. At the marina, it was a normal practice to bring a ship out of the water on a series of lubricated timbers secured in place. This was easily done with the aid of winches and pulleys. Out of the water, the ship could then be serviced or brought into a shed for storage.

In this instance, the ship was first moved as before; then stripped of unnecessary weight, such as masts and rigging and oar racks and ballast. Next it was put to muscle, with dozens in lines of ropes on each side of the ship, pulling to a cadence ... *heave ... heave ... heave ... heave.* While most pulled, some moved logs from back to front; some lubricated them; while others along the sides jammed in stay poles to keep the ship balanced.

The ship was moved, foot by foot with each beat, in a process seeming forever, across grassy expanses, sandy lanes and scrubby inclines. When the sun set on the first day, it seemed like an unbelievable distance had been covered, and it had. The ship was now well inside Gyrthafarm, over half the distance ultimately required; but muscles and backs were tired beyond memory, and the steeper inclines of the mountain remained.

A tasty meal with lusty drinks thrown in, and a good nights sleep, however, worked wonders, for in the morning, everyone was at it again. At one point when there was a combined turn with a difficult incline, one of the volunteers moving the logs excitedly called out, "Hold it . . . Stop! It looks like some of the bow planks are parting. If they do the ship will take on water."

It took a moment for people to absorb that remark; when they did, everything did stop, with some falling to the ground laughing. It gave the workers new life once order was resumed, and on it went. When the *Sea Eagle* was finally put in place with the bow facing straightaway out to sea, the mountain reverberated with people jumping and shouting and cheering, settling into wide grins and swelled chests and hugs all around.

The burying, the mounding and the celebration that followed the next day, along with moving the ship, were experiences that would be talked about for generations. In fact, what Sigurth was doing at this moment was what others in the family, and all who'd been there, had been doing from time to time ever since . . . making a pilgrimage.

Sigurth dismounted and settled by the stern, where Gyrth had been interred on the section of decking beside the steering oar. He was put to rest with the finest clothes he owned, which he rarely wore, including a magnificent vest with hammered leather plates decorating a multi-colored woven base, all made by Thora and given to him at his last Yule celebration. Beside him were placed a sword, a lance, and several other weapons, all finely crafted, none of which had been used in combat. As an afterthought, Hrolf also placed beside him a worn and weathered wooden pitchfork, and a drinking horn, both of which had been extensively used. All of this was covered with fine quilting and flowers, then an overhead decking to enclose a crypt was constructed before the mound was shaped.

Around the perimeter, the grounds had been left undisturbed, blending in with the natural mountain-scape. Assisting with this impression was what happened to the keel at the stern by Gyrth's crypt. Originally standing clear, it was now obscured by vines as well as a few scrub trees that were in abundance on the slopes and had taken root. All of this added to the solitude intended.

A certain stone, easy to miss because of the overall combination of features, and particularly since a bush had grown against it, was just to the side above the crypt. Sigurth pulled the bush away and dusted the flat surface, which revealed that the stone was actually a monument. He had carved it and placed it in a manner to be obscured, as if a special treasure, but not hidden.

The carving was in runes. This was as much as Sigurth had been able to learn. Learning to read and write in the manner that stories could be told wasn't an opportunity ever extended to him, which was a frustration he'd resigned to accept; but then he didn't know what he didn't know. Another area of knowledge that interested him because one was tied to the other, was that of poetry. Skalds who specialized in it entertained royalty and crowds at special functions throughout the land. And in many households, others dabbled in it, mainly as part of winter entertainments. Without these abilities, the runes he composed were simplistic, no more complicated than the limit of the assistance he received, in this case two lines that snaked in parallel about the flat surface of the stone. It read:

Gyrth Torkelsson, husband, father and patriarch
of generations that farmed Bird Mountain and secured its bounty.
A leader of landed men in Moer.
Died from battle wounds.

Sigurth moved the length of the mound to the bow end of the keel. This end was anything but obscure. Originally plain like at the stern, it was revised by Sigurth during the winter after Gyrth's internment. The revision was a carved wooden cover that fitted over the keel to give it a more glorified appearance in keeping with it name. The cover was an eagle with the head in a majestic pose, arching back but looking down as if to intimidate the sea it was commanding. On each side were wings, contained but semi-flared as if ready for flight. After a brief look to see how the carving was holding up, he went to another stone nearby, a stone much like that for Gyrth.

Here lie Orm and Thora.
He, small in stature but a giant among the good and talented,
a wood carver and ship builder;
She, a lovely woman whose virtue was matched by her exceeding talent,
a weaver and seamstress without equal.

Two years before, a malady of sorts had swept through the area during the winter. Most were sickened, and many died. The two were among the latter, doing so within a day of one another. As with Gyrth, except in a private ceremony, they were buried in exquisite finery along with the tools of their trade.

Sigurth stayed for about an hour, his mind reliving all the wonderful moments beginning with that first day. He talked to them as he always did, in whispers. And as with the horse, he felt there was a connect, a reaching out and embracing across the undefinable worlds that were, and he was comforted by it.

In time he stood and walked away, turning south to walk up the slope to the flattened heights of the plateau. He stopped at a particular combination of rocks that had been a favorite vantage point for he and Sveyin when they were spotting for incoming ships. It was also the place where he would ask "What do you see when you look west from here?"

It seems some things never change, and that's a good thing as he located the place where he'd often sat when they were here; so, he plunked down and got comfortable like he'd done ages ago. The big differences, of course, were that Sveyin wasn't here, and neither was Trulsi, the dog that had been his companion for many years. But then something happened that made him laugh. The horse, as if reading his mind and wanting to belong, moved up and stood with his forelegs beside him.

Sigurth leaned over and gave the legs a hug, to which the horse snorted. Let's see, Sigurth thought, they'd been together like this years ago, waiting for pirates to come down the south road . . . and he'd been deep in thought. He'd been thinking about the story he'd write if he could write.

They'd just left the Faroes, the first leg of their journey to Greenland . . . the two ships . . . the Mule and the Skaun, a ship named for the area near the marina where it had been built . . .

The two days in open water, the time it took to reach the Faroes, had seemed a long stretch when there was nothing to see. That time and the amount of boredom was soon eclipsed by the days that seemed to inch by on the way to Iceland. Although no stranger to sailing, this was putting everything in a new dimension. There were only so many subjects worthy of talking about at length to Odd, who was usually with him at the steering oar. With the Mule slicing gentle waves as smoothly as it was, there was also little in the way of direction to give to the crew— Arni, Jon, Frothi, Thor, Ondur and the others; and there were only so many reasons to skirt along the rails from stern to bow and back again.

Fortunately, adding interest to the days, there were passengers. There were Yngvi Skoptason and his wife Thyri, who had three of the children, the oldest being ten. Yngvi was a farmer, whose story was such as could be expected from anyone who was embarking on this kind of trip. He and a brother had grown up and inherited a farm not far from the Trondheimsfjord. But it was a small farm on a locked-in bit of flatland, and with two growing families, didn't offer a future worth pursuing. So they'd collected their assets, with hopes of finding more land and a real future elsewhere. For them, the sound of a place called "Greenland" had the promise of all they were looking for.

Yngvi was of average height and appeared wiry, with his usual tunic and leggings hanging loose. Being energetic, he was also bothered by the lengthy stretches with nothing to do, or of trying keep his children in tow, so he took to assisting with the animals, who in truth were less bothered by the situation than anyone else aboard.

Another couple was Dag Hringsson and his wife Dotta. They were young with a one year old baby girl who was requiring a lot of attention and making more noise than any other.

And there were the brothers, Ari and Askel Bjornsson. They were hunters and fishermen who'd been hearing of the exotic catches, like walruses and seals and white bears in Greenland, and were looking for the adventure they might bring. They were often at the rails with lines in the water, and were successful enough to provide a daily ration of raw fish to anyone who could stomach it.

Anyway, the days went by, one after the other, with the Skaun off to the right, always in view. The Mule, despite its unglamorous name, proved to be the faster of the two, so whenever the ships got uncomfortably distant, the sail was rolled enough to slow down.

Then came day six and eyes began looking for the signs that would lift spirits and give direction. Jon, who was the smallest and most nimble of the crew, scampered up the mast every few hours to give a look; but would always slide down with that gesture that said there was nothing to see.

Day seven followed and there was more of the same.

On the morning of day eight, the Mule slowed so the Skaun could approach within shouting distance. This part wasn't unusual because they started each day this way to exchange observations, give opinions of directions or anything else of interest. This morning, however, was different; they had expected to see land by this time.

"We haven't seen a thing," Sigurth yelled. "Jon went up the mast again at dawn and only saw the horizon."

Visbur nodded, "Same here. We haven't seen birds either. What we know for sure," he added, "is that Iceland is north of us. I'm at a loss why we haven't seen it."

"I have an opinion on that," Odd said.

"And that is?"

"I think we've sailed past it. For one thing, we've had excellent sailing conditions with much better time being made than usual. Secondly, we may be moving more southwesterly than westerly. With the cloud cover we've been having, it's been difficult to tell."

Visbur turned to his aide for a few moments, then swung back to say, "Lars agrees with you. We usually don't have trouble keeping up, but your boat is fast and conditions have been ideal. We could be as much as two days past.

"How are your rations?"

Sigurth groaned. "We had hoped to restock in Iceland."

"That's not an answer. Can you make it to Greenland?"

Odd laughed, but no one saw the humor in it. Then he explained, "We could waste days doubling back, because there's no telling how far we're off. So I'm for keeping going, but let's turn to the northwest to make sure we don't miss. We'll have to do half rations, so the animals might complain; but we'll make it. For darn sure we'll be sick of raw fish."

A week later they saw land. It took another day to round the skerries and dodge icebergs until they could turn north and head to where the settlements could be found. As they traveled offshore they saw treeless countryside and rocks and fjords with glaciers along the horizon.

The first question, which was asked in murmurs along the rail, was . . ."This is Greenland?"

Sigurth's eyes, that had been out of focus, saw movement, a ship entering the channel that might turn into the marina, and that interrupted his thinking.

He watched the ship, wondering what stories it could tell or what news it could bring. The latter thought could be cause to worry. Norway had been fairly stable for several years now. Olaf the Stout had been undisputed King ever since the sea battle, and had been doing his thing with regards to Christianity; but he'd been wrapped up in enough turmoil in certain parts of the country to keep him busy. Anyway, he'd left Bird Mountain and the surrounding vicinity alone.

That had been a good thing, and there'd been no war-arrows.

But word had been circulating about King Knut, who ruled Britain and Denmark, and felt because of previous relationships that he should be ruling Norway as well. So far there'd only been rumors as to what that would mean; except he'd heard that Einar Thambarskelfir, who he'd fought with on the losing side at Svolth years before, had risen to prominence since then and had gotten involved in this rulership business, siding with Knut.

Einar was supposedly the greatest archer ever to ever lift a bow, which meant he must be pretty good. But Sigurth thought he'd like to see him up against Sveyin . . . If that were to happen, Einar might not be so great after all.

Well, anyway, he didn't like it, the things he was hearing; they were like a distant thunder warning of a storm to come. He was training his boys the best he could for whatever might happen, and they were doing fine; but the many years of peace had been good to get used to, so it was his hope the skills would never be used.

He stood and grabbed the reins and made a sound that meant. *Come on horse, it's time to go home.*

Chapter 17

STICKLESTAD

Sigurth concentrated, his hands steady as he carefully shaved a slice from the complicated ornament he was carving. He sat back and eyed the result, then leaned forward to make another, when he realized Gunnar was trying to get his attention.

He looked up and grunted.

"Pa," Gunnar began, "I thought you might want to hear what this is all about."

He sat up then and looked in the direction Gunnar pointed with his head, noticing that Sverri and Garth, who were a ways away working on a boat hull, had stopped and also turned.

Two riders were approaching, one of them carrying a flag that fluttered at the end of a long shaft.

Sigurth snarled, set his tools down, and pushed his work back so he could stand.

The riders, who'd been ambling along at an easy pace, came to a stop short of the work shelter and waited as the workers gathered round. The rider carrying the flag was young, and by the look on his face, wasn't yet comfortable with being in the limelight. The other, however, was considerably older and obviously accustomed to it. He was also on the portly side, with clothes that looked impressive at a distance, but up close showed a telling amount of wear. He looked over the group as if trying to pick out a friendly face, which he was. His face blossomed into a smile as he did.

"Sigurth, is that you?"

Sigurth looked more closely, not yet recognizing the man. Then it came to him, and he nodded. The man was an older and much traveled Ashjorn.

"He can't talk," Sverri said.

"Oh that's right," Ashjorn said. "The last time I saw him was when he returned from the Hjaltlands. He was in bad shape then; but that was a long time ago."

If that was so," Sverri said, "do you remember who was with him?"

"Hmm, let me think . . . I recall there were two, a couple of tots . . . boys."

Sverri laughed. "That *was* a long tome ago. I'm sure you don't recognize them now, Garth Sveyinson and Gunnar Sigurthson here," pointing to the two.

"Oh my," Ashjorn said. "It was a long time ago, indeed. What fine young men you've grown into."

"So what's this all about?" Sverri said. "And please don't tell me that's a war-arrow."

Ashjorn shifted in the saddle, trying to find the right words. "It's not really a war-arrow; but then it is . . . kinda."

"Kinda?"

"I'm not working for anyone in particular right now, just making rounds for the Tronders to let folks nearby know what's happening."

"Are the king wannabees at it again?"

Ashjorn snorted. "That's not exactly what we call it; but it's something like that."

"Does that mean Knut isn't still in charge? The last we heard Olaf had gone to Garthariki."

"Well, yes he did . . . and we wish he'd stayed. But it seems that recently he's decided that being King was worth another chance. And that leads to why I'm here. Actually this whole affair is pretty complicated, and I need to spread the word to a lot of people about it. Is there a place where a large group can assemble? Inside would be preferred because you never know about the weather. I'm familiar with a number of longhouses around here, but all of them are too small for what I'm thinking. I'd like a place that'll hold thirty to forty people. That would include people from all the farms in this corner of the district. In a place like that I could tell everyone what's happening with Olaf, and what's being planned around Trondheimsfjord because of what he's doing."

"Did you ever see the farm where the pirates used to winter?"

"Ny."

"The farm's in the forest only a couple miles from here. It has the largest building in these parts. It belongs to Tosli Folason now; there's a long story about that, but I'm sure he wouldn't mind."

"Sounds good," Ashjorn said. "Could any of you give me a hand in spreading the word about this? It would be perfect to meet tomorrow morning at Tosli's place, if it's okay with him. So all of you here know, Olaf isn't just thinking about returning, he's returned and is in Norway as we speak, having crossed the mountains from Sweden. He's aiming at the Trondheimsfjord area."

"Why there?"

"Beats me. Maybe it's because if he can tame an area that's given him so much trouble in the past, the rest of the country will fall into line. Anyway, the farmers around the fjord want to amass such a force opposing him, that Olaf will give up without a fight and leave the country for good."

"Fat chance on that," Sverri said. "Olaf isn't the kind that backs down . . . and he's pretty clever too. He raised hell with the fleet we'd assembled a few years ago, resulting in many of our citizens getting killed, including my uncle."

"You mean Gyrth Torkelsson?"

"Ya."

Ashjorn shook his head. "Sorry . . . He was a great man. He helped us out many a time."

Two days later, after the meeting Ashjorn conducted, the families met at Gyrthafarm, Hjalmar now serving as host. From his farm were his sons Hlovir, Frey and Hroald, with Hlovir the oldest at eighteen; his brother Torkel; and four hands. From the other farm were Sverri, his sons Bjorn and Barth, both in their late teens; his brother Gunni, a like number of hands; and Sigurth with Garth and Gunnar. The wives and other daughters, as well as Rogna, who still had fire in her eyes whenever there was something challenging, crowded the far end of the room.

"Most of you weren't at the meeting yesterday," Hjalmar said. "So Sverri and I thought we should all get together and discus what's happening."

"The gist of it is that Olaf the Stout has returned from Garthariki. He's been gathering forces loyal to him, and has gotten help from King Onund of Sweden, who has provided near to 500 men. All told he may have an army of four thousand."

The only sounds were throats being cleared.

"That's a large army," Someone finally said, almost in a whisper.

"What's that got to do with us?" Another asked.

"Good question," Sverri said, then looking at Sigurth, added, "If Sigurth could speak, I think he'd ask the same thing. He'd ask why do we want to go to battle, a battle on land that can chop us into pieces, for a cause that won't benefit us one way or the other when it's over, except give us reason to grieve."

"And he might be right with the question," Hjalmar said, "but we really don't know. Olaf wasn't popular in parts of Norway, particularly around Trondheimsfjord; and we can't forget that Gyrth died from the injuries he received fighting him. We just don't know whether King Knut or whoever he appoints will be better or worse over the long run in ruling us."

"So why do we want to join either side?" Bjorn asked.

"That may be the best question of all," Sverri said. "Unfortunately, we may not have a choice. Ashjorn, who's representing the Tronders, said his people want no part of Olaf. To make sure he doesn't get his way, their plan is to assemble such a large force of resistance, over ten-thousand men, that resorting to a power play would be foolhardy. And that's the plan."

"How do the other farmers around here feel about it?

"The meeting yesterday was packed," Hjalmar said, "with the questions you're asking among the many that were raised. From all that was discussed, there was a consensus of what do do. There were a few who were anxious to go to war; but most were like we are. We've been to battle and know it's not a glorious thing, particularly when the outcome isn't likely to be of any benefit."

"That doesn't answer the question."

Hjalmar hesitated, looked at Sverri and sighed. "I don't like to answer because I don't like the choices. The fact is if we don't join the force that's heading out tomorrow for Nitharos, we'll be the only farm staying out, and that's not good.

"And there's more I don't like. The Tronder concept of a great force to intimidate sounds good; but what if the great force is mainly a group of disorganized farmers, while Olaf comes to the field with experienced warriors and a battle plan. We must remember that Olaf's been leading men to battle most of his life . . . and winning. From what I've heard, he's used unique strategies when it looked like he was in a box that baffled his opponents and won the day."

"So you're saying we should go too," Sverri said, "but that you aren't as excited about the numbers as Ashjorn made it sound."

"That's about it."

Sverri looked at Sigurth, who was sitting to the side, looking down and toying with his hands as if not interested in what was being said. But he knew that wasn't the case, and wishing there was a way he could hear what his uncle was thinking, forced the question anyway. "Sigurth . . . Do you think we should join or not?"

Sigurth jerked at the mention of his name as if surprised to hear it; then he scanned the group as all eyes turned to him. He held their gazes for a few long moments, then taking a deep breath, reluctantly nodded.

The marina had been picked as the marshaling yard for those who planned to join the Farmer's Army, as it was being called; and on the day agreed, they began to arrive early, with most on hand by mid-morning. The response to Ashjorns's appeal was universal, with over sixty ready to travel. Since there was a shortage of boats for the purpose, it was decided to move overland. This was admittedly cumbersome, taking two days just to get to Viggja. But there was no way of knowing where a battle might be, if there was one, and if there were to be as many as ten thousand in the army, an estimated number exceeding anything previous in Norway, it was felt better to be flexible with regards to getting around.

As for the leaders, the same ones who'd planned the attack on the pirates farm—Tosti, Thor Bergthorson and Guni Erlingson—were directed to lead here as well. The exception being Sverri, who was added as a replacement for Gyrth.

The Bird Mountain group was about average in size and composition, providing ten men for the army and traveling in a combination of horse-driven tented wagons and men on horseback. The men included Sigurth, Sverri, Garth, Gunner, Bjorn (Sverri's son), Hlovir (Hjalmar's son), Torkel (Halmar's brother), and three hands. The group also included Rogna, who insisted on going along, not only to fight if need be, but also to be ready with balm, stitches and bandages if there were injuries. So convincing were her arguments, that Gyrthi and Gurtha, Sverri's wife and daughter, came along as well.

Hjalmar stood along the side as the group made ready to move into the line slowly heading out. He'd said all the well wishes and words of advice he could think of to say and was about as dejected as he'd ever been.

"Why so glum, cousin?' Sverri said. He'd ridden around the group to make sure all was well before moving to the front, and reined in.

"Oh, I'm still not happy about being left behind," Hjalmar said.

Sverri looked down, took a deep breath, "I know you're not, and I wish you were up front with me. But someone had to stay and look over the farms, and since you'd already seen the hell of war, it only made sense that you stay back this time."

Hjalmar snorted, having lost the argument the night before, then said, "Oh get your ass out of here. If all of you manage to move slow enough, you might succeed in missing harvest next month."

"I see . . . that's what's got you riled," Sverri said, tugging the reins to start away. "Not to worry, we'll be back. Just make sure there's more than a horn's worth waiting for us."

They arrived in Viggja without incident, and then went to Nitharos. At each stop the going became more cumbersome because of the traffic—other parties like themselves who were converging on a yet to be defined destination. The direction kept trending northeast along the coast. As they did the mess of others along the road, and the poor and circuitous nature of the roads, made them wish they'd arranged a flotilla instead as they were seldom out of sight of the Trondheimsfjord.

It was now late in July and they'd been on the move for ten days when they settled in under some trees by a small stream for the night.

"So where are we now?" Gunnar asked Sverri as he rode up to dismount; just having left a meeting with other leaders.

Sverri dusted off and started to loosen the saddle straps, ignoring the question at first, then saying, "Can't you feel it?"

"Feel what?"

"The tension . . . We're getting closer to Olaf. We're not far from a place called Skaun, which is on the coast and a part of Vera Dale. Scouts reported that Olaf may be as close as five miles away."

"That makes me nervous," Garth said, walking over from where most were gathering around the cooking fire. "We've seen a lot of people, but also a lot of confusion. And many of the people look like farm hands who may be poorly trained for what may lie ahead."

"We're well aware of that," Sverri said, "and you're right about the people. There may be too many of them. The latest estimate puts the number at over fourteen thousand, fourteen thousand getting in each other's way. There are a number of meetings planned tomorrow to try bring order to what's happening. We've already had our meeting to insure that whatever happens, we hold together and act as a unit."

"Where's Sigurth?"

Sverri shrugged. "He was with us most of the afternoon; but when we made our stop, he disappeared. My guess is that he's somewhere up front working his way to Olaf. I wouldn't be surprised if he didn't return until dawn."

"Well, look who's here," Rogna said as the horse ambled into the campsite, light from the fire bouncing off the arrivals. Sigurth winked at her and dismounted, immediately working to loosen the saddle.

"Have you had anything to eat?"

He shook his head as he finished what he was doing, then tied up the horse and set the saddle and blankets against a tree as if preparing a bed.

"Here's some bread and cheese," Rogna said as she turned back to what she was doing, which was putting cooking gear in place. "A rooster has already made some noise, and the east is lightening up, so the others will be stirring soon. You can bet they'll be hungry, which means you'd better not run off again if you want the best bites.

"How close are we anyway? I figure you've been sneaking around out there and near enough to count Olaf's toes . . . Am I right about that?"

She turned to see what response he had to give, but Sigurth was asleep.

He slept through most of the morning, which was quiet around camp because Sverri and the men had gone to join the special meeting. It was called the Council of the Farmers, with the purpose of hammering out details for the pending battle . . . if it were to occur.

The meeting was primarily for leaders of the contingents, but everyone was welcome. One of the main features was a speech by a Bishop—Bishop Sigurth, a man who'd been with King Knut for years and was an ardent supporter of him. The Bishop was extremely hostile to Olaf, and spoke to convince the farmers they should destroy him and his invading troops, if there was any doubt about why they were here. Although it was hard to hear all that was said because of the crowd, the elegance of the speaker and the rage with which he accused Olaf of his many misgivings, with words such as "He has fared far and wide about this country with niding hordes, burned the countryside, and killed and robbed the people". . . did its work.

Sverri and the men were back around noon, which coincided with when Sigurth was up and busy communicating with the women in his manner of lip-synching and gesturing.

"Hi uncle," Sverri said as the group filtered back. "I didn't see you at the Council, so was hoping you hadn't gotten lost in the dark last night."

Sigurth scoffed.

"You wouldn't believe what happened at the meeting," Sverri went on to say. "This was about forming a battle plan, right? Well, that part didn't start out real well as the top candidates for overall leadership didn't want to lead. First there was Harek of Thjota who was named, then Thorir the Hound, both saying no. Finally Kalf Arnason, who spoke about how he thought the battle should be pursued, was selected. An odd thing about him is that he has three brothers in Olaf's army.

"Anyway, Kalf laid out the battle array, which consisted of basically three major groupings, each centered around its own standard. Oh . . . To help in unifying our actions, we have been given a battle cry. When the fighting starts, all our men are to move forward, yelling, *"Forward, forward, farmer folk!"*

Sigurth listened, nodding to indicate understanding as each detail was related.

"And this will please you," Sverri continued. "After the Council, Tosti, Thor, Gunni and I got together to discuss how we should fit in. In the past, Gyrth had a strategy of staying in the wings and not committing to combat unless unavoidably forced into it. They were familiar with it because they'd been a part of it, and agreed with doing the same in this instance. This should be easy to do because there are so many groups in addition to the main contingents, it's likely most won't see action even if they wanted to."

Sigurth clapped his hands at that.

"But," Sverri added. "We also agreed that we should think like a unit and act like a unit whatever the case. We're going to meet again in the morning before we start out, and establish who's in the shield wall, who's in reserve, who's among the archers and so on. Thor even wants a standard to identify our force regardless what happens, and he's volunteered to be stationed beneath it if we do go to battle."

That night around the fire there was a strange calm. At first there'd been questions about what anyone knew, which led to the fact that Olaf and his army were in position only a few miles away at a place called Stiklestad. Then the conversation tailed off, the veterans going silent, knowing what the morrow could bring. The others quieted down soon after that, but for a different reason; they were reluctant to express anything that would indicate the churning in their stomachs. It was quieter than usual, most checking their weapons, sharpening edges and doing whatever to take their mind off what lay ahead.

In the morning, after a meal that few had a hunger for, an area for several miles came alive with movement. The forces of Kalf Arnason led the way, with those of the other major forces on each side. The advance, however, was not uniform, taking up most of the morning to put together a front with satisfactory conformity.

Sigurth on horseback separated from the group and rode ahead, staying abreast but to the side of the main forces. He knew that Olaf's men had been in position since the afternoon before, and had stayed there overnight across a wide front under three banners identifying their groups, in a manner similar to the farmers. From a good vantage point he found, he saw where Olaf was in this array because he was conspicuous, not only by the banner at his side, but also by his shield, painted white with a gold cross, both of which were placed at the head of the central group.

By noon the farmers had drawn up so both lines were in readiness, waiting for something or somebody to initiate the battle. The first something, however, wasn't fighting. Instead there was conversation between Farmer leaders and Olaf, which wasn't surprising as many in opposing ranks knew each other. There was little else that seemed noteworthy or that he could identify, as at this point there was none of the usual action, like banging shields or inspiring words by group leaders, to get the men in the ranks in the mood. It was as if there might not be a fight. There was another figure who stood out, though, and that was because he was not only unusually tall, but also more active and giving the impression of more youthful exuberance than the others around Olaf and his banner.

Finally, and unfortunately, because of some spark, it started. Men in the Farmers ranks began to shout *"Forward, Forward, Farmer folks."* With that arrows flew and men surged forward. In response, Olaf's men cried out *"Forward, Forward, Christ's men, Cross men, King's men,"* and the fight began.

As Sigurth watched, Olaf's men, who were on a hillock, surged into the farmers and initially drove them back, almost routing them. But then the mass of greater numbers came into play and the front stabilized. Stabilized into the guttural growl of men in hel, dancing to the music of thuds and clanks and metal on metal, accompanied by muffled cries of effort and pain. From Sigurth's location, too distant for exact detail, it looked like a writhing mass of snakes, tragically entangled on a two-dimensional plane.

Almost unnoticed while the battle was progressing, was that the sky, which had been clear, was strangely changing in color, beginning with a light red that slowly intensified. By the time Sigurth became aware of it, the redness had darkened and the sun, whose brilliance was such that it couldn't be looked upon, was becoming less so. As the battle continued without noticing, the last vestiges of the blinding sun disappeared into a strange grayish orb, with a darkness, though not as complete as the night but with a few stars visible, coming over the land.

Whatever it was, possibly a heralding of significance by the Gods, this phenomena lingered through most of the fighting, then slowly began to transition back in a reversed sequence to what it had been before. Sigurth could then see that the battle may have ended, with the men who'd been fighting during the darkness either dead, wounded or exhausted. The battle area still was active, but it wasn't with continuing combat. In addition to the bodies that lay still on the ground, it included those that tossed and turned; it included men looking for and helping others; and it included a flow of stragglers limping to the rear. He noted that Olaf's banners were down, that the white shield with the gold cross was among the detritus littering the ground, and that the tall youngster so animate before was among those limping away.

The battle, however, didn't end, which didn't make sense because from all appearances, the men roaming the battlefield were from the Farmer's Army, a strong indication, along with other signs, that Olaf was dead or captured, and his mission defeated. Nonetheless, a large group of Olaf's army, that hadn't been fully engaged, moved forward, and with a zeal that characterized the troops an hour before, resumed the fight. Catching the Farmers by surprise, this new attack drove them back. Sigurth stood in the saddle, hardly able to believe what was happening, and became so animated by what he saw that his horse became unnerved and shuffled about. The attack scattered several of the Farmer units and approached another line, which happened to include the men led by Thor Bergthorson.

He moved forward paralleling the attackers, hoping that at some point they would be exhausted and stop, or be turned back by a counterattack by one of the many Farmer groups still on hand. But no such thing happened. He removed his bow and quiver, hanging them on a tree nearby, then loosened his sword and readied his lance. He reined in then and waited, continuing to hope that the Gods, *it must have been one of their antics*, would darken the sky again or pull some other trick to stop this madness. His hopes were to no avail as the shrieking mass of attackers reached Thor's shield wall.

Sigurth spurred his horse. Blindsiding the attackers only a short distance in front of the wall, he bowled men over, using his lance until it was lost in a body. Then he drew his sword while continuing to spur, slashing out on both sides at anyone within reach. He came to a point past the troops and turned his horse so violently it reared, spinning its forelegs in the air before landing. He charged back, but there wasn't an element of surprise this time. Even so Sigurth continued to spur and slash, sending red spatters all about, and while doing so contending with a gauntlet of spears and axes and swords, that for a magical time bounced off his shield or somehow missed. Then he was hit in the head by the blunt edge of a throwing axe which sent his helmet flying.

That was his last recollection, his horse kicking out with every stride and continuing on as he tumbled to the ground.

He would have been sliced to pieces by a maddened enemy; but they didn't get a chance. The shield wall, initially heavily engaged, then astounded by Sigurth's ride, exploded as he fell. With Gunnar and Garth and the Bird Mountain group leading the way and screaming like berserkers, they charged, routing the now bewildered and disorganized attackers, driving them away and ending the last element of the battle.

"How's he doing?" Gunnar asked in another of his frequent visits to the area where the wounded were being treated.

Rogna sat back and let out a sigh. "As you can see, he's still not settled.

He thrashes around like he just did every so often, so we've had a time getting all his cuts sewed up. He's going to be hurting from them for quite a while, because besides all the minor cuts and bruises, there are a couple on his legs that were to the bone. But it's the head that bothers me most. It's not caved-in, at least that I can tell; but the swelling's pretty bad . . . Just look at it, he really took a rap.

"Now don't look so glum. If he dies, he'll have died doing what he's been doing all his life, and for that he'll be somewhere on the high seat of that place called Valhalla for sure."

"Don't talk about dying . . . Don't even think about it. And what's this business about what he's been doing?"

"Oh get away with you. I'm busy and the story's too long to tell. Besides, all of you need to arrange for getting us back home. The battles over and we've won, although I'm not sure what. The rest of our great Farmer's Army, who are mostly from around here, are already there. We need to do the same, so scat."

"Have you seen your Pa?" Rogna said as Gunnar approached the shop, all dirty and sweaty.

Gunnar gave her one of those puzzled looks, like it was the kind of question he wasn't expecting.

"Ny," he answered. "I've been in the field all day. So has Garth and everybody else. I didn't think you'd just let him wander off."

"I didn't," Rogna said, "but I've been busy too if you haven't noticed. When I looked up a while ago, he was gone . . . gone, with this place and the longhouse deserted and everyone in the field."

"A while ago?"

"Ya . . . Since then I've looked every place I could think."

"How was he acting the last time you saw him? To me he's weak and still not healed up, and his head's not on straight."

"I'm not sure about the last part," Rogna said.

"Sure of what?"

"His mind seems normal enough to me, although it's hard to tell because he never says anything. It's just that he doesn't seem to be here."

"I'm not following you."

"I think his mind's in Vinland."

"Is his horse gone?"

"How would I know. When I checked the barn, there weren't any horses to be seen. What's that got to do with it? In his condition, especially those wounds on his legs, he can hardly walk . . . He certainly can't ride a horse."

Their eyes met for just a moment . . .

"I'll get Garth."

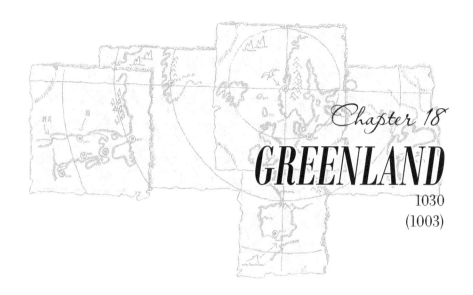

Chapter 18

GREENLAND

1030

(1003)

"This is Greenland?" (Sigurth's mind returned to 1003, beginning with when he first saw Eirik the Red's land of opportunity)

"This is Greenland?"

It was Yngvi who spoke, repeating the question being murmured by the passengers and crew who stood at the rail watching the shoreline move past. They saw a rugged coast not unlike the worst of their Norwegian homeland, or the Faroes for that matter, with contortions of every manner sloping to the water's edge. There were no trees to be seen; in places there were patches of green, but not a great deal of that either; and looming over all of it, in not too great a distance, were gloomy rising elevations capped in white.

Sigurth looked at Odd, who was quietly tending the steering oar, and looking busier and more concerned than the situation warranted . . . almost as if avoiding eye contact.

"You've been here before . . . right?" Sigurth said softly as he edged over.

Odd nodded, still busying with nothing.

Sigurth was uncomfortable about the passing scene, and smoldered when every now and then someone at the rail turned and gave one of those looks. *I didn't talk you into coming here,* he thought, *I only sold you a ride.*

"Not much to get excited about, is it?" Odd finally muttered, still concentrating on some imaginary concern.

"Now you tell me."

"I was supposed to tell you something?"

Sigurth wanted to swear at the wind . . . to hit somebody. He looked at the passengers lining the rail—Yngvi with his family, who'd he'd grown to like, who he knew were aboard with all they owned because they were looking for a new home, a home with opportunity; and Dag Hringsson with his young family, who were here for the same reason.

It didn't help when one of the children started to cry.

"You could have given a hint as to what to expect."

"Seems to me I did. Besides, there was no secret about what Greenland was like," Odd said, finally looking at him. "Ships have been plying the waters between here and Norway for several years, with every crew telling what they've seen. And I have a question about all of this . . . Why did you want to come here in the first place? It wasn't to become a farmer. Even though you'll find people *are* making a living here."

"There are no trees."

"There're scrubs here and there."

"That's just great . . . scrubs."

Odd snorted. "Look . . . You built this ship, and did all you've done for two reasons—to find your cousin Sveyin, and to find the edge of the world. That's about all I've heard you talk about. Exactly why you brought these animals along doesn't seem to fit in with that, but that's your business." He then barked orders to the crew, some responding by scrambling about ropes controlling the sail, others readying oars for action.

With this in progress, Sigurth stepped to the rail for another look at the bleak shore passing by. Turning, he saw that the *Skaun* was trailing further behind than usual, which didn't matter now as there was little need to coordinate with them anymore, other than to wave and wish them well.

"What do you recommend going in?" He asked, returning to Odd's side.

"Well . . . you want to find your cousin, right?"

"Ya, but first we've got to drop passengers at the best place for them. As for cousin, I don't have the foggiest idea where to begin."

"You said he sailed here three years ago with Leif Eiriksson."

"Ya."

"Okay, let's do this . . . Soon we'll see an opening in the shore; that will be Ketilsfjord, the first of the meaningful fjords that have farms around the banks. This will be just past a jutout called Herjolfsness. There'll be a landing in the fjord, and you'll see people gathering and booths being set up to welcome us. Ships don't come by every day, so any arrival is an occasion.

"But you want to find Sveyin, so we'll pass this landing and its people and leave them to Visbur and all who are aboard his *Skaun.* I don't think it matters to him."

Sigurth glared at him in a way that said, *We've been at sea over two weeks, and we're not stopping at the first chance we get?*

Odd interpreted the look perfectly, and said, "Now I know everyone can hardly wait to get on dry land; but what I'm suggesting is only a little farther. We'll pass a number of skerries, and then come to another fjord whose opening is marked by an island called Eirik's Isle. The fjord, if you haven't guessed, is called Eiriksfjord. It cuts inland a good ways to Brattahlid, the farmstead of Eirik Thorvaldson, Eirik the Red as he's known, the founder and leader of the Greenland settlements. You'll find the biggest concentration of farms in all of Greenland along Eiriksfjord's banks, along with more landings and booths and hopefully all you need."

Sigurth thought on it a moment, sighed and said, "Sounds good."

They proceeded as Odd described, and although the extra hours were as long as any experienced, there came the point where the *Mule* was turned into a narrow, poorly defined channel. Interest along the rails picked up quickly, as right after the turn, the sail was furled and the crew put to oars, an indication they were near the end. More exciting than this, however, was what could be seen about Eiriksfjord. There were other boats in the water—skiffs being rowed from the opposite shore to the landing coming into view up ahead, and another coming from that landing and turning to guide them in. There were men on horseback approaching from distant farms; there were people congregating along the shore and others setting up booths above the landing. More importantly to the passengers who would be farmers was the fact there were animals, cattle and sheep and goats, grazing on tufted green meadows along the way.

Sigurth was particularly drawn to the buildings. In their makeup he noticed there was little evidence of tree trunks or timbers or planking. Most of what he could see of the material he specialized in working were improvised uses of driftwood, which weren't particularly impressive. As for buildings, most were low, as if formed of sods stacked over excavations and vaulted.

He shuddered at the thought of spending a long winter here, essentially in a hole in the ground under several feet of snow.

Regardless of what had been disturbing, all that had been seen since turning into the fjord, as well as the reception at the dock as they eased in, erased those impressions. There were smiling people and helping hands, extending to not only the people disembarking who'd been cramped and tossed around and wetted and starved, but also to the animals who were nervous after being confined for so long.

"Do you see him?" Odd said. He'd been directing the crew, and noticed Sigurth standing along the rail looking over the people moving about on shore.

Sigurth turned and snapped a smile. "Ny . . . I didn't expect to be that lucky, but I had to take a good look.

Odd nodded.

"Who's in charge here?" Sigurth asked as he looked over what was, at this point, undirected but friendly confusion. "Where do we go from here."

"There are more approaching from the far end of the fjord," Odd said. "If they're from Brattahlid, we may be getting the answer to that real soon."

They watched as several men on horseback, as well as a number of empty wagons, ambled to the heights above the dock and came to a stop.

"That's Leif Eiriksson," Sigurth said, pointing to the well-built, ruddy complected man with vestiges of red-gold hair, who was dismounting. "He was in the group that left with Sveyin three years ago. I remember meeting him in a celebration the night before."

Sigurth and Odd stepped on the gangplank and left the ship, walking past all those mingled about to meet Leif and his party.

"Aren't you Leif, the son of the founder of this colony?" Sigurth said as the man was completing his way down the slope.

Taken aback somewhat, Leif said, "Ya da. Do I know you?"

"I'm Sigurth Gunnarson, the owner of the ship. I'm also cousin to Sveyin Gyrtheson. I met you while you were in Nitharos the night before you returned here."

Leif looked at him, not making a connection, then shook his head and said, "Forgive me . . . a lot has happened since then, and my memory seems out of kilter because of it. There's no way you could know, but my father died recently, and the leadership of the community has fallen on my shoulders.

"Sorry to hear that," Sigurth said.

"Oh, I'm not here to burden you with my problems, I'm here to be of service. It' always a joy to have visitors, particularly if they have goods to trade, or if they include families that want to settle, both of which seem to be the case here.

"How can we help? We have pens for the animals and shelter for your keeps. For your passengers and crew, we have the room to put them up in Brattahlid until other arrangements can be made. Now I've been at sea a time or two myself, so I know what's wanted most when first coming ashore, and that's a good bath, a warm bed and a hot meal. My wife and her staff are bustling about as we speak making arrangements for that. This will also give us a chance to talk and renew that acquaintance that was all too brief."

Sigurth hardly had a chance to respond as the passengers, who'd been lingering with the uncertainty of stepping ashore in a strange land, heard what was said and did it for him. Yngvi, who'd been trying to keep his flock in tow, shouted with joy and broke into a jig, his baggy clothes flying every which way.

"Well, just look at him," Sigurth said laughing. "Looks like we're off to a good start."

Odd broke in when matters settled. "Thanks for the offer, but as you can imagine, our ship's a mess. We can't rest until it's cleaned and readied for what comes next. With that being so, we, the crew, will put up tent covers and spend the night aboard. There is a favor we'd ask, however. If you could send down some of the hot meal you mentioned, and maybe a horn or two for each of us, we'd be as happy as can be."

Leif hooted and clapped his hands. "We can do this! But first, let's get the animals penned. While that's being done, some of you might want to mingle, meet those at the booths and see what they have to offer. Then we can load up the wagons and be on our way."

It wasn't far to Brattahlid, and once in sight, the impression of what was Greenland improved considerably. For one thing, as they passed along the rough, rutted roadway, the lush grass extending in all directions tended to compensate for the lack of trees; then there were the animals, which seemed to graze as contentedly as in any other setting in memory; and there was Brattahlid, which was reassuringly far above the hovels noted to this point. There were many building in the complex—barns, bunkhouses, storage buildings and special housing—all about a main building. The main building was not only sizable, but was also impressively constructed with stone and turf grass walls set deep in the ground, and having a steeply pitched, timber-framed, sod-covered roof.

Another building, well apart from the others, was puzzling. It was of medium size with the usual sod roofing, but it differed in that its walls were entirely of stone, and seemed at odds with everything else about.

As they approached, servants and residents and children came out of the buildings to give the arrivals another friendly welcome. Introductions were made all around, and then the parties were ushered off to where lodging was to be provided.

Sigurth watched as his passengers were escorted away, feeling relieved at how things were proceeding because of the looks on their faces, the children bouncing around with a spirit hardly seen before. He reviewed the people he'd first met, knowing he would initially forget most of their names. There was Freyda, Leif's sister, who he probably wouldn't, for she was short but strongly built, with a fiery look accentuated by red-gold locks that were more reflecting of her father, the legendary ruffian who had more than one banishment to his credit; there was Gudrid, conspicuous because of her beauty; there was the mother, Thjodhild, who seemed very much in charge despite her age; and there was the wife, who was busy with the details needing attention and in the background because of it. Then there were Leif's children, three of them, with Thorgil, the oldest, being the only name he could remember.

"You're the only one here from the ships's compliment," Leif said. "How many are there for us to still provide for?"

"Fifteen," Sigurth answered. "They're a fine crew, many of them friends. You heard Odd Snorrason, my Ship's Captain, say the crew could stay with the ship until properly cleaned and put away; but after that, they'll be needing housing as well."

Leif nodded. "That won't be a problem. Servants are rearranging one of our large storehouses, so there'll be plenty of room. This isn't unusual for us because at the end of the year, we host a Yule celebration, at which time there are many guests in need of accommodations. For now, let's get you and your goods settled; then we can relax inside by the fire."

They did soon after, being joined by his sons and a few others. The conversation was mostly between the two of them, so after servings of a few horns and generous portions of a meal, most drifted away.

"Tell me again," Leif said, "why you're here. I understand why the families made the trip, which I'm delighted about because we're in need of more people. But the animals, as I understand, belong to you. Do you intend to sell them or settle down and become a farmer?"

Sigurth flashed a smile, hesitated, then raised his horn and drained it, *"Aaah!* We both have many questions."

"Oh, I have more," Leif said. "Another has to do with your crew. I couldn't help noticing how well they worked together, and that most of them were young. My guess is they have energies and ambitions that need more of a challenge than making a trip . . . or farming."

"Very true," Sigurth said, "which complicates any answer I can give, for all of it depends on first finding Sveyin, my cousin."

Leif slapped his knee. "That's right . . . now it's all coming back. You were part of that group in Nitharos that partied hard that last night. Now, with three years gone by and many weeks at sea, you don't resemble the young man I met then. But I know you well. Sveyin often spoke of you, and in a very complimentary way."

"That's strange," Sigurth said. "All I ever heard from him were insults."

Leif doubled up laughing, and when recovered, snapped his fingers at a girl standing by, who quickly refilled their horns. Then he raised his in a toast. "Here's to friends . . . *Skoll!*"

They drank and burped and felt good all over. Then Leif said, "Sveyin told me you were many things . . . too many to really believe; but the part that relates most to the present is that you're not only a ship owner, but also a shipbuilder and woodworking artist. All of which tells me you're not going to be a farmer."

"Most likely not, but then again I did bring animals. Before trying to explain the why of that, tell me where Sveyin is."

"Of course," Leif said. "He's in Vinland."

"Vinland?"

"Ya . . . Haven't you heard of it?"

"Ny . . . Is that the place further west of Greenland? That last night in Nitharos, you mentioned something about land being there, but didn't have a name for it."

Leif nodded. "Your memory is better than mine. Let me start from the beginning. When Eirik, my father, settled Greenland, he started out from Iceland with twenty-five ships loaded with animals and everything needed to colonize a new land; but only little more than half made it."

"Did the rest of the ships sink?"

"No. One of the ships floundered and sunk, but most of the people were pulled aboard other ships. The ships that didn't make it were heavily laden knorrs that didn't handle well in the conditions we were experiencing at the time. That's as much detail I can give on what happened . . . I was only twelve then and not paying much attention to others. Not long after the twenty-five left, a certain Bjarni Harjolfsson decided to follow and did, missing entirely the ships that were returning. He also became lost and went way past where Greenland was supposed to be, coming upon lands that didn't look at all like what he expected of see. So he turned north and went quite a ways in that direction, seeing more lands of differing characteristics along the way. When he got so far north that what he saw was completely inhospitable, he turned east, finally finding what appeared to be Greenland.

"He sailed south along this coast, found our colony and joined us, retiring from his previous life at sea.

"His story about those strange lands always intrigued me. When I returned from Norway three years ago, there was still sailing time in the year, so I went to Bjarni and bought his ship, which had been in storage almost fifteen years since his last voyage. I had no trouble putting together a crew, which included my brother Thorvald and your cousin Sveyin, who was, as you can imagine, hopping to go. He was a great help in getting the ship seaworthy, I might add.

"We left in a hurry, retracing Bjarni's route. One big difference was that we made landfall at places along the way to better evaluate what we were seeing. The first stop was at a rocky, desolate and useless shore, which coincided with what he called "inhospitable." I called this land Helluland. Turning south, we sailed several more days, making another stop at a shore that was heavily forested. I called this land Markland. Continuing south, we arrived at an island that seemed to be a gateway, to what we had no idea; but we thought it might be of interest, so we turned in. It was. We sailed many more days, first west, then south, making various stops and circling islands in what we concluded was an inland sea, eventually finding land in all directions. We were elated. There were stands of timber and abundant game and great fishing, the best we've every seen, wherever we went. We even found stands of a self-seeding form of grain, and vines with berries from which it might be possible to make wine.

"I called this area Vinland.

"With temperatures starting to drop, and leaves starting to turn, we made camp on the lee side of a long island and made preparations for winter. We brought our ship out of the water and built a number of timber lodges, hardly making a dent in the forests all around. Anyway, we stayed the winter, which proved to be much milder than what we were accustomed.

"Bear with me for the story doesn't end here.

"In the spring, we put the ship back in the water because there was a need to get back to inform everyone about what we'd found. In doing so, I left with only as many crew members as needed to man the ship, leaving the rest behind to expand the settlement and find out more about the surroundings, while promising to return with more people and provisions before the end of the summer. "Included in the group left behind was your buddy Sveyin."

Sigurth sat up, concern written across his face.

"Now hold on, there's more. On the way back, not far from the gateway island, we passed near skerries and happened to spot what looked like people trying to get our attention. There were. They were stranded with the remains of a ship that had sailed for Greenland, overshot and wrecked on the rocks. We picked up fifteen survivors, including Gudrid who you met today, and her husband. "Unfortunately the husband has since died, but that's another story."

He laughed. "Because of finding this party I've been called "Lief the Lucky" ever since.

"Shortly after getting back, Eirik died. With that my sailing days came to an end because I've needed to stay at home and take his place as leader of the settlements. But Thorvald was free to go, and since he was still excited about our discoveries and there was still time in the year, he formed a new, full, ships compliment, including colonists and animals and supplies, and returned to Vinland to fulfill our promise to those left behind. Actually, two ships went. Most of the people I rescued wanted to go back to salvage as much of their ship and its contents as they could, and there were enough who wanted to go to outfit another one. Thorvald's still there, and I get bits and pieces of news from the traffic that's resulted; but I don't have all the details of what's happening. The traffic, by the way, has included ships from Norway and Iceland, and even one from Ireland, that reached here, and after hearing the news about the new settlement, resumed their travel in that direction.

"It may not look like much from what you've seen today, but a lot is happening. When your ship was about to dock, you were directed to the far end of the pier. That wasn't because of the other ship which I understand accompanied you, it was because we were expecting one of our own ships to return from Markland with a load of timber. We've found we can sail straight west and get there in far less time than using the route I originally took. The same goes for returning to Vinland; ships are being directed first to Markland, then south along the coast to the gateway island into the inland sea. A staging area has been built on the land across the channel from the island to help everyone passing through by giving an overview of the area and such directions as might be helpful. They're also able to assist in ship maintenance and repair if such is needed. This staging area, or Way Station as its being called, I have yet to see."

Sigurth sat back, trying to visualize all that Leif related. Then he reached for the leather tube he brought along, and extracted the soft leather rolls, spreading them out on the bench between them.

"I wondered what was in that tube," Leif said. "And now that I see, I still don't know."

"They're travel sketches."

"Sketches of what?"

Sigurth went on to explain about the pirate he'd sailed with the year before, and the drawings he copied from him, representing the areas of the world the pirate had traveled.

Leif looked at them, trying to understand. He pointed to various blobs, asking what they represented, nodding as each of their descriptions seemed to fit into a pattern that made sense.

"Amazing," he finally said, sitting back. "I've never seen the likes of them."

Sigurth nodded. "They are; but when the pirate made them, it was assumed what he recorded was all there was to the world. Now, with what you've done, we know it isn't."

Then he laid another roll of soft leather beside the sketches.

"There's nothing on it," Leif said.

"That's right. Greenland," Sigurth said, pointing to the endmost sketch, "is on the far edge about here. I've brought the blank along so I can add the other worlds we now know exist, and also others that may be found beyond that. This leads me to a question that's been on my mind."

"Which is?"

"The edge . . . the edge of the world. Every time anyone sails, and sails beyond what is known, they're afraid of many things—sea monsters, for one, but mostly the edge of the world and the dangers it might entail. It's got to be out there somewhere."

Leif thought on it, his eyes returning to the drawings. "I'm well familiar with the old beliefs, having been raised with them and not being converted until in Nitharos three years ago. So I know about the edge and the Midgard Serpent and all. The new religion, that of the White Christ, says only that the Lord created the heavens and the earth, and doesn't define the extent of either. It's a good question though. It's unreasonable to assume land and water can go on forever."

"So that's another objective of yours . . . to find that edge and complete this map?"

Sigurth nodded.

"Wow," Leif said softly, leaning forward to look over the leathers again. "So you're really not interested in colonizing."

"Well, maybe that too. I won't know about that until I get to this new world you've found. The world I left isn't a bad place, though, in fact it's beautiful. But it's fraught with egos and ambitions that draw most people into conflicts in which they have no interest. This happens often enough that much of what is good is ruined. I don't think I'm telling you anything new.

"Oh . . . In regards to Vinland, you told of wintering and building houses and all, but you made no mention of people. Are all these wonderful lands you discovered uninhabited?"

"We didn't encounter any where we stopped and set up camp; but there are people around as we saw evidences of them. When Thorvald returned to Vinland, more exploring was done, and in those cases, they came in contact with some—savage people, skraelings they were called. Anyway, I don't have the full story, but it seems things haven't gone as well as hoped. Fighting has occurred and people have been killed. Some of the reports are conflicting and don't make sense yet; but I am curious and hope the people that have to be contended won't be a problem.

"So given all I've told you, what are you inclined to do?"

"In my mind," Sigurth said, "there's no doubt as to what to do. There's still enough left of the summer to make it to that Vinland you mentioned. All I have to do is convince the crew to get on board again and leave."

Leif laughed. "I thought so. Here's my advice on that. You should give your crew and the animals you want to take along a week to relax and fatten up before raising anchor and heading out. This, along with what we can tell them about the new world, should have them roaring to go."

Sigurth smiled.

"Good," Leif said. Then he snapped his fingers . . .

Chapter 19

VINLAND

1030
(1003)

"You've got to be kidding!"

The crew were together for a special meeting Sigurth called. Seven days, or a week, which was a new concept of time that had worked its way into the lexicon of thinking since Christianity began its inroads, had elapsed since landing at the dock at Eiriksfjord. During that week, they'd gotten settled; they'd returned to the docks, and although they didn't have anything to trade, had visited the booths and talked and gotten ideas on what might be taken back to Norway for sale and profit. In their conversations, they'd heard of the Western Settlement, or the community in the fjords farther north, which was near to hunting grounds for seal and walrus and bear; they'd mixed with local youth, not only in drinking bouts at night, but also in games like knattleitr in the open field; they'd toured most of Eiriksfjord from the island that signaled its entry to the glacier that crowned its horizon; and they'd visited its main points of interest, including the stonewalled structure unique to Brattahlid, which was the first church built in Greenland, as directed by Thjodhild, Leif's very Christian mother. It was reported that she quit sleeping with the very pagan Eirik when he refused to be baptized.

Sigurth explained to them that he wished to load up the *Mule* and take them away from all this, and sail once more into dangerous waters, this time to a place hardly known to exist.

They responded . . .

"Sigurth, we've met many people here, and made new friends. We love it here," said Jon, the smallest of them, but among the most daring and vocal.

"Look," Arni, one of the men who'd worked with Sigurth at the Marina and was as close to him as anyone, said with a strange cadence, "If we have to leave, let's go home. I understand the winters here are long and fierce."

This went on for a bit longer.

Sigurth thought to explain that winters in Vinland were supposedly milder; but then something wasn't making sense. Frothi looked away, an old habit when avoiding eye contact; and Ondur, the most burly, the farmhand friend who was everyone's tower of strength, bit his lip.

Then someone gave the sound of losing it and the dam broke. It was a joke . . . and everyone was in on the joke, laughing and pointing at Sigurth for having fallen for it.

"You should have seen the look on your face," Thor said, who bobbed in an effort to keep his sides intact.

Sigurth shook his head as the joke pulsated a few more times until the group finally quieted.

"It's hard to keep a secret around this crowd," Jon said, "and it certainly doesn't help when one of Leif's sons decides to tell all he knows."

"So all of you knew what my plans were?"

"Ya da," Jon said, snorting another laugh.

"And what do all of you think? Are you with me?"

"Oh ya!" "Yahoo!" "Ya ya ya!" "Let's go!"

"We *are* enjoying it here," Arni said, "but we've also heard things about Vinland . . . It's got lots of fish and game."

"And trees," someone added . . .

"And Sveyin!" another said.

"That too and more," Jon said, almost bouncing as he reflected how everyone felt. "Anyway, we're ready anytime you say."

Sigurth looked at Odd, who'd been standing to the side and out of it. Now as their eyes met, Odd broke into an ear-to-ear grin, nodding.

"Okay . . . If that's the case, there's no reason to wait," Sigurth said. "There's time left in the sailing season; but we don't wish to push our luck in that regard. So Odd, how soon can we get away?"

"We can be ready to sail the day after tomorrow; but there are others to consider who could complicate that schedule."

"Who?"

"A few locals have been looking for an opportunity to make the trip, the brothers who heard about the good hunting and want to go, and another party . . . one you'd never guess."

Sigurth looked, waiting . . .

"Yngvi and his family."

"What! His wife and kids too? I didn't think there were women in Vinland."

"That's not true," Arni said. "From what I heard, some of the ships that stopped there had women and families on board."

They were ready a few days later; but as it turned out, the weather wasn't. A storm hit with gales out of the west making sailing impossible. There was therefore a wait, and an impatience, which although a part of travel at sea, was more unnerving because the time to safely travel was being squeezed.

Finally the weather settled to a favorable breeze, and with that and a shout, lines were cast, oars lowered, and the *Mule* moved. They rowed all the way out of the fjord, then unfurled the sail, caught the breeze, and entered into the open sea. The excitement of a new venture soon settled as the *Mule* moved easily along, making the quick and steady progress they'd gotten accustomed to. There was little to note until a day later, when a large white mass, the first such sighting for most of the young crew, came into view.

"We need to give that thing a wide berth," Odd said, working the steering oar.

"It looks like we'll miss it by plenty," Sigurth said. "What's the problem?"

"Doesn't look like there is one, that's for sure; but be advised that what's showing is only a small part of it . . . You never know. I've heard of Captains assuming they were safe, only to have their ships beached on a shelf jutting out below the surface. Not a pleasant thing."

Sigurth leaned against the rail, looking at the mass and giving it more respect. "Are there many those around here?"

"I don't know. Leif made mention of them, but in a casual way. I know that at certain times of the year around Iceland, you have to be on guard because these things, Icebergs they're called, break loose from mainland glaciers and float south with the currants until they melt. I suppose the same is true here. Never thought much about them until this one came along."

"Most of my travel has been to points south," Sigurth said, "so this is new to me. Should we be doubling up on overnight watch?"

Odd snorted. "I guess you haven't noticed; but we've already done that. Besides, you never seem to sleep. How do you do that?"

At the shoreline of what was assumed to be Markland, the *Mule* was turned south to follow along offshore. Another day brought them to an island, which was expected, that signaled the gateway passage. Instead of continuing through for points west, Odd turned the *Mule* south to the shore of a relatively treeless landmass in that direction, where they had been told a Way Station could be found. He and Sigurth had agreed that if there was one, it made sense to stop by for both direction and restocking.

They were only a few hours along the coast when Jon, who was high on the mast, yelled, "A ship! I see a ship at anchor!" Then as they approached, more and more detail came into view. Beyond the docked ship was another out of the water, which probably meant it was being serviced, while farther in the background shapes could be seen that appeared to be man-made. A little closer and they could see people moving about.

"Not a moment too soon," Odd said as they headed for a space beside where the ship first seen was anchored, and began making preparations to do the same. "I don't like what I've been seeing in the sky behind us. Something serious is brewing."

It was. While attention had focused on what was ahead, the sky behind segued from an inconspicuous grayness to a dark rolling mass, with lightning bolts for emphasis.

"Damn, here it comes!" Sigurth said. He and everybody aboard now had their attentions bouncing between two things, the dock ahead toward which they were rowing, and the boil of clouds rolling in behind them.

"*Ny o ny!*" Odd yelled, as he realized what was about to happen. "We'll be smashed against the landing. S*top! Stop! Row back!"*

Sigurth and Ondur, who were at opposing back oars, dug in, with the rest at oar quickly doing likewise to the cadence being called. The *Mule* slowed, stopped, then began inching backward, with Odd yelling adjusting orders to point them directly into the approaching wind, stern leading, as there wasn't time to turn around.

The action was not a moment too soon. The storm hit—a hard, cold, wind driven rain that churned the sea into rolling waves that swept past the ship. As it did, the oarsmen fought to find water and be effective in maintaining position, too busy to see that the waves continued on, smashing into the dock and the ship already moored.

While the oarsmen were in their struggle, other crewmen scampered about, putting up tents and doing whatever else that could be done, not only to provide a measure of protection, but also to minimize the water being taken in . . . all the while of which children screamed and animals shuffled and brayed and bleated.

The turmoil was intense, so much so it was hoped that the storm was just a squall that would pass quickly; but that wasn't the case. Winds and rain continued without lessening for several long hours, during which time the ship bucked and twisted and heaved. To counter this, the men at oars struggled at a level of exertion that couldn't be maintained, so there had to be a rotation with other crewmen in order to keep a line.

By the time the storm finally ended, diminishing to a soft drizzle with wave action back to its normal pulse, all of the crew, and some of the passengers, including the brothers and the irrepressible Yngvi, went limp with the kind of response that comes with having won a victory . . . which they had. The *Mule* lay, seemingly undamaged, bobbing in the water not far from where they'd been when the storm hit.

But now it was almost dark. Sigurth, still at oar, a position he'd left only once during the ordeal, groaned as he eased to his feet. He moved over to Odd, who was putting the steering oar, which had been useless in reverse, back in the water.

They looked at the dock and the station, whose detail had been masked during the storm with only the crashing sounds of the waves to indicate it was there. Now its image was almost as vague because of the fading light. They could sense people moving around, and they could see that the stern end of the ship that had been moored had broken loose and now rested askew and away from the dock. They could see torches were being lit and hear shouts, but they were too muffled by the distance to understand.

"What do you think?" Sigurth asked.

Odd was almost as uncertain. "Well, we have two choices—to anchor in the shallows for the night, or to move in and tie up. But we need to decide now, because what's left of the day is almost gone."

"Let's move in. I think we'd all feel better being on shore one way or the other."

With that orders were shouted and oars once more put to motion, this time under good conditions with only a short distance to go. Odd guided the ship in at an angle, then turned so that its momentum swung it sideways towards the dock and the row of torches guiding them in. As they closed, lines were thrown, and aided by those on the dock, bumpers were placed and ties made. With the precision of seasoned seamen, the ship was secured.

There wasn't much more that could be done that night. The men who'd helped them dock were mostly from the neighboring ship, who'd come to the dock to see how they'd fared. Then seeing the ship offshore, stayed to give a hand. All had gone well, but when the gangplank was laid out and set in place, one of them said it wasn't a good time to unload anything or anybody, because not only was it dark and confusing, but also that quarters weren't available. Facilities at the station were jammed with their ship's complement.

Sigurth was at the rail. "We have a families aboard with children. Can you take them in?"

The man who'd spoken talked to another for a moment, then turned back. "We can do that," he said. "They can crowd in with our other families . . . but hurry." With that the families aboard scampered out, the children clinging to their parents and each other as they were led away.

"That was a bad one," Sigurth said to the dim-lit figures who stood alongside the *Mule*. He and Odd and many of the crew were still at the rail.

"You do all right?" The man said.

"I think so; but it wasn't easy."

"Damn, that's for sure," the man said. Then he turned to his group and mumbled some more. Turning back, he asked, "Where you from?"

"Norway, out of Nitharos in Trondheimsfjord. We stopped off in Greenland a few weeks before coming here. You?"

"Norway, Harthangerfjord. We've been in this area over a year. Was going to return in hopes of interesting a few more people. Even left some of my people behind because I figured on coming back. Now I may have to hitch a ride if we can't get this thing back in shape. If you haven't noticed, my ship took quite a beating. It appears to be settling in the water."

"I was wondering about that," Sigurth said. "Maybe we can help. Let's take a look in the morning."

"You know anything about ship repair?" the man asked.

"A little," Sigurth replied, while Odd held back with what he wanted to say.

"Would appreciate anything you can do. See you in the morning then."

"Before you go," Sigurth said. "You've been in Vinland for a good while, you say . . . Do you like it here?"

"Oh my . . . You'll see. There are problems, but I don't think there are any that can't be worked out. By the way, to change the subject, who rules Norway now?"

"Well, its not Olaf Tryggvason; he went for a swim the other side of Denmark with all his armor."

The man laughed. "Ya, I heard about that, and that Earl Hakon's sons have taken over. Is that still the case? Doesn't much matter to me one way or the other, though. The farther I can stay away from it all, the better. As for this," he said pointing at his ship, "there's not much we can do right now. Think I'll go back and find me a few good drinks.

"Good night."

The next morning the remaining passengers were put ashore, and the animals unloaded and moved to pens. Then the ship was cleaned and inspected.

"How did we do?" Odd asked as Sigurth emerged from the hold.

Sigurth wiped his hands on the sides of his trousers and looked up, exhaling in relief. "Can't find a thing other than a few damp spots. The water we had to bail must have all been from rain."

"That's amazing," Odd said. "That was some ride."

Sigurth climbed out of the central recess and looked around to see that most hands were still busy, but nearing an end of what was needed at the time. "Anybody getting hungry?" He said.

Voices sounded in a chorus . . .

Sigurth laughed. "Me too. Odd, let's all grab bowls, go ashore and see what this place has to offer. We can always set up our own cooking fire; but what we have to throw together wouldn't be hard to beat."

They didn't get far. They'd just started down the gangplank when they were confronted by a group they hadn't noticed gathering on the landing. It was as if they were patiently waiting.

"Did you forget about us?" A man said in a voice easily recognized as the person from the night before.

"I'm Ulf Hranason, the owner of that pitiful ship next to you. And you're Sigurth Gunnarson, who not only worked in a marina, but also helped build the *Long Serpent,* one of the largest and most amazing ships ever built. You said you might be able to help us. Can you? We're honestly at a loss . . . and have been impressed how well you and your crew have been working."

Sigurth hesitated, looking at Odd, who was trying to hide his pleasure in hearing what was said.

"How did you come by all that? We may be able to help; but we're not miracle workers."

"Your passenger, Yngvi, is quite a talker, to answer your question," Ulf said. "Which gives me hope about our mess. Anything that works is going to be a miracle to us."

Sigurth was momentarily at a loss, the loudest voice being the rumble in his stomach. He looked at the man's ship, which he'd looked at at first light and seen that it had settled in the water.

"Maybe we *can* help each other," he said. "In our case, we've been at sea for over a week, working hard while eating you know what in the process. So right now we're hungry and are on our way to do something about it. As for your ship, you're in luck because it settled at right angles to the dock, which gives you a much better chance of getting it out. But trying to do that can't be done until it's stripped of all that isn't structural. The dock in front of it also has to be dismantled. When these are finished, then we may be able, by everyone working together, including those working on the other boat already out of the water, to ease it forward. When enough progress is made doing that, then the ballast can be removed, making it much easier to get it out and see what damages need to be repaired.

"Now, where can we get something to eat?"

Ulf blinked, swallowed, then looked at those around him, who were generally avoiding his glare. He turned back, half laughing and said, "Well it looks like we have work to do. As for your empty stomachs, I'd suggest you head for the cookhouse. Getting what you want isn't going to be easy, though, because everyone at the station is hungry. But give it a try and good luck. By the time you get back, we may be ready for that next step . . . and your assistance."

The Way Station was a busy place. Beside the pier, there was the logged ramp on which the ship seen before had been pulled, and on which a crew was at work with some kind of repair, which must not have been serious because structural damage wasn't noticed as they walked by. Beyond the ramp were pens, which contained more animals than they had unloaded earlier; there were a few shops and booths; a smithy; and then a series of buildings that at first glance appeared to be either storage or lodging. Although logs and timbers were visible in places, most construction seemed to be of stacked sods vaulted over floor recesses, much like that seen in Greenland. Sigurth thought this strange, because even though the immediate surroundings were flat and heavily grassed, the lands across the inlet were amply wooded.

Not surprising was the amount of activity. Soon after daybreak, those in the lodges, who were from the ship recently docked as well as those stationed on the premises, were outside away from the cramped quarters the buildings provided. And like the crew of the *Mule*, everyone, like Ulf said, was hungry. Therefore the cookhouse was easy to find. There were a number of people still gathered, smoke was still in the air, and telltale odors that said that whatever had been prepared was still being served.

"Don't get too excited about what's in those pots," said Yngvi, who'd spotted them and walked over. "If you were hoping for meat, you're going to be disappointed"

"There are animals in the pens," Sigurth said. "Couldn't any of them be butchered?"

"Aren't some of them yours?"

"Ya."

"Care to volunteer any?"

Sigurth hesitated. "So what *is* being served?"

"The big pot has a mixture of grains, garden vegetables and seafood . . . and then there's fried fish."

"That doesn't sound too bad."

"It really isn't, except for the fact there are few reserves. The bread is gone, grains are near to also, and the garden has almost been picked clean. I don't know what your plans are, but there are many people here, the growing season is over and winter is right behind. You hoped to stock up the boat here for the next bit of sailing, didn't you?"

Sigurth hesitated, not liking the news, while the men who were gathered behind him waited for an answer.

"Boys," he said." Get in line and eat hearty. There are problems to solve, that's obvious, but we can do a better job of it on a full stomach."

As they did he turned to Odd. "It sounds like there's a disaster here waiting to happen. Any ideas?"

Odd shook his head. "Whose in charge of this Station, anyway? It can't be as bad as has been described. Let's get in line ourselves. Then afterwards, find the man and get the full story."

"Ya, I'm Ingivar Sweinsson. Aren't you the owner of the ship that docked after the storm last night?"

Sigurth nodded, addressing the short, stocky man with overly large cheeks and a bald head, who he found leaving the ramp where the ship was being repaired. "That's right. I'm Sigurth Gunnarson, and this is my First Mate Odd Snorrason.

"What can I do for you?"

"We just ate, which was fine. We got the impression, however, that you're running out of food. We were planning to leave as soon as we could stock up. Will there be a problem with that?"

"Ya and ny. What you've been told is partly true. We do have problems. We have plenty of good water and hay for the animals, and there's an abundance of seafood, but that won't keep aboard ship, which you already know. We are low on meat and grain and garden goods. Next year we're just going to have to plan better; because we've been hit with more traffic than we expected and are running out of a few things."

"Any way we can help?"

"The best you and Ulf can do for us is to load up and get out. That will help a lot by getting us back to a normal population to feed. But now I understand Ulf has a problem."

"He does; we're on our way back to see if we can help. If he can get his ship out of the water, we think we can."

"That would be good," Ingivar said. "Good luck on that."

Ingivar was about to walk away, leaving Sigurth with still a number of questions, but Odd, who was standing by, sensed this and interrupted to keep the conversation going. "Is this a small island?"

"Ny o ny, It's large . . . very large."

"We haven't noticed forests like we saw when we sailed along the coasts of what's called Markland. Don't you have any here?"

"Ya da. There are plenty of trees, but the area around here is mostly grassland. You may have gotten the wrong impression from what you can see around this station, but this island is quite a place. There's plenty of game too. Unfortunately we cleared most of it in the immediate vicinity, so now my hunters have to go farther south, which is where the trees are. In this regard, we also send parties across the passage to forage in that Markland you mentioned. One way or the other, we'll have meat soon enough.

Oh, there's also some kind of grain growing wild in marshy areas. We'll be harvesting that before it gets much colder, and that will alleviate the other problem you mentioned. By the way, you came in from Greenland, so I hear. Where are you headed?"

"I'm not sure," Sigurth said. "Do you know of a man named Sveyin Gyrtheson? He sailed with Leif Eiriksson to these parts three years ago, and as far as I know, is still around here somewhere."

"You mean Sveyin the Archer?"

"Ya." Sigurth said, holding back a laugh. "That would be my cousin. Now what did that fool do to deserve being called that?"

"Oh, let me tell you," Ingivar said, beaming at the recollection. "And what I tell you is true, because I was there."

"Where?"

"In Vinland."

"Where exactly *is* Vinland? I'm confused . . . Isn't where we're standing a part of it?"

Ingivar stopped, now puzzled himself. "Well, I guess all of the area around here, and the various islands nearby, are collectively called Vinland. What I'm talking about happened on another island to the west.

"You know, or must have heard, that there are other people here. Some call them savages or skraelings. Anyway they're around, usually in scattered settlements that don't have much to do with one another, and each one is unique in its way. On this occasion, there was this group of them, warriors, who got full of themselves and decided to cause trouble where we were on that island. They yelled like banshees and attacked, filling the air with arrows. Well, we were lucky and no one was hit, although Sveyin almost was because an arrow stuck in a loose fold of his tunic. We countered and chased after them, capturing a few, the rest running away leaving a trail.

"We were about to chop off the heads of the ones we captured, but Sveyin held us back. He was, by the way, standing with that arrow hanging from his clothes, which he showed off by turning in a circle so everyone could see. Then he took the warrior who seemed to be the leader of the group, and had him tied to a large tree . . . spread-eagled and tied. This done he walked back fifty paces or so, farther back than any of the rest of us could hit anything from, and asked for his bow. Bow in hand, he draws it back, and all of us, including the other captives and the poor bastard on the tree, thought we were about to see an execution. But the first arrow missed, striking just under the man's armpit. The second missed too, under the other side. The poor man tried to be brave, but he noticeably wet his pants. Then in quick succession, Sveyin fired away, circling the man's body and head, *and crotch,* without a single arrow touching him.

"We were agog, and I have no way of knowing how the natives felt, but I can guess. Anyway, Sveyin put down his bow, walked to the tree, and cut the man loose. Then by signs and gestures, which is all we have in the way of communication, he told the man, and his companions, to leave with his blessing.

"As far as I know, we haven't had trouble from that bunch since then."

Sigurth smiled . . . nodded, "Sounds like something that dumb bastard would do.

"So where is he now?"

"I think he's still on the island. It's where Leif built the first settlement."

"How do I get there?"

Ingivar tried to describe the way, which didn't clearly answer the question, so he picked up a stick. "Look," he said, sketching in the dirt . . . "Here's the island we're on, and here's this Station. This is the island Sveyin is on, and right about here is Leif's settlement. Be careful here north of the island, as there's an opening going farther west that could go on forever. Oh . . . On the west of the island is a land mass that goes something like this, swinging around and eventually going southwest. At this point, it's my understanding that Thorvald, Leif's brother, ran aground. Last I heard he and his crew are still there trying to get the ship repaired."

Sigurth studied the marks in the sand a long time. Then said, "I think I've got it . . . Thanks."

Ulf was waiting for them as they approached the dock. But before he said anything, they could see that the dock had been dismantled in line with the ship, a ramp had been built, and the bow of the ship had been pulled out of the water and part ways onto the ramp.

But Ulf had to explain it anyway, almost hopping as he did.

"We were lucky . . . The shallows were all mud and sand, as is the beach below the dock; so no damage came from being on the bottom. It also made the next step easier, because once we got the ropes on with everyone pulling, the hull slid out right onto the ramp. Thanks for your crew; we couldn't have done it without them."

"It looks like you're unloading the ballast," Sigurth said.

Ulf beamed. "Isn't that what you said to do?"

The next step took a while; but once completed, all the men who could be mustered, including Sigurth and Odd, were back on the lines. With coordinated orders to "heave," the ship inched out of the water.

Not long afterwards, Arni and Frothi, who'd inspected the hull, came back to Sigurth with their findings. "The gunwale, or meginhufr, and the boards above it to the rail took most of the beating. They look pretty bad in a few places, and some are broken; but they're not the problem."

"So what is?" Ulf asked. He'd been following along with the inspectors, and had been puzzled, because that part seemed so obvious.

Arni led them over to a place low on the hull. "One or more of the waves must have lifted the ship high enough to hit the leading edge of the dock. Right along here planks cracked and a few bolts ripped loose. When this happened, the planks separated along this line enough for water to pour through. It took a while, but with water roaring through in thin sheets, it was enough to sink her."

Sigurth thought of Hjorungarfjord, and how quickly one of the ships in their fleet had gone down.

"What needs to be done to fix it?" Sigurth asked.

"We need to add cleats on the inside, and pull the planks back together, recaulking and rebolting them in the process."

"How long will that take?"

"We should be done by the end of the day."

Sigurth turned to Ulf, who was all smiles, "Okay, we'll fix the leak, but then you're on your own. We're going to help the Station Master by getting out of here, which you should also do as soon as you can."

Then he turned to Odd. "Get the ship ready and notify all the people. I want to be back in the water first thing in the morning. You know where we're going."

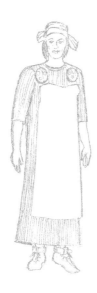

Chapter 20

SVEYIN

1030
(1003)

Sigurth leaned against the rail, straining to see what Jon high on the mast had just confirmed, that land was still in sight north of them. That would be Markland, at least all he'd been told indicated it was. He recalled what Leif said about the makeup of the Vinland region; and he memorized what Ingigar sketched in the sand, which showed that the Markland coast turned west above the gateway island and continued that way for as far as anyone knew.

Still feeling uncertain about all of this, he'd gone to see Ulf the night before leaving to double-check his impressions.

"Ulf, you said you'd sailed all over Vinland. I've been told it looks something like this," making a quick sketch in the sand duplicating what Ingigar had done, "with the station we're on being here on this island, Leif's settlement being here on this one, and this being the Inland Sea separating them. Is this how you'd draw it?"

Ulf had looked at the sketching, cocking his head as he traced the lines in his mind. "Which way is north?" He asked.

"This way."

Ulf looked some more, finally pursing lips and nodding. "Makes sense . . . Ya, looks good. This island we're on . . . It's big. I've been all around it and I know. The east side is a mess; it catches heavy wave action from the big-ocean storms coming its way, so the shore is nothing but rocks and cliffs. We only went ashore once and that was enough.

"Now if I understand all of this, the place where Leif's brother Thorvald ran aground is about here. Last I heard they're calling the place Keel Point because of it."

"How long should it take to get from here to Leif's settlement?' He'd asked.

"If conditions are good and you know exactly where to go, three, maybe four days. But to make sure I found it, I'd follow the southern coast along here of what's called Markland, and overshoot a ways past this island. Then I'd turn south because that coast could go on forever. Anyway, by doing this you will hit this north shore, which you can follow returning sort of east. The shore will soon turn south and eventually take you alongside the island you're looking for."

Sigurth had followed Ulf's recommendation, and the *Mule* was cruising along, making good time. *Two or three days to the first turn,* Ulf had said. His mind reeled. It had taken three days to the Faroes; twenty days from the Faroes to Greenland; ten days from Greenland to the Way Station. Then it got more complicated as he tried to recall the days to Hjorungarfjord, the days to Wendland and the days to Narvesund. All of this related to the sketches he'd been making. *Are the shapes anywhere near to what they really are? Are the distances in realistic proportion? And the two or three days to where both Ulf and Ingigar said could go on forever. My o my . . . Forever, that's a long way. Forever, that could lead to the edge.*

"Is something wrong?" Odd said, breaking his concentration. The two were only a few paces from one another, with Odd as usual at the steering oar.

"Eh? What did you say?" Sigurth mumbled, jerking up from the rail.

"Is everything all right? You seem to be wrestling with a problem."

"Ny . . . ny . . . nothings wrong," Sigurth said. "Just trying to guess when to turn south. What do you think?"

"Well, by next morning three days will have passed. I think that will be a good time to turn if we're clear of this island that's coming up on our left. We sure don't want to do it after dark, which is only and hour or so away, and risk crashing into something we can't see, which could be either the island or the north shore."

Sigurth nodded. "We don't know how far it is to that north shore, do we?"

"Not really."

At first light the next day a turn was made, the south shore they'd been paralleling soon disappearing from view. Then for a while they were once more with water in all directions; but it was to the west that Sigurth took interest. From time to time in his shuffling around on the deck, he'd stop at a rail and gaze at the endless horizon that rarely had anything of interest, and say to himself . . . *So this is what forever looks like.*

Later in the day, a little past noon, he was in the hold, crammed in among the animals and exchanging a few words with Yngvi, who was routinely checking them out, when he heard Jon. Jon was on the mast again and had shouted, "We have shoreline!"

Sigurth climbed back out, kicking off the usual, and stepped over to Odd, who was already reacting. Orders were relayed and the crew responded, adjusting ties that turned the sail so the steering oar and canvas worked seamlessly to take *Mule* into a gentle turn.

"Any idea how much longer, Mister Sketcher?" Odd asked.

Sigurth snorted. "You know as much as I do, and I'm going to guess a few more days. We'll find out soon enough."

"Ya, that's so. Like we agreed when we left the Station, this way's probably the longest, but it's better than trying a shortcut whereby we could end up lost in the open sea. We wouldn't be the first."

They followed the distant shore as it rounded, gradually turning from east to south to several degrees southwest. Doing so, however, was confusing, because the shoreline was deceptive, with large, tempting inlets beckoning them to follow. The first was highlighted by a distinctive flat-topped rock that shot out of the sea at least three hundred feet.

"Well just look at that," Sigurth said, which wasn't necessary to say as it was unusual enough to catch everyone's attention.

"Should we give it a name?" Odd said.

"What?"

"A name. I mean it's a good reference point, and seems to be guarding the inlet."

Sigurth nodded, thought, then said, "Okay, since that's the case, let's call it Sentinel Rock."

They passed the rock and stayed a simple course and it paid off, as eventually, land that had disappeared came into view again. Two days after sighting the north shore they came to what they were hoping to find, a point at which they could see land on both sides. The left side would be the island on which Leif's settlement was said to be located.

As it happened, they didn't find the settlement. It was more like the settlement found them. They were cruising steadily, still under sail, and maintaining views of land on both sides, when Jon, who'd fashioned a rope-seat at the top because he was going up so often, shouted, "I see a ship!"

Actually, it wasn't a ship, it was a small fishing boat. But it was under sail and those aboard had seen them first and one was standing on the bow waving something to get their attention.

A quick order from Odd and the ship came alive as men raced to stations, some adjusting ropes to furl the sail, others reaching for oars. There wasn't much conversation about what was happening, except that one was heard to say, "Put a move on Jon, or we'll have your ass cocooned until next spring."

The *Mule* slowly glided to being dead in the water, with the entire complement taking to the rails to watch as the fisher come alongside.

"Welcome to Vinland," the man who'd been waving what turned out to be his tunic said as they came together. "You picked a good day. We've had some nasty weather lately."

"We know about that," Sigurth said.

"Where you from?"

"Norway, out of Nitharos in Trondheimsfjord. Left about six weeks ago, stopping by Greenland on the way here."

There were only four men on the small boat, and when Sigurth answered, the faces of the other three seemed to brighten. They scanned the row of people along the rail. Then one face exploded with a smile, "Ari! Askel! I knew it was only a matter of time before they threw you out?"

"Who is it that thinks he knows us?" Askel said.

"Bovi . . . Bovi Syverson. Don't you remember me?"

"Bovi! Well, I'll be damned. We'd heard you'd run off, but we didn't know to where."

"I was crew on that ship Leif Eiriksson returned to Greenland on three years ago, and also on the one he took here. Been at Vinland ever since."

Sigurth wanted to butt in and talk to the man who'd waved them down, a thin, weather-beaten man with stringy hair tied in back, now putting on his tunic; but it seemed everyone was enjoying this renewal, so he held back.

"How's the fishing?" Ari asked.

"Oooh, the fishing! You're going to love it . . . The biggest salmon you'll ever see, and all kinds of other fish. In addition there's lobster and clams and crab and oysters and shrimp and scallops. If you love seafood, you'll think you're already in Valhalla or Heaven or whatever's your pleasure. And we'll have a boatload of it by sundown."

"And the hunting?"

"That's another story. It's great too; but you'll have to go to either Markland or the mainland for the best of that."

"Okay, that's enough," Sigurth said, half laughing, as others groaned at the interruption. "We can't drift around all day." Then directing his comments to the man still standing on the fisher, he added, "How much farther do we have?"

"A couple miles maybe. You can't miss it. By the way, what's your name?"

"Sigurth Gunnarsson."

"And you're from Nitharos."

"We sailed from Nitharos. I'm from a farm at Bird Mountain a ways south of there."

"I see. Well, you really did the right thing by coming here instead of staying in Greenland. There's no comparison, you'll see. And that goes to the families you have aboard. They'll love it too."

With that he pushed off.

Sigurth watched as the boats separated, the breeze catching the sail of the fisher and moving it away.

"Okay Odd," he said. "Let's get *Mule* moving."

The settlement, which was the most significant in all of Vinland, wasn't much more at first glance than the Way Station had been. Sigurth stood at the rail while the gangplank was set in place and the disembarking begun, scanning what could be seen from where he was. There were pen's nearby, which had become a standard feature in many of the docking arrangements. Further inland and through the trees were a few buildings, which he guessed must have been what Leif had built that first winter. He was relieved to see they were wooden, above the ground structures rather than mole-holes he'd seen elsewhere. Beyond that there was little to see as trees and the terrain effectively blocked the view past a few hundred feet.

What he could see, however, and that was of more interest to him anyway, were the people who'd gathered along the shore. As usual some were there to help, but most were there to see what was happening. Regardless, they were people.

"Well," said Odd, who sidled up to Sigurth knowing what was on his mind. "Have you seen him yet."

Sigurth shook his head.

"He could be in any number of places, you know that. It isn't as if anyone was expecting us. Go take a walk, you're not needed here anyway; and I know you're not going to rest until you get an answer."

Sigurth did, first nodding to a group on the bank. Most nodded back; but no one stepped forward as he moved on. He noticed that Ari and Askel had gotten into a spirited conversation with a few locals, and moved away from them also, knowing what that was most likely about. He saw Yngvi and his family just ahead, not seeming to be doing anything; but he noticed the children only standing when moments before they'd been bouncing around. Then he saw other children—locals, also just standing—each group eyeing the other. Sigurth snorted *some kind of juvenile stand-off.* He wasn't going to get into that either.

"Where do we go from here?" Yngvi asked as he tried to walk by.

"Don't know yet. We've come in unexpected, so it may take a while for the word to get around. Don't worry. Odd is cleaning out the ship now that the animals are out. If we have to, we'll set up tents and stay back on board."

At the pens, Arni, Ondur and Thor were finishing with the animals. It's always fun to see how they act when they get off the ship," Ondur said as Sigurth approached. "They're almost like kids . . . prancing around and kicking out."

"I feel the same way, don't you?" Sigurth said, bouncing him on the shoulder.

"Ya, I guess no." Ondur said, a big smile lighting his face. "By the way, have you seen him yet?"

Sigurth shook his head.

"You might talk to that man heading down to the ship," Arni said. "He helped us at the pens. You two must have passed each other because my guess is he's looking for you now."

The three watched as Sigurth returned to the ship, catching up with the man they'd pointed out at the gangplank. An obviously cordial conversation took place after that with Odd being called from the ship, and others being summoned from the spectators, with much nodding and gesturing and pointing going on. Finally they broke up, everyone smiling, and each turning as if to proceed with some sort of mission. Sigurth went first to where Yngvi was waiting, then returned to the pens.

"What's up?"

"Everything's fine," Sigurth said. "There have been a number of ships docking here over the past three years, so they've learned to be prepared for it. They have a couple barracks building just for that purpose; and the man I spoke to was leaving to make preparations for taking everyone in, along with a good meal to welcome us."

"Sounds good . . . And did you find out about Sveyin? Is he anywhere around here?"

Sigurth beamed. "Ya. He's here all right; he's with a work crew out in the field. They're haying, so I'm on my way to see him now."

"Mind if we go along?"

"Of course not. Let's go!"

They'd just started when Sigurth said, "Hold on a second," a strange smile on his face.

"Oh oh . . . What's this all about?"

"Well, if you know Sveyin, you know he's always pulling one stunt or the other. He knows all of us, but he hasn't seen us in at least three years. My thought is to grab tools, go in the field and start working without saying a word to him. Let's see how long it takes for him to catch on."

They stopped by the barn and found what they wanted, enough to make a show anyway, and headed to the field, which turned out to be over a half-mile away. As they walked, Sigurth looked about at what seemed a meeting of new farm with old wild. For the areas that had been planted, the gardens and fields, most clearing was complete with only a few stumps still to be rooted out. *Someone's been doing a lot of work,* he thought.

There were level changes along the way, with rock formations through which paths had been struck to get from one area to another. It was after one of those that came to an open expanse that harbored the hay field.

They stopped.

"There he is," Ondur whispered, pointing to a group of four who were spread out along the far corner of the field. "He's the second from the left."

Sigurth nodded, likewise keeping his voice down and pointing, "There's an area over there that hasn't been worked. If we start on the edge of it and work to the right, we'll eventually come together. Remember now, no talking."

They dug in, unable to withhold a few restrained giggles at first, which prompted a few "shushes"; but then they settled down.

Sigurth wielded a long handled sickle, which was his favorite tool, and for him it felt good. With two months having passed since he'd worked hard, the muscles he began to feel made it seem as if he were back home. Even the sweat and chaff and bugs felt good. As he moved and slashed and got into the rhythm he'd developed over the years, his only fear was that his hands had softened to a point where they'd be blistered and torn. Regardless, he got so much into what he was doing, while also concentrating on not looking up, that the coming together caught him by surprise.

His first notice was a certain tension, a feeling that someone had stopped; but he kept working, his back turned.

Then he heard Sveyin, who was now close by, say, "Ondur . . . is that you?"

Ondur was a big galoot with an easily recognized two-furrow stride. Sveyin repeated, "Ondur, is that you! *What are you doing here?*

"And you, Arni! And you, Thor! Am I going crazy?"

Sigurth kept turned and kept working. Then he heard Sveyin say, "Oh shit! *Oh shit!*" in a rising crescendo . . . and footsteps, running footsteps.

Sveyin was on his back, and they were spinning and falling and rolling like idiots and laughing. Finally they got to their feet, and after a few more beats on the shoulders, settled down, with the other three closing in.

Sveyin shook his head. "You know, you bastards," looking around at each of the four in turn. "I've met every ship that's docked-in for as long as I've been here, hoping someone from home would show up. So when did you get here? I've been in the field all day."

"About an hour ago."

He shook his head again, looking at Sigurth. "I'm still having trouble believing this. My o my, do we ever have a lot to talk about. Fortunately, I've been brewing a few kegs which haven't yet been tapped. Now couldn't be a better time, so all of you, follow me."

"What about the work here," Ondur said. "This mess we made needs to be bundled and tied."

"It can wait," Sveyin said.

"Ny . . . You two have a lot to talk about, and as for me, I need the exercise."

"Same for me," the other two chimed. "Besides, I'm sure these guys wouldn't mind the help. We'll catch up with you later to help with those kegs."

Sigurth and Sveyin started back, seeming to jostle one another every other step for as long as they were in view.

"There must have been a lot of work getting these fields ready," Sigurth said, starting the serious conversation as they left the hayfield.

"That's for sure. When we first got here, there were a few open spaces, but most of the land was forested. That's to be expected most places around here."

They stopped at one of the level changes and took seats on the rocks that bordered the edge. A few cattle, sheep and goats mingled freely in the area below them, which with its grass, shrubs and trees had the look of virgin territory.

"Leif told me about the first voyage to these lands, and of wintering over," Sigurth said. "But he didn't mention animals. Oops, yes he did, he said Thorvald returned with some before the summer was over. Did he bring all of these?"

"Some he brought," Sveyin said, "and other ships brought more, some of which we've been able to keep to grow our stock."

"I don't suppose you brought any," intending the comment to be a joke.

"Actually we did," Sigurth said, listing all that he had.

"Really . . . I wouldn't have imagined you being a colonist. What do you have in mind, and why the mules?"

"I'm not sure, to be honest. One reason is that I reasoned animals would always be of value, either to use or trade, or in a pinch to eat. As for the mules, I really wanted horses, but they're too big."

Sveyin laughed. "I know how you love to ride, and have a picture in mind of you on a horse, but its hard to imagine you on a mule."

Sigurth shook his head and changed the subject. "It looks like you're building up your stock. Does that mean hunting isn't very good here. A young man named Bovi Syverson, who we met on a fishing boat on the way in, said the best hunting is elsewhere."

"Oh there's some game. There's enough to keep a few bears and a pack of wolves interested. And when our crops are up, deer as well as all kinds of critters show up. But Bovi's right, it's better on the mainland."

"I'm surprised," Sigurth said. "You're on an island, and yet you say many animals are here. How do you suppose that happened?"

"Well, for one thing, the passageway between lands freezes during the winter. For another, the lands almost come together farther south, so just about anything can come across, including natives."

"Aah, the natives. Tell me about them."

"Let's see now," Sveyin started, Sigurth suspecting by the look on his face he was going to put a spin on it, "they're very native."

Sigurth refused to laugh. "And?"

Getting serious, Sveyin said. "They're primitive, and that's a fact. They live in shelters near the water, and eat, it seems, mostly seafood, which we also do when we run out of farm goods. They don't have boats like we do; instead they have round shells of stick framing and leather skins which they paddle around close to shore. We haven't gotten to know them as well as we should. It seems to me they're more interested in us than we in them, and I think that's a mistake."

"Have they been a problem?"

"They were in the beginning; but not for a while since then."

"So I understand, Sveyin the Archer."

"Sveyin almost choked, then he doubled up laughing, "How did you hear about that?"

"Ingigar at the Way Station."

"Oh yes . . . He was here at the time. He's a good man."

Sigurth nodded, "He was a great help to me, as was the Way Station. How'd that come about?"

"The Station was Thorvald's idea. He came back that first summer, you know, and although he should have known the way, he got lost and wasted almost a week before finally making it here. Another ship came before winter set in, and they'd had the same problem. You can imagine what the discussion was about during the winter that followed. Anyway by spring Thorvald had his mind set that we needed something right across from the island where traffic would pass, and Ingigar volunteered to set it up."

"I see," Sigurth said. Then after flicking a pebble at a goat that happened to be nearby. "Tell me about all these animals."

"That started with Thorvald like I said. When he returned he had quite a few aboard, as his intent was to start a colony with all the features of home. That made sense, so in the spring most of us went to work clearing trees and creating spaces for the fields and pastures that would be needed. In the meantime, Thorvald left with the rest of the crew to help Ingigar."

"The animals have multiplied to the extent I see in just three years?"

"We got a few more from another ship; but it's been mostly natural growth. We're trying to get animals to a number where we need to start culling; but we're not there yet. In that regard it's helped that we haven't needed to butcher any in order to survive, because we're getting along quite nicely with game, and of course seafood."

"You've mentioned other boats coming here."

"Ya, not a lot, but some. They come and stay a bit, mostly to get their bearings, then they're gone, usually to sail around and find out more about this world. A few stopped by again on their way back to Greenland, so that's given me a better picture of what's around; but others haven't, and I don't know if they've been lost at sea or done in by natives."

"Ah, the natives again."

Sveyin didn't comment.

"What about Thorvald? Ingigar told me he'd run aground somewhere. Is there a story there?"

Sveyin snorted. "Ya sorta. As I said, when he returned, he brought all these animals. But the settlement we have here is really Leif's property, and that bothered him. So after the Way Station was settled, he set sail to find the place he could establish as his own. I don't know all of where he's been, in fact I don't know much more than you. A ship passing by saw his ship on this shore about two days southeast of here. They sent a skiff in and found out what was happening, which was that Thorvald and his crew were intending to stay and repair their ship. And that's the last I've heard.

"What about you? When I was preparing to leave Nitharos with Leif, you were getting ready to join the crew of the *Long Serpent*. What happened with that?"

Sigurth told of the voyage to Wendland and the disaster at Svolth; then the lengthy adventure to the land of the Moors, during which time his sister Rogna was rescued; and finally the building of the *Mule* and the voyage up to the docking a few hours before, answering all of Sveyin's questions as it went.

Standing, Sigurth said, "This has left me as thirsty as I've ever been, and I'm not done yet. There's got to be a lot more to tell about in the three years you've been here, and I want to hear about it all. Besides, I want to stop by the boat and pick up something to show you."

They left the rocks and walked the barely discernible trail through the pasture, with on occasion one reaching over to squeeze the shoulder of the other, or the other butt-kicking the one.

"So you have a surprise of sorts for me," Sveyin said.

"Of sorts . . . You might find it interesting."

"Well, I have a surprise for you."

They headed for one of the buildings Sigurth had seen from the ship, but they were interrupted . . .

A young woman Sigurth hadn't noticed on his initial way through was sitting on a blanket under a tree, playing with a toddler. As they approached, the toddler, a little girl with curly blond hair, excitedly staggered to her feet, and lurching like a drunken puppet, ran to Sveyin, babbling *"Papa, Papa, Papa"* all the way.

Chapter 21
REUNION
1030
(1003)

Sigurth froze, his jaw dropped and eyes popped as Sveyin picked-up the curly haired cherub and hugged her, spinning a few times and making her giggle. Still agape, he slowly turned his head to see the young woman, who'd gotten up, dusted off and now moved to join them.

Then his face transformed into a big, beaming smile, "My o my . . . my o my," is all he managed to say. Following that and shaking his head, he said, "I see you've found a way to deal with long winter nights."

"You've got that right," Sveyin said, all puffed-up as a proud papa could be. "This is little Yrsa, and this," reaching out to bring the woman closer, "is my wife Bergljot."

Sigurth looked at her, really seeing her for the first time, and nodded, not able to think of anything more to say, anything appropriate, that is. She was slender, almost as tall as Sveyin, with a pleasant face, blond hair, big blue eyes, and a mouth momentarily pinched.

This changed as she broke into a smile and said, "This must be Sigurth, the gallant warrior of Svolth."

Sigurth's jaw dropped again. Turning to Sveyin he said, "You ass-hole, you asked all those questions as if you were hearing about the battle for the first time."

"Just listen to him," Sveyin said, addressing his comment to Yrsa as he bounced her about. "His dander's up because I didn't tell I'd heard about it . . . and after the stunt he pulled on me in the hayfield."

Bergljot stepped forward and gave Sigurth a hug, then, backing away, said, "When I saw the two of you approaching, I knew right away who you were. Sveyin's told me so much about you. As for this Svolth thing, you're more famous than you realize. The story of the battle eventually spread all over Norway, reaching us from one of the ships that stopped by. So we knew we lost, and that a number of men were captured and spared, including Norway's supposedly greatest archer, Einar Thambarskelfir, and a young man who'd displayed incredible feats of valor, named Sigurth Gunnarson."

Sigurth stood, almost blushing, but rebounded, saying, "So much for bullshit. Look, this is great . . . absolutely great," gesturing to the three of them. "But Bergljot, you should have talked to me first. The things I know about him."

Then he shook his head. "Of course I'm kidding . . . So this is your surprise?"

"This is it." Sveyin said beaming.

"You could talk for hours about all kinds of nonsense without mentioning a thing like this?"

"Ya da. I'm still not sure we're even," Sveyin said. "But you said you had a surprise too."

"It doesn't compare to this, so it can wait," Sigurth said. "I'd rather get to those drinks you promised. I feel a few toasts are in order, among other things.

"By the way, what happened to Arni and the rest. I thought they were going to finish up and join us?"

"They did," Bergljot said. "They finished and have already been by, taking another route. You two just talked and talked while all that happened. Anyway, they've gone to the ship to get cleaned up, which reminds me that I smelled you two before I saw you, so you best be thinking of doing the same thing. While you do that, I'm heading for the cookhouse to help out. Thorth Folason, the leader of our little community in Thorvald's absence, who I understand met you at your ship earlier, intends a good meal for all of you as a welcome."

There was excitement in the air, and people scampered about to get ready because of it. There were no indoor spaces of any size, so whatever was to happen was going to happen outside. For this, benches were contrived and placed in a circle, with stones arranged within that circle and firewood stacked in its center. Other than that, the food and the expected words of welcome, it was for the people to make it what it could be.

The *Mule,* being the largest object in the vicinity had been an item of interest since it arrived, now became no more than a backdrop. It lay in the water securely tied, gently moving with the creaks and groans ships make as they react to the motion of the water. The word about was that the ship wasn't going anywhere for a while, maybe not until next spring, so intents were to take it out of the water in the next day or so and make ready for winter storage. Until then it was necessary for someone to be on board, and tonight, while everyone else prepared for the special meal, Jon and Frothi stayed.

As it turned out, it wasn't a bad assignment. Ondur and Thor brought them generous amounts of the fixings, which were more of a treat than they'd hoped. The fixings included the usual gruel of grains, garden produce and scraps of meat, along with a loaf of coarse but fresh bread; there was also fried salmon, steamed oysters and even roasted meat since a deer had been bagged that morning. As good as all that was, the toppers were the bulging bag of grog that accompanied the meal, and the new friends that joined them, the ones that had been made in the dust and chaff of the hayfield earlier.

For everyone else, there was a banquet of sorts around the fire with more conversation for most than had been experienced in a long time; there were attempts at poetry, and, as drinks took their effect, a spirited contest of insults with explosions of laughter that scattered animals in the pasture more than once. In all, almost sixty people mingled and enjoyed.

At one point when they'd been alone, Sigurth grilled Sveyin with "How did you two meet?" "How did you win her hand?" All reasonable questions to a man without holdings or connections of consequence in as remote an outpost as Vinland.

After enough horns to loosen his tongue, Sveyin finally opened up.

"Sigurth . . . It's hard to explain because it's hard to believe."

"Well, try me."

"Ya, ya, okay. When Thorvald came back that first year here, there were animals aboard, but you know that. There were also a couple families along, and Bergljot was among them. You can imagine the interest a pretty girl of age can make in a place with many men, but only a few women. Before the winter was over, more than one, including a Ship's Captain from the second ship, approached her parents to bid for her hand.

"Nothing ever came of any of it, which only added to everyone's frustrations, and certainly mine because I couldn't help but be interested, even though I had nothing to offer. Our eyes met on occasion, which didn't make it any easier because I really wanted to get to know her. Fortunately there was a lot of work to be done, so I poured into that.

"Then there was this attack in the summer by those savages, which you've heard about. I got pats on the back for what I did, but I didn't think much more about it. A little while afterwards the strangest thing happened . . . her father came and talked to me. Apparently Bergljot had been in danger that day, and she not only felt saved, but also impressed by what happened at the tree. Before that she'd been appalled by arrangements almost made for her, so after the incident, she took matters into her own hands."

"You're telling me she picked you and you reluctantly relented."

Sveyin almost rolled over laughing at that.

"Where are Bergliot's parents? It's too late to warn them, but at least I could give them my condolences."

"They're gone. Two years was enough for them here, so they caught a ride on a ship stopping by. They want to return to Iceland."

"Oh."

"What about you?" Sveyin said, changing the subject.

Sigurth shrugged.

"Hey now, don't hold out on me. You were the scourge at the festivals as we grew up, with girls giggling like fools every time you went by. Seems to me you were pretty interested in more than one."

Sigurth only rocked a bit without answering, then took another drink. "So?"

"Well . . . Just being a farm hand with nothing to inherit doesn't make you very attractive. You understand that because you were in the same situation."

"You're kidding . . . even after Svolth and all those carvings? What about Katrin?"

Sigurth sat, seeming frozen, then said in a whisper, "Oh ya Katrin . . . We had something going, you know. But . . . well, her Pa married her off to a farmer in the east whose wife had died."

"And?"

"One more," Sigurth said, lifting his horn.

He and Sveyin were the last of the celebration, which had been quite an event. But all parties come to an end and this one did, gradually at first, but then decelerating soon after dark when temperature dropped and the first flecks of approaching winter danced in the air.

"You are one lucky bastard," Sigurth said, clicking horns and downing it in one long gulp.

Sveyin downed his as well and settled back. "Aaah," he said, then burped. "Let's see now . . . that's about a dozen times you've said that."

"Well, it's true. She's a beautiful girl, and she seems so nice. You're a lucky bastard."

"I agree," Sveyin said. "In fact, I agree so much, I'm asking why I'm outside freezing my ass off, with only a drunk and an empty keg to keep me company, when only a short distance away is a warm bed and you know who.

"You're welcome to spend the night in our cabin," he added, getting up and burping again.

"Ny," Sigurth said struggling to his feet. "Ny e tuk, my gear's over at the bunkhouse, so I'll head there."

With that and one last shoulder bump, they parted. Before they had gotten far in almost opposite directions, Sveyin stopped to say, "Is that where you have your surprise too?"

"It's not really a surprise. It's just something I thought you might find interesting."

"But do you have it?"

"Ya."

"Good . . . See you in the morning, then."

Sigurth eased into the bunkhouse as quietly as possible, an effort wasted because everyone inside was long asleep, emitting soft sounds of heavy breathing. He laid out his blanket, fashioned a cushion and settled into place. For only a moment, however. He was too tired and too much under the influence to reason why, but for him, this wasn't right and he couldn't stay.

Easing back up, he added a hooded layer, extracted his sword and bow from his stowage and went outside.

He'd been inside just long enough that the cold night air caught him with a bite. Then he adjusted to it and it was good, the area all about quiet with only an occasional movement of air to rustle a leaf. It was also overcast, the absence of light resulting in a uniform darkness that almost blotted out anything that might normally be seen. Then his eyes adjusted and faint outlines slowly come into view. With that he moved out.

There'd been torches at places where people had gathered earlier; but they'd burned out, as had the fire built in the center of a sitting area. Except for a few coals still glowing in the circle, there was nothing . . . and with the settlement asleep this didn't make sense. There were buildings with people and pens with animals and pastures with even more, all of them being in hostile territory, and yet there was nothing in the way of security. He sighed.

He moved past the pens, which were likewise draped in darkness and a corresponding silence. One of the animals did sense him, resulting in a faint snort to let him know.

The only other sound was the *Mule*, which creaked slightly as he passed, but that was it. He shook his head and smiled. When he and Sveyin had taken a walk early in the evening, there were sounds coming from aboard that caused Sveyin to speculate that the best of the party that evening was under the tent. *Was there anyone awake and on duty now as there should be?* He was about to move in closer and see; but then he sensed movement. *No, the only way to keep a secret is to make sure no-one knows a secret exists.*

Sigurth moved along the shore past what could be defined as the settlement, moving slowly south. Sveyin had said at some point in that direction, lands from both shores extended to form a narrows, a narrows across which both men and animals habitually crossed. How far the narrows was he wasn't told; he only knew that the farther he went the closer he would be to it, and that was good enough.

He'd only gone about as far as half of what he wanted, intending to return before daybreak, when the sky changed from almost blackness to a blackness mottled with lighter shades as the cloud cover seemed to be breaking. This had an effect on the landscape, and although subtle, created patches with varying detail. With this change, Sigurth changed his tactic, moving from one dark area to another as the clouds moved, in almost a game in case someone or something else was out there and moving about.

He eventually came to a point that he considered far enough. Nothing had been seen in all the distance covered, or heard for that matter, which was more important because sound on or near water travels with amazing clarity.

Before he could turn, however, he sensed movement. Did he imagine it? He stopped, held his breath while focusing every sense. Then there it was again . . . It was real. Whatever it was also stopped, and in the almost absence of contrasts, seemed to disappear. Soon after that there was another movement, very subtle, and another behind it . . .

Wolves!

Sigurth strung his bow and notched an arrow with slow, deliberate movements, during which time the movements stopped.

Those animals are much smarter than I am, he thought. *They can see better, hear better and smell better.*

One of them, probably the leader of the pack, inched closer using the same tactics he'd used earlier. Then a path of light crossed exposing the wolf and the wolf froze, legs crouched and ready to fly at the first sign of danger.

The arrow hardly made a sound, even when it hit. The wolf folded with the impact, managed a few weak yelps while in a drunken dance blurred by darkness, then settled into a heap where its only movement was a tail that slowly wound down.

The other phantoms accompanying the leader vanished without a sound.

"Hey, since when have you started sleeping half the morning." It was Sveyin nudging Sigurth in the now empty bunkhouse.

"What?" Sigurth said, moaning as he rolled over, trying to sit up and rub eyes at the same time.

"Is this Sigurth, the great warrior who used to be able to outdrink anyone around?"

"Oh good grief," Sigurth said, now sitting. He looked about trying to get his bearings. "What bad thing have I done that the first thing I see in the morning is you?"

Sveyin laughed . . . "Very funny."

Sigurth managed to stand, rubbed his eyes again and yawned. "So what's happening?"

"Not much . . . not much at all. But the cookhouse is open and some leftovers and broth are available. Let's go over and have a bite. Then we can get into what you thought I might find interesting."

That didn't happen for a while. Odd and several of the crew were also at the cookhouse.

"From what I hear," Odd said as they walked up, "the two of you had quite a reunion last night."

"That we did," Sigurth said. "That we did. How about the rest of you . . . Did you have enough to eat?"

"Sure did. It was so good, that as you can see, we're lined up for more. But I'm glad you came by at this time, because if you didn't, I was going to come find you."

"The ship?"

"Yes the ship. Are we about through for the year? If so, we should get it out of the water before the weather gets much worse."

Sigurth looked at Sveyin and asked, "You folks were stranded until we came along. Are there any trips that need to be made?"

Sveyin shrugged. "Not that I know of, but let's see Thorth, he's approaching as we speak and may have something in mind."

"Thorth," Sigurth said, "we were just talking about our ship and the need to get it out of the water before winter sets in. Since there is still some time before the water freezes, is there some trip, a short one, that needs to be made before it happens?"

Thorth thought a moment, then shook his head. "We've been stranded so long we've become fairly independent. I'd like to find out how Thorvald is doing, though, and whether he needs help. The last I heard was that they were okay, but that their ship had run aground and been damaged. They were staying to make repairs."

"How far are they away?"

"I've been told two or three days, somewhere along the coast southeast of here. I'd hate to ask you to find him in a short time though, as these coasts go every which way. I'm sure Sveyin will back me on that. When we made that first trip with Leif, the main thing we learned was that what he called Vinland is a very big place. Outside of that there's not much in the way of detail because we bounced around and only touched on places we sighted, really not getting enough information to record how one related to the other.

"We haven't even explored all of the island we're on. To be honest, one of the reasons has to do with the natives. We haven't had much trouble, with thanks to Sveyin for that; but other ships making explorations haven't been as lucky.

"Back to your first question . . . We do have many needs, but if I were to list them, we'd find most of them would come from Norway or England or some other developed area, and tops on the list would be women. So Sigurth, why don't you hold off for at least a week. If we can't come up with a pressing need in that time, then put the ship away."

Sigurth and Sveyin left soon after that, returning to the bunkhouse. Once inside Sigurth went to his goods and pulled out the leather cylinder.

"That's it?" Sveyin asked.

Sigurth ignored him, unrolling the drawings.

"What are these . . . and there's nothing on this one?"

Sigurth went on to explain what they were, travel sketches, who he'd gotten them from, and why the one representing Greenland and beyond was blank.

"And what are you going to do on the blank one?"

Sigurth rolled out a third sheet of fine cloth. "This is how Ingivar at the Way Station described Vinland. I've yet to put it on the leather."

"Why?"

"Because I'd like to not only verify the shapes and distances he outlined, I'd like to add neighboring lands and features as well."

Sveyin looked at him with that look that asked *What are you doing?* Then he squinted as if he hit on to something. "Are you looking for the edge?"

"Maybe," Sigurth said. "That was a big part at first, but . . ."

"But what?"

"I'm not sure."

"You brought along animals . . . and mules. Why the mules?"

"I didn't have room for horses," Sigurth laughed.

"Seriously, it looks like you intend to colonize."

"That's also a possibility. I'm sick of the situation in Norway. We lost a lot of good men at Svolth, the cream of the crop . . . and for what?"

Sveyin sighed, looked down at the drawings. "You said you had something I might find interesting."

"Ya."

"Well, I'm interested."

The sun at its zenith was as low as it was going to get for the year. It was cold, freezing cold, and as a result the passageway at the narrows was now closed.

On the west bank a party of men in leathers and fur and carrying spears and bows, stepped down to the frozen surface.

"This is a mistake," one of them said. "We will be killed."

"They have animals," the leader said. "All we want are a few animals. We'll be gone before they find out."

The party crossed the narrows and headed north following the shore. About half way to where they knew the settlement to be, they came to a particular tree. From one of its outstanding branches, the carcass of a large wolf hung, swaying in the breeze.

They turned around.

Chapter 22

STRAUMSFJORD

1030
(1004)

By the time the third ship docked, people in the farthest reaches of Vinland were scrambling.

"Three ships?" Sigurth asked as the youngster ran by shouting the news. He was among a group who'd been busy with spring planting, which included turning the forest into a field. When he heard the shout, Sigurth was with Andur as they worked to dislodge a stump. They gave a last effort, using a thick branch as a lever, broke it free and turned it over.

"There," they exhaled, catching their breaths; then they chopped the remaining roots tying the stump down.

"Three ships," Sigurth repeated as he pitched-in to drag the stump to where a pile was accumulating. "That's three too many to ignore. Let's break and find out what they're about."

They weren't the only ones excited about the news, because as they dusted off and slipped on their tunics, they saw others moving from what they'd been doing. No one was disappointed. When the *Mule* arrived and a celebration held to greet them, a grand total of sixty people were assembled. Now as those in the last ship disembarked, there were two hundred milling about, the bulk of whom discovering how small the settlement was, and how little their chances were of getting relief in the way they wanted. The animals, however, had empty pens waiting; so that, at least was something.

Jon saw them approaching from the field and motioned them over, "You've got to see this; they had an awful time getting it off the boat."

When they'd gotten through enough of the crowd to see, Ondur said, "By the Gods, a bull . . . and not only a bull, but one of the largest I've seen."

And it was—a mean looking, heavy-humped, sharp-horned bull, that pawed the ground and snorted, seeming on the verge of charging the flimsy fencing that separated it from where it wanted to go. As they stood, for the moment fascinated by the animal, Sveyin joined them, shaking his head.

"What's wrong cousin?"

"Haven't you been listening to the conversation over there?" Sveyin said, snapping his head to a group on the bank near where the lead boat had tied. "What I've heard so far is hard to believe."

Sigurth turned in that direction, hearing little he could understand as the words were blurred by all the other chatter, but he got the gist of what was being said by the body language, and recognized a few of the people involved. There was Thorth; there was a fiery red-headed, short but firmly built woman who seemed to be doing most of the talking; and there was a distinguished-looking man with white hair, bearded to match. The striking woman beside him, however, was the one that got his attention. She was Gudrun, the woman he'd met at Leif's Brattahlid the year before. Her husband had died, as he recalled, so her being here now seemed strange.

"I'm having trouble following this," he mumbled to Sveyin. "Let's get closer."

Moving up they not only heard better, they saw more. The fiery-haired woman was stomping around while others were trying to reason with her, and by the looks on their faces, to just shut her up.

"That's Leif's sister," Sveyin whispered. "Her name is Freydis."

"Aah, ya," Sigurth said. "Now I remember . . . I met her briefly."

"You're lucky. She's a bitch if there ever was one. She's saying that this settlement is Leif's land, and that means that since Thorvald isn't here, she's in charge. She wants to move her people into the buildings, and whoever's in them out."

Thorth was so angry he was almost unable to talk. He'd spun out in a huff and made a circle back. But then the distinguished-looking man spoke, "Look . . . we're not going to force anybody out. We're here for only a short time, and then will be gone; so we don't wish to create a problem. There are ways you can help us, though. You've already taken in our animals, and we thank you for that. We'd also appreciate any food you can spare while we're here."

"The animals in the pastures are mine," Freydis blurted.

"Ny . . . *they're not!*" Thorth answered, his face red. "They belong to a number of people, and they aren't going to be slaughtered on your say so."

A rumble rose from the residents. The animals they'd been working to keep alive as well as increase in numbers, were also being nurtured.

Most of the arrivals, not understanding what was happening, mainly glanced awkwardly at one other. They'd looked forward to arriving and getting off the boat, and didn't like how this was going.

Then a woman from among residents who'd worked their way close to the leaders, spoke. It was Bergljot, who addressed the distinguished-looking man, saying, "Sir, I take it you're the owner of some of the ships."

"That's right," he replied. "I'm' Thorfinn Karsefni, and this is my wife Gudrun Thorbjarnardottir. We, and Bjarni Grimselfsson with his partner Thorkall Gamlason, have two ships with full complements of people and animals. The third ship is captained by Thorvard, standing over at the side, the husband of Freydis Eiriksdottir, who all of you have been hearing."

"Well," Bergljot said. "Welcome to Vinland, if somebody hasn't already said so. You've caught us by surprise and we're ill prepared; but as we speak, many are scrambling to see what we can do in the way of helping all of you. As for food, we're preparing baked fish along with assorted other seafoods, and also pots with something hot and hopefully tasty. Regarding meat, we'll just have to see what we can do, but we're working on it too.

"Another thing . . . We see you have a number of women and children. We're woefully short on quarters, but we think we can squeeze them in somewhere."

The effect was immediate; faces that had been glum lit into smiles, with a result that people began to mingle and make acquaintances.

Sigurth turned to Sveyin, a sly smile tugging the corners of his mouth. Nodding in Bergljot's direction, he said, "I was thinking you had your hands full with that one; now I know for sure, because your little lady has saved the day." Getting serious, he added, "It looks like things are getting settled over there, so let's go down and see what it's settled to."

They forced their way to where Thorfinn was standing, and at the first opportunity Sigurth, who was leading the way, said, "I'm Sigurth Gunnarson, the owner of the ship out of the water over there, and this is my cousin, Sveyin Gyrtheson, who's been here at Vinland since it was founded."

"These are the people I was telling you about," Thorth interrupted.

"*Aha!* You have some information, I understand."

"Sir?"

Thorfinn laughed. "I've been grilling Thorth on everything he knows about Vinland—Vinland and its surroundings. You see, if you already haven't heard, we're only here to say hello and restock, then we're on our way. So anything you can add to what we've been told would be helpful. He also said you had exhibits to aid in our understanding."

"I'd be happy to show them for whatever they may be worth to you. But if you've already talked to Ingivar at the Way Station, you know as much as I do. "By the way, where *are* you going?'

"I thought we'd go south. I'm told if we do that, we'll pass Keel Point where I understand Thorvald is stranded. Beyond the corner of the land he's on, we'll turn southwest, where we expect long stretches that may have good places to settle. What do you two think?"

"Makes sense," Sveyin said. "We don't have much information from our own experiences, other then my first voyage with Leif Eiriksson, because since then, we've been mostly learning about this island we call home. Other ships have taken the route you're suggesting, though, and have spoken of it. They've mentioned a fjord in that direction, and also that the sea is a little warmer."

"Well, what do you think?" Sigurth said after they'd parted company with Thorfinn and the Captains.

"What do you mean with 'what do I think'?" Sveyin responded, sensing something in the way Sigurth said it. "*On ny o ny!* . . . Are you suggesting *we* follow them?"

Sigurth didn't say anything, he just walked along fending off a smile.

"I guess you've forgotten I have a wife and child, and can't go sailing anywhere and anytime I get the urge."

"So you have the urge."

"I didn't say that."

Sigurth roared and bopped him on the shoulder. "But you were thinking about it weren't you?"

"You asshole . . . Of course I was; but I can't go, and that's that."

"Ya sure. Well, I'm going to grab Odd and the crew and tag along when they go. But we're traveling light. We're not taking animals or families, maybe the hunting brothers, Ari and Askel, though, if they want to go along. In the months we have in summer, we should be able to see most what there is to see and still return by late fall."

"What do you expect to find?"

"How should I know? I like the idea you had about plotting our locations each day on a drawing, then connecting the dots so we get some semblance of what the shape of things is really like."

"It just makes sense to do that. By the way, you aren't really looking for that edge are you?"

"If it's there, it's there."

"Well, have fun."

"I spoke to Bergljot earlier and she thought you should go."

"You bastard!"

The four ships left a few days later, with the *Mule* having a unique problem—It was not only faster under normal circumstances, it was also carrying a lighter load. To counter this, the lines and canvas and steering-oar were continuously manipulated so they wove in and out, giving them a better idea of the coast as they passed than any of the others. With Jon atop the mast in his improvised seat much of the time, he was first to spot Keel's Point where Thorvald's ship and crew were located. They dropped anchor and settled in, Sigurth and Sveyin boarding the skiff to catch up on the news.

"How are things with you, then?" Sveyin said to the party that met them on the shore as they eased in.

"Is that you Sveyin?"

"Ya . . . Good to see you Soti; and Magnus, Bui, Ola. How's it going?"

Bui flashed a big, toothy grin, "Well, if it isn't the archer. Shot any big trees lately?"

"Haven't had much reason to in a while," Sveyin said, returning the smile. "By the way, all of you, this is my cousin Sigurth, and this is Jon, the best lookout anywhere. We'd have probably swept by and missed you completely if it wasn't for him. Like I said, how's it going?"

"Well, we're almost ready to get back in the water," Soti said.

"It looks that way," Sveyin said as he glanced at the ship nestled on the ramp nearby. "So where is everybody? Where's Thorvald?"

Most are hunting or fishing right now. As you can tell by our ribs, this hasn't been a land of plenty."

"That's where Thorvald is? Hunting?"

"Ny . . . Thorvald's under a pile of rocks a ways inland."

"Dead?"

"Dead."

"What happened?"

"Skraelings."

"The natives? The natives attacked you?"

"Well sorta."

"Sorta?"

Soti fidgeted, seeming to be picking words to make sure he said the right thing. Then. "A while back, about a dozen of us, including Thorvald, went exploring the banks of the inlet a ways over . . . it's like a narrow fjord.

Anyway, Thorvald saw some land that really looked promising to him; in fact he thought it would be a good place for a farm. We were returning another way when we came upon three boats, you know the native kind that look like round baskets with stick frames and leather covers, upside down on the ground. Something seemed strange, their being there like that, so we turned them over. We were surprised to find three men under each of them who'd either been sleeping or hiding. You can imagine how it all happened as well as I can, but with the confusion that resulted, people jumping around and yelling, someone struck the first blow. Then there was full blown stabbing and chopping until all of them were down, except for one who managed to get a boat in the water and paddle away.

"We were fairly sure what was going to happen after that. We got back to the boat, prepared defenses as best we could, and waited. Sure enough, they came—many boats filled with warriors rowing down the fjord, mad and yelling like banshees. We were seriously outnumbered, so we hunkered down behind the rail, and only raised behind our shields every now and then to stab with our spears to keep them at bay, or to let fly an occasional arrow. All they could do, besides make noise, was to shoot arrows that ended up sticking all over the ship.

"Finally they either ran out of arrows, got tired, or had too many injuries. At any rate they left and we haven't seen them since.

"We were lucky. No-one was hurt, except Thorvald, that is, who caught an arrow under his arm. At first we didn't think the wound was serious, but then we found that the head had broken off, with the point deep inside. We eventually got it out and cauterized the wound, which was as much as we could do. But nothing we did seemed to help. Thorvald grew weak, his color turned, and ten days later he died. Before he did he made two requests. The first was that he be buried on that site he thought so beautiful, and that the site be called Cross Point with crosses at both the head and foot of his mound; the second was that the rest of us return to Greenland and tell Leif not only what happened, but also what had been learned in our travels.

"So we buried him. I'll show you the site if you'd like; it's only a few miles from here."

"Ny, not now anyway," Sveyin said. "You see the ship out there waiting for us? We've got three other ships to catch up to."

"Where's everyone going?" Soti said.

"Generally south or southwest of this point. We're doing what you were doing . . . exploring. The other ships are loaded with animals and provisions needed to make a settlement or two; but we're just tagging along to get an idea what's in this part of the world."

Soti nodded, screwed his face like he was searching for something to say. He looked at Sigurth, "Are you the man from Svolth?"

Sigurth blinked, and shaking his head, said, "News seems to travel far."

Soti said, "Ya . . . that's good because we're starved for news. Like when Magnus stubbed his toe on a burlwood root the other day, it was hardly worth talking about."

Sveyin laughed and clapped his hands, then said, "We'd better get going. Will you be returning to Greenland, then, when you get back on the water?"

"Ya, that's what Thorvald wanted. But we intend to stop by Leif's settlement on the way."

"Good, I was hoping you would. Say hello to Thorth . . . the poor guy had his hands full when all three of the ships we're following came to Vinland on the same day. And give my love to Bergljot and Yrsa. Tell them we're doing fine and still on schedule to be home in the fall."

They caught up with the three other ships at the corner of the land mass, turning from southeast to southwest. As before, the *Mule* moved faster, darting in and out along a coast that was at this point generally straight.

It was easy sailing, with Odd and the crew managing the boat with little involvement by Sigurth, which worked well all around. He was able to spend time, at least in regular intervals, doing what he most wanted to do, which was working with the drawing and locating the next dot.

Locating the dot was a complicated process. It involved aligning with the shore, made easier at this stretch because it was fairly regular; checking the boat wake; measuring the sun angle to estimate the time of day; and listening to any argument anyone else might make . . . that person usually being Sveyin. Most important of all considerations was the distance of travel since the last dot, which was estimated by guessing their speed as might be affected by ocean currents. At night, if the sky was clear, locating the north star verified their direction.

There was one overriding impression that began to work its way into Sigurth's mind as the days eased by. The world in which he'd grown up in was mountainous and rocky; it had fjords cutting deeply into the countryside, breaking land into segments with only small portions usable for farming, and much of that on steep inclines.

He'd seen other lands, like Denmark and Wendland and the coasts on the long voyage to Narvesund, that were otherwise, but nothing had impacted him like what he'd been seeing since leaving Greenland with its Norway-like fjords and ice-capped ridges. In Vinland there were rugged shores, and fjord-like cuts in places; but there was a difference. There were hills in and about, but not dominating, pinnacled mountains. There were trees, but in endless forests instead of patches. And now, as he leaned on the rail going through the exercise of locating the next dot, he gazed across at the sanded shorelines he'd been seeing for days—a length already named Furdustrandir, or Wonder Beaches.

Vinland and its surroundings were in a way like Garthariki, with vast stretches of the world. But it was better than just big because it had abundant waters as well as land and wood and game. Ya sure there were problems, but were those problems that bad, and didn't this world provide endless opportunity?

They missed a turn. All the captains had been told that at some point the shore would turn to the right, either north or northwest; but wherever that point was, they reached it at night and sailed by. In the morning they were greeted with a panorama of water on all sides; so without a need to discuss the matter, the lead ship, which was the *Mule* as usual, cut back in a direction Sigurth's dots told the shore had to be, and in a reasonable time, Jon affirmed it with a hearty "Land Ho."

This new line was followed; but before the end of the day it could be seen that the shore was turning again, this time in a gentle arc back the way they'd come. They circled about and eased in beside the Karsefni ship, the *Reynines*, named for his home in Iceland.

"Do you think we're near the opening to that fjord we heard about?" Thorfinn shouted when the *Mule* came alongside.

"Possibly so," Sigurth answered. "And Jon says it's faint, but he thinks he sees land straight ahead. If so, then we must be there."

"Could you go ahead and verify that? We'll follow in case there is, because its a good time to start looking for a place to settle."

The *Mule* moved forward, spending the next two days not only reaching a shore, but also circling an island almost fifteen miles long that stood off the mainland. They found the other three ships at anchor off the southern tip of the island.

"What you see before you is an island," Sigurth said as Odd coaxed the *Mule* in so close the rails had to be bumpered. "The mainland is roughly ten miles away. You have some good choices. Either has all the room you need. Fishing will probably be good wherever you go; but Ari thinks hunting will be better on the mainland. We didn't see savages anywhere we went.

"Oh, and you'll find out soon enough, but there are strong currents in these parts."

The ships skirted past the island that they named Straumsey because of those currents, and proceeded along the shore northeastward into what they considered a fjord, which they named Straumsfjord. A short way further they found an area that looked too good to pass up, so they landed, unloaded and set up camp.

"Well what's on your mind now, Captain?' Sveyin said. He, Odd and Sigurth relaxed around a fire, the rest of the crew doing the same a short distance away.

Sigurth sighed and looked up, "Oh nothing . . . just thinking."

"Well ya," Sveyin snorted. "That doesn't answer the question."

"Okay, for what it's worth, I'm feeling a little out of sorts with the other crews. They're busy building quarters and making ready to stay, while we're not doing much of anything."

"We've taken a few good hikes, and passed on the information to Thorfinn, who seemed genuine in his appreciation."

"Everyone enjoyed the venison from those deer Ari and Askel bagged," Odd added. "And there are some nice skins stretching out because of them."

""Ya, ya, I know . . . everyone's pitching in to help. It's just that I feel there's something else we should be doing. This seems to be a good place, so that isn't it; game and fishing are good, and all the birds . . . there are eggs all over the beaches around here."

"Do you want to explore more?"

"Maybe that's it. We've seen a lot these past weeks, but it's only a part of what looks to be a big picture."

Sveyin nodded. "Actually, as much as I'd like to take issue, I agree. When Leif did his thing, we spent the whole summer sailing around, making stop after stop in what turned out to be all directions. But we didn't pinpoint locations and record data like we're doing now; so we didn't have much of a way to relate one place to another. Ingivar did a better job of that later when he set up the Way Station.

"Before that though, Leif told me about Eirik, his Pa. He had a dark side and had been banished from Iceland for some killings, the details of which he didn't go into. Anyway, Eirik, having to go somewhere, sailed to Greenland, which he found to be much like we've seen it, rugged and wild and uninhabited. He spent three years, the whole time of his banishment, traveling the southwest part of it, from the southern tip to the ice fields up north, and in that time became familiar with every fjord and part along that stretch that had potential. That sounds like what you want to do."

"Not unusual and makes sense," Odd said. "Iceland also wasn't settled until explorers had taken years sailing around and testing every shore. I think it's even more complicated here because there are so many good choices, whereas in the other instances, the opposite was true."

Sigurth sat rocking on his crossed legs, his chin pinching as what he'd heard filtered through. "When you think about it," he began, "we've picked up information along a month's line of travel that seems like a fishhook. It looks to me like this so-called fjord is pointing back to where we started. Can that be?" There are great unknowns on both sides of us, but it makes sense to me to clear up this one first. Anyone disagree with that?"

No one spoke.

"Odd, how soon can we be ready to sail? I'll go to Thorfinn and let him know what our plans are, and see if he has any thoughts. There's a chance that by the time we get back, it will also be time for us to return to Vinland.

"This is weird," Odd said.

It was the second day on the water, and Sveyin was on the stern near Odd, while Sigurth was close by on the opposite rail, looking over a table he'd set up on which was mounted the marking cloth.

"You mean the currents," Sveyin said.

"Ya, I've never seen anything like it. At times we're being carried forward and making good time; at others we're only holding our own. Jon says what he sees is amazing. Sometimes the water reaches into surrounding forests; at others there are wide beaches with sand bars and muddy islands, or sharp cliffs and incredible tall pillars. Those pillars would tear the bottom out of the boat, and is one of reasons I'm staying far offshore."

"It's got to be tides causing all of this."

"That's what I've thought. I've just not seen anything like it."

Sveyin looked over at Sigurth, "How are the dots coming?'

Sigurth looked up from his board, then motioned him over, "Check me out on this last one."

The sheet had both north-south and east-west lines serving as guides. The dots usually represented a couple readings each day and another at midnight if there was a clear sky. The line tying them together had previously outlined a fishhook; but when they sailed from the new camp, they followed the north shore, Sigurth naturally locating his dots in relation to it. This was in contrast to the dots placed previously from what had become the south coast. He recognized the disconnect, assuming they'd have to tie it all together later.

"Remember when I said it looked like we're heading back to our starting point?"

"Ya."

"Well, it looks more like that all the time."

"The only thing for sure is that the one won't cross the other," Sveyin said, knowing the obvious would irritate him.

"We'll see."

"I think that's the end of it," Jon said from his perch, pointing to a line of something beginning to show only a few miles away.

They'd followed the port-side shore since leaving the new camp, with clear water on the other. Then land appeared in the distance on the right side as well. Finally it was seen that the waterway narrowed, then split. With the right side not yet showing an end, it was taken, only to find its channel narrowing to less than a mile. Not wanting to head into that straight with all the uncertainty they felt, they anchored for the night.

"What do you have in mind?" Odd asked as the day broke the next morning.

Sigurth leaned on the rail searching the shoreline for anything of significance. "Why . . . are you nervous?"

"Ya da. The tides we've seen are the highest I've ever experienced. I'm trying to visualize what they might be like at the end of these narrows. Have you ever heard of the maelstroms?"

"You mean those currents around some of the islands on the coast of Norway that at times go into dangerous swirls and whirlpools?"

"Ya . . . We could be looking at something like that going forward."

Sigurth turned away, looking at the stretch ahead that seemed harmless, but may not be. "Damn," he muttered.

"What is it?" Odd said, almost afraid to ask.

"I'd like to go ashore at the end. Is it even possible?"

Odd swallowed. "You ask a lot?"

Sigurth didn't respond.

"What's so important on shore?" Odd asked.

"Nothing . . . What's important is what I might see inland a few miles."

"Oh."

"Is it possible?"

"We'd only know after we'd tried it. How many would go ashore?"

"Everyone who wasn't needed to sail the ship."

Odd shook his head. "If I anchored far out at low tide, you and your party would have to wade a long way in the mud to reach shore. If I anchored in close at high tide, the ship would ground when the water receded, and not be moveable until the next cycle."

"When's the next high?"

"It's on its way in now. In keeping with the cycles I've been tracking, it should peak in two hours."

Sigurth looked at the sun, only a short ways above the horizon. The wind was slight, but supportive. He thought if they rode the surge with help from that wind, then he could be right where he wanted to be.

"Okay, let's go."

Sveyin had spent the night in the hold, but was awake and on the steps coming up when he heard the conversation.

"Why are we doing this?"

Sigurth hesitated, and realizing that in all his thoughts on the matter, he hadn't shared them like he normally would, said, "Sorry, but this is the only way I can think of to make sense of the studies we've been making."

"You mean connecting the dots?"

"Ya. If we've been close to accurate with what we've been doing so far, then the waters we sailed when we started out should be just past the land in front of us."

"How important is it anyway? People could get hurt."

"It could be important, you never know. As for the getting hurt, there's always a chance of that in anything we do. I'd hoped to minimize that, however, by dashing inland about five miles, ten at the most; and if I don't see water by that time, scoot back and be at the boat when the next tide rolls in. But you're right, there is a danger, and I don't want you to go. No one else has to go . . . going alone might work out best anyway."

Sveyin looked at him as if he was nuts. "Of course I'll go. You'd get your ass full or arrows if I wasn't around."

When the announcement was made, everyone wanted to be a part of it, so Odd became the bad guy and had to pick the eight men he needed, leaving ten to eagerly slip over the side. Every man was told to carry his favorite weapon and shield, but for strictly defensive purposes; and everyone understood this as a dash-in, dash-out exercise, and not an exciting military maneuver.

That's what Sigurth said, anyway; but there was nothing that could be said that could mask the fact that this was much more exciting then the endless hours of near to doing nothing aboard ship. So everyone volunteered, and the ones that had to stay behind were disappointed. All that is, but Odd. It wasn't that he didn't want to go . . . he didn't want anyone to go, and he didn't want to stay either. They and the *Mule* were soon to be beached in the mud, in the center of an amphitheater of shoreline, with every human being, if there were any in the vicinity, knowing they were there. If they were there, they, the natives or skraelings or monsters, had twelve hours to assemble and come out of the woods and do what they could. And he had twelve hours of watching that tree line and wondering whether they were going to do it.

All that concern vanished as soon as they raised anchor and started forward. Not long into the channel, it became obvious to Odd that he wasn't steering the ship, especially when it began to turn sideways while accelerating forward with the current. He shouted orders, the crew jumping with their own awareness as well as the tone of his voice, and in quick time the sail was furled and oars extended.

"Jon . . . Are there any rocks in our line?"

"Not that I see."

"Keep me posted."

The oarsmen dug in on command, and although it seemed an exercise in futility, there was an element of control, at one time the *Mule* evading an ominous boil it was heading for. Towards the end of the run, with more confidence in what could be done, Odd ordered moves that turned the ship around. Then he ordered full forward, with the result that when the tide peaked, the peak being really a quiet lift rather than a splashing surge, the *Mule* was facing the way it had come.

Sigurth dropped his oar and looked across at Andur. They burst out laughing, as did the rest of the oarsmen and the crew. It was as if they had wrestled with a monster and were still intact, which is about the way it was.

Then it was over the side for the ten, a splash and a wade to shore. Sigurth held a short meeting there, mainly to count heads, make sure everyone was okay and repeat the simple nature of the mission. That done, and with a quick wave they were off.

Sigurth set a fast pace . . . not running, but stepping out with an authority that said this was serious business. They disappeared into the woods, angling towards the first ravine they came to, which they then followed, staying below the ridge line as much as they could.

The going was like untamed forest anywhere, with rises and falls and rocks and fallen logs and thickets combining into an obstacle course that had the party stretching out and snaking its way inland, generally in an east by northeast direction. At uneven intervals, Sigurth stopped, somewhat to check his bearings, but equally to catch his breath, see how the rest were doing, and make sure the trail was being marked as they passed.

"How far do you think we've gone?" He said to Sveyin, who he'd asked at the start to keep that in mind for him.

"Maybe a mile so far."

"Is that all?"

"That's my guess."

"Everybody okay?"

All he got in reply were mumbles and nods.

"Okay, let's do another mile before taking a break," Sigurth said, and the march resumed.

A small creek trickled through the ravine, and at times the logical route swept beside or across it, and it was at a point beside it that Sigurth moved past without seeing what he'd almost stepped on. But his passing did flush out what was there—two young boys who'd been into something at the water's edge, had frozen at the sound of something unknown approaching, and finally panicked when they realized what it was. Sigurth didn't see enough quick enough to do any good, but Thor was next in line with Jon right behind, and the two, seeing what was about, jumped ahead to cut them off. The rest, who sped up hearing the commotion, completed the entrapment with the boys quickly being held with mouths clamped.

"We sure don't need this," Ari said beneath his breath as he climbed to the nearest rise to see if anyone else was around.

"Damn . . . what now?" Someone muttered.

"Well, we're not going to hurt them," Sveyin said. "They're just kids out doing what kids do."

Sigurth stood, letting his shield slide to the ground while he looked at the boys. The two, who'd been wild-eyed and struggling against stronger arms, settled down and stared back. His mind whirled as everyone went quiet. Not long before, they'd survived a maelstrom of sorts; now, although they'd been careful . . . this. What's going on? *Are the Norns working against Him? Is Loki messing around?*

"Sigurth?" It was Sveyin. "We've got to tie them up, and either take them along, or assign someone to stay here with them."

"They'll slow us down," Ari said.

"Ya, and I don't want to be left behind on guard," Thor said. "We can imagine what will happen if their men find us."

"There's only one smart thing to do," another whispered, a comment followed by several mumbling in agreement.

Sigurth blinked out of his stare, then stepped over to the boys and knelt. Speaking softly, but loud enough for all to hear, he said, "Look, you two, I know you're scared and don't understand, but we don't intend to harm you. We're going to tie you up, and then put a rope around your neck.

We want you to travel along with us, and if you cooperate, we'll let you go and everything will be fine . . . okay?"

While arranging for doing this, several of the party fanned out to see if there was anything to indicate anyone else was aware of them. There being nothing, the party started out again, this time, however, at a slower pace. This wasn't good. Being in enemy territory was one thing; but being unable to move quickly and stealthily and control every movement was another. Now those abilities were gone and progress became more of a drudge. The next few miles, therefore, seemed like forever, with something ominous waiting at every turn.

"How far do you think now?" Sigurth asked as they stopped by a small pond to take a rest.

"It's nowhere near five miles yet," Sveyin said. "It's hard to tell with all the turns we've taken."

Sigurth inhaled and slowly blew out. He could see in mind that the *Mule* by now had settled on the bottom, and could only guess how that was going. *Was the bottom gradual in its slope? If not, would the tide rolling back swamp her before she had a chance to float?*

"I have an idea," Sveyin said, breaking into his thoughts.

"Ya?" Sigurth said, relieved that someone had one.

"Why don't a few of us take off, traveling as fast as we're able. The ground looks higher up ahead. I can't tell how far that ridge is, however, maybe two more miles. If we don't see water from there, then we can decide whether that's far enough. Right now we're in limbo with a feeling of no end in sight."

Sigurth looked up, his brow raised. "Who?"

"You, me and Ari. He's a fast mover and a good shot."

"Sounds good to me," Ari said. "This pace is driving me nuts."

"Okay, let's go," Sigurth said. "Thor, you're in charge here. Take care of my boys."

With that the three left, breaking into a trot at first but then settling into a pace still faster than the way they'd first started. When they got to the high ground, they were disappointed, because as often happens, the only thing to be seen from one ridge is the next one.

"I smell something," Ari said.

"What?"

"Water, the next ridge . . . there's going to be water. I just know it."

No one argued. They pushed on, dropping first into a shallow valley and skirting through the usual matter of the forest, which now seemed to take longer than intended because they'd already gone farther than planned. Finally they reached the crest, and it was as beautiful a sight as they could ever recall—water, blue water stretching across the horizon, with beaches and islands and all kinds of features ripe for identification.

Sigurth grabbed a roll from inside his tunic, spread it out, oriented it properly, and said, "Okay, dammit, where are we? Where do we put the dot?"

The way back was no less filled with anxieties. They debated on letting the boys go at the start, but decided to keep them until they were closer to the shore when they could then make a dash for it.

It didn't work that way.

At a point, with still miles to go, Jon, who was leading, stopped and held up his hand, the rest bunching up behind.

"I hear voices," he whispered.

They stayed motionless for a while, straining to hear, but there was nothing. Then Ari crept to a nearby high point, camouflaging his head in leaves before easing it over the edge. He slowly retracted, turned and mouthed, his face contorting as he said, *"Oh Shit!"*

"They know we're here," he whispered when he returned, "because as they talk they keep pointing in our direction. And more are coming all the time."

"Okay, then let's move out," Sigurth said. "Jon, keep the lead but pick up the pace. Everyone, set your shields up on your shoulders like this, and stay as close together as you can. We'll keep the boys with us for a while longer as that might keep the natives at bay. Anyway, move out, I'll bring up the rear."

They did, awkwardly at first; but then Andur and Thor picked up the boys and threw them over their shoulders, and this worked out much better.

The way back was generally down, which was a help; but there was still the obstacle course of the forest—rocks to sidestep and water to cross and tree trunks to hurdle, all the while sounds like attack dogs started and built up not far behind them.

This went on for seeming an eternity, lungs heaving and legs going numb. They came to an open area where the shelter of the forest disappeared for both groups, the ten reaching the far edge of it just after the now numerous natives emerged from the other.

"Hold up!" Sveyin said.

They did; but Ari said, "This is crazy . . . We're in the open and they've got a clear shot."

"This is a good time to let them go," Sveyin said, looking at Sigurth.

Sigurth hesitated, then accepted the thought because he didn't have a better one. He moved to where Andur and Thor were standing, and then, one by one, helped the boys off their shoulders and cut the bonds.

The boys didn't know what to make of this and stood as wide-eyed as they'd been at first.

Sigurth knelt, and with hands on each of them said, again softly as if speaking to a friend, "This is as far as we're going to take you. You're free to go. May we meet again in better times."

Before he could turn them and send them away, Sveyin said, "Hold on a minute." Then he stepped forward, raised his bow, and sent three arrows into the knurl in a tree just above where a large group of natives were gathering.

They reached the shore without further incident, a fact that made clearing the last bit of the forest and wading into the water almost anticlimactic. But that wasn't the case with those on board the *Mule* who'd been anxiously tracking the hours. They yelled, cheered and jumped about from almost the time they came into view. Even Odd wore a grin that he couldn't get rid of until the last one was safely over the rail.

That last one was Sigurth and their eyes met.

"Well," Odd said.

Sigurth smiled and winked, saying, "What are you waiting for? Let's get this bucket moving."

They did. In only minutes, all oars and hands were in tune and the *Mule* was on its way even before the tide ebbed its way to escort them out. Sigurth was at oar and too busy to see, but Sveyin was at the rail and turned back.

"Look!" he said to Odd, who was at the steering oar; but everyone heard and those who could strained to see.

There on the shore that was quickly receding were natives, many of them. He began to count, but then he saw two boys among them. He waved, a lusty wave as one might to old friends.

The boys waved back.

The return trip to Vinland was as uneventful as return trips usually are. Sigurth and Sveyin continued to plot dots on the drawing, mainly to see how closely the new dots retraced the pattern they'd plotted before. They were surprisingly close.

They hadn't reached the eastern end yet of what had been called Furdustrandir when a storm hit. They were at a point where they knew from earlier side excursions that the shoreline cut way in and might offer protection, so they sailed into the cut, which did provide a haven. The cut turned into a sizable bay penetrating far to the north. Exploring this after the storm abated, they found a channel that continued in that direction, eventually opening to another bay that at first didn't make sense. But then when they rolled out the drawing and studied the dots, they saw that what they'd apparently done was taken a short cut from a southern bay to a northern bay, also noted previously, eliminating a need to circumvent Keel Point and spend several more days at sea.

The real test came later—to locate a dot from the east that coincided with the dot from the west, the one they'd scrambled from the far end of the Straumsfjord to locate. While the three who'd made the last dash roamed the rails looking for clues, and even Jon on his perch who'd been told what to look for, the *Mule* glided on, passing the southern tip of the island they knew Vinland to be on. At that point they veered to the western shore, knowing the features they were looking for were best seen from there.

"I can just feel it," Ari said, pacing the deck.

"That's good," Sveyin said. "Seems to me you had a feeling before, and it turned out to be right."

"What are you looking for?" Askel asked while following his brother around.

"We were on this ridge," Ari said, "looking down at an expanse of water with many small islands offshore, much like we're passing now. On that ridge was a stand of trees, with one tree in particular apart from the stand to the north, apart and taller than any of the others. We thought that combination would be silhouetted against the sky and be distinct enough to recognize from afar."

Just then Jon yelled.

Chapter 23

HOPS

1030
(1005)

"Oh, there you are." Sveyin said as he reached the edge of the bank and looked down at the dock where Sigurth was standing.

Sigurth looked up and nodded.

Sveyin half-slid down the icy surface of the bank to join him, grabbing his wrap to tighten it as a gust whipped up, scattering anything loose every which way.

"They said you'd probably be down here."

"Who, the men?"

"Ya."

"They're still in the game?"

"Ny. They were about to break up when I came by looking for you. This weather's a pisser."

"For sure. The ice *is* breaking up though. It shouldn't be much longer."

"You were looking for me?"

"Ya. Bergljot baked bread, so its fresh; and now she's cooking a pot of stew that smells like party time. Thought you might be interested."

"Oh I don't know," Sigurth said acting the fool, his mouth already watering. "If you can throw in a good horn or two, I might."

Sveyin snorted, "Did I forget to mention that?"

It was dark inside, as usual, even with a central fire and several lamps burning; but it was snuggle warm. It was also a busy place, with sixteen people and three dogs calling this structure, one of the original first winter ones, home. Like most buildings, home, whether longhouse like this was, or bunkhouse, there was little privacy, a fact everyone was accustomed to, even though in this case a few outcrops, sheds and special purpose buildings had been added to make it more livable.

After a few words with those in the main chamber, the two settled in with cushions on the ledge near the corner. They were still into the first horn when the door opened, sending a cloud of winter rolling in, as well as Yngvi and two of his kids. Yngvi removed his wrap and stood for a moment beating and stomping and adding to the organic material already floating around. Along with that, enough smell wafted about to let everyone know where he'd been, which was obviously to the animal shelter, his favorite haunt.

"Well, look who's here," Yngvi said as his eyes adjusted to the dim. Seeing how comfortable Sigurth and Sveyin were, he signaled to Thyri in one of those ways that eliminated conversation, and ambled over to joint them.

"My guess is that you two are itching to get on the water again," he said, squatting on the ledge across the aisle from them.

"This one has the itch, no doubt about that," Sveyin said pointing at Sigurth.

"You mean you're not going?"

"I didn't say that," Sveyin answered. "I said *he* has the itch. I'm just going to make sure he doesn't get lost."

Sigurth rolled his eyes.

"I know this has been talked over every which way since you two got back," Yngvi said. "But I'm still not clear on what you'll be looking for this time. You're returning to the last place you were at, aren't you? Then what?"

"You ask the same questions I ask myself," Sigurth said. "But as uncertain as the answers might be, there are enough reasons to go. One is that we skimmed the coast most of the way, bypassing scores of places that may have treasures laying around." He laughed at that thought, adding, "You never know. Anyway, we could stop at some and take a better look."

"We'll have more time to do that if we care to," Sveyin said. "On the way back last fall, we found a short-cut saving a number of days."

"Ya, that was something," Yngvi said. "There's a lot about that trip that has us all talking. The drawings you two made . . . What are they called? And locating that same spot from two directions. I don't know much about those things; and haven't found anyone else that does either. They are amazing, though."

Sigurth bounced his head from side to side while crunching his mouth, not sure how impressive it all was. While doing this, he happened to catch

Bergljot's eye at the far corner, so held up his horn with a stupid grin, then settled back. "I really don't know what to expect, if that's what you're trying to find out," he said. "We've told all of you about the fjord whose tides were higher than anyone had seen before. The question before us now is whether there's something more amazing farther out."

"Like the edge?"

"Anything's possible."

"You know we stopped by that landing where the other three boats were before we returned," Sveyin said.

"Ya . . . You told Thorfinn Karsefni and the other captains about what you saw farther down the fjord and all."

Sveyin nodded. "The thing that surprised me is what Karsefni told us in return. He said the place they'd selected for their settlement, which he called Straumsfjord, you know, isn't bad at all; but he *still* isn't satisfied with it. And when we were preparing to go, he said to hurry back in the spring, because his intentions are to go further west down the coast."

"That'll be farther than anyone's ever been, won't it?"

"Talk about perfect timing," Thorfinn said as the gangplank of the *Mule* was eased into place. "As you can see, we haven't put our ships in the water yet; but we were about to."

"Is everyone leaving?" Sveyin asked, balancing his way off with the first load.

"Ny . . . Just two ships. It makes sense to leave at least one here, and Bjarni and his boat will be the one. If the truth be known, he's not keen on going farther anyway."

The *Mule* was unloaded, shelters were erected, and everyone prepared for what was to be a short stay. The crew was hosted to a dinner, with generous amounts of venison as well as the expected seafoods.

"Ny, we didn't go farther into the fjord to see what you'd reported," Thorfinn said as they settled around the fire. "We had a good look around here though."

"But you still want to move on." Sigurth said.

"Ya. For one thing these tides have me unsettled. They ease in and out rather than rolling in in huge waves, so it's mostly a matter of getting used to them. But around one of the islands west of here, we found a whirlpool that formed at unpredictable times. It's a big one too, one we didn't wish to get close to. It's scary, because there's no telling what other surprises we could run into."

"And the natives?"

"They're curious, like I understand the ones have been everywhere else; but they haven't been a problem. Ny, if you're trying to find out what we don't like about here, there's not much to tell. The winter was mild; there's land aplenty; there are grapes in the wild and stands of self-seeding grain as well. The fishing is as good as it was in Vinland; and the hunting is . . . well, the brothers that travel with you will love it."

"But you still want to see more," Sigurth said, not intending to, but making it sound like a stupid question as he looked about the clear, blue sky which framed the sparkling spring day. "This is as close to Valhalla as I've ever seen.

Thorfinn snorted, looking up at him through the white brows that framed his eyes. "Just listen to you . . . And why do *you* want to keep going?"

"I'm just curious," Sigurth said. "This island or whatever it is is large, we know that already. But how large? And what else, besides what we already know, is there that may be of interest?"

"Or amazing?"

"Or amazing."

Thorfinn looked at Sveyin, who hadn't said anything to that point; but Sveyin looked away.

"There's more here, isn't there?" Thorfinn said, his head tilting while looking sideways.

Sveyin straightened, thought a moment, then said, "Cousin's mind is still Old Norse."

Thorfinn sat back and looked at Sigurth. "Aah, the Gods . . . and the world of the Gods. You think there's an edge out here somewhere, don't you?"

Sigurth met the gaze.

Thorfinn said, "Well, I'm Christian. But to tell the truth, I'm curious about that too. Let's find out if it's there."

A few days later they left, three boats, two of them laden with all the animals and provisions they'd carried before, the things they'd need to start a new colony. As expected, Bjarni and the forty who'd landed with him stayed behind.

The *Mule* led the way, darting in and about while the others kept a more steady course. As this was happening, with Odd and the crew making it happen, Sigurth and Sveyin were at it again making a game, or rather a contest, of locating a dot each day to record the ships position, and also sketching a corresponding shape of shoreline or feature of particular interest in relation to that dot.

Every point of land along the way had its uniqueness, and in that its sameness, because it didn't matter. They sailed past regardless, with the *Mule* coming about on the *Reynines* each day to mainly say hello. After almost two weeks, and having traveled far, they made landfall and set up camp. There was nothing unusual about the area, which also didn't matter, for the purpose of stopping was only to service the animals, clean the boats and restock supplies. By the time the natives in the area became curious or brave enough to come forward in any number, the ships were loaded, launched and on their way.

The *Mule,* continuing to range ahead, and with Jon atop as he often sat, was able to make progress much more efficient for the other two. One time Jon saw they were approaching low lying lands in three directions ahead of them, so Odd directed a turn, and, signaling the other ships to follow, diverted everyone around what turned out to be a large, far-ranging fishhook-like shape of lowland. After skirting this and the islands beyond the southern edge of the hook, they returned to the general southwest direction they'd been on. A day past that corner and Jon could see land on both sides, but not ahead. Since this could be a long river or deep bay, another turn was made until land appeared only on the right, and then the direction resumed.

The flotilla came to a point where the shores looming ahead blocked them, forcing another change in direction, this one to the south. Being the time to stop again anyway, they did.

Before they'd come to this, however, Sigurth noticed something in Sveyin. He wasn't the same buoyant self, who didn't enter the game of dots they'd been playing with the same enthusiasm as before. At other times he'd fall into a trance along the rail, gazing without sound or expression at the endless sea that was always there, and usually looking back in the direction they'd come.

They'd circled the corner where the landing was to be made, and saw that the corner was a collection of islands into which at least one major river flowed, creating at its outlet shallows that required attention in managing. But a good landing site was found on the south side of either the mainland or a large island, so that's where the ships headed. Sigurth had Odd hold the *Mule* offshore to let the others in first, their cargos being the more demanding. While they were dead in the water with oars at rest, Sigurth stood up out of his seat, stretched, and walked over to where Sveyin leaned on the rail . . . again deep in thought.

He put his arm on Sveyin's shoulder and said, "You know, cousin, I've about had it with this. Everything is just looking the same with no end in sight, and certainly nothing to indicate that edge you keep accusing me of looking for. If we don't quit farting around, we might miss the fall parties back home. I'm ready to turn around. What do you think?"

Sveyin stood without moving, or even turning his head to look back. Then he chuckled, that subtle kind that said he knew exactly what Sigurth was doing, followed by swinging his leg behind and kicking Sigurth in the ass.

"Ya, I understand," Thorfinn said after Sigurth explained their intentions. "This is a long way for sure. But stay a while, at least until we get settled. This place, at first glance, is as promising as any other we've come to, so it deserves a good look."

They did, setting up tents while eighty people from the other ships hustled about making their preparations, like clearing areas and chopping trees and constructing shelters for a longer stay. During this time, the crew of the *Mule*, once settled, hiked further inland as well as along the shores, establishing that where they'd settled was really a large, long island. They also saw that the narrows separating it from the mainland extended to the long river or deep bay they'd averted before, and verified the nature of the other islands in the make-up of the area.

With all this information in hand, Thorfinn called the area "Hops" in deference to the tidal pool nature of the central bay that tied the islands and the river to the ocean.

"Here they come again," Ondur said, standing up to get a better look as several boats approached from the west.

"They sure are a curious bunch," Thor said as the crude boats unloaded, and both men and women approached the settlement.

"Wouldn't you be if you were in their shoes."

"I like their shoes," Jon said.

"They don't call them shoes."

"But wouldn't you be?"

"Wouldn't I be what?"

"Curious. Imagine if you were here when several ships, larger than anything you'd ever imagined, sail in, stirring up your fishing area, and stop. Then strange people come ashore, mostly funny looking men with scraggly, light colored hair and scruffy beards, carrying stuff around they've never seen before . . . and bringing animals, the likes of which they've also never seen, like that damned bull, to chew up your plants and crap on your countryside. Wouldn't you be curious?"

"Well, I'm not curious about them."

"Why not?" Sveyin said, wondering how they managed to be such a great crew.

"They look weird."

"Ya . . . and every time we land, the savages seem to resemble one another."

"Maybe they think *we* look alike."

"You looking for a fight?"

"Sure hate to see you guys go," Thorfinn said while Sigurth and Sveyin were at his cabin informing him of their plans.

"Well, all of you have settled in pretty well," Sigurth said, "while we haven't. But then as we told you before, we never intended to stay."

"I know, I know; but you're just good to have around, particularly when we get on the water again.

Sigurth nodded in appreciation. "So how's all of this "Hops" looking to you?"

"It's fine," Thorfinn said. "But now that the hardest work has been done, and even before the weather begins to turn, a sad reality has grown in my mind."

"The natives?" Sveyin said.

"Ny, not them," Thorfinn answered. "In fact there's a couple boat-loads coming ashore again right now. They love, of all things, our milk and the foods prepared with it, things they've never had before; and want our colored fabrics, which they're trading fine furs for."

"I've heard they want metal products, too, particularly knives and axes and swords."

"Oh ya . . . That's the case at Straumsfjord too; but we never trade them. They have stone clubs and stone-tipped arrows, and that's enough to contend with if things get out of hand."

"When they approach in their boats, they hold poles in the air and swish them around. What's that supposed to mean?"

Thorfinn shook his head. "Who knows. I suppose they have their weird gods and beliefs too . . . like some other people I know.

"Or like those with Chariots of Fire and Heavenly Angels," Sigurth said.

Sveyin made a loud sound something like a bull in heat and everyone laughed.

"But you said something about a sad reality," Sigurth said when they settled.

"Ya," Thorfinn said. "There is one. The pathways here could be lined with gold, and fruits could drop from every tree, and it wouldn't matter. The fact is that Greenland is so remote, it has a problem in that it may not be able to prosper or even survive in the long run. And here we are, many times worse in remote. We may not have reached the end of the world, but we might as well have because I don't think we'll get visitors. We think we'll do fine once we establish trade with those back home. But that trade may never happen. If that's the case, the only way we'll succeed here is to become independent, which may mean combining with the natives. And those fascinating drawings you two have been making are really handy to look at to find where you're going; but anyone with any sense has got to realize the distances between each of them represent another day in water so cold each drop stings and a bunch kills, where mountains of ice crush, where whales wreck, and where storms sink."

Neither of the two blinked, the comments hardly debatable. After a moment, Sigurth said, "Whales . . . We've been hearing about them and sea monsters all our lives, but I've yet to see the first one."

"Oh didn't anyone tell you? We hadn't seen any in the Straumsfjord last year when you were there either; but in the winter we saw lots of them, and they were a sight. Fortunately all of them were seen from shore."

There was another lapse as the thoughts were chewed.

"I think I've sailed through all the bad stuff you mentioned," Sigurth said, "and it didn't seem to be something we couldn't handle at the time. However," he added, "If I found myself sinking for any of those reasons, I'd agree with your every word."

Thorfinn laughed. "Well, I may have made it sound a little grim; but there is truth in it. The biggest question is why would anyone travel this far with all those dangers, for the only thing we have to offer, wood and furs, when they can get the same thing next door? If those thoughts aren't enough, it just so happens I have something else to consider right now."

"And that is?"

"It's Gudrun. She's pregnant, which means this isn't a good time for us to turn around and return anyway."

Sveyin, his eyes giving away that his humor was rekindled, said, "At a time like this, it must be reassuring to have someone like Freydis around."

Thorfinn almost choked, his mouth only making motions but conveying his thoughts anyway. Finally he spoke, "Oh, there are other ladies here, so we'll be all right in that regard . . . *wise ass*."

"That's another thing you can add to your list of problems here in the remote, though," Sigurth said.

"What's that?"

"Women. There aren't enough of them . . . and men are getting restless."

"You're right about that. We have only ten, and two of them are really children. I've heard rumbles, some men thinking there should be a sharing. Is your crew having a problem with that too? You don't have any."

"I don't know about the crew; but a certain acquaintance of mine has been away from his lovely for a couple months now. It's gotten so I have to take my bedroll up into the trees at night."

The rap on the shoulder was harder than usual.

The *Mule* left a few days later. Being alone, their only concern was their own progress, so they were able to concentrate on that, using the drawing to take shortcuts rather than retracing the route taken before. They had loaded the ship with more than the usual amount of provisions, intending to stop only at Straumsfjord. It didn't work out that way. The kind of storm Thorfinn had spoken about struck just as they were rounding the fishhook of sands, forcing them to take refuge inside the bay, which they barely managed to do.

The bay, unfortunately, wasn't much of a refuge because it was over ten miles wide, with winds and waves of almost the same size as in the open sea; so the only relief was close in on the lee side where wave action was lessened. Since the water was much more calm there, they were able to anchor and ride the storm out there rather than be driven across and against the far shore.

"I think we've seen the worst of it," Odd said as he and Sigurth completed a walk around the rail, stopping at the stern.

Just then another gust hit that lifted the ship and dropped it again, forcing them to duck down behind the rail and hang on.

"Are you sure?" Sigurth said, mocking him as he struggled to stand up.

"That was just an opinion," Odd said. "We'll see."

"Oh, I think you're right . . . At least I hope so. How bad is the sail?"

Odd shook his head. "We had to keep it up longer than we wanted to fight our way around the point. If we'd been driven on shore it would have been the end of the *Mule*."

"I know . . . Just asking."

"Well, I won't know until things settle so we can unfurl it again."

Work began on the sail as soon as the sea calmed. But there was little they could use from the point, so oars were extended and the ship rowed across the bay to the mainland, where at least wood and fresh water were available.

The result of all of this was that they sailed into the settlement at Straumsfjord almost two weeks later than hoped, which was also well past when they'd departed the year before. It was their intent to be back on the water as quickly as they could, but their reception was something they hadn't expected.

"Are we ever glad to see you," Bjarni said as they tied in.

"Why, is there a problem?" Sigurth said, leaning on the rail as the crew lay the gangplank and began unloading."

"Yes and no," Bjarni said. "Finish what you have to do and then join me. We're doing well enough that we can give you a proper welcome."

The light was beginning to fade by the time Sigurth and Sveyin made it over to where Bjarni and Thorkall Gamlason were waiting.

"Many thousand thanks for the meal," Sigurth said. "The men may have outdone themselves with so many tasty things to eat."

"Oh, we all know how hungry a crew can get after weeks at sea, "Bjarni said. "A good hot meal can be the greatest thing ever."

"You're trying to bribe us, aren't you?" Sveyin said, only half joking.

"Of course we are," Thorkall said. "We're hoping you don't just turn around and leave again."

"Yes, that is what we said we'd do," Sigurth said. "We want to get home, and we don't want to be sailing in winter. What's the matter with our doing that? I mean, is there a problem that our staying will help solve? Is it the natives?"

"It's the natives all right," Bjarni said. "Nothings happened yet; but I'm not the only one who feels something's going to. Before all of you left in the spring, there were quite a few people here, and lots of activity, evidently impressive to them. Then three boats left, and things weren't as impressive any more. We've noticed it in their attitude. It's not in what's been said because we don't understand each other; but, as you know, body language says more anyway."

"So what's happened?"

"Nothing yet."

"What do you think's going to happen?"

Bjarni shrugged like it was hard to tell. "They're coming by in greater numbers all the time. At first there was peaceful trade between us, and that was good. Now it's not so peaceful, and we've had to constantly be on guard because things are disappearing. These people are damn clever.

So much so the real fear is that something is going to happen, and happen fast when we're most vulnerable. We even hear sounds at night, which our imaginations tell us something's afoot . . . and because of that we're losing sleep."

"I was under the impression they didn't fight at night," Sigurth said.

"I wouldn't count on that."

Sigurth sat back and looked at Sveyin, then turned to Bjarni and asked, "And how is our staying a while going to help?"

"More people, first of all," Bjarni said. "And not just people. You may not realize it, but your crew is a pretty impressive bunch. If we see that, those savages are smart enough to see it too."

"And secondly?" Sveyin said.

"Well, we know you want to get home. We'd leave ourselves, but it's too late in the year to start a long trip. What might be good for us is if you stayed until the leaves fall. Then there'll be no place for them to hide, so the chances of their mounting a surprise attack will be slim; besides, they'll need to get ready for cold weather themselves. By spring we'll be out of here whether Thorfinn shows up or not."

"What do you make of it?" Sveyin asked later back at their tent. "They're obviously on edge, because they have guards up all night. In addition they've erected "fire walls," as they call them, that are good defensive stands just outside the bunkhouses in case they're attacked at night. They're also working on a stockade."

"Well, they're doing what they should," Sigurth said. "In fact, I can't think of anything better, and was going to suggest we do some of the same. I'd hate to see any of us hurt because we weren't prepared."

"You mean fire walls?"

"Ya . . . Our tents aren't much in the way of protection. But I'm not happy about staying around until the leaves are down. Early winter storms can be as bad as any other, and aren't ones I'd care to chance, especially with the sail in the condition it's in. Despite the repairs that were made, it's not as strong as it was."

"You know how I feel about staying later," Sveyin said. "But I heard the sounds last night Bjarni'd talked about."

Sigurth grumbled. "The bastards were quiet for a while after we landed, but I guess they've gotten their nerves back up."

"Do you think they'll attack?"

"They'd be stupid to, and they're not stupid. It seems like a game they're playing to keep us rattled. If they could amass a few hundred warriors, though . . ."

Sigurth eased out a few hours before the time he'd heard sounds the night before. He moved slowly, not steadily, but in stages from shadow to shadow, with the first objective being to avoid his own sentry. That was Thor, who paced along the rail of the *Mule* which was anchored close in offshore. Then he entered the woods, where he could move faster, in time reaching a point beyond where he thought sounds may have originated.

He really didn't have a plan, except he hoped that whatever he could do, it would be something that might make the natives think again about what they were doing. In case that something meant killing, he'd brought along a knife, an axe and a bow; but he'd also brought along ropes in case they could serve a better purpose. He knew how Sveyin felt about killing, even savages, so he hoped that wouldn't be what he got into.

It was difficult to tell how far he'd gone, moving as he did, when he was stopped just as he was about to step out towards another shadow, by sounds so close they startled him—whispers, smooth movements and subtle footfalls expertly placed, that approached and glided past like a cloud in the night, there one moment and gone.

Ten, Sigurth counted to himself. That was more than he expected, and was all he knew because he couldn't identify face or feature . . . He'd stared into a tree all the while they moved past to avoid eye contact. *Ten men, not enough to mount an attack; but certainly enough to scare, very effectively, if that was their purpose.*

He stayed until the sounds disappeared in the direction of the settlement; then, still not having a plan, resumed in the direction he'd been moving. Eventually he came to water, which he expected was out there somewhere, and in the water, boats. *There had to be more.* It didn't make sense that the boats weren't guarded, so he remained where he was and soon he saw movement. It seemed to be only one person, and a small one at that. *This was almost too easy.*

Sigurth could have killed with an arrow, but he didn't. He could have moved close and thrown an axe, with which he was also expert, but he didn't do that either. Instead he walked in the manner of one who'd left and was returning, which got the reaction he expected because the small guard stood to greet him. In moves too quick to follow in daylight, he threw the guard on the ground, turned him on his back, pinned him and clamped his mouth.

The guard was an unarmed boy.

"Oh ny o ny," Sigurth mumbled to himself, *what now?* He took his hand away and the boy began to scream, so he clamped again, saying, very softly, "Shhhhhhhh," which could be understood in any language. He continued this until the boy remained silent, which allowed him to sit the boy up, bind, gag and blindfold him, all the while speaking softly, hoping his tone would make the boy cooperate. It worked.

Now what?

He heard sounds in the distance which meant whatever was going to happen was happening, and also meant he didn't have forever to do something that might leave an impression. Staying with the hope of not having to kill anyone, he also rejected the thought of ruining the boats because he wanted them to get away. Instead he dragged them out of the water, standing each against a tree. Then he shot an arrow into their bottoms, pinning them in place. If it worked the way he hoped, they'd still be able to get away; but doing so wouldn't be easy, and they'd be bailing like crazy while they did.

As a final touch, Sigurth tied a rope to each of the boy's wrists, then each rope to a separate branch overhead. When he left, the last thing he saw was the boy dangling well off the ground, uninjured and safe, but with body twisting and legs flailing every which way.

"Where were you last night?" Sveyin said, shaking Sigurth, who finally groaned and rolled over in his bedroll.

He sat up, rubbed his eyes, and said, "You mean when all that noise was going on?"

"Ya, we looked all over for you."

"I'd gotten up to pee, then walked over to see how Thor was doing."

"Thor said he never saw you."

"Ny, I never made it," Sigurth said yawning. "All that ruckus started, so I hussled into the woods a ways to see what I could see."

"You damn fool! We all had our bows out . . . We could have skewered you."

"Oh, I thought of that, a little late, admittedly, but I thought of it, so I circled back. You were gone when I did; and since the yelling had stopped, I just crawled back to bed."

"You what? We stayed up the rest of the night, ready to shoot anything that moved . . . and you went back to bed?"

"I expect that's what them dumb bastards expected you dumb bastards would do."

"What?"

"Let's go get something to eat."

There weren't any sounds the next night or the next, or ever after that, and the daytime visits for supposed trading didn't occur for a while either; and when they finally did, it seemed with a difference. As for Sigurth and

Sveyin and the crew of he *Mule*, the delay could have been maddening. But they saw in this a chance to take the sail down, and borrowing material from Bjarni and Thorkall, make it as sound as it had ever been. That done, and with any other repair that could be made out of the way, the days then began to drag, with patience being tested as well.

Sigurth was on his way to talk to Bjarni, to tell him that in his opinion, matters had eased enough that their presence was no longer needed. He never got there, as someone shouted, resulting that those within hearing ran to shore to see two sails plainly in view. The ships of Thorfinn and Freydis were returning.

The *Reynines* was in the lead, so it came in first, only to realize the tide was running out, leaving a long stretch of mud. Because of this, it was decided to hold back whatever the hours needed for high tide, then to move in and anchor, being able to shuttle, at least the people and dry goods, a short distance without getting wet. By the end of the day, both ships were docked and secured, and everyone and thing ashore, tired and hungry.

Since disembarking was so complicated, it wasn't until the evening, that Sigurth and Sveyin were able to meet with Thorfinn to hear his story. It wasn't a private meeting because many were interested, and the questions that had been bouncing around since they'd landed had led to many misconceptions. Finally, with unpacking completed and having eaten, a group assembled around the fire, horns in hand, to hear what was the truth.

"You've all been asking what happened," Thorfinn said, "and it seems like I've answered over and over. But the questions keep coming, not only to me, but to everyone who was there at Hops. Let me tell it one last time, and if any of the others wish to correct me or add details, listen to them as well, as each of our experiences is different.

"All of us, at least all of those in the two boats that arrived today, thought we were going to stay the winter. Our little settlement was in a place that was so beautiful, that one of you felt it was equal to Straumsfjord here, which was his picture of Valhalla. It was beautiful, and we settled in, building our lodges and making ready for the long term.

"Ya, there were natives. We thought we could live with them and work out our differences, which we felt was essential to making our colony successful. And all went fine for awhile. But only for awhile. Something went wrong, and for reasons we may never know, they attacked. Many were killed, and although more of them were natives, we felt a great opportunity had been trashed. We therefore have returned to a place that also has great things to offer. We shall just have to start over with the same objectives in mind."

"What a bunch of bullshit that was," Sigurth said as he and Sveyin walked back to their camp.

Sveyin laughed so hard he staggered, bumping shoulders a few times before settling down. "I wondered if I was the only one who heard it that way," he said. "I don't feel I know what happened at all."

"Well, he skillfully left out the details, the bastard . . . and that's where the story really is."

"Let's talk to our crew," Sveyin said. "They've been mixing it up with those from the ships. My guess is they'll know a lot more."

The fires were still burning when they returned, and the impression was, as well as the reality, that as long as there was something to fill horns, the fire would continue to burn.

"You two are back early," Ondur said, the words spoken around a burp that almost got out of hand. "Did Bjarni run out?"

"No, nothing like that," Sveyin said. "It's just that we got one version of the story back in Hops, and thought all of you might have gotten another."

"Another what?"

"Another version of what happened to make them leave."

"It was the natives," Jon said with an exuberance as if he knew the answer to a riddle.

"We know that much," Sigurth said, trying not to laugh. "But how did it happen?"

"They attacked . . ."

"They attacked, that's it?"

"Look," It was Thor, who seemed to have been in a trance watching the fire, and just snapped out. "Remember how they came to visit, paddling their weird boats and twirling poles in the air?"

"Ya . . ."

"Well, no one seems to know what led up to it; but on this day, a large number of boats came, each filled with warriors who were screaming like crazy and twirling those damn poles. Thorfinn and Thorkall's people were caught by surprise, not knowing what it all meant until spears and arrows started to fly."

"And people were killed?"

"Oh ya . . . The men tried to put up a fight and some did, but most ran into the woods. They almost lost everything."

"So what saved them?"

"You'd never guess . . ."

Sigurth gave Thor one of those looks.

"It was Freydis."

"Freydis!"

"Ya . . . She went out of her mind, and if you've ever seen her do that you'd know that's scary. Anyway, she was having a fit about the men running away like they did, and was chasing after them when she came upon a dead man, Thorbrand Snorrason it was, he'd been hit by a stone projectile they'd launched, lying there with his sword beside him. She picked up his sword, stripped to the waist, turned on the natives and attacked, screaming and slashing with red hair stringing and tits flopping. It was quite a sight to see, and it drove them, with finally some help, back to the boats and away.

"When it was over, Thorfinn was disgusted. The women and kids, including his wife Gudrun, had cowered in one of the buildings and weren't hurt, but they were scared to death, as you can imagine. It wasn't long afterwards, just after the bodies were buried, in fact, that Thorfinn said this wasn't going to work, so start packing."

There were more details, with others adding aspects of it that they'd heard, but now Sigurth wasn't listening. He'd heard enough to give him visions of Freydis in action, particularly because she'd given him a look earlier that day while disembarking. That look had all kinds of possible meanings, none of them good. He looked at Sveyin, "What do you think?"

"This is your decision to make."

He saw Odd, who'd been quiet but attentive through all the conversation, in the shadows on the other side of the fire. "Odd," he said. "You're sitting there without saying anything, but I know your mind is spinning. I have a question . . . What's the soonest we can be back on the water?"

Odd responded too quickly, as if anticipating the question, "The first high tide after daylight will be mid-morning tomorrow. I can be ready if you can."

"Then spread the word. We're leaving."

Sigurth was among the last to board. The *Mule,* at the time, was floating freely with all hands at their stations, and only the last stays and the gangplank tying them to Straumsfjord. He was still on the beach because a group, including Thorfinn, had stopped by earlier, and were still there.

"I keep wishing I could think of something to say that would keep you here longer," Thorfinn said. "But it looks like I've failed."

"Ny . . . you haven't failed," Sigurth said. "I'd really like to spend more time with you as well, there's so much to discuss. But I have an obligation to my men, who I've promised that we'd return before winter. And you know as well as me, that that promise is already in jeopardy."

Thorfinn sighed, then said, "You feel the natives here are no longer a problem . . . Why do you say that?"

"Just a feeling. Their nighttime antics ended suddenly, for one thing. And small groups have only started to return. I remember what you said at Hops about working with them. I think that doing so is a good idea; good luck with it here . . . sincerely."

"Ya," Sveyin added. "You don't know how good it is for me to hear cousin say that, because he tends to be the warrior. Obviously I agree. There's a small group approaching your settlement right now . . . who could be a start."

Heads turned to see three men and a boy walking slowly in the distance. At the sight of them, Sigurth almost betrayed himself because his immediate inclination was to stand tall and wave at someone who looked familiar. But he held back, remembering the best way to keep a secret is to keep it a secret that a secret exists.

A round of goodbyes, and the last few walked to the gangplank, the stays being reeled in as they boarded.

It was late in the year, with the days almost as short as they would get. The temperature had dropped, and although there was little wind, a light rain began to fall.

Yngvi spotted her while on his way from the pens to his lodge, and wasn't surprised. She'd been there often, particularly these last few days. But now the weather was turning, so he walked over and said, "Bergljot, my joints are old and getting decrepit, but they're also wise. Right now they're telling me the weather is getting colder. So why don't you go inside where it's nice and warm. I'll stay here awhile, and if something shows up, you'll be the first to know."

She turned, the pretty face under the hood managing only a weak smile.

"Look," Yngvi continued. "The *Mule* is as fine a ship that's ever sailed, and that crew, they're really something. There's nothing that's going to stop them, so try not to worry."

She nodded, reached out and touched his arm in a way of saying thanks, and started towards the longhouse, when there was a sound on the water.

"What was that?" She said quickly returning to the bank.

"It's just Bovi and the boys," Yngvi said. "They've been fishing and are hustling in to get out of the weather."

"Any luck?" Yngvi said as the boat came through the mists from the north.

"Oh, you would call it luck, would you?" Bovi said as the sailer eased in and scraped to a stop on the shore. "The fact is we're loaded. Take a look at these," proudly holding up one of the strings.

"*Ooooeee!* That is impressive," Yngvi said. "Do you need any help?"

"Ya sure," Bovi said. "When we get unloaded, we could use a hand getting the boat up and turned over. The temperature's dropping and that could mean anything.

As they pitched in with what needed doing, the rain turned to ice crystals, and finally, as if by some magic, morphed into large white flakes that floated down in a heavenly display.

"Well look at that," Bovi said. "What did I just say?"

Bergljot watched as the men, jabbering as men do when they worked, furled the sail, lifted the mast and proceeded to turn the boat over. That done and with no more to see she turned to leave.

Then there was a strange silence. Spinning back she saw that everyone had stopped talking, and Yngvi was holding up his hand as if to say, "Hush."

"What is it?" Bovi whispered.

With visibility only a stones throw in the heavy snowfall, but with sound somehow amplified, there *was* a sound—the sound of something in the water, a rhythmic sound, almost a splashing, faint at first, but as everyone held their breaths, growing. It grew and grew until finally the grey silhouette of a ship emerged within the cascading whiteness. Then there were waving arms from the rails and shouts from voices they recognized, and before the *Mule* got close enough to the pier to tie in, the Yule Celebration had begun.

Chapter 24

SETTLEMENT

1030
(1006)

It had been a hard day with spring planting, and now that the day was over, with everyone old enough to lend a hand cleaning up for the evening meal. Everyone except Bovi and his crew who were on the water, and the brothers, Ari and Askel, who were on the hunt. Toweling off, then hanging the towel around his neck, Thorth walked bare-chested to where others were lounging, waiting for the iron to be rung at the cookhouse. He sought out Sigurth and Sveyin in particular, who he found under one of the large trees providing shade in the area. They were still in the process of putting their clothes back on, snapping them in the air first to clean off what they could.

"We got a lot done today," Thorth said, "which I should be happy about."

"Should be?" Sigurth said, stepping into his trousers. "You mean you're not?"

Thorth snorted. "Ny . . . Another day like this and you'll start packing."

"That's true, nothing's changed."

"And all because of Freydis."

"Oh ya . . . She's a bitch all right," Sigurth said, shaking his head. "But she's only part of the reason. You know, of course, that Leif considers Vinland his property, which probably means the whole island. So the longer we stay, I mean any of us, the more time we waste, accomplishing nothing for ourselves when we have better choices, seemingly without end, and free for the taking."

"Free, except for the natives that you might be taking it from," Sveyin said.

Thorth chuckled as Sigurth rolled his eyes. "But you don't know where you're going."

"Ny . . . Like I've said before, there's a big opening north of here."

"A big opening all right," Sveyin said. "I saw it with Leif when we sailed around the area, and we had the same impression others came to, which was it could go on forever. That's a mystery and a challenge if I ever heard one."

"I've heard that too," Thorth said, "but the challenge seems to be more appealing than scary, since darn near everyone here wants to go along, which *is* a problem."

Sigurth nodded, not having an answer.

"Have you determined who goes first?" Thorth asked.

"Like I said before," Sigurth said. "Everyone who sailed with me from Greenland has first choice. So far no one has said they didn't want to go. We're able to take a few more," he added, nodding to Sveyin, "but there's a limit to that. When we find a good place and settle in, we'll sail back for another load. That trip should coincide with harvest time here, allowing us to load up with vegetables and grains from the planting we're about to finish. At that time we'll take on more animals and anyone else who wants to join to the extent we can.

"What I've outlined sounds simple enough, except that it's not, because we don't have a clue as to what to expect. The trips made south these last two years had all kinds of surprises."

"So we don't know how long it will take to find a good place," Sveyin added.

"Right."

"What if Freydis and her crew are here when your ship returns?'

Thorth said. "As I recall, she had around forty people aboard . . . You'd be seriously outnumbered if there's an issue."

Sigurth groaned, then said, "I'd tell Odd to lay offshore and try to work out something from there. It would be pointless to fight about it, regardless the number."

"But she'd claim she owned everything—buildings, fields and gardens, and whatever animals left behind. Remember what she said the last time she was here?"

"Ya," Sigurth said, holding up his hands to show he didn't have an answer. He looked around to see if anyone else did.

After an awkward silence, Thorth responded, "The best I could do to help is to lie. I'd simply say you're gone for good, and try to keep that you're planning to return under wraps. That part might not be easy because you never know who might blab. Anyway, it'd be worth a try, because if it works, she might use this place as just a stopover and keep going."

"Maybe. There sure are a bunch of ifs though."

The day before leaving, they rounded up the animals intended to be taken and stored then in the pens. They also packed hay in the hold, and stocked feed, water and food on the dock. At first light the boarding began, with the animals to fill the hold coming first, the provisions next, and finally the people, who filled every nook and cranny that wasn't necessary for the crew to do their work.

The leaving was a community affair because everyone in Vinland was there, those not going nonetheless helping any way they could. When the stays were reeled in and the oars put to work, the remaining population lined the bank, exchanging best wishes and waves, and not leaving until the ship had all but disappeared.

Thorth was one of the last to walk away. As the others had earlier, he thought to count the numbers. Vinland now had fewer than twenty people.

"You don't want to turn in and take a look?" Odd said toward the end of the first day sailing north.

Sigurth shook his head, "You asked me the same question over two years ago. The inlet may have something of interest, but it wouldn't matter. I don't want to settle this close to Vinland."

"Why? There'd be no legal claim to anywhere you settled in there, and there might be advantages to having a friendly neighbor."

Sigurth gave him one of those looks that said *you really don't get it do you?* Then turned and walked away as if he had something important to do, which he didn't.

Odd looked across the deck to Sveyin who was listening and trying not to laugh, which didn't quite work. Then Odd, pinching his forehead, said, "I'm missing something, aren't I?"

Sveyin settled down too and thought, then said in hushed tones, "Sigurth's a very complicated person in ways I don't completely understand. You had no way of knowing, but most of his family was murdered when he was a tot, and he was given away to strangers on another farm far, far away. That worked out well enough, it seems, even though there had to be lingering effects of the trauma. Then there's a deep resentment, maybe even hatred, which we've both inherited from our families, for the so-called royalty who fight among themselves with other peoples blood to see who can command the riches of the land."

"That's something we're all tired of, but it's always been that way. Would you say he wants to start an independent colony . . . with no ties?"

"That could be it," Sveyin said. "And if so, I'm going to help him."

"There's our Sentinel Rock," Odd said on the second day as the bold feature named on the way south came into view. They passed it, and as it disappeared they rounded the same gradual turn they'd made on the way to Vinland, and entered the wide expanse heading west . . . the one that was rumored to go on forever. Instead of following this southern coast to wherever it led, Sigurth had Odd divert in a northwest direction, which was maintained until the expected northern coast was sighted.

'Well just look at that," Ari was heard to say as the *Mule* got in close enough to see detail.

Sigurth looked up from what he was doing, which was what he and Sveyin had done before, locating dots on paper to represent the ships's location and recording characteristics of the land near to that dot.

"Seals," Sveyin said. "Lots and lots of seals. I'm sure our hunter friends can hardly wait to go after them."

After noting what they could, a turn was made to the southwest, starting what was to become a zig-zag pattern. From this exercise, they could see that the channel, which was so wide at the beginning that land wasn't in view, and therefore over fifty miles wide, was getting narrower with each new combination of sightings. They also noticed that it was turning in a southwesterly direction. By the end of the week the channel had reduced to only a ten mile width; but then even that width ended.

They passed what they guessed was a large island that split the channel, with the southern portion, which they were on, reducing to a miles width, then expanding again to several miles as the island was passed. Sigurth ordered Odd to furl the sail, the *Mule* slowing to a drift. From where they were at the southwestern corner of the expansion, which was like a bay, the channel continued westward, but in much narrower a form.

"What are you looking for?" Sveyin asked.

"We need to stop somewhere and give everyone a break," Sigurth said. "Around here might be as good a place as any. Any suggestions?"

Sveyin looked to the mast, where Jon had climbed when the sail was taken in. "See anything of interest," he said.

"Ya, lots," Jon said after scanning in all directions. "I see high ground and bluffs on both shores, but you probably see that too. It looks like there are low lands before the bluffs, but I can't tell the extent of them . . . which means we'll have to get closer. The best of flat lands seems to be on the island."

"Anything else?"

"Ya . . . Look at the north shore. We're not close enough for me to be sure, but what I see might be boats . . . and there seems to be movement."

"You mean people?"

"Could be, unless bears are a lot smarter here. We'll have to move in closer to see for sure. Oh, there's a large waterfall east of where I'm talking about."

"Fresh water, then."

"Ya . . ."

"So?" Sveyin said, turning to Sigurth.

"I'm thinking of more than a stop," Sigurth said.

"A settlement?"

Sigurth nodded. "What do you two think. We know we intend to set up somewhere, and I rejected that first bay because I thought it too close to Vinland. Now we're not only a good deal farther, but also so far that if we don't stop somewhere around here, we could discourage the possibility of trade from home. If all our charting is near to accurate, we're now as far from Greenland as Greenland is from Norway."

"Good point," Odd said. "I Remember what Thorfinn said about that."

"Ya," Sveyin said. "Let's take a look all around. The island looks good, particularly for farming; but then the other shores might be too, if there's enough flat country in front of the high ground."

"And no natives."

"Ya . . . We should be so lucky."

They made a loop under oar, heading first to the south shore, then following it westward along a line one hundred yards away. At the continuation of the channel westward, more like a river one-half mile across, they turned north following the shore, which then turned northeasterly. It was along this stretch that Jon's sightings were verified, as the people aboard the *Mule* packing the rail came eye-to-eye with a growing number of natives who crowded the shore. He was right about boats too, as there were many of them. They weren't like the crude tubs seen near Vinland or Straumsfjord or Hops, however, these were long and narrow with pointed ends turned up.

About four miles farther they passed the outlet of a river, whose background included the stately waterfall they'd seen earlier. Beyond the river they turned south and crossed the channel to the island, where they cast anchor and tied up for the night.

"Anything around here look good to you?" Sigurth said to Yngvi after he'd stacked his oar. Yngvi had been at the rail like everyone else, and was edging past in the crowded confines to get down to the animals.

"*Ooooeey!*" Yngvi said. "I'm excited like everyone else at what we've seen. I'm not crazy about mixing it up with the natives on the north shore, though, so am eager to see what else there is. And I can tell you the animals are just as anxious as we are."

Sigurth turned and looked to Sveyin and Odd, who were close by on the stern. "Well?"

"Well what?" Sveyin said.

"What do you think?"

Odd snorted and shook his head. "They're all looking the same to me. Just don't ask me to land on rocks."

But Sveyin said, "I've been seeing things I've liked ever since we left. There have been bluffs and ridges and mountains, but nothing as rugged as Norway or as stark as Greenland. There have been trees, lots of trees, and rivers and flat lands with rushes and grasses and all sorts of stuff. I think that when we finish our tour tomorrow we'll have a number of good choices."

By noon the next day, a choice was made. The island was a strong consideration, because being over four miles wide by almost twenty miles long, it would have had endless possibilities for farming. In addition, being surrounded by water, it would seem to be more secure. An area across the channel to the south of the island's point, however, was chosen. This area, although backed by a ridge, still seemed to have enough flatland to provide more than enough to satisfy farming interests for years to come. It was also felt the high ground a ways beyond didn't complicate basic needs; and the fact the area was a direct tie to lands in three directions without indications of a native population, made it the winner.

Odd guided the *Mule* in carefully to a sideways landing into an area clear of overhanging foliage, with the bow pointing upstream, a move aided by the fact the shore was beside a slow eddy that nullified the current. From the tour they made the day before, he noticed only a slight tidal affect, which seemed to be near to the last of it in the long channel they'd sailed. Remembering some of the other landings he'd contended with, he smiled, thinking this selection was looking better all the time.

When the *Mule* was as close as made sense, several of the crew jumped over the side and waded up on shore to receive the ties. Then with men at the ropes, the ship was eased in closer and secured. This done, the gangplank was slid into place, the docking being so close to shore that it was able to reach dry land. As this was taking place, there was a rush to disembark.

"What now?" Sveyin asked as he stood by Sigurth in the stern, watching the people almost hopping as they waited their turn.

Sigurth didn't answer at first. He was half smiling at what was happening, but his eyes were darting about, looking past the immediate shore to the more inner reaches. He looked up at Jon, who had been doing the same, and when their eyes met, Jon gave a thumbs-up to indicate things were okay. Then Sigurth turned to Sveyin and said, "There's no reason to change what we agreed to earlier.

"Ari and Askel have already taken off . . . Did you see them go? They couldn't wait to test the area, so they went and won't be back anytime soon. Regardless of them, we'll do what we usually do at a temporary landing, and that's to set up shelters, make pens for the animals, establish our perimeter defense, and start cooking a meal."

"I'll stay on board," Odd said as he tied the rudder in place out of the water.

Sigurth nodded. "I expect several people will. Once we get the animals out and the hold cleaned, with the tenting we have this may be the best place to be for a while anyway."

Sigurth was one of the last to go ashore, following Sveyin with a load to where Bergljot was waiting. By this time, those first off had ranged through the woods and brambles and were circling back.

"Like anything out there?" He said to Yngvi, who was returning to where Thyri and his children had settled.

"Oh ya," Yngvi said, still bouncy with the joy of getting off the ship. "I didn't go very far, but what I saw looked good . . . A lot of work to be done though."

"We figured that to be the case wherever we landed."

Yngvi nodded. "But there's more."

"More?"

Yngvi pointed up the shore to somewhere hidden by a thicket and said, "We're not the first to come here. There's a clearing and a campsite on the other side of those bushes. It looks like it's had a good amount of use too."

Sigurth looked at Sveyin to see his response, but Sveyin had wandered off like everyone else, taking in the area to see where it seemed best to settle. Then he heard a comment that drew his attention and saw someone pointing west. Turning to see what that was about, he looked to the high bluff less than a mile away, close enough for those with keen eyes to see movements.

"Oh shit," he muttered.

"What did you expect?" Someone said, and he turned to see Bergljot sitting on stowage, trying to keep track of Yrsa who was into going every which way.

"We spent the better part of two days sailing around the bay," Bergljot said, "so every native in four directions knows we're here. By the way, has any other ship come this far?"

"Not that I know of."

"Then you can imagine the impact the *Mule* made."

Sigurth nodded. He turned back to see Sveyin returning from one direction, Ondur and Thor from the opposite, and others in between. Instead of waiting for a number to assemble, he went back to shore and the *Mule,* where not unexpectedly, Odd was leaning on the rail waiting for him.

"Do you think there'll be a welcoming committee?" Odd said.

"Anything's possible," Sigurth said, "but nothing's changed. We'll set up temporarily as planned, then go from there. You can be a help by putting Jon atop from time to time to see what's happening across the bay."

"Ya . . . already thought of that," Odd said. "Those small boats on the north shore, they're a different kind, longer and sleeker than the tubs we'd seen before. My guess is the natives there can cross the bay any time they want.

"That could be a problem."

Sigurth turned to see a group had gathered where Bergljot was seated. "It looks like its time to get organized," he said. "Let's join them."

The next month saw a level of activity that most would remember the rest of their lives. From the first hint of dawn to the final fade of day, everyone was involved as if the work was essential to their survival. Bushes were cleared and burned; rocks were moved and stacked; and trees were cut and trimmed, with logs and every limb deemed usable dragged to a stacking area. As this was occurring, stumps, which now protruded like warts all around, were dug up and hauled away.

The mules, which had been the butt of jokes from the start, turned out to be invaluable. With simple harnesses developed earlier at Vinland, they were worked as teams to drag logs, extract stumps and do the heavy pulling. When grounds were cleared and the uses of land determined, simple plows were contrived, again hooking up the mules to prepare for planting.

"*Haaaii!*" Sigurth shouted, snapping a whip over the mules heads for effect, then grabbing handles to wrestle the improvised plow as it moved forward, cutting through an eon of tangle and turning over an uneven furrow to layer against the one before. At the end of the line, which was the last one for the field, he stopped to catch his breath and shake out muscles. The mules, although welcoming the stop, turned their heads and looked back, almost as if saying, "What's next ass-hole," in a way that made Sigurth laugh as he stood wiping his brow. Since this was the last row for the day, he unhitched them, and began to lead them by rope towards a crude corral, which was easy to do because they understood perfectly and almost ran over him as they approached.

Sveyin met him as he headed to where most of the men were gathering, which was at the shore near where the ship was tied. "That about wraps up the first stage," he said.

Sigurth stopped and turned to look at what he was referring to—acres and acres of uneven but cleared land with only a few specimen trees remaining. What had once been scrub forest was now mostly open ground, punctuated by scattered piles of debris.

All this was part of what Sveyin proposed the day they'd landed. In his opinion, partly based on his experiences at Vinland, it was a mistake to worry about permanent lodging at first. After all, he argued, it was summer, so tents and lean-tos, along with the ship, could provide shelter well enough for months to come. Instead he felt the fields be given top priority. Therefore as much of the forest as determined should be cleared, and then fields and gardens planted with hopes of a harvest before the end of the season. If they could also collect a harvest from Vinland, they'd be in excellent shape for their first winter. When the planting was done, there would be the time for constructing lodges and other more permanent facilities for which timbers would already be stacked.

Sigurth agreed, the plan Sveyin outlined made perfect sense. And now that the first part of it was over, a weak "yippee" was all he was able to say.

"I think we should all take the day off tomorrow," Sveyin said. "Maybe have a special meal . . . I mean, everyone deserves one."

"Okay by me," Sigurth mumbled, slipping off his clothes and wading into the water to join the rest who'd already done so, and who seemed too tired to do more than wallow.

"Did I hear you say, 'No work tomorrow?'" Ondur said, recognizable now after ducking under several times and rubbing off the dirt and grime and sweat streaks that had made him anybody. "Please tell me that's what I heard."

There was a chorus of similar comments, mostly in jest, but with a hint of pleading.

Sigurth didn't answer. Instead he slipped below the water, and after ridding himself of generous amounts of soil and its workings like Ondur had done, held his breath and let the coolness of it sooth him to the core. Rising slowly, he rubbed his tangled hair another time, as if it accomplished something, then looked around, pretending to be surprised at all the stares.

"Whaaaat?"

"Tomorrow," Ondur said. "Did you say no work tomorrow?"

Sigurth pinched his face as if that was a very serious thing to consider, then broke into a big, wide, shit-eating grin, all of which was rewarded by hoots and well-aimed splashes.

He fell asleep quickly that night, doing so shortly after eating, still sitting cross-legged beside a small fire, and might have remained there about to tip over if Thor hadn't thoughtfully nudged him, at which time he went to his bedroll under one of the few trees remaining. Later, however, some time between midnight and dawn, for a reason he never questioned, his eyes blinked open. He sat up, taking several moments to focus on what he could see at the time, which on this occasion was a lot because of a near to full moon and an almost cloudless sky.

He heard a sound by the edge of the clearing to the north, and knew that Yngvi was out there somewhere, it being his time in the rotation. Looking to the *Mule*, which was quiet and lonely, he detected a movement that was probably Jon. All seemed well, which should have satisfied him, but for the same reason he awakened he couldn't go back to sleep. So he dressed, collected a few weapons and headed out, moving with the shadows towards the bluff, which seemed to be the concern drawing him on.

He'd been to the high ground once before, so he didn't have to invent a way in the dark across the stream that ran beside it and then the slope. That hike had been on a day before the heavy work in the fields started, and during it he'd learned the top presented views in all directions. It also appeared that it was a favorite spot, and may have been for a number of years, for the natives this side of the channel.

He reached the top, moving into the shadows of a small area to the side, where he stopped. Seeing or hearing or sensing nothing of concern at first, he started to move to another shadow, when he heard a cough that sounded like it came from the north end. It took several minutes to circle around to that part, the top being irregular with only a few hundred feet in one dimension, but he succeeded, arriving where he could see who it was. The who were four in number, bundled and sleeping around what had been a small fire in a hollow sheltered from view.

He knew little about either of the nations on opposite sides of the river as he'd been giving his attention to everything else since landing. Those from the south had been seen on the bluff he was on from time to time, and groups of them had come to the edge of the settlement as well; but when they did they'd only watch the busyness, with few attempts at communication.

Sigurth stayed for what must have been the better part of an hour, a long time when trying to be quiet while unsure of what to do next. He didn't want to attack, that much he knew. Both Sveyin and Bergljot had spoken at every opportunity about the fact that if we were serious about a settlement, then we needed to . . . what were the words? . . . intermingle or coexist with them. Splitting a few skulls didn't seem a good way to start; and some kind of communication, as friends, was hard to imagine at this time.

He decided to do nothing. He wanted to find out more about these people, and reluctantly, which spoiled the fun, he admitted the best way to find out more was to keep from revealing he might be lurking about. So he retraced his steps down the bluff and back into the settlement, catching a few more hours of sleep before the noise of a new day awakened him.

It wasn't really the normal noise of the morning that caught his attention; it was the presence of two people who sat cross-legged nearby in quiet conversation, waiting for him to stir.

Sigurth listened for a while, but was unable to hear enough to make out what they were saying, so he eased up on his elbow, yawned and rubbed his eyes, saying, "I thought this was to be a day of rest. What are you bastards hounding me for now? The sun's hardly up."

"We may have a problem," Odd said. "I've alerted the crew."

"Alerted the crew?"

"And I've sent word to everyone else," Sveyin said.

Sigurth sat up with that. "What's this about?"

"Our neighbors," Odd said.

Sigurth snapped his head to look at the bluff, not understanding because he'd seen nothing of concern just hours before.

"No not them," Sveyin said. "It's the ones across the bay."

"How so?"

"You know," Odd began, "that not long after we settled here, they got real curious. Actually, they'd probably been curious since that day we sailed by their shore. Well, recently their curiosity ramped up. We told you when it did, that two of those slender boats of theirs had paddled by, the natives in them looking us over. It was easy for them to do because they could follow their shore, cross the channel at the narrows west of here, then swing by."

"Recently, a couple of them came ashore and walked around," Sveyin said.

"Ya, I saw that," Sigurth said. "We were all working our asses off in the fields and didn't pay as much attention to them as we should have . . . the friendly waves our women made not being enough."

Odd nodded. "Well, they now probably know as much about us as they feel they need to know . . . and that is that we're a small group with a large ship and many other things they'd like to have."

"Who'd be easy pickings," Sigurth added.

"Exactly," Odd said, "and that's why we're here. Jon climbed to his roost at daybreak this morning, as was his custom, to scan the water for any movement. "Well, today he saw some."

"Where? How many?'

"Right where you'd expect . . . at the narrows. It was too far for an exact count, but he could make out a line of them that extended all the way across."

"Remember now," Sveyin said. "We counted over two dozen boats on their shore the day we passed by."

Sigurth was up now, getting dressed. "And you're concerned we might have a hundred or more warriors on our shore in another hour or so."

"It doesn't look good," Odd said. "Anyway, we need to be prepared. We've been so busy doing our own thing, we haven't done as much with our neighbors as we probably should have. We don't know, for instance, if those across the bay to the north are friendly with those to the south. They could be teaming up with them right now."

"I don't think so," Sigurth said.

"Why do you say that?" Odd said.

"Just a hunch."

"I'd agree," Sveyin said. "Bergljot has made an effort to communicate with the ones who've stopped by, and she didn't get the impression they were aggressive. She also said she noticed they were apprehensive when they saw one of those long watercraft paddling past offshore."

"What are your ideas about what we should do now?"

"One idea is to load up the *Mule* and sail into the bay," Odd said. "We would be able to defend better there than anywhere else . . . and even sail away if we chose to."

"And throw away all we've done?" Sigurth said, his voice rising.

"We've got some bad choices," Sveyin said. "We also don't wish to throw away lives."

"Well, we'd probably throw away Ari and Askel," Sigurth said. "They're hunting again and will be stranded. And we'd be throwing away the dream of not only those here right now, but also those waiting at Vinland."

"Ya da," Odd said. "We've thought of that too. But we need a plan everyone can agree on."

"You mean we need to take a vote?"

"It's your ship, so you either tell us what we're going to do, or we do what most people want."

Sigurth swore. He was in the process of putting on his scabbard sling, but he stopped, dropping it by his bedroll, kicking up dirt instead. "Okay, get off your asses. We've got to get everyone together . . . and fast!"

"So that's the story," Sveyin said to everyone gathered on the shore beside the landing. He'd explained the situation, which most were already aware of, and described the options that were available. "What would you like to do?"

"You mean we have a say in this?" Yngvi said.

"Yes," Sveyin said. "If most of you want to leave, Sigurth will offer his ship."

"What's the plan if we decide to stay and fight?"

All eyes turned to Sigurth, who was trying hard to keep his feelings in check. He took a few deep breaths, and said, "We want to be at peace with our neighbors, so we'll start by doing what we can to promote that. But if we don't succeed, and they attack, we'll fight back as if our lives and all our dreams depend on it, because they do. The natives know what we know, and that's that they have four times as many men as we do. What they don't know is that our crew is not only heavily armed, but also extensively trained in combat. If a fight starts, the first thing we'll do is kill their leaders. Hopefully that will cause them to give up the fight and leave. If they don't, we'll just have to do our best and see what happens."

There were a few moments of mumbling within the group, which settled with Yngvi speaking out, "I'm for staying. I'm not as heavily trained as others might be, but I can fight. I'll live here or die here, but I won't choose to run away from the most delightful situation, with the most promise, that I've ever been in. Sure things are going to be rough from time to time; but we expected that, and we can't expect it to be different anywhere else."

"Ya, ya" . . . "I feel the same way" . . . "Let's fight the bastards" . . . "Count me in" . . . resounded from the rest.

Sigurth swallowed, at a loss of how to respond. He'd expected otherwise . . . not from the crew, who he felt would do whatever he asked, but from the others who had wives and family to consider. He looked over the small crowd, almost choking, thought a moment, then said. "Okay, we stay! . . . Now listen up, this is what we're going to do."

They came. Later in the morning Jon announced he could see movement at the narrows again. It was as if the craft had collected there for the leaders to refine a strategy before moving on. A little later, he confirmed this as the lead group turned the point west of them and headed their way, followed by group after group until there was a solid array of boats and men and splashing oars. If that weren't enough to generate nervous swallows, it could be seen that faces were painted to look as fearful as imaginations could contrive.

The leading boats could have beached anywhere, but they continued onward, the ones behind them following, towards the *Mule* and the landing where the settlers could be seen together, everyone yelling and waving to get their attention. Another attraction was the small skiff anchored fifty feet further offshore of the *Mule* with a man standing up in it. Except that as the natives approached, they could see that the man was really a stood-up log dressed as a man, with a head-like top made up with crude but identifiable facial features.

The crafts covered the half mile distance after making the turn in a time measured in heart beats, and soon there was an armada clustered four rough lines deep in an arc centered on the *Mule*.

Sigurth thought, *Oh shit . . . this better work!*

Aboard the *Mule*, both men and women were standing at the rail, smiling and talking and waving as if they were greeting old friends. Sigurth was on shore doing the same thing, but behind his smile he was seeking to identify those who were the leaders. When he concluded what he could from shore, he went on board and continued the same there, coordinating with Sveyin on his findings.

Finally it was time. He went to the rail, and smiling his best-friend best, peered eye-to-eye with each of the leaders identified, and said words of welcome with readable tone and inflection. Then he called attention to Thor, who was with a group on shore west of the ship, standing behind a concealed shield-wall that would pop into place if fighting began. Thor picked up his bow, looked in the same manner as Sigurth had at the leader nearest him, then drew back an arrow and shot it over and past the crafts, whose riders ducked, only to see the arrow "thud" into the mannequin on the skiff. Next Sigurth pointed to Ondur, who was east of the ship, and he did the same. Then Sveyin, in quick succession, sent three arrows home, with Sigurth completing the show with a final shot to the pitiful head of the now porcupined log.

The meaning of all that had happened was hopefully clear—that we wish to be friends, but will kill you if you choose otherwise, starting with your Chiefs.

There was an impasse. There was no more to say, the settlers now standing in stony silence, while the natives began to stir, mumbling amongst themselves. One of the craft edged in close to the skiff, with a brave standing and putting a foot aboard to straddle and withdraw the arrows. At this, Sveyin yelled *"Ny o Ny!"* and loosed another arrow, whose impact startled the man, causing him to fall back, tipping the craft and spilling all four on board in the water.

There was an uproar from one end of the armada to the other as those in other crafts stretched to see what was happening; but there was little said from the settlers, as the few who started to laugh were quickly shushed.

After the scene calmed, there was a period, like a small eternity, when the man singled out as the leader, who was sitting in a craft near the center of the armada, and Sigurth, standing at the rail with his arms crossed, stared at each other. Then, slowly, Sigurth broke into a welcoming smile again, and with arms extended, beckoned for the Chief to approach the ship. The Chief was startled and looked about, but Sigurth kept on with his appeal. With little choice now, the Chief had his craft paddled around and through those between him and the *Mule*, stopping below the rail where Sigurth stood.

Sigurth addressed him, speaking in the tone of one friend to another, loud enough so most could hear, and using sweeping gestures to assist the meanings, said, "Sir, we welcome you to our land. We have come from afar to settle here and make this our home. We hope we can be friends . . . good friends who will live together in peace and share the fruits of our labor. Towards that end I give you this." He reached below the rail and lifted out a sack. From the sack he pulled out a wooden eagle, a project he'd worked on during the long hours the winter before. The Chief was stunned, not knowing what to say or do.

"Now go," Sigurth said, pointing to convey his meaning. "But go as friends. We look forward to meeting again when we are better prepared to show you the hospitality we intend."

Nothing happened at first, the Chief looking at the eagle, a magnificent carving unlike anything he'd ever seen, then at Sigurth, and back again.

Finally he stood, which caused no little consternation for the others in his craft because the craft appeared easy to turn over. Once stabilized, he began to speak, quietly at first, but growing in volume as, it seemed, his thoughts became better organized. Then he removed a highly fashioned necklace, probably an amulet, and gave it to Sigurth. With that he spoke again, directing his comments to the other craft, sitting down when he'd finished.

As quickly as the armada had rounded the point and amassed before them, it turned around and paddled away.

"A day of rest, my ass," Ondur said as the last of them disappeared around the point. "We just about went to war."

Sigurth and Sveyin looked at each other, not laughing, and like most everyone who had sense enough to realize what had just happened, exhaled in relief. Then calling Odd over to hear, Sigurth said, "We ducked the arrows this time, and the impressions we made may last. However, they might not, and if that is the case we need to be better prepared and stronger. I think we should put together a small crew and return to Vinland right away. Before a month is over, we can have everyone together again, with work well underway on permanent and more defensible quarters."

With that Sigurth left, as did almost everyone else, to begin thinking about what the next challenge would be. Sveyin, however, stayed on board with Odd to work out the details for the quick trip Sigurth suggested.

"What he said makes sense, don't you think?" Sveyin said.

But Odd didn't seem to be listening.

"You don't agree?" Sveyin repeated.

"Oh that . . . of course I agree. It makes perfect sense; and with Jon's eyes and your sketches, I can retrace our route blindfolded. I'm shaking my head at what just happened. It's hard to believe we're standing here without blood and guts all around. And the carving . . . Where did that come from?"

"From Sigurth," Sveyin said. "He just happens to be an excellent carver, but that's another story. Anyway, back home in the marina near Bird Mountain is a ship called the *Sea Eagle*. We've both been to battle on it, as have many others in our district. Sigurth said that if he ever returns to Norway, he'll carve a fitting keel-head for that ship. The carving he gave away was a small version of the carving he intended."

Chapter 25

WE

1030
(1007)

Boats were't a problem. Sigurth had been working on boats, including all their components and designs, for as far back as he could remember. But buildings, that was another matter; and that was the problem, because when the *Mule* sailed away, the next need was for permanent quarters, which fell on those left behind.

Sveyin had reasoned earlier that clearing and planting should be the first order, and that recommendation had been followed. Now everyone looked again to him for direction, for he had the only experience in this sort of thing, that being the Vinland buildings. Only those buildings weren't impressive, even Sveyin not caring for them. So there were several problems: Where to build, how to build, and what to build.

The first, the where, was easy. The small creek that snaked its way out of the high ground and passed below the bluffs to the west before emptying in the bay, was the logical place to start because of easy access to fresh water. The bay's water, although near to being fresh, was still somewhat blended with the ocean.

The next problem wasn't only how to build, but also how much to build. When the *Mule* left there were three dozen to provide for. When it returned, and depending how many decided to join from Vinland, there could be as many as sixty. This speculation segued into a form of entertainment, in which the discussions on how to proceed turned out to be mainly arguments between Sigurth and Sveyin, who turned disagreeing into an art form to the delight of most everyone else. Neither of them liked the structures at Greenland or the Way Station, where buildings started as holes in the ground, and ended with sods arched around to complete an enclosure.

"I'll lay out under a tree before I'll crawl into one of those damned gopher holes," Sigurth said, and most agreed with him.

In the end, they settled on building in a manner with which they were familiar, replicating what they had seen around the farms in Norway, with an exception to the use of nails and metal fasteners. There weren't any, so shaped, interlocking intersections with wooden plugs, joints somewhat reflective of those in ships, were devised. Then on the first selected site, for a multipurpose Community Building, a base platform to serve as the floor was raised and leveled. Large, flat rocks were next set in place as the foundation for the walls, with log posts following. All posts for a sixteen by forty foot building had been set, and the log rafters forming a gable roof for half its length framed, when a call was heard.

"A ship, a ship . . . I see a ship!" It was from Ygg, one of Yngvi's children, who was high on a tree and had a clear view of the channel to the east, the channel to the sea.

Sigurth was on a wall beam at the time, working with Thor and Ondur to wrestle one of the rafters in place and complete it intricate anchorage. He couldn't stand up and look until finished, and when he did, he understood the reason for the more than normal excitement.

"Just look at that," he heard Bergljot say from below.

By then the *Mule* was clearly in view, still too far away to hear the yells from the smiling faces lining the rail, but close enough to see that the ship was jammed. It was more than jammed. Beside it was the fisher, under its own sail but till tied, and farther astern something else.

"What's behind the *Mule?*" Sigurth said while straddling the rafter and trying to balance on the wall beam.

Sveyin was now there, having climbed the scaffolding to get a better view, and was standing on the beam while hanging on his cousin. He began to laugh.

"What is it?"

"I think they're towing a barge," Sveyin said, continuing to laugh while jumping down and racing off to the landing. Sigurth had to wrap up what he was working on before following.

At the landing, there was about as much turmoil as six dozen people could generate, with people and animals and stowage intermingling with delighted, and often surprised reunions. Among the latter was Thorth, who stood along the rail, beaming at all the commotion.

"Thorth," Sigurth said as he finally joined the throng, "What are you doing here? I didn't expect to see you, or this many. Who did you leave behind? And how'd that come about?" He added, pointing to the strange vessel being unloaded beside the *Mule*.

"There's much to tell," Thorth said. "Let's get all of us settled in somewhere, then we can relax and talk. Looks to me like you're kind of busy anyway."

That was good advice, with the result that in the remaining hours of the day, while the arrivals unloaded and set up tents and other make-do accommodations, those not needed to help continued with what they'd been doing. When word was given to stop, the log framing for the main building was complete, standing with skeleton ribs in the fading light, and the sites for the next two buildings were leveled and ready for construction to begin.

Sigurth was the last to join the group that included Thorth, Odd, Sveyin and a few others. "I've looked over those that came with you," he said, plopping down on an improvised log bench, "and can't think of anyone who isn't here."

Thorth nodded. "That's the part that's even hard for me to believe."

Sigurth looked at Odd. "You look as relieved as I've ever seen you. How did anyone smooth-talk you into dragging this weird flotilla along? You must have had the great God Thor beside you all the way to pull it off."

"Don't think I don't know it," Odd said. "I'd protested at first, and was close to being right about it when along the way winds got rough. A couple times we almost cut the barge loose before the damn thing took us all down. But it was hard to resist trying to help with what they were doing."

"Which was?" Sigurth said, returning to Thorth.

Thorth was trying not to smile, but was obviously pleased with what had happened. He said, "Being left behind wasn't a good feeling. When you sailed away your words stayed with us . . .The ones that said,'the longer we stay here, the more time we waste.'"

"But I thought you were going to stay. I mean, weren't you sort of Leif's agent?"

"Ya, that's true. Several others intended to stay as well. But then they got infected too and soon we were all talking about how much we could take away if we had the chance, the takeaways being the fruits of our labor."

"And the barge?"

Thorth laughed. "We left Leif's buildings and the bunkhouses, but we tore down everything else—the sheds and storage shacks and all. From these we made a barge so we could bring along as much of what we couldn't squeeze on the *Mule* as possible."

"Looks like quite a lot," Sigurth said.

"And a good thing too." Thorth said. "I see what you've been able to do so far, and have a good idea how much more is needed to get us under cover by winter. My guess is that everything we brought is going to be put to use."

When the first snow fell, they weren't ready. Beside the main longhouse, two bunkhouses, several barns and pens, a cookhouse, a shop, and a shelter for the *Mule* were all thought to be necessary; but only the first few were complete. So the effort for the rest, which had been intense before, rose to even a higher level with chopping and sawing and chipping continuing past dark, at times being conducted under torchlight. It wasn't until what was recognized as the shortest day of the year and the time for a Yule celebration, that enough had been completed so that relaxing could be considered.

Yngvi stepped in and quickly shut the door, a cloud billowing past him into the room. He stamped his feet and beat the snow from his wraps, at the same time relishing the warm air that rushed to envelope him. *"Ooooy,"* he said.

"The animals okay?" Svein said, knowing where he'd been.

"Ya da," Yngvi said. "The barn still needs work, and snow is drifting in in spots, but at least they're inside, crowding together and glad to be there.

"Damn, this weather is something. I've never seen so much snow."

"Is it still falling?" Sveyin said.

"Ya . . . and drifting too. If this keeps up we'll be getting from one place to another by way of tunnels."

Yngvi removed his scarves and wraps, hanging them up, then walked over to the central fire where Bergljot, Thyri and several children were gathered. "How is it going with our guests," he said, nodding to the three native girls who were among them.

He was referring to a special project of Bergljot's that had begun soon after starting the settlement. She had reasoned, really drawing from what others had said, that if the colony was to succeed and survive, it needed to mingle with the natives, and mingling meant learning their language and customs.

Since that day when the largest ship ever seen appeared, and then made its parade around the bay, the settlers had been the foremost item of interest to natives in all directions, most particularly those to the south. Groups from there were the most frequent visitors, stopping to see what wonders were developing in one of their fishing areas. For most of the settlers, who were usually busy, these visits, since they weren't being made by bedecked warriors waving weapons, were of little concern and generally ignored.

Not so for Bergljot, who mindful of the special need, took it upon herself to be a welcoming committee to whoever came near. She greeted them with a smile and comment, and although never understood by word, always conveyed the messages of peace and friendship. She invited them to sit and converse, and usually laughable results, and treated them to simple fare from the cook-pots. In all of this, Yrsa's scrambling about helped no little amount.

In the course of a number of those visits, Bergljot singled out three young girls who she thought might be the bridge to the mingling that was needed, the boys with their manly complications, and older visitors with their inhibitions, seeming less of a way to go. This led to invitations to stay over as guests, which if understood, were initially rejected. But the girls became regular visitors, and in early winter after the first snows disappeared, a final visit was made, this time with tote-bags. Little was known about their nation, or of them, except that their names were Potanchachee, Salanaias and Nychanachia, listing them from shortest to tallest, and that they were ten to twelve years old.

"They're doing fine," Bergljot answered, then turning to the girls, said, "Say hello to Yngvi."

To which the girls understandably said, "Hello Yngvi," then giggled.

"Do you happen to know where Sigurth is right now?" Bergljot asked.

"No, he wasn't with me," Yngvi said. "My guess he's in the bunkhouse where he's been staying No-one's outside right now if they don't have to be."

"Any idea what he's doing?"

"Not really. He could be carving again. He spends a lot of spare time with that. Why?"

"Well, I've been working on the loom," Bergljot said pointing to the assembly against the wall. "I need more yarn, and was going to teach the girls how to spin on a distaff, but remembered Sigurth was supposed to be expert at it."

"Sigurth? Making yarn?"

Sveyin, who couldn't help but hear, laughed, saying, "Sounds weird, doesn't it?"

"Ya Sigurth, the mighty warrior . . . making yarn?"

"Strange as it may seem, he does, or at least he did. He grew up in a craft-shop with as great a seamstress as you'll ever meet. She employed and taught local girls how to do that, and guess who was right in the middle of it all. The girls used to tease him about his attempts at doing what they were doing, so you can imagine what happened . . . He got better at it than any of them.

"Would you like me to see what he's doing?"

"Oh, I hate to send anyone out is this weather."

But Sveyin was already up, slipping into wraps. "I've patched and sharpened everything I own, and am bored, bored, bored. This weather can't be that bad." The words had hardly time to hang in the air when he was gone.

It took longer than the going and returning should have taken, so in time the hope of getting assistance was all but forgotten. Then there were sounds from outside, sounds that penetrated the heavily built, insulated and now snow-banked walls, sounds that could have been of battle except for the tones that went with them, followed by the door opening and two snow-covered abominations bursting in.

"*Whaat?*" Sveyin said to the gaping stares.

"He started it," Sigurth said, rosy cheeks above his snow covered scruff, with more snow scattering from every wrap he untangled. Sveyin was still laughing, or at least it sounded like Sveyin, which wasn't confirmed until he'd discarded enough to be recognized. During all of this Bergljot shook her head, but Yrsa squealed and ran down the aisle to tackle her daddies legs.

"So what is it you'd like help with?" Sigurth said as he walked as if his entrance was perfectly normal to where the girls were gathered.

"With making yarn," Bergljot said, still not settled and rolling her eyes. "I was going to teach the girls, but somehow thought you might be better at it."

"Oh my," Sigurth said, holding up his calloused hands, then wringing them together as if to loosen them up. "I don't know about that . . . It's been a long time."

"Well, give it a try."

"*Hmmm* . . . Let's see."

He picked up a bundle of wool wrapped around a stick and looked at it, turning it around and around until he found an end that looked like a place to begin. Then he took the distaff wheel that Bergljot was holding. Getting started, however, didn't go smoothly, with the bond breaking with the first few spins.

When Nychanaachia giggled at the look on his face at the first failures, with hardly realizing what he was doing, he reached over and bopped her on the head, the rest in the group almost bursting sides while the poor girl's face turned red.

Finally, he made a good connect and began spinning, his eyes focussed and his fingers somehow finding an amount of nimble that worked. Bit by bit the material spun out and a thread grew, the distaff slowly dropping. When this sequence had been repeated with several lengths now on a skein around the wheel, he stopped and said, *"Ta daaah!"*

Several hours more were spent as he worked with each of the girls, showing them how to hold the bundle, how to connect, and how to spin the distaff, all simple looking but difficult to perform. This could have gone much longer, but Bergljot came to the rescue.

"That's enough for now," she said. "We'll practice this more tomorrow, but this has been a good start. Besides, we're getting hungry and there's a pot to fix. Sveyin, could you find some of that grog you've been hiding while I fix something for us and our guests to eat?"

Sveyin was moving before the last words were out, and was soon back with a small cask and several horns, returning to the ledge in the corner where Sigurth and Yngvi settled.

"Skoll!" Sveyin said after the first pour, then after all had been drained, added, "That was quite a show. I'd never seen you do that . . . had only heard that at one time you had."

"That was a long time ago," Sigurth said, half laughing. "I really didn't think I could do it again. It's not like the kind of thing I've been thinking about."

"So what have you been thinking about?" Yngvi said.

Sigurth held out his horn. "It takes more than one to loosen my tongue, don't you know."

Sveyin poured all around and sat back.

"Actually, there's a lot to think about," Sigurth said.

"Like?"

"For instance, how's it going in here. I mean with languages?"

"It's slow," Sveyin said. "The native girls are doing better than we are. Which forces me to bring up the fact that you aren't taking part. It's just as important that you learn their language as the rest of us."

"Ya, ya." Sigurth said nodding.

"No seriously. When are you going to spend time here trying to learn more?"

"Okay, I'll come over."

"What else is on your mind?"

Sigurth sighed. "It's more than their language. It's what they're all about."

"All about?"

"You know . . . What are their skills? How do they live and survive? What do they believe in?"

"Well, we've got to know how to talk, to understand each other, before we can really get into those things."

"You might be right," Sigurth said.

"Darn, so what does this mean? Does it mean we can agree on something?"

Whoops, that's not likely."

"Which means it's time for another horn."

By early spring, everyone was on edge, eager to get outside and into the pile of work waiting. Sigurth leaned on a rail forming the corral, and looked at the melting snow, the water meandering by in a thousand rivulets wherever it could go on its way to the bay, much of it settling in shallow ponds as a step to making mud.

"The ice is gone out there," he said, almost to himself as if no one was listening.

Yngvi nodded. "I don't know what's on your mind, but you're thinking, and I'm all ears"

"There's so much to consider. Like which comes first?"

"What do you think?"

Sigurth said, "Whatever we can do I guess. We're all itching for something. After a long winter being cooped up, we're mostly just anxious to get to work."

"Ya, the animals are like that too. I can sense that they'd like to get out and move around, maybe find something fresh and green to eat."

"Don't see anything green popping up yet."

"Ny, not yet, but soon," Yngvi said.

"Have we set aside enough land for pasture?"

"Oh I think so. But if it isn't, I know where we can turn."

"The island?"

"Ya, the island. From what we've seen from the ship, it's flat with grasses from one end to another. I'd love to go there and see for sure."

Sigurth nodded. "That's one of the trips on my list. It's really an easy thing to do because we could get Bovi to take you over in the fisher. Moving animals in the barge wouldn't be difficult either. The problem I see with animals over there is safety. We don't know whether wolves are about, or bears, or those big cats we've heard about. Then there are the natives across the bay. Remember the way they were painted last year? I don't think we've seen the last of them."

"Ya . . . You said 'one of the trips.'"

"Ya . . . Nobody knows we're here. So another trip should be made, at least one to the Way Station. Informing them where we are could lead to traffic in our direction."

"What about Vinland. Don't you want to go there?"

"Not really. I don't care about anything Freydis is a part of. Many of those on her ship are good people though."

"You said 'at least' to the Way Station," Yngvi said.

Sigurth didn't answer at first, then said, "Greenland . . . That's a long nasty trip in open water; but it's one that may need to be made for no other reason than women."

"Women?"

"Ya . . . It's not right the way things are. I have a great crew, many have worked with me for years either at the marina or on our farm; but they're men, and it's not fair to keep them from having a life. As far as I'm concerned, it's a top priority for them."

"Oh Bullshit!"

"What?"

Yngvi doubled up laughing. Then he straightened, still with a smirk as if he'd been really funny. "Oh, I believe you're serious about the men, but you haven't said anything about what you want to do for yourself. You want to sail the river going west, don't you?"

Before Sigurth could answer, there were sloshing sounds, and the two turned to see Sveyin, Odd and Thorth approaching.

"There you are," Sveyin said. "It looks like we might be able to get going on a few things."

"Tell me about it," Sigurth said, watching as they picked their final steps through the mud up to them.

"We're all itching to do something," Thorth said.

"We've been discussing the same thing."

"Well, we can't do this yet, and we can't do that either," Yngvi said, pointing every which way. "So while we're all tippee-toeing through the mud trying to figure out what we can do, why don't we get the *Mule* back in the water and see what there is along the river going west. An awareness to what it has to offer might mean a great deal to all of us here."

"West?" Thorth said.

"Yngvi's just baiting you," Sigurth said. "He knows I want to see more in that direction. But what we were really discussing were actions to consider now, and putting the *Mule* in the water was part of all of them."

After repeating the options, Thorth spoke, "Sigurth, it's your ship and your crew, and most everything about coming here has been under your direction, so I guess you can do anything you want. The options just mentioned sound good; but on the other hand, what's been done here to date has the making of a large farm, not a community. Do you intend to be a Chieftain or King like we've been used to, or something else? When you mentioned the word "we" in your statement before leaving Vinland, you got all of us excited."

Sigurth bristled and Sveyin laughed.

"I can answer that," Sveyin said. "We're both, and I think the rest of you feel the same way, sick and tired of the mythical concept of royalty. So that's the farthest thing from his mind. The arrangements built so far are my fault, if there's a fault to them as they were intended as a start to get us all into shelter as quickly as possible. Beyond what we now have, plans need to be made for the farms and businesses that will make up our community, and bring the concept of "we" to front and center.

"I also don't think we should try to solve all of this while standing in the mud and hanging on this rail. There's a large tree back by the buildings with the largest area of dry ground available around it. Let's hold our own first Althing there right now and invite everyone to participate. I think a consensus on which option to take will be easy to reach, particularly once the concept for the community is explained. As for the trip to the west, I'm curious about that too; but now might not be the time."

They sloshed their way back to the tree, made announcements at each of the buildings and wherever people were gathered, and soon the population of the settlement was outside and gathered. Sigurth looked at Thorth and Sveyin with a silent appeal to lead the discussion, but Sveyin deferred to Thorth, who'd been the leader of such things at Vinland, and with that the meeting, the first Althing in the new settlement, began.

Thorth repeated what had been discussed at the rail, which included Sveyin's comments on community. With those words it was as if the sun broke through on a cloudy day, the light coming from faces as the concept of "we" hit home. It was obvious, that although only discussed in whispers if discussed at all, the concept had been on their minds, with hopes that it could be.

Several other topics were volunteered and discussed, the most notable being by Bergljot about her passion for coexisting and integrating with the native population. The three girls were beside her, and although none were yet confident enough to speak, their expressions said all that was necessary.

A trip intended to be quick was made to the east with only as many on board as needed to manage the ship, and with Odd and Thorth directing what was done. The first stop was at the Way Station.

"Where have all of you been?" Ingivar said to those lining the rail as the *Mule* eased in. "And where's Sigurth, doesn't he own this ship?"

Aside from the crew who jumped off to anchor the ship, Thorth was the first down the gangplank, going immediately to greet the portly friend he hadn't seen in five years.

"I can't tell you how glad I am to see you, "Thorth said. "In remote places like we've been in, you never know who's still alive."

Ingivar laughed, grabbing Thorth's hand and almost crushing it. "You're a sight for sore eyes. There's got to be a lot to tell."

"There is, but we're only here for a quick stay, so tell me what's happened."

"Not so fast," Ingivar said. "We haven't had traffic in over six months; so if you expect to get any news out of me, you're going to stay long enough to lift our spirits. Besides I told those at the cookhouse to start preparing for guests as soon as I saw your sail."

It wasn't a pleasant day, with a stiff wind in from the east with temperatures still just above freezing, so Ingivar led Thorth into one of the mounded longhouses that composed the Station, settling on a ledge near the center, even though the fire was only embers at the time. A quick hand signal to a servant girl had her scurrying for horns.

"Where's Sigurth?" Ingivar said. "And where's everyone else?" It looks like you barely had enough aboard to get here. What you have now certainly couldn't have handled the storm we had when the ship arrived the first time."

"Ya, I heard about that. As for Sigurth, he's alive and well. Right now he's at our new settlement, as is everyone else not with the ship. They're into spring planting and all that goes with it as we speak."

"Ah . . . the new settlement; now we're getting somewhere. Where is this settlement?" Ingivar said. "I've been told that Sigurth and his shipload, as well as you and the people of Vinland, disappeared without a trace."

"Who told you?"

"Freydis, of course. She came through late last fall on her way back to Greenland."

"What did she say?"

"A lot. She told about the long trips to Straumsfjord and Hops, and the good and bad of all of that. She also mentioned that Vinland was deserted, with only a few turds laying around to suggest anything had been there. She was half spooked and half pissed."

"Her's was the only ship to come through?" Thorth asked. "There had been three."

"Ya, there had been three. She said all of them left Straumsfjord together; but when they got to the turn by Keel Point, Bjarni continued on, intending to go directly to Iceland without stopping. Karsefni turned north with her, but didn't follow her to Vinland. He came by here first."

"Other than those two, no-one else has been by?"

"Ny, and it's boring. It's also not healthy, specially during the winter when we're cooped up. A few of our people died, and others want out. We didn't expect this to happen when we setup the station, you know. Which brings me back to my questions. Where is this new settlement? And why are you here?"

Thorth smiled. "We're here to answer those very questions. First, you know about that opening in the inland sea just west of here?"

"Ya."

"Well, keep going west into that opening almost a week more, and that's where we are."

"Why there?"

"Because we thought it was as far as we should go. If we had gone farther, we thought we would have exceeded how far anyone would travel to visit and trade with us."

"Makes sense."

"And we're here for two reasons. Te first is to let you know where we are so you can direct ships our way. The second is to find people to join us, particularly women. We're badly proportioned in that regard."

Ingivar snorted. "We sure can't help you there. Some of the men who want to leave may want to join you, but I'm more inclined to think they want out all the way back to Iceland or Norway. As for what you might find in Greenland, I can only guess. Do you intend to continue there?"

I haven't decided yet. It's a long way and I hate to be gone too long."

"I understand," Ingivar said, then. "There is another alternative, you know. You've been around as long as I have, so you may be guessing what I'm about to say. Ever since our ocean-going voyages started in earnest a few hundred years ago, several things happened. There was raiding, of course, which gets so much attention. But more signifiant to me was the settling that invariably occurred. It's been the same in Garthariki, in Francia, in England, Scotland and Ireland, where invaders and traders settled down and disappeared into the local population, leaving only names and a few unique characteristics as evidence they'd been there. The same may be the way for you, even though the thought of doing so with the natives, or skraelings as they're sometimes called, may not be attractive to all of you."

"We're aware of that," Thorth said, "but haven't moved in that direction accept to start learning their language."

Thorth rocked for a moment on his haunches, then said, "I don't like to consider what I must do after what you've said; but it leads me to the next logical move."

"To go to Greenland?"

"Ya. I'll tell the men to eat well and get a good rest, because we'll push off at first light. It's for more than the women. The tools we have are getting hard use, so it wouldn't hurt to stock up on a number of them. How are you in that regard?"

"We're doing fine, but don't have any to spare. However, if we were to close down, you'd be welcome to what we have."

Sigurth watched as the three walked past—the girls returning home for the summer. As they did, he picked up a pebble and plunked it at Nychanachia, who turned and gave one of those looks only a teenager could.

He was going to miss her. True to his word, he'd spent more time attending language sessions, and in that time had learned to appreciate not only her quickness, but also her budding sense of humor as they became comfortable with each other.

Their leaving brought up the other questions, however, those about the society of their neighbors, whoever they were. A few nights later his need to know more bubbled over. He left at midnight, moving quickly on a pathway that had by this time been worn into the woods and up the rises to the heights beyond. Miles later, maybe five or six, he stopped for the first time, not having seen anything, but thinking it a good idea. After a minute of study, he moved on, but repeated the stop and go, eventually moving from shadow to shadow.

He hadn't learned anything so far, except that the only creatures about during the evening hours were an occasional nocturnal animal, which was nothing new. He'd asked Ari and Askel what they knew of this area, but they'd been careful to avoid going where the natives might be hunting, which meant they knew nothing about where he was now.

By the time the sky tinted light in the east, he stopped with what would be a final time and sought a place to hide. He soon heard sounds of activity, the awakening of not only a community, but also of animals, especially dogs. He stayed in hiding all that day, mostly because he'd accidentally ended up as close to what he'd been looking for as he cared to get. From his hideaway, a large tree surrounded by thick, brambled bushes, a place that reminded him of hiding places as far back as memory would go, he eased up from time to time to see a fragment of what there was to see. By late in the day, he had a mosaic of images and sounds that combined to form an impression, an impression of a village of closely packed houses, usually rectangular of stick construction, with barrel-vaulted roofs. The village was circled by a frail wall of vertical pointed sticks tied together. Sigurth couldn't see how this wall could do any good; but then again he just didn't know. There were also fields and gardens and communal features, most of which were imagined by way of sounds and smells because these were things he couldn't see.

Imagined . . . Sigurth hated the thought that the most of what he felt he knew about the village was the product of his imagination based on bits and pieces of glimpses. He'd been in the process of deciding how and when to back out of his hiding place and head back, when defying all logic, he changed his mind.

He crept around to what appeared to be the entrance to the village; then after there being no traffic for a few minutes, he stepped into the opening, stood and waited.

He didn't have to wait long as a boy happened by, probably on his own little game. The boy glanced at Sigurth, then continued on, only to stop and look again, almost coming out of his skin. He yelled and raced farther into the village, where he stopped and turned, pointing and yelling words Sigurth couldn't completely interpret, but understood. He also understood other reactions as people everywhere stopped what they were doing and stood if they weren't already standing, other people streaming out of the buildings like bees swarming from a hive.

Sigurth walked into the village, slowly, and he hoped, calmly, the people assembled spreading out to let him through. He continued on, walking past what seemed like a ceremonial area with a number of posts arranged in a circle around a central feature, really looking for what might be the leadership of the village. Unfortunately what he saw was the look of emotions turning from astonishment to anger, and that wasn't good.

Finally he came to a few who had gathered squarely in his path. They were older than most, and were festooned a bit, although simply, but enough to indicate they might be the leaders he hoped to find

He tried to speak in their language, saying, "I'm sorry to barge in this way, but I was out on a hunt and accidentally came by here. So I thought I'd stop in and say hello as a friend and neighbor." He might as well have said, "Up your asses you wrinkle-faced coots!" Because the next thing he heard was an angry scream. He reacted enough to see a wooden bat being swung, getting his arm up in time to take most of the blow, the rest bouncing off his head and sending him reeling. As he stumbled, he instinctively shed his bow and quiver, then turned expecting another blow. It came, but Sigurth ducked under and let it fall on his back, at the same time grabbing the man by both an arm and his mid-section, raising him up and slamming him on the ground, the dust billowing in all directions. He stood over the man, who was trying to catch his breath, and stiff-arm pointed at him with a glare that said, *Move, you bastard and you're splattered.*

He stepped past the man as if he wasn't there, turned back to the elders, and said, "I come in peace."

He tried to say more, when he heard a soft feminine voice say what he thought he had just said, only it sounded different, and he realized someone was interpreting for him.

It was Nychanachia.

He continued to speak, now in Norse, with his phrases being repeated. He paid no mind when the man at his feet rolled over and disappeared into the crowd.

He spoke again of his hunting, the elders nodding as if this made sense. Then he repeated, "I come in peace. Our people and our people are friends . . .

"We need to do more together, because there are things we can teach you, just as there are things you can teach us . . .

"I see you have fields and gardens, like we have fields and gardens. But they are different . . .

"For instance, I see a tall, long-leafed plan with a strange, long-husked fruit that is not known to us . . .

"We have grains and vegetables an animals that are probably strange to you. It would be of mutual benefit to remain friends and share with each other what we can."

The elders whispered among themselves for a moment, then one, who was probably the oldest because of his white hair, wrinkled skin and missing teeth, spoke, like Sigurth, in phrases, with his words being translated.

"You caught us by surprise, and we are sorry for how some have reacted . . .

"Ya, we are friends, and ya, we would like to share with you the things we know . . .

"We are amazed at what your people have done, so look forward to learning from each other . . .

"You are bleeding. Are you all right?"

"Ya, I'm fine."

"We would be honored if you'd spend the night. We'll prepare a feast for you fresh from our garden."

"Thank you, but ny. My friends are expecting me back and will worry."

With that, the elder spoke to a woman nearby, who immediately scampered away.

"Then," the elder said, "please accept a package of the fruit you found fascinating. They can be eaten raw, or better boiled, which softens them. I think you will like them."

Sigurth accepted the package when it was brought to him and gave generous thanks. Then he turned to Nychanachia, who'd been serious faced through all of this. "Thank you for your help."

She nodded, almost blushing.

"Are you returning for the winter?"

Her eyes darted from side to side, as if not knowing how to answer.

"You really need to," Sigurth said. "Because you saw what a mess you've made with what I'm able to say."

Nychanachia's expressions flashed from shock to an urge to respond, but she wasn't able to say anything because someone tapped Sigurth on the arm.

It was a young man extending Sigurth's bow and quiver, who said, "Are you the man who fired the arrows at the post on the small boat last year?"

Sigurth thought a moment, then said, "Oh, you mean when all those from the north came to visit."

The man nodded.

"Did you see what happened from the ridge to the west of us?"

The man stood, not knowing how to answer.

"Are you one of the four men who sleep in the hollow at the far end?"

At this the man's jaw dropped, and Sigurth immediately regretted he'd said something that violated a basic premise. Rather than linger an allow things to get more awkward, he turned back to the elders.

"I look forward to what we discussed. I will tell my friends of this, and know they will be pleased. As before, all of you are welcome in our village."

With that he turned to leave but not before catching Nychanachia's eye and winking. He was almost to the entrance when a small pebble bounced off his head. Without turning he burst out laughing, able to tell by the sounds behind him that the crowd was confused.

Hours later he reached the edge of the forest that defined the extent of what was the settlement. He stopped there long enough to sense where the person who might be on duty might be, then continued on as if on a stroll.

"So how'd it go?" Said a voice from the shadows as he passed, the deep, husky voice easily recognizable as Thor's. "Ondur said you might be about."

"Okay, I guess. I'm still in one piece." Sigurth said as he pivoted to where Thor was standing in the shadows.

"There are still a few waiting up for you."

"You mean by that fire I see?"

"Ya."

Sigurth nodded his goodbye and threaded his way through the field and past the corrals to the Althing tree, as it was now being called, where the small fire burned. Even in the poor light he recognized Sveyin, Ondur and Yngvi, who were half asleep when he ambled up.

"What's the matter?" Sigurth said. "Couldn't sleep?"

Sveyin almost jumped, turning in his direction. "Well, it's about time. Where have you been?"

Sigurth plunked down to join them, letting out a long sigh. "It's been quite a day."

"We expected that much," Sveyin said. "You've been gone since midnight. And isn't that blood on the side of your head?"

Sigurth nodded. "Ya . . . It's along story."

"So tell it. That's why we're here."

"Well, I didn't intend to, but I ended up visiting the village of the natives to the south."

"Where the girls come from?"

"Ya."

"Just like that . . . unannounced?"

"Ya, I just walked in."

"It's obvious your surprise wasn't welcomed. How did you get out of that?" Yngvi asked.

Sigurth explained, and when finished opened the bag he'd set down beside him.

"What's this?" Ondur said.

"Don't know what it's called, but it's a food crop."

Ondur pealed back the husk to expose the fruit, which gleamed white in the flickering light. "Hmmmm," he said.

"I was told they can be boiled to soften the kernels."

"Maybe so," Ondur said. "But I'd like to take a few of these and flake off the kernels. They must be seeds. There may be time in the season to have a late planting. What do you think?"

But Sigurth was no longer in the conversation. He was asleep.

The *Mule* returned in late summer with eight new settlers, five of them women. A celebration was held as quickly as it could be planned, with the newcomers marveling at the abundance laid before them. The gardens had just been harvested, as had some of the fields. Then there were the variety of seafoods in addition to fish, and the meat from a recently successful hunt.

There was ample reason for many horns of what had been brewed, for besides all the introductions, were the stories that were exchanged. Sobering, but hardly ruining the spirit of the celebration, was the fact that there had been sickness during the return trip, and that a woman from Greenland and a man from the Way Station had died and been buried at sea.

A few weeks later, Sigurth was about to burst.

"What's gotten into you?" Sveyin asked. "Are you okay?"

Sigurth didn't answer . . . instead he said, "How long do you think it will be before the first snow?"

"Four, maybe five weeks. Why is that important?"

Sigurth looked at him.

Sveyin looked back, brow pinched, then said, "Oh, it's the trip west, isn't it?"

"Well ya!" Sigurth said. "We've been to the Way Station, sailed to Greenland, gone to the island, and built an entire settlement. The west may not be on anyone else's mind, but it's foolish to ignore that it's there. It might be of utmost importance."

"Okay, okay," Svein said, laughing. "I agree with and want to go along. Let's go to Odd and see how things are."

Another intended to be quick trip was made, with just enough of a crew to manage the *Mule,* and with both Thorth and Sveyin aboard to share in what could be seen along the way. What was seen was more of the same—more of endless possibility, water and trees and mostly unpopulated shoreline. The sailing part of the trip came to a halt when they arrived at a waterfall, ending what the *Mule* could do. Then a party, led by Sigurth, spent a few more days hiking the shoreline farther west, learning only that more rapids and turbulences corresponding to the rising terrain existed, possibly like what they'd heard of in a certain river in Garthariki, so they turned back.

They returned to dropping temperatures and flecks in the air, and to the work needed in preparation for another winter.

Chapter 26
KANATA
1030
(1008)

"There's no need for you to go," Sigurth said. "It may be a long trip. To be honest, I have no idea how long . . . maybe years."

"Until you find the Edge and the Midgard serpent?" Sveyin said.

"You know that's been on my mind," Sigurth said.

"What about traveling until there's reasonable evidence it doesn't exist?"

"Are we negotiating something?"

"Ya," Sveyin said. "I want to go along because I'm just as curious about this world as you are; but I won't go if you're set on finding something that isn't there. In that case we'll *never* return."

"But why *do* you? You have Bergljot and Yrsa and another about to pop."

"I know that," Sveyin said, "and Bergljot knows that. She wants me to go just like she wanted me to go on those other trips. She knows I'll regret not being a part of something that could be great, and she doesn't want that."

Sigurth looked at his cousin long and hard. "You know that I can be a stubborn bastard."

Sveyin laughed. "Everybody knows that, so what's new? That aside, is there anything I can do to help? It seems most of what you've been doing this winter has been for this trip; and the only reason I haven't done as much is because you haven't asked me."

"Ny . . . I'm in good shape. But I'm glad if you're going, in case you're wondering. You just need to get ready too."

"I am ready, particularly for hiking. Last year we spent only a few days at it. This time, knowing how nutty you are, we may be gone quite a while."

Sigurth shrugged. "No way of knowing; but yes, it could be quite a while."

"And you're taking along the mules, I understand. You couldn't have had this in mind when you left Norway."

"Of course not," Sigurth said. "I really wanted horses because I like to ride; but they were too big. The mules, which did fit in, were taken because they might be good as draft animals, which they've been. Then when I thought about all we might want to carry if long hikes were planned, the mules on hand came to mind. Actually, Yngvi suggested it. They'd be perfect as pack animals, he said, and that thought brought up several possibilities."

"Like what?"

"When I thought about the cargo needed before sailing from Norway, I tried to anticipate what might be needed in either Greenland or the Vinland I was hearing about. One concern had to do with boat repair. That led to more tools than usual, and also a supply of metal components that might not exist in a remote port. Instead of rocks for ballast, I used sacks of iron rivets like those to anchor hull boards. There are enough of them to build a small ship."

"You expect to build a ship on this trip?"

"Don't know. We know the *Mule* won't go up river past the rapids we came to last fall, and we know there are more rapids beyond that. But that's as much as we know. We could find open water at some point, which wouldn't be the first time that's happened . . . Remember what we've heard about that river in Garthariki? Anyway traveling by boat will be a lot easier than hiking."

Sveyin stood, his head bobbing from side to side as he tried to follow those thoughts; then he said, "Who do you think should be going?"

"That's been a tough one because we shouldn't take away too many from the settlement. For instance, I'd love to have Ondur and Thor; but they need to stay behind and provide muscle helping Thorth. Here's what I have in mind. First, everyone has to be in good shape because of the cross country travel with heavy loads to carry; then there's boat building, which is very possible. That means Frothi, because he's not only experienced in that, but also strong at oar; there's Askel, who's a hunter plus being strong at oar; and now there's you along with me to fill another two slots. Bovi can manage the steering oar and direct Jon and Arni at sail. Then there's Nychanachia, who can not only be our interpreter, if one's ever needed, but can also help in living off the land, which we'll have to do; there's Asa,

Trygvi's oldest daughter, who's become Nychanachia's best friend over the past few years, who'll manage the mules as well as the cooking; there's Offar, who can do many things and is awesome strong; and there's room for one more."

"The girls . . . You think they can keep up?"

"No doubt in my mind," Sigurth said. "I can see by the look on your face that you're skeptical. Well, all other considerations aside, Nychanachia saved my ass once and could do the same for all of us before this is over."

"Okay," Sveyin said. "It's not for me to question something you've put so much thought to, but I do have a question."

"Just one?"

Sveyin laughed. "No seriously. A group of us were talking the other day about what we're called. We, our settlement, I mean, aren't called anything; we don't have a name."

"Hadn't thought much about that. Any suggestions?"

"Ya . . . We thought of Freeland and Norseland and Fjordland, none of which sounded very exciting. We also thought that maybe you wanted something like Sigurthland."

"Oh ny o ny, *paleeeeze!*"

"There are native words, like "Kaniatarowanenneh", which means "big waterway." It's somewhat appropriate, but way too long. There's also "Kanata," which means "settlement"."

"Kanata," Sigurth said. "I like that."

They left soon after spring planting. This time there were differences with the quick trip taken the fall before. Many more people were along; the mules, that had been useful during spring, were aboard, as were more supplies. With the previous trip, stops had been made along the way to see what the shores and lands beyond them had to offer. This time the *Mule* sped through, not making a meaningful stop until they reached the rapids.

As before, they tied the *Mule* in along the south shore because the north shore was more complicated with a sizable river flowing into it just below the falls. It was late in the day by the time everything had been unloaded and the camp set up. For the crew of the *Mule*, it was also the last chance for a warm meal.

Fortunately the weather cooperated, the sky being clear with temperatures dropping to a pleasant cool as often happens in early spring. When the sun set and the stars came out, there was no hurry to retire as everyone gathered and settled around scattered fires, the thought of the next day very much on their minds.

"I have a question," Odd said at one fire where Sigurth, Sveyin, Jon and Arni also plunked. "You're going to lands each day that haven't been seen by anyone else from our home countries. You've already settled in this place we're going to call Kanata . . . The question is whether you hope to find a place even better; and if that's so, what would it take to make it so much nicer that you'd want to resettle?"

Sigurth laughed. "That's a loaded question if I've ever heard one."

"Now let's think about that," Sveyin said. "Didn't Karsefni say it wouldn't matter if paths were lined with gold and fruit hung from every tree?"

"Right . . . He meant that being too far away wouldn't work. Besides we've seen a lot in the past few years, so much so that eventually even the variations begin to take on a sameness. The settlement we have continues to look as good as anyplace we've seen."

"Which brings me back to the question," Odd said. "What are you looking for? What do you hope to accomplish?"

There was a lengthy silence, almost an embarrassing one as eyes turned to Sigurth for an answer. He sat like a lump for more than a moment, until finally he said, "Aren't you curious about anything?"

Odd fidgeted.

"For instance, what *is* the moon, or the sun that just dropped out of sight, or all the stars that are popping into view above us? People have been wondering about all of them since as far back as we go, and have only products of the imagination to go by. Why do geese fly back and forth each season and do it in formation? Why does the tide in Straumsfjord rise and fall as much as it does? Why do the natives in Hops twirl those damn sticks the way they do? And what other mysteries are there in this strange new land we're on? Is this land an island like Greenland seems to be, or is it a huge land mass like Garthariki, going on forever? I guess it's the last question that's the answer to what you ask, along with . . . is it the end of the world?"

"Oh ya," Odd said. "The edge again."

Sigurth nodded as if to admit that was a possibility. "At least we'll know more when we return."

"Let's drink to that," Odd said. "*Skoll!* . . . to your safe return."

The next morning they watched the *Mule* fade into the distance. It was the easiest part of sailing as the ship, high in the water with a minimal crew and little cargo, caught the current just offshore and rode it, the oars out but used mainly to correct whatever Odd didn't like.

Before it disappeared, Sigurth called the group together.

"There's not much new I can tell you," he began, "but it's necessary that I go over certain things again. First . . . We're a small, vulnerable group traveling through unfamiliar, and possibly hostile, country. Second . . . We don't want to hurt anyone, and we don't wish *to be* hurt by anyone.

"Now, I've asked all the men to bring along shields, spears and swords, even though half of you haven't had much training in combat. The reason for those weapons is what we'll resort to if we're attacked, and that is to form a shield wall or circle, from which we might do enough damage to survive. We'll practice that in a moment, but we hope to never have to be in that position. As for travel, we'll proceed in a line with a certain order, with two scouts, usually Jon and Arni, out front, the mules tied together near the end."

They didn't start out until almost noon, following the plan that had been explained, snaking in and around and up and down in a manner that soon became routine. They followed the river as closely as possible, which at times wasn't close at all but out of sight, and penetrated woods, climbed heights, sloshed swamps and portaged streams along the way.

The river was followed, not only because it gave them a reference point, but also because it was an extension of what they had been on since leaving Vinland. At some time during each day, usually at the end if not before for some reason, Sigurth pulled out a cloth, and he and Sveyin went through their exercise of locating a dot, representing the distance and position in relation to a previous dot, with squiggles to show shorelines or prominent features in the area. This was the same exercise, almost a game, they'd played when on the water. Of special interest this time was the nature of the river—its width and speed of flow, and its unique features like sandbars, islands and turbulences. Rapids in particular were studied, with the question always asked as whether a small ship, barge or raft could survive running them . . . and if so, how?

There were many of these to consider. Some were minor blips; some were lengthy but smooth drops; some were violent but short falls; and one in particular was a wide and lengthy tempest-boil, spellbinding to watch.

Progress was anything but consistent. On a good day, with no interruptions or complications, over ten miles would be traveled. Then at other times there was the weather or a geographical feature that slowed them down. On more than one occasion a halt was called because natives were spotted fishing the shore in front; so they hid and waited until the way was clear before proceeding. In one place a village was on the same shore they were following, so they were stymied until a route around the village, taking two days to circumvent, was made.

Although there were variables in weather and landscape, there was also a sameness, especially in routine, for when the sun set and light dwindled, they'd set up camp and make ready for the night. Part of the routine was security, which meant that each night someone had guard duty. This was done in shifts, with all of the men sharing in the assignment. The only difference was that more often than not, Sigurth would take the early morning shift. The others protested because they felt he was taking on an unfair amount of the burden; but he shrugged, saying he usually didn't sleep well during this time anyway, so it didn't bother him to do more.

On one night in particular, they'd camped near the bank of the river, which was as usual. The sky was clear with the stars in all their glory, and the moon was full, a combination that brought a particular beauty to the night with shades of grey throughout the forest. These shades shifted as the moon moved to the west, all the while contrasting with the sparkling current that slid by with its soothing sound to what otherwise would have been eerie silence.

Sigurth had been sitting at the base of a tree, wrapped and warm but vigilant, silently marveling at the beauty of the surroundings, when he heard a sound from within the encampment and then saw movement. He watched as the person, also bundled, made their way towards him, and when near, sat down as if to chat.

It was Nychanachia.

"What are you doing up?" Sigurth said in a whisper.

"I couldn't sleep."

"You should give it another try. If the weather holds like it is right now, we'll have a hard day tomorrow."

She didn't comment.

After a few moments trying to think of what else to say, he said, "It's very quiet . . . Do you hear spirits at times like this?

"Are you making fun with what we believe?"

"Ny . . . Just trying to understand what it is that you believe."

"We do believe in spirits. For us there are many mysteries. Bergljot says that much of what we believe she calls superstition; but added that that's okay because no one has the answer."

Oh my, Sigurth thought. *What have I gotten into.* He leaned back and looked at the sky just as something streaked across it and disappeared.

"Did you see that?"

"Ya . . ."

"Do you think it was one of your spirits or one of our gods?"

"You think it's a God, don't you?"

Sigurth snorted. "I don't know. But Bergljot is right. We believe what we were brought up to believe, but we don't know anything for sure."

"But we're doing what we're doing . . . trying to find the end of the world, because of what you believe."

"That's partly true. I'd like to prove or disprove something one way or the other."

"What's the other part?"

Sigurth thought, then said, "This land . . . your world. We love it here. I'd just like to find out as much as about it as I can, that's all.

"Now that's enough; we might disturb the others . . . so get to bed."

By late summer, the constantly changing scene that usually fell into a certain sameness, began to differ. The north shore changed from matching the south, to a widening into which island after island appeared, a situation they couldn't define from what they saw from where they were.

After days of the unusual but fascinating views along the way, Sveyin said, catching up to Sigurth who at this point was up front, "Any thoughts what this is leading to?"

"It's been different, no doubt about that," Sigurth said. "But I don't know what to make of it. Jon and Arni are ahead. The last I saw of them they were climbing that bluff over there to see better. They may have something to tell."

A half hour later, they were beside the bluff. The river, as usual, was visible to their right, but the way ahead was obscured by a thicket. They stopped when they heard yelling from above, and looked up and saw the two scouts waving but not coming down. This meant there was something to see.

The caravan also stopped, everyone plunking while Sigurth and Sveyin snaked their way to the top.

Once there, the scouts didn't say anything. Jon simply swept his arm to the west. Before and below them was the end of the river, or really its beginning, for the river had turned into a wide channel with the many islands it held. Beyond the channel was nothing but blue, a wide and glistening blue to the horizon.

Sigurth turned to Sveyin. "Pick out a good place to make camp . . . I mean a place to spend the winter."

"And let me guess," Sveyin said.

Sigurth smiled. "Ya . . . You know why. This is where we build the boat."

Like with the first weeks at Kanata, their settlement, there followed here a furious period of activity. Trees were downed, chopped-up, segregated and stacked as the essential first step, a step that wasn't stopped until Sigurth felt he had enough of the proper combinations. Then the work began in much the same manner as it always had, with first forming a ramp and laying the keel. In the beginning everyone was involved; but when work progressed past the initial stage, Sigurth, Frothi and Arni, who'd worked together at the marina back home, became the principal workers.

The ship Sigurth originally envisioned was a small version of a warship like the *Sea Eagle*, not a deep-hulled knorr like the *Mule*. After seeing the spectrum of river features, he was more convinced then ever of the choice, altering it only slightly to be a little shorter but wider than normal proportions. When finished it would be thirty feet long, with three oars each side and a single sail. It would be a shallow draft vessel, like a byrding for coastal travel, and hopefully like the *Sea Eagle* with the ability to skim the surface at an impressive speed.

While this was underway, Sveyin led whoever else was available in the construction of a winter shelter. For this he chose a site on the side of the bluff, then had it hollowed out to provide its back wall and sides. With only eleven people and four animals to provide for, the building didn't have to be large and complicated. Even so, much work was required, the result being that by the first snow, quarters were snug with only minor tweaks remaining.

The ship, however, which took on the name *Waterbug*, still had a ways to go. The frame and hull were finished, which was a lot; but the decking, the mast, the accessories and all the finished touches remained. There was something else.

"What is it?" Sveyin said as he noticed Sigurth standing beside the hull and facing the cold wind churning up the expanse of water before him.

Sigurth started to speak, only didn't at first, turning back a ways to think awhile, then, "I'm missing something."

"Like what?"

"If I knew," Sigurth said half laughing, "it wouldn't be missing."

"You're looking at the water."

"Ya. On all the other boats I've worked on, the hull was formed on skids close to the water like we've done here, and there never was a problem."

"Well, for one thing the building of those boats was in summer."

Sigurth nodded. "That's part of it, but there's more."

"Ice creep?"

"Could be," Sigurth said. "What do you know about it? I've heard of it, but never seen it."

"We had a good bit of creep at the Vinland that first winter, particularly on the northeast shore of the island. It happens, I guess, when ice covering a large area starts to melt, and is driven ashore by a combination of tides and wind. Now that you mention it, it could be a problem with the long, low shoreline we're facing here. Let's extend the skids and pull the hull in as far as we can, then tent it over."

After the first snowfall, the weather warmed, allowing for more work to be completed. But then around the shortest day, it closed in with heavy snows, dropping temperatures and driving winds. The next months were hard. Although the shelter was almost as snug as any other lodging in the new world, the weather outside was difficult to contend with. Work on the *Waterbug*, of which much still remained, was therefore advanced by shaping pieces inside.

Food was another problem as fishing was limited to chopping holes in the ice; and hunting was fruitless. The situation became so serious that one of the mules, much to the dismay of the girls, was slaughtered.

Finally the weather turned and the world began to melt. With this welcome turn, there was also ice creep, which was more fearful than imagined. It came in a seeming relentless series of crunches that moved slabs across the beach almost to where the ship was sheltered.

"It looks like it's finally stopped," Sveyin said, sighing as he stood on the edge of the closest slab.

Sigurth standing nearby shook his head. "This has been as weird a thing as I've ever seen. But I think you're right. It seems to have stopped moving, although it's still scary. Another twenty feet and it would have turned our ship into kindling."

Arni and Frothi walked over, Arni saying, "What are you guys doing? We've been waiting for the word to get back to work. That ship will never get finished with everyone standing around."

The *Waterbug* was in the water a few days after lake ice disappeared. Then, after testing the hull, the improvised rigging and all systems, they were ready for loading.

"What about the mules?" Asa asked.

"They need to stay," Sigurth said. "We'll leave the shelter open so they can come and go as they please . . . and they'll have this whole area in which to forage, so they'll do all right."

"When we return, will we be coming back this way?"

"Most likely . . . We may give that river we've been following a try on that return. It might be we'll be able to take it all the way home."

"Will we pick up the mules, then?"

"We'll see."

They didn't cast off until two days later, mostly because of Bovi, who suggested that it would be better to wait for a favorable wind. It wasn't much better after the wait, but patience being what it was, they left anyway, rowing at first until the rigging could be adjusted to move them along. As they settled in, all eyes turned to the receding shoreline, with its mounds of drift ice still scattered about the shore, and the bleak shelter dug into the bluff. The mules, who'd at first enjoyed their freedom to roam the area, were now watching them go with what seemed a forlorn awareness to something they didn't understand.

Sigurth and Sveyin stood back by Bovi at the steering-oar, feeling better with each moment as the *Waterbug* easily slid through the water.

"You want to head west past those islands, right?" Bovi said.

"Ya," Sigurth said. "We've been looking at islands north of us since last fall, never getting close. I don't expect anything unusual, but you never know."

They stayed on that tack all through the day, coming within a few hundred yards offshore in several places, with Jon once more taking a high seat to see what might be important. There was little of unusual interest, except for two riders in one of those long, thin, multi-colored watercraft with pointed ends similar to others they'd seen since coming to Kanata. The two gawked as the *Waterbug,* huge in their eyes, slipped past within a stones throw, a row of smiling faces lining the rail.

They furled sail and tied ashore that night at a spit of land that doubled back to form a fishhook, similar but considerably smaller than the one passed years before.

"It was a good first day," Sveyin said. "Everything's been working fine."

Sigurth smiled, spreading his hands out on the roughly chiseled rail as he watched most everyone scrambling ashore. "Ya, a good day."

"Are you uncertain with what you might find?"

"Of course I am. We've already spent a year looking at some very interesting country, but it's differences have been just that, with nothing particularly unique. We've seen more and more of land that would be wonderful for farms and pastures and gardens and fields. I mean we could move entire communities from the scraggy coasts of Norway and Iceland and Greenland, and know they'd be delighted with their new homes. We've seen all that; but we haven't seen anything to indicate it's not going on forever. Now we're continuing the direction we've been on, but doing it many times faster and therefore many times farther; and ya, it's making me nervous to think we won't find anything other than what we've already seen."

"But we are finding something. We've been locating dots, like we just did, and when we finish and return, we'll have a picture of this world that few, if any other, have ever had."

"And what good will that do?"

"That remains to be seen."

The next day they cut back to the south, almost southeast, passing several islands and connecting again with the south shore, then proceeded along it west.

"Are you thinking about angling over to the north shore again?" Sveyin asked.

"Ya . . . That makes sense, because if we don't find land in a reasonable time we'll turn back, knowing the body of water is large . . . Why?"

"It just makes me nervous, that's all, for a different reason you might have. During the winter I watched gales rip across the water from the northwest. They were vicious. I couldn't help but think about what those winds would do to a small ship in open water."

Sigurth nodded. "But we faced the same possibility every day when we crossed to Greenland . . . and again to Vinland."

"But the *Mule* is bigger and sets more firmly in the water."

"Okay, you have a point."

They did head northwest again into open water, sailing until they were out of sight of land, which had Sigurth and Sveyin skittish for different reasons. For Sigurth, it was that they might be approaching an unimaginable something; for Sveyin, it was that a gale might strike them. As they stood side by side at the rail, both absorbed in their thoughts, Sveyin broke the silence with, "Why don't you fish for it?"

"What?'

"Fish for it . . . the serpent, you know, Jormungand. Like Thor did when he went fishing with Hymer the Giant."

"You're being stupid."

"Why?"

"Everyone knows the serpent is in the ocean . . . and this is fresh water. Besides, I don't have an oxen head as bait."

They both chuckled and cuffed each other with elbows.

After a few moments, Sveyin said, "It's hard for me to put much stock in those stories we grew up with . . . the gods, giants, trolls, dwarfs and all, and the magical things that supposedly happened. There's been nothing anyone has seen to support any of it."

Sigurth listened, respectfully, and stayed silent for a moment, then replied, "I guess walking on water and turning water into wine are much easier to accept."

Sveyin snorted in a way of saying he also had a point, then said, "Okay, let's call it a draw."

After another interval Sveyin added, "You know, of course, that I spent a year with Olaf and his ministers at Nitharos, and during each day was pounded with the bible and the glory it contained. I wasn't happy about it, at first that is, with many parts about it easy to question like you just did. But then other parts began to stick . . . and that's where I am."

Both let out a sigh when Jon sighted land, for it gave them a chance to change the subject. This led to another dot being located and a shoreline being drawn to connect to the one outlined previously.

They turned southwest again, returning to that shore, then followed it for a few days. While on this tack they passed a large opening in the high ground following the shore, from which a river of impressive size exited. They noticed this feature but continued on. Later they saw that the shoreline was turning northward, then completing a turn such that they could see they were now following the north shore going east.

"This most likely returns to the north shore we touched last week. If so it means we're on a very large lake," Sveyin said as Sigurth directed Bovi to turn back in a certain direction and cruise for the night. "Any thoughts about tomorrow?"

"I'm mostly set on what I don't want to do," Sigurth said.

"Which is to go ashore and explore? Does that mean you've had enough?"

Sigurth glared at him.

"You're heading for that river, aren't you?" Sveyin said.

Sigurth nodded. "We should be near the mouth of it by first light. You've got to admit it's been the most interesting thing we've seen since getting on the water. No telling what it leads to."

"Could be nothing."

"Could be something."

Shortly after daybreak they were there and in position.

"It looks interesting, all right," Sveyin said peering ahead beside Sigurth at the bow. "It also has a heavy current."

They threaded their way back to Bovi, looking at the water to see what direction the breeze was from. "Will the sail do us any good?" Sigurth asked.

"A little," Bovi answered. "But it's going to be tricky. From what I can see, the river's not real wide and the shore's mostly rocks. I don't have to tell you, but you know we'll have to have close coordination between rowers and those managing the sail . . . and we're short handed."

"We can row again," Asa said listening to the conversation.

"Actually, we may need you two," Bovi said looking at the girls. "But if you don't row correctly in concert with the others, you can do more harm than good."

"You saw us row yesterday," Asa said, "when we were just making a game of it in open water."

"Line us up the way you think," Sigurth said to Boi. "We're going in."

In a matter of minutes, everyone, after but a little jockeying around, were in their places, concentrating on doing as they were directed. By the time the *Waterbug* entered the mouth, it had reached an alignment near the center-point, with oars working effectively in unison. There were a few adjustments, but not many as the ship moved in a way that seemed relentlessly to the observers on the cliffs above the river, who, like the natives earlier, could hardly believe what they saw.

Concentrations were such that the first few miles swept by with most hardly noticing features along the canyon walls drifting by. Then a certain awareness came to everyone, first to those standing and free to move about, then filtering to those at oar. The awareness was that this was no ordinary river, even disregarding the cliffs. Initially only a feeling, they all felt it without knowing why. Then there was a mist far ahead that necks strained to see, joined by a sound that grew as the mist began to take form.

The form became a waterfall, actually two falls in line, the likes of which they'd never seen or imagined . . . so stunning the rowers broke cadence.

"Keep rowing!" Sigurth snarled.

They did, falling back to a rhythm which Bovi renewed directing. He shouted to not let up because he saw what others hadn't, a swirl of water off to the right. The sound of his voice was such that he didn't have to explain.

They passed the first falls, which was astounding but almost ignored because there was something more ominous ahead. A little farther and there were questioning murmurs and heads turning to one another. But Sigurth felt the letup and with teeth gritted, screamed,"*Keep rowing! Keep rowing! Keep rowing!*"

Again they complied, moving the craft near to the base of the larger falls, which enveloped them in mist and thundering sounds that beat at their senses like nothing before. After reaching a numbing point where best efforts took them no farther, and after a lingering that seemed forever, including a moment when Sigurth stood beside his oar with his every feature distended and roared as if challenging the Gods, Sveyin countered with, *"Enough! Bovi, turn us around!"*

Bovi, who'd been stunned into inaction, came to, and realizing the boat was drifting back, barked orders so the turn was orderly and not heading towards rocks.

Sigurth, who seemed mesmerized and hadn't participated in the turn, then returned to his oar and shouted to Bovi,*"Bring us in!"*

Bovi did. Seeing an opening along the shore a quarter mile past the first and smaller falls, he brought the *Waterbug* to a halt, then edged it sideways until there was a gentle crunch, at which time lines were thrown, Jon and Askel jumping out and securing them.

As the ship settled in its place, so did the rowers, who straightened up, took a deep breath, and shaking from the drenching they'd received, looked around at each other not knowing what to say.

Not so Sigurth. He immediately rose from his seat at oar, stepped to the rail opposite Bovi and stared at the rumbling cascades a short distance away.

"Well?" Sveyin said, joining him.

Sigurth hesitated, then said, "We may have been close to something."

"What do you mean may have?" Sveyin said. "We *were* close . . . and it was a waterfall."

Sigurth looked at him, took a deep breath, and said, "There was a feeling of awesome power. It may have been more than that . . . and I've got to know."

He picked up his shield, his weapons, his roll and a few supplies, and stepped over the rail.

"Oh ny," Sveyin said. "You're not . . ."

"Ya . . . No one else needs to go. I'm going to the top, and then as far as it takes to find out what this is about . . .

". . . and what are you doing?"

Sveyin had collected his things and stepped over.

"You're not going," Sigurth said.

"Oh, ya . . . If I didn't, you'd shoot yourself in the foot."

While they were into it, the others looked at each other not knowing what to think. All except Nychanachia, who quietly gathered her things and wasn't noticed until she was also over the rail.

Sigurth and Sveyin stopped bickering, mouths dropping; but Nychanachia ignored them and said, "You'll need me," staring down a look from Sigurth.

After a few moments of impasse, Sigurth turned to the rest and said, "Okay . . . Frothi, you're in charge. Set up defenses and get comfortable. I don't know what's up there," he said pointing to the heights, "but we're going to find out. If we don't get back in a reasonable time, say a couple days, or if you're in such danger you can't stay, then cut loose."

With that the three picked up their gear and climbed, snaking back and forth along what turned out to be a well-worn trail. They disappeared at the top with a final wave.

Sigurth took a moment to look around once on top. There was a lot to see—the river below them splitting a plateau to form cliffs on both sides; the swirl in the river that had scared Bovi being a dangerous whirlpool; and the two rapids, the latter of which dominated the scene and sent billowing clouds of mist in the air. Seeing no immediate danger, he led them toward the first cascade, and soon they were there, standing by the corner where the water swept by and tumbled over. They could feel the fall's awesome power reflected in the ground by a continuous tremor.

There being nothing that had a meaning relating to what he was seeking, Sigurth said, "Let's go," with a twist of his head to indicate he wanted to follow the river above the falls. They did, soon passing the small island that divided the falls to see the full river, now a mile wide, moving relentlessly along.

Sigurth thought *this could be it . . . the river is intense, powerful . . . It could be from an unimaginable something.* They hurried on for another hour, only to come to a point where the river split again, this time in a significant way with the forks seeming to go in opposite directions.

Sigurth stopped and sat on a log. As the others did likewise, he said to Sveyin, "How far do you think we've walked?"

"Maybe four miles."

"Any thoughts?"

"Look," Sveyin said, "this is your idea. I see interesting scenery; but it has no special meaning as far as I'm concerned."

Sigurth looked around, and then squinted at the sun. "This has been quite a morning. It's about noon, so let's have a bite and rest for a while. We haven't seen anything to slow us down, so we should be able to go a good ways before dark."

They did. With nothing out of the ordinary holding them back, and moving with a steady pace, they followed the fork eastward about five miles where it turned south, and then a few miles farther to a southeast turn. At times along the way they saw natives by the shore, but they skirted past hoping to go unnoticed. That didn't always work because once they saw someone stand and watch them as they moved.

By the time the sun approached the horizon, they reached where the river forks came back together, once more being a mile wide.

"Sigurth, our legs are dead," Sveyin said, plopping on the first object providing a seat. Nychanachia did the same, almost in tears, trying to hide the fact she was as tired as she was.

Sigurth settled down too, and not reluctantly.

"It must have been another fifteen miles around that damned island," Sigurth said, almost in a whisper.

"That's about what I figure," Sveyin said, then added, "So where does that put us in your mind?"

Sigurth groaned and got back up, walking stiff-legged to the bank to look at the water moving by. He turned and said, "You two have done more than I could ever ask, and I wish I could say I'm giving up, but I can't. So let's do this . . . You two start back in the morning. I'll go it alone until noon tomorrow; If there's no more to see by that time, I'll turn around. You'll be getting back to the boat within the two days I suggested and can hold it until I return."

Nychanachia shook her head.

Sveyin groaned, thinking of Bergljot and the kids. "I don't like it either way."

"But it makes sense."

They were too tired to argue, so they agreed to discus it in the morning, having a meal and settling into their bed rolls instead as soon as it was dark. The only thing of note was that Nychanachia moved her roll to be beside that of Sigurth.

An hour or so after midnight, Sigurth's eyes, as usual, blinked open. He eased out, leaving his roll in place so as not to disturb anyone, and carefully picked up his other gear and tip-toed away. The going was easy because the sky was not only clear with the stars out in full array, but there was also a good piece of the moon to add its light along the way. He'd traveled possibly two more miles, when he heard a sound up ahead.

Could that be a dog? He thought. *Damn! . . . That would mean a village.*

He moved ahead further, maybe half a mile, when there was another sound, this one from behind with more than one person involved by the sound of the footfalls; and whoever they were were in a hurry. He ducked behind a tree and eased out his sword, hoping whoever they were would race by.

They did; but as they passed, Sigurth recognized Sveyin and Nychanachia. He now had to chase down and stop them without making too much noise; which wasn't easy because they were not only carrying their packs, but also what Sigurth had left behind.

"You sneaky bastard," Sveyin said in a whisper when they were back together, everyone gasping to catch their breaths.

"Okay, I'm sneaky," Sigurth sputtered, "but it doesn't matter now. What does matter is that there's a village in our way. And it's on the river."

"So let's go around it."

With that they turned east, going at least a mile before turning south again. The way was much more difficult than usual because they were not only walking through a forest at night with all its confusing aspects, they were also doing so without the river as a reference. Despite this, by the time the sky began to lighten in the east they were on the other side of the village. They were also at a different river that was too wide and deep to wade, one that snaked its way westward.

"My guess is that it empties into the main one," Sveyin said.

"Could be," Sigurth said as he stopped to pick off burrs he picked up going through the last stand of bushes. "But let's keep going. We don't know how close we are to the village, but we can expect the early risers to be moving soon, particularly those who might go fishing."

"That could be to where we are."

"Ya . . . So let's move."

The river made another turn, now going northwest in almost the direction the village might be. Along the way another half mile and the topography flattened to the west, opening up a view the men didn't see at first; but then Nychanachia, who did, grabbed Sigurth and pointed.

Sigurth stopped and looked, as did Sveyin. They both scrambled up a short rise nearby to get a better view. Across the river and the flat spit of land beyond it, as far as the eye could see in both directions, was water.

Sveyin looked at Sigurth, who was staring, almost as if mesmerized by something he never expected. He held that gaze, just staring, for more than a moment. Finally he sighed and turned, saying, "Okay . . . it looks like I've gotten an answer. This certainly isn't the end of the world."

"Ny," Sveyin said. "It looks like another great lake, just like the one we left yesterday."

"I agree."

"Does that mean we can start back?"

Sigurth was about to answer when he heard a sound and turned to see two young men, boys really, come through the bushes nearby. The boys continued on until they were almost in their midst before realizing someone was there. They stopped, eyes popping . . .

"Don't be afraid," Nychanachia said in her language.

Before she could say more, however, first one, then the other, dropped gear and exploded in retreat, their feet churning sand as they picked up speed, one falling down in the process. Then they were gone, their footfalls fading away.

Sveyin, also stunned, swallowed and said, "Let's get out of here."

But Sigurth didn't move . . . instead he looked up the river.

Sveyin, wondering what might be of interest at a time like this, turned, and then he saw. About a hundred yards ahead, partly hidden by bushes along the bank, were several of the long, slim watercraft seen in this part of the world.

"You're not thinking of . . ."

"Cousin, we're looking at the only chance we have," Sigurth interrupted. "Even if our legs weren't dead, we couldn't outrun a village coming after us."

They stood for a moment, then as if in silent accord, headed down to the shore. There were three of the craft, all about the same size, but one in particular seeming in better shape.

"We can't wait," Sigurth said. "There's still a ways to go before we reach the opening to the lake. If they cut us off before then, we've had it."

"I hear you . . . but first, let's get rid of these," Sveyin said, grabbing one of the craft, all of which were upside down and off the ground on crude stands.

They sent two of them away with violent pushes that had them skimming the water almost to the far shore. Then they eased the chosen one in most of the way.

"Careful now," Sveyin said. "These things appear to be made of tree bark, which means they'll be fragile. One wrong step and there'll be a hole."

"Okay, okay . . . So show us how it's done smarty. You get in first."

Sveyin did, stepping carefully on sections that appeared to be for that purpose, settling in on a seat near the front end. Nychanachia stepped in next, taking the same caution. Then Sigurth handed her the weapons and gear, finally easing the craft all the way into the water in preparation for getting in.

"Take it easy," Sveyin said. "This craft is squirrelly . . . Don't tip us over."

"It can't be that difficult, the natives didn't seem to have a problem"

"Well, be careful, that's all I say."

"Here I go," Sigurth said, stepping into the craft with one leg. Then he tried to figure out what to do next.

"Don't poke a hole in the bottom!"

Sigurth stepped out and pulled the end back so it was almost on sand, then stepped over the edge, finding the seat and getting his second leg in.

"Push us off, we need to get going!" Sveyin hissed.

"Paddle you damn fool!" Sigurth answered, trying not to shout.

"I'm paddling!"

Sigurth jammed his paddle into the sand and pushed, the craft slowly breaking free and moving. Then he started paddling furiously.

"Ny o ny!" Sveyin shouted. *"You're turning us upstream. We need to go the other way!"*

So it went until they reached the mouth of the river and the lake. By this time the knowledge of rowing in ships and the coordination and teamwork it required had its influence, and the two figured out what worked and what didn't.

About the time they heard a sound.

"What's that?"

"They're drums," Nychanachia said.

"What do they mean?"

"It means they know we're here and are calling everyone together."

"Let's go for open water," Sveyin said. "If those kids are the only ones that have seen us, they may start after us by going way back to where that was."

"Sounds good, but let's also try find the river we were tracking last night. It's our way back . . . and has to be somewhere ahead."

They paddled in a northwesterly direction, distancing themselves from the where they'd been seen. When they got within a half mile of the distant shore, they turned north.

"The river must be around here!"

It was, which was only of momentary relief, because they could see it was also narrow . . . with what had to be a tremendous volume of water flushing through. When they got closer their fears were confirmed.

"You two sit on the bottom," Sigurth said. "I think the river is going to do what it wants with us; but maybe, if we're low enough, we can ride it through. I'll do what I can from back here."

On entering the river they were drawn in as feared and swept along, with Sigurth working furiously to keep the craft pointing with the flow. After a gauntlet of time and distance that couldn't be measured because of the intense concentration to stay afloat, the river widened and eased. When Sigurth saw that the river was splitting, he thought he might know where he was, so he shouted for Sveyin to get back up and paddle and fight to get out of the main flow into the fork he felt they'd hiked the day before. They made it, and soon were cruising along, almost relaxing.

They didn't see it at first, but as they moved, more with the current than by paddle, they happened to glance at the shore, and there it was, the village they'd walked around in the middle of the night. There wasn't a problem, however, because the people watching them glide by were mainly women and children, who stood gawking as if they couldn't believe what they were seeing. Sveyin guessed that the men were off in the opposite direction where the boys said they could be found, so they smiled and waved and disappeared.

By late afternoon, now traveling west, they saw that they were almost around the large island they'd hiked the day before, with the river about to join into a single flow again. They pulled over, knowing the falls were somewhere ahead and not wanting to get caught in a current they couldn't handle. Once back on land, Sigurth and Sveyin, neither of whom could hardly walk, stumbled up the bank and plopped, groaning with the pleasure this seemed to give. Nychanachia, however, regardless of the tired, scrambled about doing what needed doing, like beaching the craft and unloading it.

The cousins looked at each other, shaking their heads first, then breaking out laughing. They sat, not wanting to move even if they could, even reluctantly sitting up when Nychanachia brought them water and the last remnants of food.

"We were very lucky," she said. "I didn't see any other craft on the river, nor anyone chasing us even though they'd seen us. This may means the people here have a great respect for the river, and that what we did was amazing to them."

The men nodded, wanting more than anything to lay back and rest.

"Ny . . . we can't do that," Nychanachia said. "We're close to the end; but if we dawdle, we can still run into trouble. Word gets around, and there may be many from other parts who come to see what they've been hearing about. There could be a problem."

The men groaned and struggled to their feet.

"How much farther?" Sigurth asked.

"My guess is we're near our first stop, which means we still have three, maybe four miles left to the *Waterbug*."

"Okay, let's get going."

They stopped at the falls again, giving it one long, last look, then followed the rim retracing their steps. They didn't get far.

"Oh ny!" Sveyin said as they rounded a stand of shrubs and were able to see ahead. Word had gotten around, and as a result there were a few dozen natives gathered on the rim overlooking where the *Waterbug* was tied. This came as a surprise because the noise from the falls had drowned out any other sound. But there were other sounds because the natives were milling around, peering over the edge and doing manly things like shouting, throwing stones and threatening to shoot arrows.

"Any ideas?" Sveyin said.

Sigurth only said, "Damn . . ."

"Most of them have bows . . ."

"Ya . . . I see."

Before they could think of doing anything that made sense, Nychanachia left them, walking confidently towards the men who didn't see her until she was almost upon them. As Sigurth and Sveyin watched, she spoke to the group with gusto, gesturing and pointing back to them. Occasionally they could make out a word or two.

Whatever she was saying, however, didn't go smoothly as several of the men took issue, likewise gesturing and pointing back at them, and beating chests and stamping feet. But Nychanachia held her ground in the midst of the anger growing around her, until she turned and motioned for them to come.

They did, holding shields casually to the side, but loosing scabbards for quick release.

"I told them you are great warriors from far away," Nychanachia said, "that you come in peace, and that you're only here to experience the unique beauty of this world. I also said we're finished with our travel and wish to return to where we've from."

One, who seemed a leader, partly because of his demeanor and partly because of the band around his head with a large feather in it, said, which was interpreted, that, "If we let you go, you will return with more people."

"If you don't let us go, more people will come for us." Sigurth said.

After more of this, the leader said, "Your woman said you are great warriors. Show us how you are great."

Sveyin smiled, saying out of the corner of his mouth, "I've been wondering about that myself. Let me see one of your tricks."

Sigurth glared at him and thought a moment. Then with a flurry, he pulled his sword out as if creating something magical and shiny out of nothing. Actually, this *was* astounding because the natives had never seen the likes of the marvelous object that gleamed as light hit it. Next he went into stances, really hambone nonsense they'd gotten into as kids when they were playing around, all the while moving over to a small tree, its trunk about three inches across. In a finale with hops and swirls, he made a slashing movement too quick to follow, and the tree fell to the ground.

While the natives rumbled in awe, Sigurth sheathed his sword with a flourish and sauntered over to Sveyin, whispering "And what are you going to do smart-ass?"

Sveyin responded by turning to Nychanachia and saying, "Tell them we've got to go now."

She did, but the leader stiffened and said something that obviously meant he wanted to see more.

Sigurth laughed, the natives not at all understanding.

Sveyin, now trapped, looked about, his gaze settling on another tree, this a large one about fifty feet away. *Perfect!* He guided the leader over to the tree, adjusting his head band and feather so the feather was directly in front. Then he walked back, strung his bow and notched an arrow. Turning quickly, he fired before the leader realized what was happening. The leader ducked, the arrow sticking and vibrating three feet over where his head had been.

Everyone laughed, eventually even the leader; but Sveyin wagged his finger and motioned the man to get back in place and stand still. When he did, his eyes dancing with uncertainty, Sveyin drew again, the arrow splitting the feather and hitting the tree behind, splattering pieces of bark.

While the leader stood, shaking so badly he was unable to speak, the three picked up their gear and took to the path leading down from the rim.

"What's been going on up there?" Frothi said when they were close enough to hear over the sound of the falls, which was an unrelenting din.

"We'll tell you about it later," Sigurth said. "What do we have to do to get ready to leave?"

"We've never been unready."

"Good . . . Let's load up and cast off."

With that they did, the few miles to the lake moving by more quickly than any they'd ever traveled. When in open water and moving smoothly, the adventure of the last two days was told.

"We were beginning to worry," Jon said. "We didn't like the idea of leaving when it came to two days."

"That's good to hear," Sveyin said. "If the truth be known, we were a little worried too."

"Sigurth," Bovi said. "All of you started back when you saw the second lake. Does that mean you're not ever going to go farther?"

Sigurth looked up, surprised at the question. He looked at Sveyin, who he knew didn't want to address this again, and said. "Ny . . . No more trips like this. If there's something out there, I leave it for someone else to find. I don't have an answer to all the questions that might be asked, but I hope that when Sveyin and I put together the sketches we've been making, it may do for some of them.

"Where are we going now?"

"Home, to Kanata . . . as fast as we can."

They reached the eastern end of the lake in four days, making only one night stop along the way. At the shelter, where they came ashore, it was like returning to a home of sorts.

"Where are the mules?" Asa said.

Askel, who was the first out tying down the lines, said, "We'll look around. I see plenty of tracks.

"They're not the only tracks around, though," someone else said, a comment echoed by several as they unloaded and carried stores up the beach. By the time they'd settled in, they'd identified a host of animals in addition to the mules, including a number of human footprints.

"The inside of the shelter is in good shape, as if that matters," Sveyin said.

"Which means?"

"Well, I don't know about you, but I want to get home. That means moving out as soon as we can decide which way."

There were only two options, and everybody knew them. One was to retrace their steps paralleling he river; the other was taking the *Waterbug* and running the river, taking a chance they'd make it. At the dinner fire a little later after things had settled, the river was the main topic of conversation. Not surprisingly, everyone was anxious to return.

"You've been holding back, Sigurth." Bovi said. "We know you must have an opinion."

"Well, I do. I just thought I'd hear what all of you had to say first."

"Okay, now you've heard. Most of us hate the idea of hiking again, or of spending another winter away from home. But the river *is* scary."

Sigurth nodded. "Yes it is. Sveyin and I made notes on every part it that could be a problem on the way up. We went over those notes since getting here, trying to make up our minds."

"And?"

"We're taking to the water. I mean Sveyin, Nyhanachia and myself are going to give it a try. I don't want to leave the *Waterbug* behind because it's too valuable a ship, one that will be very useful back home. Besides we think we can make it. As we told you we stole one of those small boats the natives use and managed to survive some very rough water, even though it was frail when compared to what we have. If the rest of you prefer to hike, and if we make it, we'll meet at the bottom of the last falls where we started out from last year."

It was quiet for a moment, then Bovi said, "That's crazy! You can't make it with three people."

"Ya . . . I know. But like I said, I don't want to leave the ship behind. If a few others will join, it will make our chances better."

Frothi said, "Count me in, and Arni too. We helped build the damn thing and know how sturdy it is."

Soon everyone was for sailing.

"Think about it," Jon said. "If it works, we'll be home in only a fraction of the time. And if it doesn't . . . well, there must be something we can do"

"There is," Bovi said. "We can package the things we need in a way they'll float; that way we can retrieve them if things go wrong, and continue on."

"What about the mules?" Asa said.

Sigurth winced, "They're not here. Even if they were, we couldn't take them because we can't tie them down on our small open deck. That being so, they'd stumble all over in a turbulence, probably hurting someone besides going over a rail. I'm sorry about that because they've been very useful, and are like family."

"But they're not here," Askel added, "and they're not likely to be. We saw all kinds of tracks around here, and many of them human. Those mules wouldn't stand a chance if a hunter went after them."

Bovi laughed.

"What's so funny?"

"Just thinking. Remember what we did when we left Vinland?"

"What? Oh, you mean the barge."

"Ya . . . If those mules showed up, I agree with Sigurth that we can't take them aboard the *Waterbug*. But we could make a small barge, a raft."

"Aaaah," Sigurth said. "That's it. If the mules show up, we'll take an extra day and make a raft."

Sveyin listened to the conversation without commenting; then when everyone dispersed to make ready for the night, he walked by Sigurth and whispered, "The sneaky bastard strikes again . . . You know those mules will never show"

Two of them, however, stood outside the door the next morning to greet the first person up.

They left two days later, every bit as weird a convoy as that that had arrived from Vinland with Thorth. Managing the *Waterbug* was one thing, but the raft tied behind it was another, making everything much harder. The main problem was that if the *Waterbug* slowed or was hung-up, the raft could crash into it. They made arrangements best they could to counter this possibility, and entered the river and an adventure that could have been written into legend.

The beginning was actually easy, with a gentle current flowing past an amazing parade of islands that had only been glimpsed when hiking past the year before. There were temptations to steer into one of the labyrinthian channels along the way to see more, but Sigurth told Bovi to follow the south shore, fearing that any of them could be a snare and their undoing.

Then there were the rapids. They approached the first with the dread of knowing this was the end, only to slide through a dip and splash and bob to the surface without any problem.

Each of the rapids thereafter was different, with what was seen and noted while hiking of little use for getting through them. The largest and most awesome seen before turned out to be the easiest, as both crafts eased through with barely any special action needed. Despite the numbing and trying situations, there were periods of gentle flows and eddies, so stopping for the night or to attend to a particular issue was never a problem. There were also views from the water during those periods of gentile flows that allowed them to see much more of what the river held in all its verdant beauty, then they had been able to while struggling on land.

The last of the falls, the one that ended the part of the trip aboard the *Mule*, was one of the worst, and everybody knew it. After the many gut-wrenching experiences getting to that point, there was a growing feeling their luck couldn't hold forever. Before tackling it, they drifted to a stop along the bank where an eddy provided calm waters.

"What do you think?" Sigurth asked. "My recollection is that there were turbulences that had to be from rocks below the drop. In fact they seemed to extend all the way across."

"There were," Sveyin answered, looking again at the first sketch made when they started. Then he said, "There seemed to be a slight trough that started its drop sooner and extended farther about a third of the way across."

"That's it . . . Bovi, listen up."

When they approached the falls, all were tense, because after the last command from Bovi, there was nothing to do but pray to the God they felt most hopeful and hang on. In keeping with those fears, the *Waterbug* followed the drop into the trough, the prow disappearing and water billowing up and over and in and drenching everyone and everything. Then tense seconds later, that seemed like an eternity, the prow rose as if resurrecting and leveled out to float peacefully downstream.

They entered the bay at Kanata and turned the corner leading home before anyone saw them. And seeing them didn't mean recognizing them, because the *Waterbug* never existed before. It wasn't until someone heard the mules bray and made a correct guess, that word was screamed and a stampede started towards the landing.

Chapter 27

NYCHANACHIA

1030
(1010)

It was good to be outside . . . not that the weather was good, because it wasn't. It was as bad as it gets, with banks of snow and freezing temperatures and drifting winds and flaky skies. But Sigurth was well wrapped and bundled, and even though conditions pinched his cheeks and made him squint, it felt good. It felt good because the last month inside with its dank dimness and lack of privacy, even of thought, were getting to him. Those conditions weren't unusual for winter; but then again this wasn't the usual winter.

For one thing there was sickness. Winter never was a healthy time, with sickness and even death sometimes a part. It seemed to be more prevalent this year, however. After returning and the celebrations that followed, it was disturbing to hear of those who'd died while they were gone, with more following since then. Kanata had few people to begin with, and now there were fewer. The strange thing relating to this problem was that animals were doing fine. With those brought from Vinland, the numbers had been increasing and were on their way to being impressively sized flocks.

Strange.

For another, and this was what really had him booting frozen clumps about, was Nychanachia. He remembered when he'd first really noticed her, a lean sprite among the other girls he was instructing on spinning yarn. Since then he'd frequently been drawn to her, not only because of her pleasing face, but also for her quick wit and sparkling eye, a combination that often had them playing little tricks on one another, something like with he and Sveyin, only different. Since then they'd also shared saga-worthy experiences in which she'd played important, even crucial roles. All of this was complicated by the fact she'd taken to putting her bed-roll next to his, which meant he could do anything he wanted to do . . . and he wanted to; but for some reason, which he hadn't resolved, in the right way.

In Norway, and also in Greenland and Iceland for that matter, there was a right way . . . sort of. If a man was interested in a woman, he would go to the father and ask for her hand. Then, if deemed a suitable fit, there would be negotiations and agreements, followed by a simple ceremony and party. More often than not, the marriage was for convenience, business or politics, with emotion or mutual attraction not a factor.

It had to be different here, being so far away as it was with completely different cultures, but in what way was it or should it be? The only precedent among his people in this remote colony was Sveyin and Bergljot, where she'd gone to him. He didn't have a clue how Nychanachia's people treated this kind of thing. He didn't know her parents, for instance, or whether they needed to be considered. He'd assumed that the circle of poles he'd seen in her village were there for ceremonial purposes, but he didn't know if those purposes included marriages.

All he knew was that Nychanachia was no longer adolescent, now fourteen to sixteen years old, and that he wanted to get on with his life, with her, and in the proper way. He also didn't know who he could talk to. So he'd churned in mind, which had been difficult while stifling inside, the only persons coming to mind for advice being Thorth, who was older and liked to be considered a leader, and Bergljot, who naturally was. He decided to talk to Bergljot, mainly because she said she wanted to talk to him.

Bergljot eyed him, a somewhat puzzled look on her face, "Don't you know her parents are dead?"

"Ny, I didn't know," Sigurth said.

Bergljot shook her head. "What do you men ever talk about? You never seem to know what you should."

"How'd *you* find out?"

"Duh! We talked. She told me about that the first winter she stayed over."

Bergljot walked over and gave Sigurth a big hug, kissing him on the cheek and saying, "This is so sweet. Thank you for coming to me with the problem . . . I'm honored. And you must know how Nychanachia feels about you. She's managed to be somewhat coy like women are prone to do, but Sveyin and I have laughed about how obvious it is to us. Let's do this, if you can wait."

Sigurth cocked his head, "I'm waiting . . ."

"Did you remember that I wanted to talk to you?"

"Oh ya."

"Well," Bergljot said, "It may be that the two can be linked together."

"Two what?"

"Your plans and our plans."

"And what are your plans?"

"While all of you were gone, one of the things a few of us women tried to do, was to get better acquainted with our neighbors. You know I've felt we should be coexisting with them ever since we've gotten here."

Sigurth nodded.

"Well, we made some progress, but in my estimation, not enough. So Sveyin and I have decided that we and the children are going to live with them . . . in their village."

"Sveyin agreed to that?"

Bergljot laughed. "After all those long trips with you, he could hardly refuse."

"When?"

"As soon as the snow melts."

"You mean just for the summer, I suppose," Sigurth said.

"I can't answer that. We may want to stay until we understand each other fully. There's only so much Nychanachia and the girls could do to help us reach that point."

"Okay," Sigurth said, but more as a question. "So how does that link with us?"

Just then, little Garth, the son born while the trip up the river had been made, began to stir, causing her to jump. "I'll let you know," she said.

It seemed like forever, but it wasn't long at all before the weather warmed, the snow first imperceptibly shrinking, then transforming full bore to water, flooding the landscape and making a mess. And Sigurth was nervous. He and Sveyin had both been rounders, beginning about when hair began to grow where it hadn't before, and extending, almost to renown at fairs held each year, as well as at Nitharos before Greenland and points west interrupted all their play.

But this was different.

The trip had changed many things. It had removed from mind a concept of the world he found hard to believe, but which he couldn't let go until he'd tried his utmost to either prove or disprove it. That was now behind him.

There were the parties that followed, and the telling and retelling of the many experiences from different points of view.

There was Garth, now able to walk and everybody's darling, particularly his and Nychanachia's, who the boy seemed to bounce between as much as with his parents. During the winter with its long hours, Sigurth carved toys that had the boy hopping.

And especially there was Nychanachia, who'd shared the trials of the journey, not only doing as well as any of the men, but also adding to its success in ways none other could. Then upon returning, she blossomed further in a manner astounding as much as pleasing to him.

So he was on edge, waiting for Bergljot to "let him know," with the only way to get relief being to work. So that's what he did in earnest as soon as mud turned to dirt.

"Are you ready?" Sveyin said, walking up and surprising Sigurth, who hadn't seen him since he, Bergljot and the family had left weeks before. At the time, Sigurth's head was down, concentrating on spring planting which he'd been into for hours.

"Eh? Ready for . . ." not finishing as he saw the smiling face before him and could guess.

"You planning to work all day? Everybody else is already there."

"Well, dammit, this is a fine time to tell me. I can't go anyplace or do anything right now . . . I'm a mess."

"That you are. But I don't think they can get along without you, so let's get you cleaned up and on your way."

"Way to where?" Sigurth said.

"To where Nychanachia is."

"Which is where?"

"Her village."

"Her village? I didn't know she was gone," Sigurth said.

"I guess I forgot to tell you."

"You bastard!"

Sveyin laughed. "It's a lot more fun this way. Come on, let's go . . . I may be able to find some grog to get you in a better mood."

"I'm not in a bad mood . . . It's just that no one ever tells me anything."

They arrived after dark to a village scene that was eerie because of the many torches lighting the central area. A crowd was gathered within that area, and among them Sigurth could see Bergljot and the kids, Thorth,

Yngvi and his family, Thor and Ondur, and everyone who'd returned in the *Waterbug*.

Sigurth hated not knowing. He now knew what this was about, but didn't have a clue as to how it was going to happen; and correctly suspected Sveyin was supposed to tell him, but didn't and was thoroughly enjoying letting him dangle. The only good part so far was that he was clean, even having shaved and trimmed his hair which had gotten to wild-man long, and wore a special, beautiful tunic sewn by Thora that he'd never had the occasion to wear.

They stopped at the poles, the poles he'd noticed the only other time he'd been at the village, that were eight in number forming a circle maybe twenty feet in diameter. A few girls, including Nychanachia, were in the center, while young men, sometimes two, were at each of the poles . . . except one. Sveyin, smiling like an idiot, pointed at the vacant one, obviously meaning for Sigurth to go there.

Once in place, there was an explosion of sound as the men at the other poles began whooping it up and dancing, kicking their legs high and spinning around almost as in the antics of Yule-fooling. Sigurth heard Sveyin goading him to do the same, so he started to shuffle, managing a mild "whoopee." The tempo increased and the other men, from time to time, broke from a pole and rushed in to grab a girl, only to be driven off and back to where they'd come from.

"Oh I get it," Sigurth thought, so he stomped a little higher, then rushed in and grabbed at Nychanachia.

But she drove him away too.

"Damn!"

Back at the pole, he hesitated for a moment, still not sure what he was supposed to do. Then he let go his inhibitions, jumping and swirling and kicking and whooping the likes that had never been seen. When he figured he'd made as big a fool of himself as was possible, he rushed in again and picked up Nychanachia, still protesting but aglow with a radiance she couldn't hide, and carried her to stand before where the elders were assembled.

Words were spoken, some of which he didn't understand; but the meaning was clear. He'd guessed right, no thanks to his best friend Sveyin, because when the simple ceremony was over, pretty girls moved in to place flowered garlands over their heads, everyone then moving in with genuinely smiling faces to hug or beat shoulders or do something that was somehow fitting.

After that it was like weddings everywhere, a social experience with good food, here under torchlight, and bits and pieces of conversation with different cultures trying to be cordial and understanding of one another. But there was no grog, so the point when one could no longer think of anything to say came sooner than usual. That and the fact the guests from Kanata didn't have places to stay like those they were accustomed to, led them to decide it would be better to return. So they said their goodbyes and left by torchlight to walk the long way back, which they did as soon as Sigurth and Nychanachia disappeared for the forest hideaway prepared for them.

A few days later, they were back in Kanata, moving into the Longhouse where Sveyin and Bergljot had been, which was somewhat better than the bunkhouse Sigurth had been staying in before. Nychanachia was okay with whatever it was like, but Sigurth wasn't. Privacy was better than it had been before with drapes and partitions Sveyin had devised; but it still wasn't what Sigurth wanted.

What did he want?

He didn't mind farming, and had worked hard at it every summer he could remember; but woodworking was an interest that kept him busy much of the winter, and was something he regretted putting aside when spring chores took over. Now that he was approaching what was considered middle age, all of 28 years, and was delightfully married, he began to think more seriously of what he wanted to do with the rest of his life. There really wasn't a struggle in mind about this, because the first home he could remember was a craft-shop, and the first thing that had given him delight was working with tools and carving. He explained this to "Nikka," which he had taken to calling Nychanachia, and she was as enthused about it as he was. Her experiences had been much later in her life, but she'd been astounded at spinning the yarn, working the loom and learning to make the things that grew from those skills. When she saw the tunic worn at their wedding, her interest in learning more about things like that exploded.

After Kanata had survived its first winter, and the concept of "we" reinforced at the Althing, the next step had been to determine what the next step should be. There had been an immediate clamor for what people could call their own, with some even taking the initiative and staking claims. This, however, was going to lead to nowhere but trouble, so Sigurth did the only thing he knew to do in this regard, and that was to appoint a few to manage the problem. The first he picked was Sveyin, who'd almost gone into hiding when he heard what Sigurth was doing, then adding Thorth for maturity, Ondur for muscle and Trygvi for fairness. Except that the group wasn't considered complete, at least by the women of the community, who selected Bergljot to represent their interests, and no one had the courage to argue.

Sveyin thought that Sigurth appointed him to get even for something he'd done; but that wasn't the case. During the voyages he'd shown an aptitude for not only locating dots, but particularly for representing on parchment features the landscape relating to those dots looked like. To do what the selected group had to do, a good idea of what Kanata consisted of needed to be understood. So Sveyin went to work locating dots for this, that and the other in relation to a reference point, and after considerable effort, one of the first, if not the first, master plan in this world came into being. From this roadways were located, generally amorphous to follow similar levels and formations, and properties were outlined. The wisdom of the group determined that most properties should be reserved for future growth, which wasn't a problem as there were still enough good choices to satisfy those that were there. Some areas were reserved for community purposes, some for business, and some for special purposes like the marina. Most of the planning had been completed before the long voyage was made. Based on these studies, a few allotments were initially made, but the majority were concluded afterwords, and all settled by the time Sigurth returned with a bride and a look to his future.

The site he had been given was no larger than any other, but it was abutting where the marina would go, and extended to a business site near the community longhouse.

It was on the business site where he next went to work. He chopped trees and cleared land, stacking materials as if he were building another ship, except that he wasn't. He was going to build a craft-shop, somewhat like that of his early memories, but more like that later built at the family homestead, with all the improvements he could remember Thora wanted to have. By midsummer, the shop was framed, and he was beginning roofing operations, when Ondur, who was assisting, nudged him.

"What?"

"Well just take a look," Ondur said.

Sigurth crunched his face in question, until Ondur pointed . . . pointed to Nikka who was a ways away in the garden, and seemed to have collapsed to a sitting position, but leaning forward with one arm propping her up.

"Is she sick . . . or is she pregnant?" Ondur said.

Sigurth sputtered, his mind having difficulty switching from what he'd been concentrating on. "Pregnant?" He managed to say.

Then he dropped to the ground and trotted to where Nikka was sitting.

"Are you okay?"

She straightened as he approached. "Ya. I just had a dizzy spell. I'm fine."

He looked at her, then still looking, turned his head and asked, "Are you pregnant?"

Nikka snorted and tried to be gruff, saying, "Sigurth Gunnarsson . . . You must be the most unobservant person that ever was. You haven't even noticed?"

Sigurth tried to explain but only babbled, finally giving up and breaking into a broad grin. "You're pregnant!"

"Ya, I'm pregnant, and have been for at least two months."

Sigurth didn't know what to say. He shuffled a bit, asking questions that were way too late in coming, and only succeeded in irritating her more.

"Oh get back to work," she said. "If this baby comes and there's not a roof over her head, we're going to be really mad."

Sigurth spun around with that and returned to where Ondur was waiting.

"Well?"

"She's pregnant all right," Sigurth said. "And damn . . . I'm in trouble."

"You didn't know?"

"Ny! Nobody tells me anything."

Ondur roared and shook his head, finally saying, "I guess we'd better finish this building."

They did, because Ondur spread the word and assembled others who could break away before harvesting began. When finished, it was larger than either of the other craft-shops had been, with a shanty-roofed section on the north side to host a number of other functions, including the rare luxury of sleeping with privacy.

An open house celebration was held and everyone was there. A lamb was slaughtered for the purpose, as well as the new "maize" harvested from the garden. Almost all the grog in the community went down in the course of the party, which included presentations of the kinds of things that would be conducted in the shop . . . and all was well.

"I've got to tell Sveyin and Bergljot," Sigurth said the next day while they were still on a high from the opening.

"That's a good idea," Nikka said. "I'd like to see them too, and the village again for that matter."

"Oh ny o ny," Sigurth said. "I'm going alone. It's a long way to walk . . . too long for you now."

"I'd be fine."

"You're fine now and going to stay that way, which means you're not going. I'll leave in the early morning and be back before dark."

"If we took our time and stayed overnight, it would be easy. I've walked it may times you know."

Sigurth shook his head. "No way."

"Is this the same man who didn't hesitate to take me over one waterfall after another?"

"That was then. For now the answer is ny, ny, ny. I'll find someone to be with you while I'm gone, but you're not going."

Sveyin saw him before he'd passed the flimsy walls of the village. Actually, he'd been working on an outdoor cover for the cooking fire, when one of the youngsters gathered around to watch what he was doing said, "Look," and pointed, and that's how it happened.

As Sigurth approached, Sveyin put down what he was doing to greet him, and after a quick hug and a bunch of nonsense, Sveyin said, "Pa told me on many occasions that you walk just like uncle Gunnar. So whenever I see you in the distance, I think of that."

"Which all proves you don't have much on your mind."

And so it went for awhile.

"Seriously," Sveyin said. "It's good to see you; but why did you come at this time?"

Sigurth then told him of Nychanachia's pregnancy and the completion of the craft-shop and all else he could think of, all of which Sveyin was interested in, asking many questions. The conversation ended when there was a shout, and Sigurth looked up to see Bergljot and the children approaching, the shout coming from Garth, who rushed ahead and jumped into Sigurth's arms.

"My o my," Sigurth said, finally getting control of the youngster, "Who is this anyways. I was told a bear took you away."

"Ny ny ny!" Garth said, pulling away with eyes about to pop.

"Ya du . . . One of those black crows told me," Sigurth said. "They like to do that. Didn't anyone tell you I talk to birds?"

"Ny ny," Garth repeated, shaking his head. Before this could go any farther, Sigurth put him on his shoulders and took a wild run around the area, circling in and around the poles.

When they returned, Sigurth put Garth down and hugged Yrsa and Bergljot, bantering with them for a while before sitting down to visit.

Sigurth watched as Sveyin helped Bergljot onto some cushions, shaking his head as he did.

"What's wrong?" Bergljot said.

"Oh nothing . . . It's just me. I've been so wrapped up in what Nikka and I've been doing, I'd forgotten that when all of you left, you were pregnant."

"Who's Nikka? Is that what you call Nychanachia?"

"Ya . . . Anyway, how are you feeling? You must be getting close."

"I am," Bergljot said, laughing. "Kind of you to notice. But seriously, I'm fine and am dying to hear the news from home."

"So Nychanachia is pregnant too."

Sigurth nodded, retelling all he told Sveyin earlier, then saying, "That's about it from my end; how are things going here?"

"It's different," Bergljot said.

"Well, we knew that."

"Ya," Bergljot said, and didn't at first elaborate. "As you know, we came here right after the spring melt, to initially set up for your wedding. And we have stayed ever since. At first, things went well enough with Yrsa and I both speaking the language. Even after the wedding it seemed progress was being made. But then there was a sickness, with many being ill, and even a few dying."

"Like we had last winter," Sigurth said.

"Ya," Bergljot said, nodding. "Sigurth, these people are very superstitious. We don't fully understand yet all they believe in; but they have their ceremonies, during which time they look to the heavens, reaching out to what they call the "Great Spirit" for a number of considerations. And the wind and weather and many other aspects of nature have their influence too."

"Do you want to pack up and return to Kanata?"

"Ny o ny!" Bergljot said. "I never expected it to be easy here. I just never knew in what ways it would be hard. The sicknesses have been a setback."

"You mean they blame you? Surely they've been sick before."

"They have . . . sort of. Ya, they've been sick before; but there's a coincidence here."

"Let me explain," Sveyin said. "Remember the natives to the north . . . the ones we almost went to war with?"

"Ya."

"Well, they're not exactly friends with the natives here. But they're not sworn enemies either, and get along in a sort of peaceful coexistence way. They're both into fishing, which is one of their staples, and so it's not unusual for them to come across one another from time to time. They don't speak exactly the same language, but they understand one another. So guess what the fishers from here found out recently."

"I don't have a clue," Sigurth said. "The fact is we haven't seen much of them since that encounter off our shore. Small groups used to stop by and walk around, but that's stopped; and Yngvi, who's taken animals to the island, hasn't seen any of them."

"Exactly," Sveyin said. "The reason is sickness. They've had a few bad winters in that regard since our settling in, so guess who they blame. Anyway, they've broken camp and moved farther north."

"Damn!"

"Ya."

"So what *are* your plans?" Sigurth said turning to Bergljot.

"We're going to stay as long as it takes," Bergljot said. Because we can't quit, not if we ever hope to make a success out of being here. On the bright side are the women. I've been working with them, teaching them to spin yarn and work the loom; while they've been introducing all kinds of things from their world. "Maize" is just one of them. And the girls who wintered with us, including Nythanachia while she was here, have been wonderful assistants. So it's not all bad."

"Is there any way we can help?"

"I thought you'd never ask. We've already exchanged garden goods and grains, so that's been great; and the sewing and weaving have been started, but have a way to go. Sharing domesticated animals would be good because that's something that's astounded them as much as anything; but the biggest thing to bring our people together would be the sharing of metal weapons, tools and devices."

"They're in short supply right now," Sigurth said. "And they're very precious to us. They're also the only advantage we have against overwhelming numbers if things go bad."

"That's a tough one," Sveyin said. "The only way I've been able to get around it is to not have any of it around, which means we've really gone native, which isn't easy. One thing I've told the men here is that someday we'll jointly learn how to get metal out of the soil, which will then solve the problem."

"Very good," Sigurth said. "That would be great."

"But I don't know much about doing that, do you?" Sveyin said.

"Ny . . . not much. We'll just have to find those that do know, that's all. In the meantime, is there anything else I can do to help?"

"Ya . . ." Bergljot answered, speaking in such a way that it seemed both were reluctant to speak up.

"Ya?" Sigurth said.

"Actually, it's Sveyin's idea; but we're both having trouble with the thought of asking."

"Which is?"

"It's Garth," Sveyin said.

"Ya Garth." Bergljot said. "Things here are a little tense right now, with me about to pop any day. Yrsa is doing fine and will actually be a help; but Garth is a handful. Could you and Nychanachia look after him for awhile?"

"Sigurth was tongue-tied for a moment, but recovered, saying, "We'd love to have the little rascal around . . . for as long as you'd like us too."

"It shouldn't be for long," Sveyin said, then added. "When things settle here, probably after the baby and the harvest, we'll come by and rescue you."

"Look what followed me home," Sigurth said as he came up to Nychanachia, who was sitting outside on the sun side of the craft-shop and working on her chores.

"Garth . . . Oh ny o ny! What a pleasant surprise," she said, giving him a big hug. But before she could say much more, the boy broke free and ran over to where the goats were penned.

"What happened?"

Sigurth explained the visit and Bergliot's strange request.

"I suppose you want *me* to look after him."

"I'll help," Sigurth said. "What do you think of my building a small goat-powered wagon for him to ride around in?"

It was late in the year and the harvests were in, but most were still outside, particularly the men, who were doing the things needed to prepare for winter. The first freeze had already happened, followed by almost two weeks of balmy weather, so when the skies clouded over again and a chill wind blew in from the north, everyone felt that snow was on its way.

Sigurth was finishing a few details on the animal shelter, which was near the shop, and from time to time looking south to the trail disappearing in that direction. There'd been a little traffic recently, particularly the girls who would winter over, so he'd heard that Bergljot had delivered another boy to be named Sverri, and that all had gone well. This was fine, except if it was their intent to travel to Kanata and retrieve Garth, they'd better hurry with the weather acting up like it was. He was even considering making a trip to help them return.

The last thing he expected to see came from the opposite direction.

Someone rang the triangle at the cookhouse, which coming at an odd time made those within hearing listen up to hear *"A ship! A ship!"*

Sigurth though a joke was being played; but he put down what he was doing anyway and walked around the corner, where he could see the bay and the river extending eastward. The shout was true, a ship coming into view, its sail and hull tilted to work the wind and move against it.

By the time the ship reached the dock, with its sail now furled and oars out, most of the settlement was there to assist any way they could. Despite less than ideal conditions, the landing went well as lines were thrown and the ship tied and bumpered without incident.

Something was familiar about the ship, but Sigurth at first didn't see anyone he recognized . . . and then he did. Standing beside the man tying in the steering oar, with his stringy hair flopping out in the air highlighting his round, cheeky face, was Ingivar from the Way Station.

"I thought you, of all people, would have more sense than to sail in weather like this!" Sigurth shouted.

Ingivar broke into a grin and waved to indicate he was coming ashore, picking up his gear and working his way across a deck of busy people to balance his way down the plank.

"I'd almost given up," Ingivar said, his expression one of great relief. "You can't imagine how good it was to finally see your settlement."

"Weren't my direction good?" Thorth said, walking up to also greet him.

"They ended up being good," Ingivar said. "But it wasn't like we came straightaway here. It's a long story, so why don't you folks tell us where to go first. We can get together later."

"No problem," Sigurth said. "We have plenty of room. Thorth, how about you directing the ships' complement to the bunkhouses, and alerting the cookhouse about the number of guests."

He turned back to Ingivar. "I assume you're not going back on the water again soon."

Ingivar laughed and shook his head, "No way."

"Okay then," Sigurth said. "Once you've unloaded, we'll help getting your ship out of the water; which we can probably do tomorrow. I see Odd over there giving a hand, so I'll go over and talk to him about that. Why don't we meet at my place after that for dinner. Thorth knows the way. You hinted at a story . . . and we're anxious to hear it."

It was dark with icy flakes dancing in the air by the time Ingivar and Thorth entered the shop.

"My, look at this," Ingivar said as he eyed the spacious interior, framed with the usual timbers, but in a unique way. Its vaulted volume looked exotic by the light of the cooking fire in the center and the array of candles spaced along the length of the aisle.

Sigurth smiled, more than a little proud of his handiwork, saying, "It's sometimes amazing what happens when you can't do things the usual way."

"What do you mean?"

"We didn't have nails, so everything's interlocked and doweled."

"Welcome to our home," Nychanachia said, coming out from behind a screen where she'd been preparing dinner, and surprising Ingivar, whose eyes had been on the overhead details.

"This is Ingivar," Sigurth said, "the Captain of the ship that arrived today. He's also the head of the Way Station you've heard me talk about. Ingivar, my wife Nychanachia."

Ingivar babbled an awkward response upon seeing the pretty face with its unmistakeable features of dark-toned skin, dark eyes and black, ponytailed hair. Then, trying to recover, he swept into an overly formal, sweeping bow, which from his porky figure wasn't exactly elegant, saying, "So charmed to meet you."

Thorth broke out laughing, as did Sigurth, who said, "Welcome to the New World." Then he added, "Let's relax on the ledge over there. I'll get some horns to start us off, then you can tell us what brings you here at this unlikely time."

"It's like this," Ingivar said, once they were comfortable and downed the first horn. "Do you know about the latest attempt to settle Vinland?"

"Ny," Sigurth said. "Yours is the first ship to come this way, so we're really in the dark."

"Okay . . . Well, what I'm going to tell you is going to be hard to believe; it would be for me if I were in your shoes, but it just happens to be true. It all started over a year ago, when two ships stopped at our Way Station, one being Freydis' and her complements, almost the same that had sailed with you to Straumsfjord and Hops; the other, a larger knorr. Both ships were heavily loaded with roughly thirty men and five women aboard.

"The second ship was owned by brothers named Helgi and Finnbogi, who were from the eastern fjords in Iceland. They'd been to Greenland, wintering there, and had been talked into joining Freydis on a trip to Vinland, in hopes of either restarting a colony or finding a way to turn a profit.

"Neither ship stayed long at our station, the ship from Iceland leaving first, and Freydis the next day. There's not much to tell about that, and they were gone.

"We saw nothing of either of them the rest of that year, and naturally nothing over the winter. Then in the spring, the spring of this year, Freydis returned, stopping by on her way back to Greenland, but in the other ship. When asked about that she said the brothers had decided to stay, and since there was much to carry, they'd traded ships because theirs was the larger.

"This sounded reasonable enough; but later as the summer wore on, in discussing the matter among our people, questions began to surface. Actually nothing specific, just feelings, because several stated that when they tried to converse with Freydis' crew members, many of them avoided eye contact. So it was, you know, only questionable body language.

"Eventually curiosity got the best of us, so we loaded our ship, which isn't the greatest thing afloat and used mostly for short coastal trips, and sailed to Vinland.

"Would you mind another horn?" I'm beginning to shudder with the recollections."

Nychanahia, who'd been by the fire but straining to hear every word, rushed over to refill.

Ingivar downed his in a long series of swallows, then settled back, it not clear if he was trying to remember or trying to forget.

"When we arrived in Vinland, the first thing we saw was Freydis' ship. It was firmly tied at the dock, slowly rocking with the pulse of the water; but other than the creaking of wood and rope that ships tend to make, there wasn't a sound. If this wasn't spooky enough, no one came to assist us.

"The situation had all of us imagining things; but we made it in fine and tied up, then disembarked.

"We hadn't gotten far inland, when it hit us . . . an awful smell; the kind that once you've been exposed to, you'll forever know what it means. The smell got worse as we approached the buildings, and many birds, blackbirds and vultures mostly, scattered as we got closer.

"Some of us gagged before we came on the scene, it got so bad. Then we saw . . . a sight that was as horrible as the smell coming from it—several dozen men scattered in heaps by the sides of the buildings."

"What could have caused the fight?" Thorth said, jumping in when Ingivar paused to catch his breath.

"This was no fight," Ingivar said.

"But . . ."

"They were murdered. Somehow they'd been tricked and tied up so they were helpless; then their throats were slit."

The room went silent as the scene was imagined. Then Sigurth said, "You mentioned men . . . What about the women?"

"Oh, the women," Ingivar said in almost a moan. "Yes, there were women, and we found them too. They were inside and were not tied up, but they were just as dead. By their wounds, it looked like they'd tried to defend themselves, but failed. We guessed an axe had been used."

Ingivar sat for a minute, his voice having cracked at the last comment. Taking a deep breath, he continued. "Nature does quite a bit in a short time; and this time wasn't short, so you can guess what it was like. Anyway, we collected the bodies and put them in the building where the women were. Next we collected wood from around the area and piled them over the bodies; then we set it all afire . . . I mean all the buildings.

"We felt the place was cursed and wanted to erase all of it from the world. In a few years, with weeds and trees tending to take over the way they do, it may be that all traces of this so-called Vinland will have vanished. We also didn't wish to stay any longer than we had to, nor care to go back to the Station. Then we thought of you. Since Freydis' ship was bigger and better than ours, we moved all we had to it and cast off. We should have gotten here sooner, but we didn't want our ship left behind, so we tried towing it, an attempt that almost did us in. We got as far as the large bay with a huge rock at its northern corner and stopped, pulling our boat ashore and tenting it over so we could retrieve it later. Then we got back on course and followed the shore as it turned west. Another week passed and the weather began to turn, and finally we spotted your settlement."

There was a lull, the story being hard to believe.

Ingivar changed the subject. "As I made my way over here after unloading, it looked to me that your community if off to a good start. Does it have a name?"

"We call it Kanata."

"It's a nice name," Ingivar said, holding out his horn.

The next day it snowed—large flakes that filled the air in a picturesque display that could have been enjoyable, except it wasn't exactly endeared by the men who had to get the ship out of the water and tented for the season. In the days following, it continued to snow, not as pleasantly, with winds kicking in and temperatures falling, so that by the time of Yule, Kanata was deep in snow with little that could be done outside. That didn't mean to Sigurth that he couldn't be outside, which he frequently was, and not to get into the winter games like the younger men did. His main interest outside was to the south, which he scanned each day for signs of movement on the trail. He even tried to walk it, or where he thought it was, but the going was too slow and labored to make sense for trying to go all the way. This led to attempts at making snowshoes, which didn't go well because the saplings needed to make the shapes weren't to be found this time of the year.

What did happen from time to time, particularly late in the afternoon and hours after sunset, was for a few men, usually Thorth and Ingivar, to gather in the shop, drink a horn or two, and discuss what should be done for the benefit of Kanata, particularly as impacted by the lack of traffic, the incidences of sickness, and Freydis.

One night Sigurth unrolled the sketches he and Sveyin had made, and together with the ones he'd copied years before from Audn, tacked them together on the wall, assembled in such a way that they related to one another.

"What are these supposed to mean?" Ingivar asked.

Sigurth explained how the sketches had started by a pirate who'd traveled far and wide and recorded his findings in a form of an earth plan.

"What's this?" One asked.

"That's the coast of Norway."

"Really?"

"And this?" And so it went until there was some understanding of what each of the shapes represented.

"What I've tried to do here, and that might be hard to understand too," Sigurth said, "is to draw them, and assemble them, so that the distance from here to here, is near to the same as from here to here."

"And this is Garthariki?"

"Ya."

"And this is Byzantium?"

"Ya."

Ingivar went to the wall and put his hands on Norway and Byzantium. Then he turned, and trying to hold his hands the same distance apart, moved from Norway west, making two moves to where Kanata was indicated to be.

"Are you trying to tell me that it's twice as far from here to home, as it is to the farthest place I've previously heard of?"

"Something like that," Sigurth answered.

Ingivar paused, shuffled away stroking his beard, then turned and shuffled back to the sketches. "Why would anyone want to sail that far to get here?"

"Apparently they don't," Thorth said. I've been hereabouts ten years now. At first when we set up at Vinland there was a lot of enthusiasm for what this could lead to. There were several ships that came by those first few years. But they came and went never to be seen again. Then there was you, Sigurth, followed by three more groups, most noteworthy the one led by Thorfinn Karsefni, who made serious attempts to start a colony. After a few years, however, they packed up and left with no intention of returning. All, that is except Freydis and the brothers who gave it the last try."

"Some last try," Ingivar said. "I don't know what she said when she got back to Greenland, but she won't get away with what happened, which has her madness all over it. The people on her ship who were probably sworn to secrecy. But with that many, the truth will come out, and when it does, it may cast a pall on more trips sailing this way."

"You're making it sound like we're marooned," Sigurth said, after a long silence.

"Ya."

Chapter 28

MISSION

1030
(1011)

It was another trying winter, snow piling to such a height that getting from one building to another was by way of steep-walled pathways needing frequent shoveling. At the craft-shop, Sigurth had a unique problem . . . on the north side where the shantied sections of rooms abutted, snow had piled up to not only cover the walls, but also overlap onto the roof. Since some of those spaces needed exterior outlets, shoveling was more complicated, ending with tunneling that was both difficult and dangerous.

He was near to finishing what he could do in the back, when he heard noises from the front, voices he couldn't understand from people he couldn't see. He worked his way back into the storage room, whose door he'd made workable earlier, and after stamping and brushing off most of the snow, stepped into the main room to find that Ingivar and Thorth had just entered.

"Have you ever seen the likes of this?" Sigurth said.

"Oh ya," Thorth said, grunting as he stooped to slip out of his boots, still with snow clinging all about. "I've spent time in Halogaland, and it sometimes got like this. In fact it was worse because the sun never made it into the day."

"Ya, ya . . . We sure know about that," Sigurth said. "So what brings you here? If you're bored, I have some more shovels."

Ingivar laughed. "That's not what we had in mind. And how are things with you, then, Nikka . . . are you feeling okay?"

"I'm fine, thanks; but someone inside of me has been trying to get out."

"Oh, but that's a good sign. And how's little Garth behaving?"

"About as well as you'd expect a boy to," Nychanachia said. "We went for a walk to the longhouse earlier; but as you know, this isn't good weather to be out in, especially if you can only waddle along. How are things with you?"

"We're fine, and the men are too. They just finished a game in the snow, returning to make a mess of the bunkhouse; so I thought it a good time to get out."

"And you're probably thirsty and didn't have anything to drink," Sigurth said.

"That's not why we're here," Thorth said. "The fact is we've talked a lot since the last time we were together, and have some thoughts you might like to hear."

"But you wouldn't mind if Nikka just happened to have something on the pot."

"We didn't say that."

"Well, come have a seat," Sigurth said. "I wouldn't want your fine thoughts to escape before I had a chance to hear them."

"I see you still have the sketches on the wall," Ingivar said, stepping up to view them in the dim light.

"Ya . . . I leave them there and look at them from time to time in hopes they'll trigger a bright idea; but so far it hasn't worked. What is it that's come to mind with you two?"

"It's like this," Thorth said. "The more we think about it, the more we feel we can't rely on people coming this far. Therefore we *are* marooned, and if we don't take action, our choices are to pack up and return home, wherever that might be, or disappear into the native population. Oh speaking of that, did you know that Jon and Ondur are going to wed Potanchahee and Salanaias?"

"Ya," Sigurth said, "Nikka knew about that some time ago."

"That's fine," Ingivar said, "but it doesn't alter what we're thinking."

"Which is?

"Well," Thorth said. "We asked ourselves what it is we need if we are to prosper as a colony, assuming no one is going to drop in and solve the problem for us."

"You made a list?"

"Ya."

"Okay . . . Go on."

"First on that list is, of course, people," Thorth said. "And not just a few people, but maybe a few *thousand* people."

"And not just anybody," Ingivar added. "But people with special skills, like people who can show us how to extract metal from soil for instance.

With the time we've had at the Way Station, we've tried our hands at it, but with unimpressIve results."

"And that's it?" Sigurth said after a pause. "Just people?"

"That's the biggest part," Ingivar said. "But we should also have horses and cattle and chickens and pigs and a number of other things to make our community complete."

"I agree with everything you've listed so far," Sigurth said. "In fact, I've had the same thoughts. The problem for me is the how. Have you thought of that?"

"Ya, that too," Thorth said. "Animals are the easy part. Greenland is short on wood, and we have plenty. We could trade with them, and in only a few trips strengthen or complete what we've started."

"And people?"

"That's the hard part," Ingivar said. "So let's think about it. Sigurth, when you went with Olaf Tryggvason to Wendland, how many ships went, and how many people?"

"Over a hundred ships and maybe four thousand people."

"And when you went to Hjorungqrfjord?"

Sigurth nodded. "Similar numbers . . . many ships and many people."

"How many ships did Eric the Red have when he colonized Greenland?'

"I've been told the first group consisted of fourteen ships that made it, with four, five hundred people or so."

"Exactly!" Ingivar said, his voice rising. "We can't think too small, like in one or two ships. Eric sold the people of Iceland that what he was offering was opportunity in a fine new land that he cleverly named Greenland, exciting enough of them to pack up and give it a try. But what is Greenland, really? Do you think it compares to what we have in Kanata, or what you found in Straumsfjord or Hops or in your travel up the river?" When I look at your sketches I see an area, although only roughly defined around the edges, that's as big as Norway and Sweden combined, with who knows how much more laying beyond where you traveled, with timber and farmland and game and seafood like we've never seen before . . . and with a gentler climate than Greenland or Iceland or Halogaland."

"That's true," Sigurth said. "But are you forgetting there are people here. We found natives at every stop."

"Ny . . . We're not forgetting that," Thorth said. "Because it shouldn't be a problem."

"It certainly drove Thorfinn Karsefni away."

"And he was wrong," Thorth said. "The naives have been here for as long as we've been in Norway. Now, we've moved into their land, not the other way around, so we need to respect what they are and blend in with them, just like Sveyin and Bergljot are trying to do right now, even though they're not as well developed as we are in certain ways. But we've already learned that by sharing with each other, each of us will end up better than we were before.

"What makes doing this possible is the fact the natives aren't organized into large nations with armies and such. They're really individual settlements, usually small, each with a general area that's recognized as their territory. They have a language and religion similar to other neighboring villages, but substantial distances between them result in villages being strangers . . . and often enemies."

"Which means?"

"Which means we might be a unifying and beneficial influence to them."

Sigurth laughed. "We don't know as much as we should about their customs and religion; but then how much is that a factor when we're divided ourselves in what we believe?"

"Oh my, let's not muddy the water over that."

"That's for damned sure," Sigurth said. "And as long as I have a say, there won't be eyes gouged or hands lopped to make people believe a certain way."

"I think we can agree on that," Thorth said, "but we're getting away from the main part of the concept."

"People?"

"Ya, to move a large number of people here, enough so that we can weather the slings and arrows of starting over in a new land, and to adapt peaceably with the scattered natives we find as neighbors. All of this free, by the way, from the blood lines and politics that drive us nuts at home."

"My, you two *have* put a lot of thought into this," Sigurth said.

"Ya, we told you. Now, having heard it all, what do you think?"

"I'm intrigued, certainly," Sigurth said, "but how do you propose to make it happen?"

Thorth and Ingivar looked at each other, as if neither wanted to take the lead, then Thorth said, "Someone needs to go to Norway and talk to many young people, mostly young marrieds, showing them the sketches and describing the beauty and opportunity of each of the areas explored."

"And remember," Ingivar added. "What's being offered isn't just hunting and fishing and farming, it's also independence and freedom."

Thorth nodded, then continued. "The objectives should be to get as many ships committed as possible, and then, like the armadas of those other trips you were on, sail here to a new nation with fertile soil and endless possibility."

"Sveyin and Bergljot would be great doing that," Sigurth said.

"So would you and Nychanachia. You're well known, so several have told me, and Nikka would be a wonderful representative of a people most Norwegians have only heard of as skraelings."

Sigurth looked at Nikka, who was listening. Just then the shop shook from a gust that pounded the walls and sent a sprinkle of snow down through the smoke hole.

"What you've suggested is very interesting," Sigurth said after he'd eyed the ceiling to make sure everything was holding together. "I'll run it by Sveyin as soon as I see him."

"Good," Ingivar said. "We'd like his take on this too . . . and we certainly can't do anything until the weather clears anyway."

Sigurth didn't think much more about what had been discussed, not because he wasn't interested, but because another matter began to take over. Nychanachia became larger, to amazing proportions in contrast to the slim creature she'd been, and reached a point where he was told to summon the women who were standing by. And they came—Thyri, Tryvi's wife, and Dotta, part of the quiet couple that had made the trip eight years ago, and of course Potanchachee and Salanaias. There wasn't much Sigurth could do except get out and take Garth with him, which is what he did, going to the longhouse where he tried to get into the games and such that were in progress. But that didn't work, not for him anyway, so he left Garth in the care of others to pace in front of the craft-shop, hoping for someone inside to tell him something. At one point, the door flew open and Thyri appeared; but instead of saying anything or acknowledging he was there, she emptied a container, throwing its content into the nearest snowbank, then turned and slammed the door behind her.

It didn't help that the snowbank was now streaked in red.

Finally, after the wind had picked up, sending snow in swirls all around and turning him into a snowy abomination, the door opened again, and smiley faces he couldn't recognize because he couldn't see much through frozen lashes, ushered him. He was unwrapped and wiped off and led to the end of the room, where lighted by candle, was as beautiful a sight he was ever to remember . . . Nychanachia, weak but aglow, holding a tiny, rosy-cheeked cherub.

"It's a boy," she said proudly.

"I thought we'd call him Gunnar," adding, "What do you think?"

As soon as the weather warmed enough for most of the snow to melt, but before mud disappeared, Sigurth left for the native village to see Sveyin and his family. He didn't take Garth along because the main purposes for leaving so early was to see if they'd weathered the winter all right, and to discuss with them what Thorth and Ingivar had suggested. He also didn't want to pressure them into taking Garth back, for several reasons, one being they'd more than enjoyed having him around.

When he entered the village, however, he was shocked to find that it was deserted, and that by the look of things, with snow piled in ways that didn't show the effects people would make, the village had been vacated before the heavy snows fell.

"They're gone!" Sigurth said to Nychanachia as he returned to the shop and found her outside with the children. He almost forgot what he was going to say when he looked at Garth, who, completely taken by his little cousin, was blabbering at Gunnar whose eyes widened and rolled in amazement.

"Gone?" Nychanachia said, puzzled at first. Then, after Sigurth described the condition of the village, she explained that there was another village over a week away, straight south on a lake, that was part of her people. She'd been there when so young she could hardly recall it, knowing it existence more from visitors who stopped by since then.

"Why would they suddenly leave and go there?" Sigurth asked.

Nychanachia didn't know.

"Well?" Thorth said when Sigurth walked up. "What did Sveyin say about our plan?" By the look on your face he didn't like it."

Sigurth shook his head. "There's nothing to report. The village was deserted and probably had been before winter set in."

"So you didn't see Sveyin?"

"Ny. What do yo think would cause a village to pick up and move like that?"

"Did you ask the girls that wintered here?" Thorth said.

"Nikka did, only to find out they were surprised too."

"Hmmm . . . We know they're very superstitious, and we know they've been bothered by more sickness than usual."

"And we heard the natives north of the bay left for that reason," Sigurth said.

"Maybe that's it," Thorth said. "Maybe one more sickness tipped the scales. Maybe with that their spirit-man or whatever they call him went into a tantrum and "poof."

"Could be," Sigurth said. "I just wish Sveyin had sent word some way."

"He would have if he could have . . . I know him too, you know. We just don't know the circumstances at the time."

"Ya."

"Where does this put us?" Ingivar asked.

"In limbo I guess."

"Ny o ny, guess again! Thorth said. "Let's not let that happen. We need to survive and we have a plan to do so; but a plan's no good if you don't act on it. Let's do this . . . As soon as spring planting is in, I'll take the *Mule* with a load of lumber to Greenland. If all goes well, we should be back in four to six weeks with some of the animals we want. That should be enough time for you to prepare for Norway."

"We'd need time to overhaul the ship after you get back."

"Not if you take Freydis' ship. It's similar to the *Mule* and is in good shape, at least it was when sailed here last fall. Besides, Freydis thinks it's still in Vinland, so I wouldn't want anyone to find it here."

"But Odd's accustomed to the *Mule*."

"Odd wouldn't go. Ingivar is the logical person to take you, not me; and he has Stig, who sailed the ship from Vinland . . . Remember?"

The months slipped by too quickly in Sigurth's mind; but everything progressed well, it now being mid-summer with eyes turned east looking for the *Mule* to return. As for preparations for the longer trip, that had fallen mostly to Ingivar, who'd done his part. He'd taken Freydis' ship into the bay and checked it out, and now it floated at the dock ready for loading.

Sigurth paced outside the shop, alternately looking east and seeing nothing, then south with the same result. Just then Garth left the game he'd been playing to run over and tackle one of his legs, so Sigurth picked him up and threw him in the air, catching him as he fell squealing with delight. Sigurth put him down and patted hm on the butt to send him back where Nikka was feeding Gunnar.

Oh shit, he thought. *What was he going to do?* It wasn't as if anything had changed, because it hadn't. He needed to go to Norway, and he needed to take Nikka and Gunnar even if the tot was still feeding. But Garth . . . Should he take him as well? He was a real charmer and not much trouble, and would be a wonder to Gyrth and his family. But what if Sveyin and Bergljot returned after they'd gone?

The best guess he could put to the trip was a years duration for a round trip, and possibly two depending on the success he'd have in attracting boatloads of settlers eager to return with him. How nice it would be to have Sveyin and Bergljot along. Having them would make the selling much easier, because Bergljot was the best statesman of any of them.

Sigurth sighed, looked at the sun and headed for the door.

"Where are you going?" Nikka said.

"I've got to make another trip to your village."

"It's pretty late to be starting out."

"Ya, I know . . . but I can't settle down until I do. The days are long now so I should be back by dark."

He stepped inside, picked up his weapons and a few needs, like a water pouch, gave everyone a quick hug and was gone.

The day was warm, so with what he carried and the speed he was traveling with strides just short of a trot, it wasn't long before he stopped to slip off his tunic and tie it around his waist. By late afternoon he was at the gate glistening with sweat.

He walked the length of the village, past the ceremonial poles and the Chief's quarters and almost to the stick wall on the back perimeter to the structure that Sveyin and Bergljot called home. Nothing had changed, but everything looked different. The mud and dirty remnant of snow seen earlier had been replaced by dirt and clumps of weeds, with everything seeming to sag. Rabbits and chipmunks scampered from one hideaway to another; birds flittered about; and a coyote on haunches watched over all of it in the distance.

He went inside, sat on a bench and looked around, the structure seeming so frail, built of small branches rather than timbers. He couldn't imagine how there could be comfort during the winter, even considering that the walls were no longer complete, with skins removed and taken along because they were too valuable to leave behind. The surroundings gave him a feel for the sacrifice Sveyin and Bergljot were making to achieve what they felt was necessary.

He scanned the surface of the hut, as if somewhere, somehow, there was a clue to what had happened; but he saw nothing with any meaning. *How would a message be left? What would he do in a similar situation?* All questions that had no answer. Neither did stepping out and looking at the sad remnants of the village again.

It took Sigurth longer on the return trip. Rather than speed along in hopes of good news on the way over, he now plodded. While he was saddened by what he'd seen, he was also apprehensive of what lay ahead more than he'd felt before any of the battles he'd been in, because with the trip being proposed, everything depended on him. The latter emotion wasn't wasted because waiting for him at the shop were both Thorth and Ingivar, while in the distance at the dock, the *Mule* was being unloaded.

"I see no point in waiting for the perfect moment," Ingivar said. "We know what needs to be done, and each day we remain here, the closer we get to that time of the year when we don't want to be on the water . . . and that rules out spending another month trying to get Sveyin involved.

"So let's go!"

It rained the next two days, which did nothing but make them fret about what needed to be done, all arrangements otherwise made and on hold. Then skies cleared in the night, the stars coming out in all their glory, and everyone was alerted. By the time the sun broke the horizon to reveal a perfect day, loading was already underway.

All that needed doing was soon completed, the crew seeming to move as if each action was well practiced, with the result that before the sun was halfway to high, lines were pulled and the ship pushed off. Sigurth and Nychanachia were at he rail, each with a child in their arms, waving as the population of Kanata slipped away.

The travel plan was simple. It was to stop at the Way Station, but only for a day to rest and refresh, and then continue eastward. Greenland would be bypassed, with the next stop Iceland and another short stay. The final leg would be to Trondheimsfjord in Norway, scooting by the islands along the way that normally would be considered stopping points.

Sigurth was uneasy at first. He'd gotten accustomed to Odd and the crew of friends he'd assembled and sailed with years before; but now every aspect, including the ship, was different. Fortunately, it didn't take long to relax as Ingivar and Stig and all their men proved to be just as capable as his had been, and the ship, although not seeming to slip along quite as well as the *Mule*, still made good time.

The first leg to the Way Station was uneventful, which was good, with the best part being able to get back on land, if only for a few hours, walk about, have a hot meal and relax.

"How have things been here?" Sigurth asked Ingivar when he, Nychanachia and the kids joined the crew at the cookhouse.

"Just so so," Ingivar said. "As you can see there's not many here, and they're pissed. When we left last year, we said we'd be coming right back; and of course we didn't. So they've felt abandoned and marooned, with the only traffic being the *Mule* earlier. Oh, by the way, it's finally gotten around to me that some of the people here had spoken to some of Odd's crew when they returned from Greenland. It seems Odd's crew had talked to crew members from the Freydis ship, the one we're using that had been at Vinland, and that a story they'd tried to keep secret was now out."

"So what happened?"

"It was all Freydis. She fabricated a story that Helgi, Finnbogi and their men had treated her badly, insulting her when she'd stopped by to visit. Well, she shamed her gutless husband to do something about it, and he got his men to trap the others when they were sleeping, tying them up. On further orders, the men, now helpless, were murdered. When everyone refused to kill the women, Freydis took an axe and did it herself.

"Can you imagine that . . . almost three dozen people murdered for no reason other than madness? Those were people from Iceland we would have loved to have at Kanata."

"What's being done about it?"

"Not enough in my estimation," Ingivar said. "The crew have been left to live with their disgrace. That includes ones who didn't participate, because although they didn't do anything, they didn't try to stop the slaughter either. Leif was disgusted, so I understand; but he didn't execute Freydis and her husband like he was tempted to do. Instead he castigated them by sending them into exile."

"That may be why no-one's come this way since then," Sigurth said.

"Well, think about it," Ingivar said. "Coming here always was and always will be risky. When what happened at Vinland was made known, taken together with Thorvald's death and exaggerated stories about skraelings, it must seem like there's a curse over here . . . all of which makes what we're setting out to do much more important."

The next leg to Iceland was also uneventful, with long days and nights seeming to follow without end. It was hours and hours of gazing at the endless ocean as the ship glided along, and of saying meaningless comments to crew members who were always on alert for something to do. But it was also an opportunity to spend time with Garth, to play silly little board games he wasn't yet old enough to grasp, and to hold him by the rail and marvel at a fish that occasionally swam near the surface. It was a time to pick up Gunnar and walk about with him, because to him everything was new and wonderful, evoking big expressive eyes and excited expressions that weren't yet words. Then there were his first steps. Sigurth had been sitting on the deck with both boys in whatever nonsense they could think of, when Garth got up to get something that had rolled away. Gunnar watched him go, then without coaching, rolled over, stood, and took out after him.

And it was a time for Nychanachia. Although with a sly and ready wit, she was normally quiet, not usually the one to start a conversation. This wasn't the case, however, as the days dragged on. She had marveled about the tunic he'd worn at their wedding, which stimulated her interest in weaving and sewing that had started with Bergljot; and so she was eager to learn more, and looked forward to meeting Thora. She didn't stop there. She asked about Orm and all he'd done, and of Rogna and other family members. She had to know about Bird Mountain, and what he and Sveyin had done as they'd grown up together around it. So they talked and talked and the days flew by.

Then there were signs land was near.

"Any further thoughts?" Ingivar asked. They had discussed previously the options of going to Breidafjord, then to Hvammsfjord, where there were a number of settlements, or heading into Faxafloi Bay and quick-stopping at Laugarnes, all options know to Engivar and Stig from their experiences. With the first option there was exposure to many people, and possibly an opportunity to interest enough of them about Kanata to fill a ship or two.

"Ny, ny, ny," Sigurth affirmed. "With each moment that's passed, the urge to go home gets stronger and stronger, so let's go to Laugarnes. My preference is to stay there like we did at the Way Station . . . only long enough to freshen up and enjoy a hot meal. Then as soon as we can, be on our way to Norway.

"And not to the Trondheimsfjord, by the way. South of there is a small inlet leading to a marina near a number of farms, including mine. That's where I want to go because we can set up there, enlist help from our families and friends, then strike out for Nitharos and bigger markets."

"You know the way?"

"Oh ya," Sigurth said smiling. "I could find it in the dark."

They did as Sigurth wanted, stayed only long enough to refresh and restock, then set sail, rounding the southern tip of Iceland heading east.

Standing at the rail watching Iceland disappear, Ingivar asked, "Weren't you tempted to look up Thorfinn Karsefni?"

"I thought of it," Sigurth said. "Because he's a good man and I enjoyed being with him on the trips we made. He's also the one who first recognized the problem with settling in the new world. My guess is that he's prominent in Iceland; and if that's so, would be a help with what we want to do."

"Where's he from?"

"He lives at Reynines, which should have been easy enough to find."

"But you only thought of it?"

"Ya, and you can guess why. Besides taking time, it would jeopardize the last good sailing weather of the season. We've done well so far so I don't want to mess with that."

Ingvar nodded. "I don't blame you. What's your home like?"

"It's nothing special, but it's home. It's a farm on the side of a plateau called Bird Mountain. The farm Sveyin grew up on is on the other side."

"And you're cousins."

"Ya," Sigurth said, snorting. "We've played and tangled every which way since we were able to crawl."

"How about you . . . where is it you call home?"

Ingivar didn't speak at first, then said, "I didn't want to think about it. I'm from the south, east of the Vik near Sotaness . . . Do you know where that is?"

"Ya, been by there."

"Okay . . . Well, I was just a kid, but remember what happened like it was yesterday. They came, pirates out of the Wends, and took everything we had, burning what they couldn't carry. They killed Ma and Pa and a bunch of relatives and neighbors, and took away most of the young including my brothers and sisters. I made it into the woods and hid until they were gone.

"I've been on the go ever since. So when you talk of feeling for home and seeing it, I admit to a tinge of envy. The truth is, what you're doing at Kanata has a feeling as near to home as any place I've been."

Sigurth felt good about what Ingivar said. It was as for the first time he fully realized what he and Sveyin and the others were doing, doings that brought hope and promise to so many others.

The ship skimmed on and all was well, with the sail full and the bow slicing the water, and the horizon to the east like an optimistic beckon to their purpose for being there getting closer and closer. As the sun set behind them, Sigurth stepped down into the hold where Nychanachia waited to a scene that reminded him of another in a manger where there was a babe, so innocent and fair, bundled and sleeping in a mother's arms, with another tot beside her with his head on her lap.

Nychanachia put a finger to her lips as Sigurth eased in across from her.

"Don't make a sound," she whispered. "They're both asleep but it hasn't been easy, so be careful."

He nodded, marveling at the scene, that in his mind was as beautiful as any he'd ever seen.

"You okay?" He said, not able to find the words he wanted.

"Everything's fine," she answered. "Just be careful."

He nodded again, but couldn't stay away. He eased over, picking up the boy, who groaned but didn't awaken, and put him on his lap, then moved beside her, reaching his arm out and around to bring the all together. He gently kissed her forehead, then her nose and finally her lips, to which she almost melted.

"Are you getting anxious?" He whispered.

"Of course I am," she said softly, almost mouthing. "I'm only a few days from being in the company of complete strangers. I can't hide the fact that I'm different . . . What will they think of me?"

"What will they think of you? They're going to love you, just like I do . . . or else." Then he gave her a light squeeze and kissed her again.

It hit in a rolling front no-one saw because it came several hours after midnight, with most bundled and asleep. The lead gust swirled in from the northeast, catching the ship at full sail, which pushed it into an immediate tilt almost putting the far-side rail under water. The force was so great, that had cargo aboard been loose, the ship would have tipped at that moment.

Sigurth had just awakened and was slipping out of his roll to make a tour of he deck when he had to grab a strut above him to keep from being thrown against the far side of the hold. Others, including Nychanachia and the children, weren't so fortunate and ended in a bundles mess, the children too astonished to cry out.

The ship righted itself momentarily, then dove into a trough that appeared out of nowhere, beginning what was to be a fight for survival. Wind and rain came in uneven sequences and strengths, and the sea as a result bucking like a tormented bull, with the ship almost helpless to respond.

But almost goes a long way when it's the only option. By the time the ship righted after the first blow, every member of the crew was at his station responding to orders being screamed. Lines were altered and the sail turned to a point most neutral to the wind, then under the most difficult of conditions, furled and tied. Since the steering-oar was now useless, oars were extended, but only to point the ship downwind and run with it.

"Any idea where we are?" Sigurth said, shouting at Ingivar to be heard over the wind.

"Stig says we're past the Faroes."

Sigurth didn't ask any more, not liking the answer. With the direction they were being pushed, he would prefer there was open sea for a long way, and that may not be the case where they were. There being nothing he could do on deck, he returned to the hold to comfort Nychanachia and the kids, and to make ready for what might come next.

Hours later, little had changed except the direction of the wind, which slowly rotated, requiring the ship to adjust accordingly. By daybreak, the direction was more southerly. At times it seemed the winds were easing, only to have new surges pound just as intensely as before, with the sea responding by forming a roller coaster of mountainous highs and deep valleys. So it went, each sequence of this combination seeming a miracle in surviving.

The center of the ship was tented, as it had been since the trip began, with the area of it covering the hold. There was no way under conditions of the storm, however, to drain he decks in a normal way, so much of the water worked its way into the hold. When Sigurth returned and splashed in the water, now knee deep, he grabbed a bucket and yelled for others to join him. It was during this time, a period of intense bailing, that he heard Ingivar calling.

"What is it?" Sigurth said, rejoining Ingivar and Stig on the stern.

Ingivar was grim-faced, his hair stringing straightaway with the wind, his round cheeks pinched. He pointed to the front past the prow, to something that couldn't be seen at first in the distance. But when the ship rose on a crest it came into view, the faint outline of something that wasn't the ocean.

"I was afraid of that." Ingivar said.

"Is it the Hjaltlands?"

Ingivar shook his head. "They're skerries offshore of the Hjaltlands."

"How can I help?"

Ingvar didn't answer directly, finally saying. "We've got men at the oars. If it looks like we're on our way into a skerry, we'll try to work our way around it. Bit we might not be successful, and we're not, things can happen fast. Since that's the case, I want you and your family up here by the skiff. If we crash, we'll launch the skiff and put all of you aboard."

"I won't do that," Sigurth said, stuttering.

"You must," Ingivar said, grabbing Sigurth, looking him in the eye, and growling. "Look . . . What you and Sveyin started could be just what most of us have wanted all our lives—a home with opportunity and freedom. You must do as I say. The future of my home depends on it."

Reluctantly Sigurth obeyed, and soon Nyhanachia, holding a bundled Gunnar and a similarly wrapped Garth, huddled by Sigurth on deck beside the skiff, holding on as the ship lurched along.

They watched as Ingivar and Stig and the crew tried several things to direct the ship. Oars worked to get the ship pointed downwind, but did little to move it out of line, actually making it more prone to tip when tried. What worked better was to turn the rolled-up sail at an angle, then unfurl it a bit. This caused a tilt but changed the direction the ship was going, the result being that when the first rocks came in line, with menacing explosions of water all around, the ship glided by safely to the side.

A few crew members cheered and shook their fists as they passed; but Ingivar continued to stare ahead. He was aware that the Hjatlands consisted of many islands with surrounding shoals and skerries, and that the waters they were passing through were dangerous on either side.

Another hour passed, an hour of tense minutes while winds roared and seas bucked and the ship heaved. While they did, Sigurth shielded his family as they huddled on the floor. There seemed to be a coziness to the huddle, trading warmth with one another as the ship rose and plunged, and each rising as if born again in a process eventually taken for granted.

Then at the low point of a plunge there was a sound . . . not much of one, but one followed by a subtle shockwave, just enough of one for Sigurth to feel it, awakening him from a light sleep he'd drifted into. He eased to his feet beside the rail and looked across the length of the ship, at first sighing in relief because the ship rose and fell again as it had been doing. He looked at Ingivar to see if he reacted the same way, but saw gritted teeth instead. So he looked back, this time seeing water and people and bundles burst out of the hold.

Sigurth jumped, knife in hand, and began to cut the stays holding the skiff. Just as quickly Ingivar and Stig were beside him and in short seconds the skiff was freed, lifted over the rail, and dropped in the water, still tied to the ship.

"Over with you!" Ingivar growled, pushing Sigurth across first.

Sigurth did and settled in, set his balance and reached up expecting Nychanachia and the baby; but she handed him Garth first, who he took and placed on the floor, wedging him against the seat behind him. Turning, he reached for Nychanachia again. She was now half over the rail, handing him a bundle with one hand and reaching for him with the other, while Ingivar behind was helping, and Stig to the side was holding the last tie to the skiff with knife in hand.

Just then the ship, heavy with water, that had been on a crest when the transferring started but was plunging into a trough, hit the wall of water at the bottom. The result was an explosion of water and debris, a mess into which the skiff was thrown. The mess included oars that snapped like twigs going every which, some of the jagged ends hitting Sigurth, one of them in the throat just as he grabbed the bundle. He was pitched backward, falling on top of Garth.

The ship barely made it out of the trough. When the sea rose again it was to the rails in water with everything not tied down bobbing, including people in a melee of heads and splashing arms.

The skiff, also taking in water, sprung to the surface and spun away, with Sigurth sprawled but still aboard. He lay dazed, clinging to the side rail with one hand while coughing blood and holding a bundle that wailed with the other. As he struggled for control, little Garth squirmed below him.

A fishing boat left harbor on the western side of the main island later that afternoon and headed north. Aboard were Harald, the owner of the rig, and Holti, Erving, and Haki, friends who'd been on the water together for years.

"This doesn't make sense to me," Holti said. "We'll only get in a few hours at best."

"Oh, you know Harald," Erving said. "He was all set to leave at first light, but then the storm roared in. He just hates to give up when he's set to go, so it drove him nuts having to wait it out."

"That was some storm."

Haki nodded. "No doubt about that . . . and we were lucky."

"How so?"

"Well, think about it . . . You know the olden Norse believed Norns pulled strings that determined their day-to-day fates. If so, they sure held us in favor, because if we'd been out like Harald wanted to be, and the storm, which came up so fast, hit . . ."

Holti shivered at the thought. "We'd have had it. The storm rattled our house and woke me up when it hit. It tore up some of our roofing."

"You should have seen the bay," Erving said. "I'v never seen waves like that. Thank you Norns."

"Where's Harald going now? He's not heading to where we were going to fish."

The three swung around to see what lay ahead in the new direction. They saw in the distance a small skiff with several people aboard, two of them rowing. As they approached, they furled sail, drifting until the two boats butted.

When held together, Harald stood up from beside the tiller and made his way forward. He looked at those in the skiff, as miserable a sight as he'd ever seen on the water. There was one man curled and unconscious up front, two others shivering and almost blue at oar, and a bundle of people in back, which with a closer look turned out to be a man holding a young boy in one arm and a well-wrapped baby in the other. As he scanned the faces, pinched and cold, he settled on the ones in back, whose expressions made the crusty old mariner soften as he muttered, "Oh my."

Then he turned and said, "Well, don't just sit there, help these people aboard . . . and get blankets, they're half frozen."

On the way back, Harald asked, "What happened?"

"We got caught in the storm."

"I guessed that much, "Harald said. "Are you the only survivors?"

"Ya. We were lucky. We just happened to come up beside this skiff, which was drifting away too fast for anyone else to reach."

"I don't think your mate is going to make it," Harald said, looking down at a man on the floor. Then, "And who's the man with the kids, he hasn't said a word."

"He can't talk right now. Something smashed into him when the ship plunged into the wave at the bottom of a trough; it hit him in the throat."

"Ya . . . I saw his neck. Who is he?"

"He's Sigurth Gunnarson, the leader of Kanata. That's where we're from."

"Never heard of it. Anyway, he must be hurting real bad because he looks like he does."

"He lost his wife, too."

"Oh . . ."

When they tied in at their small fishing village, a few men with nothing to do strolled down to greet them.

"What's going on, Harald?" One said. "We thought you nuts going out so late as you did. Now you're back towing another boat."

"There's been a shipwreck. A ship bound for Norway got tossed onto some rocks north of here in the storm."

"How'd you know about that?"

"I didn't. We were just going out to salvage a part of the day. Ran into these poor folks instead."

"This is what's left?"

"Ya . . . Well, don't just stand there, give us a hand. These folks need help, food and a place to stay."

"This one don't."

"But the rest of them do, particularly the one with the kids. He's hurt and needs attention; but my concern is for the kids. It's some kind of miracle any of them are alive."

"What's that strapped to his back? Looks like a quiver."

"It isn't a quiver. I don't know for sure, but the others said it holds some drawings. Must be important to him because it's the only thing he came off the ship with . . . besides these kids."

The two other survivors went with Erling, who had a cabin near the water and enough room to put them up. Sigurth went with Harald, who was also nearby, and had a wife.

"Harald Thorgannison," Gersi said as she watched her husband escort the three, wet and shivering, to the door. "We hardly have room for ourselves. Now you bring these along."

Harald didn't say anything. He didn't have to. Garth, who was cold and tired and hungry, started to cry, holding onto Sigurth's leg as if he were looking at a witch. As if on cue, Gunnar wailed too.

They got through the night with everyone fed, cleaned and to a bed of sorts; but it wasn't a happy time with Gersi grumbling through it all. It didn't improve in that regard as Harald left early the next morning, gathering his crew and pushing off. Although fishing was a pretext, it was clear that they were heading for the shipwreck area for whatever might be found. Harald knew word would get around, and that others would try to do the same thing, so an early start was important.

This left Sigurth alone with a wife whose last word to her escaping husband was that she wasn't going to stand by and take care of a worthless stranger's snot-nosed, crappy-bottomed kids. All he could do was stand by, watch over the boys, and try to contend with his own pain and misery. The pain was the least of it, even though it was intense and he was continuing to swallow in order to breath; and he hadn't been able to eat anything other than a few spoonfuls of broth. When Gunnar fell asleep after a reluctant feeding, he took Garth outside, mainly to get away from the hostile household, and walked about the stead which turned out to be quite a humble place. The two got into simple nonsense games which Sigurth strained to show interest in. Then Garth became drawn to chasing animals in the pen, allowing Sigurth to sit and think. Except this wasn't good either because the vision he kept seeing was Nychanachia with eyes wide open, reaching to him and being almost in his grasp . . . then disappearing. Gone and then a cloud of vague images and crying children and men splashing nearby and almost tipping the skiff as they fought their way out of the water. Neither was there a ship to see in the mountains of water that rolled by with the wind, except briefly the last of the mast with its furled sail . . . no Ingivar or Stig or other of the crew or, this part making him try to shout, causing more pain and blood instead, no Nychanachia.

It was a long day with the only diversion, other than the boys, coming when he noticed a gate in one of the pens sagging and out of a hinge. So he scrambled around in one of the shacks, found tools and made repairs. This led to a few other bits of ignored maintenance, which helped him in the doing more than it helped his hosts.

When Harald returned late that afternoon, the mood of his hosts was the opposite from what it had been in the morning, with Gersi almost civil because of the work he'd done; but Harald grumpy because all he'd found in the area he'd searched were a few bundles. Sigurth ignored what he brought in, thinking it a sickening reminder of something he'd rather forget. But then when Harald unwrapped one of the soggy packages, he realized it was his. So he stepped forward with gestures that indicated the fact, which didn't make Harald any happier. He ignored Harald and completed the unwrapping. In it were spare trousers and tunics that were ordinary; there was a wooden eagle, a replication of the one given away to the native chieftain a few years before; and there was a fine tunic. He put this tunic on and stood before his hosts, wearing the piece Thora made that he'd worn at his wedding the year before. The tunic, so beautifully crafted, had his hosts agog.

After standing with it on for a moment, and remembering, he took it off. Holding it out in the dim light in the house one more time, he turned and handed it to Harald.

Harald choked, never having seen anything as beautiful before. After examining it closely in all its detail, he set it down and asked, "Who are you?"

Sigurth tried to speak, but managed only a hurtful whisper, then stopped.

"The other survivors weren't much help," Harald said. "They told me they were part of a certain Ingivar's Way Station, but spent almost a year at this place called Kanata. They said you were the leader there and that you were being taken to Norway on some special assignment."

Sigurth nodded.

"Are you of royal blood returning to claim a throne?"

Sigurth shook his head.

"Well, there's not much I can do for you in any case. Those of us around here are poor fishermen in a small community. If you want to go to Norway, you'll have to get to the port on the eastern side of this island. All traffic, whether to Scotland or Norway, leaves from there. Would you like to go to that port?"

Sigurth nodded again.

Harald sat back and thought, considering the options. At length he leaned forward. "The island we're on is very long; but it's also narrow in places. To sail to where you want to go from here is a round trip of roughly one-hundred fifty miles, which is a long way for my little rig . . . and as you know the sea can be nasty. A better choice is to sail out around the coast nearby going south and then east maybe ten miles to the largest port on our side. From there it's only a walk of two miles across the narrows to where you want to be.

"I think the other two survivors should go with us. There's nothing for them here, and they might find something to do where you're going. Since it's such a short walk, I'll go along. I don't have any great connections; but it won't hurt to have someone around to explain a few things. Oh, here . . . take back your tunic. I'll look silly wearing it in this place, and it might do you some good at the eastern port."

Sigurth stood, not knowing what to say if he could say it. He nodded, mouthing "thank you," then picked up the eagle sculpture and handed it to Harald, exchanging it for the tunic.

The weather turned foul with wind driven rain, so the trip was postponed for a few days. This meant sitting around, which outside of tending to the boys, Sigurth didn't care to do. So he stepped outside, and, almost embarrassing Harald with the things he found, made a number of repairs and improvements.

Sitting around the table the night before leaving, Harald said, "The wind seems to be easing up, so I'll inform the boys to be ready early in the morning. Is that okay with you?"

Sigurth mouthed, "Oh ya."

Harald laughed, saying, "I sure wish you could talk, because there's something here that's missing. You're obviously handy with tools. Did you carve the eagle?"

Sigurth nodded.

"Well, it's beautiful. And what do you have in the cylinder you carry?"

Sigurth undid the top and eased out a series of sketches, some of them large and complex, but the others smaller and simpler, with dots and squiggles drawn on each one. Although tied together, like on the wall, they told a story, none of them made sense by themselves. Harald picked up one of them, turned it very which way and asked, "What does all this mean?"

Sigurth looked about, but saw no wall surface on which to assemble them. And since trying to mouth words wasn't working, he finally shrugged, rolled up the sketches and returned them to the cylinder.

Harald wasn't done yet. "You say you're not of royal blood?"

Sigurth nodded.

"But you're on a special assignment."

Sigurth's eyes glazed, not responding except to look down.

Harald, not knowing what else to say, muttered, "I guess whatever you were to do went down with the ship."

When Sigurth groaned with what he said, Harald saw the face of a man in torment, and he kicked himself for forgetting that this man who amazed him and who he was beginning to like, had days before lost not only his ship and its crew, but also his wife and mother of his children.

Grasping for something to say he turned, then said, "Just look at that." He was referring to Gersi, sitting in the corner feeding Gunnar, who was sparkling and giggling over the way she was playfully doing it. "It's only been a few days, but I can tell she's going to be heartbroken to see all of you go."

The trip was easy, going just as Harald planned, even though he crowded all of the survivors on his small boat. They docked at the western port before noon, then made the short hike to the eastern shore. Arriving around noon, they walked among the cluster of buildings, piers and wharfs that were part of its seaport, being somewhat impressed with it size, which though small, was still bigger than the other settlements on the island. Harald led the way, asking people as they walked who he should talk to about travel on the water. He was directed by most comments to a nondescript shack on the water beside the longest wharf, and told to talk to Lars.

Lars turned out to be a small, wrinkled, balding person who looked like he'd never left the place that was his world.

"I have a group that wants to get to Norway," Harald said when he entered the shack. "What do you know about ships going that way?"

"Where in Norway?" Lars said, looking up from something he was working on which he pretended to be important, which it wasn't.

"Trondheimsfjord."

"You missed one passing through right after the storm."

"Damn," Harald said. "When's the next one?"

"Hard to say," Lars said. "I don't know of anything right now; but sometimes ships come in and go out without much notice. How many to go?"

"The man and his kids, for sure. The other two are undecided. They could stay or go any which way that's available."

"Why isn't the man speaking for himself? It doesn't seem that you're the one who's going anyhow."

"Ny, you're right about that. I live on the west side. We picked up these people a few days ago. They're the only ones to survive a shipwreck in that storm we just had. The man you're referring to was injured when his ship went down. He was hit in the neck and can't talk."

"Really! A shipwreck! Hadn't heard of it. What ship? Out of where?"

"From what these two said, it was a knorr out of somewhere far west, near Greenland, with twenty people aboard."

"Going to Norway."

"Ya."

Lars held up his hands as if to indicate there was nothing available at this time and he didn't know when there would be something.

"Well," Harald said."If that's the case and a trip could take a while, where can he stay while waiting? And is there work he could do in the meantime? He's a handyman with exceptional woodworking skills."

Harald didn't leave until he'd gotten Sigurth and the kids settled and fed for the night; but the best he was able to manage for settling was a barn, with an understanding with the farmer, whose farm was on the edge of town, that he'd help in any way he could.

This understanding, however, didn't amount to much of anything. When the sun rose the next morning, with the boys hungry and Gunnar announcing it to the world, neither the former or his wife stepped outside to see if they could help.

It was a situation where Sigurth couldn't wait. After hunger tantrums he wasn't able to mollify, and far more than he could stand, he corralled one of the nanny goats and milked her. Then combining milk with bread he's saved from the night before, made a meal for both the boys.

Knowing this was only a temporary solution to a problem that might not be short, he cleaned the boys best he could, wrapped Gunnar in a blanket, then picked them both up and walked back to the waterfront.

As expected, he found Lars in his shack with nothing happening. By means of gestures he asked Lars if he could store his gear, his cylinder of drawings and the package Harald had retrieved, in the corner.

Lars couldn't imagine what this was about, but he nodded his okay, forgetting for the moment that Sigurth was the only one who couldn't talk. Then he sat back and watched with fascination as Sigurth continued to move about as if there was something to do.

In Sigurth's mind there was, or at least he had to make some work. So he placed Garth in the corner, gave him wooden toys, and by signs indicated for him to stay and play. Next, with Gunnar bundled and tied to his back, he picked up a broom and began to sweep the floor in the shack.

Lars sat up in his chair saying, "What are you doing?"

But Sigurth kept sweeping, finishing the floor and moving out into the wharf, where he was when Lars got up to stop him.

"I didn't hire you to do that," Lars said, "and I'm not going to pay you."

Sigurth stopped, rubbed his stomach and pointed at the kids. Garth, who was obediently sitting in the corner, detected something he didn't like in the tones he was hearing, and began to cry; and Gunner, once again on cue, followed suit.

"What's going on here?" Said one in a group of men walking by. "Is everything okay?"

"Not really," Lars said. "This man's in a fix . . . and I don't have the means to be of much help."

"What's the problem?"

"His ship was wrecked in that storm a few days ago. Only a few survived, including he and the kids. But he lost everything, and wants to get off our island and return to Norway. Since he has nothing to offer, he's willing to work any way needed to survive and make the trip. He's supposed to be an excellent woodworker; but oh, there's a complication. He's injured and can't talk."

The men nodded, the one doing the talking saying, "We just heard about the wreck. Two men were at the Inn last night talking about it. They were in the same fix; but being just crew members, have hired out on a fishing boat. This guy doesn't look like the owner of a ship, though."

Sigurth straightened up with that comment. He walked back into the shack, and when he returned a moment later, he was wearing Thora's tunic.

Things improved from there, with word getting around that an excellent woodworker was about needing work, and willing to do so for only his basic needs. Many took advantage of this, with the result that Sigurth and the boys survived.

For the next month Sigurth sawed and repaired and cleaned and mended and dug, doing anything that was offered to him, usually only for food and lodging, but sometimes for coin. And each day he stopped by the shack to see Lars and find out what was happening.

And things were happening, mostly fishing boats and an occasional ship to Scotland; but nothing yet to anywhere near to central Norway.

Then one day he was hailed, and when he looked up from what he was doing, he saw Harald and Gersi coming his way carrying a basket and a container. It hadn't been a particularly good week, with temperatures falling and the ever present wind biting harder than usual; but when he saw those two he almost melted. What they brought was food and milk, and more than that, a caring that generally missing in a community pinched with its own day to day survival.

After quick hugs, they went to where the boys were kept, and sat, Gersi turning her attention to the tots whose eyes immediately sparkled, not only for what she brought, but more so for the bubbling affection she extended to them.

"How are things going?" Harald asked, knowing he was only going to get a shrug for an answer. "Lars says you're staying busy, but wonders how long you can last since you don't get much to eat with your throat and all, and you seem to be awake at all hours. You've lost weight, that's plain to see. Look . . . I'll do the talking," and with that opened the basket, "and you do the eating. It'll do me good to see that you're getting something down your gullet."

They left after a short visit, needing to get back to their boat so they could return home before dark. As they were parting, Harald said, "Any chance of travel to Norway will be gone when it starts to snow. When that happens, I'll come back and see if you're still here. If you are, you can spend the winter with us."

More weeks went by with a monotonous sameness, with there being plenty of people ready to take advantage of Sigurth's situation. The problem was that the shortage of food and rest, and the constant exposure to Hjaltland's winds as the weather declined, were pushing him to the limit. Then when he was at a point of walking in almost a zombie state, and looking to see Harald arrive to make good on his promise, he saw Lars instead, excited and running towards him.

"Sigurth . . . Get you things together! A ship just came in, didn't you see it? It's a knorr that's short-stopping here on its way to the Trondheimsfjord. The owner says they're landing at Viggia, which is as close as you're going to get.

"Hurry!"

Sigurth did, dropping what he was doing and dusting off. Then he picked up the kids, some meager rations he'd accumulated, and his belongings, and scrambled down to the wharf and the ship. It didn't occur to him that he and the kids looked more like refugees than travelers, and if it had, there was little he could have done, because with the level of activity at the landing, it was clear the ship was going to leave as soon as everything was ready.

"This is the man I was telling you about," Lars said to the man pacing about on the deck, the one hurrying everyone along. He was the owner, a gruff-looking Scotsman named Malcomb. He turned, and seeing Sigurth, bedraggled and worn and holding two pitiful looking urchins, swore under his breath.

"This isn't a charily cruise," he growled in horribly accented Norse. "Whose paying their fare?"

Sigurth dug into a little packet fastened to his belt and produced a few coins.

"That's not enough," Malcomb said, almost as if he were insulted.

Lars stepped into his shack, returning with a few more.

Malcomb shook his head and turned away. But Sigurth put out his arm and stopped him; then he reached into his bundle and pulled out the tunic Thora had sewn.

The trip across to Norway was smooth, the weather turning to something unseasonably pleasant for this time of the year. The problem for Sigurth was that the food he'd brought along didn't go far, and soon, besides his own hunger, he had to contend with young ones who didn't understand and wailed with their pangs, that even contributions from other passengers and crew didn't always satisfy.

The day was still sunny and warm when they docked at Viggia a few days later, which was a good thing. But Sigurth was hardly aware of it, being very troubled. He was about at the end of what he had to give, with no food, no money and hardly enough energy to walk. And he was in Viggia, where he's sailed away from seven years before with his own ship, his own crew and bountiful provisions and coin, a place at least two days hard walking from home.

This was on his mind as he made his way down the gangplank. As he plodded, he saw a couple on the landing looking at him in a strange way, at first not recognizing them. Then he straightened and focused, not able to believe his eyes . . .

The two were his foster-parents, Orm and Thora.

Chapter 29

FROM BIRD MOUNTAIN

1030

"Garth! **Garth!** Gunnar waved and yelled at the group trudging along and rounding the corner of the corral, finally getting Garth's attention.

"What is it?" Garth said breaking away and running up.

"It's Pa! He's disappeared!"

"Whattaya mean disappeared? He can hardly walk."

"Well, he's gone, that's what I'm telling you . . . and so's his horse."

"The devil!" Garth growled, then turning, ran into the pasture with Gunnar at his heals. Getting the horses they wanted wasn't easy thing to do because the horses were satisfied and very content with what they were doing, which was grazing and swatting flies and farting and doing what horses do. But finally they got two of them back to the barn and saddled.

"He's most likely on Bird Mountain," Gunnar said as they started out.

"Ya for sure . . . but he may be on the far side, where the *Sea Eagle* and the graves are, so let's go there first."

With that they whipped flanks, the horses responding and they were on their way, thundering through the pasture and across the fields all the way to the far edge of the farm. They didn't slow down until they came to the rough back-trail that circled the heights of the plateau now on their left. Here the going was difficult with boulders and trees and a small gully with a trickle of a stream, making the way more of an obstacle course than a pathway. Ordinarily it was a favorite place for them because it was one of the first places in memory that Pa had brought them to play, but now it was something else.

Shortly before, Sigurth stood up from the stone marker by the mound under which Orm and Thora were interred. He'd dismounted and dropped by that of Gyrth first, and now having visited and conversed with all of them, he stood by the eagle carving on the keel end and cleaned it off until it sparkled in all its glory.

He looked at his horse enjoying itself with what was growing around the rocks, and sighed. He wanted to go to the top, but didn't like the thought of walking. At the same time he didn't want to ride either, as getting up into the saddle had been quite a chore earlier. He grimaced to even think about it.

Deciding he wouldn't even try, he patted the horse and started walking, each step, it seemed, being harder than the last. Finally and not gracefully, he made it after passing rocks and ridges and scrubby shrubs he'd never noticed before, and eased into his favorite spot with an exultant "Aaaaah."

It was a beautiful day, or at least it had been with the sun dropping to announce it was soon to be over, and hardly a whisper of a breeze to remind there was a thing like air. The terns were there, of course, lifting above the rim, almost as if to see who had invaded their space, then tilting and drifting in a dance that was always fascinating to watch. Far out beyond, the ocean, the Norwegian Sea, smooth with hardly a ripple, was now shiny, reflecting light from the sun low in the sky.

It was a sea he'd never forgiven.

He shook off that thought, remembering a question he'd asked Sveyin years and years ago . . . *"What do you see from here?"* Then he answered it himself . . . He saw seas that stretched out seemingly forever, challenging a mind that supposedly had intelligence to continue on until finally there was something, and that far-flung something initially was Greenland. But Greenland with its inviting name wasn't what one would expect. Ya sure, it had green grass in the summer, enough to feed sheep and goats and cattle, and enough dirt clinging over rocks to allow fields and gardens, but it was treeless with short summers and long winters and ice that was aways in view.

It was beyond Greenland that there really was a treasure, incredibly, beyond even more water. But there it was . . . a place with gentle shores and seafood like clams and oysters and lobsters and fish of all kinds . . . and land, land that went on forever, fertile land with trees of every kind in forests with game and fur and plants . . . plants with infinite qualities . . . and rivers, long rivers, rough rivers with rapids and waterfalls. Oh, the waterfalls, some with heights that are hard to believe in the telling, so high the air around them is filled with mists, and so thunderous they pound the senses as if you're at the gate of another world you don't have the strength to enter.

And there are people, people some call skraelings, mostly because they're different, and they are. They're darker skinned with black hair but beardless, and the live in huts unlike ours, and have small boats and strange customs and don't have metals. But then, once you get to know them, you find they're just like we are in more ways than not. We have fields and gardens, and they have too; and we have grains and vegetables, and they have near the same with special delicious ones we've never seen before; and altogether our settlement, our Kanata, is being formed.

Then he saw a face, a pretty face of a young girl with a pleasing voice, a sharp wit, sparkling eyes and a cheery smile . . . and he reached out to a hand that reached to him, and then she was gone and a ship was gone and the promise was . . . and he fell back, his eyes flooding.

Sigurth sat for a while, now almost drained. Then he thought of the cylinder on his back biting into him as if to make itself known. So he slipped it off and removed the cap, easing the sketches out. He looked about for a smooth surface, finding the only one anywhere close to what he wanted being a large, smooth but rounded boulder. Struggling to his feet, he took the sketches and carefully reassembled them on the boulder, being able to keep them in place in the still air by placing pebbles on the corners.

He looked at the rounded mosaic for a few moments, retracing the dots and crooked lines, and tying them to scenes and experiences he could recall. Then a thought came to him, one that caused his cheeks to pinch and his eyes to squint as he looked at the sketches on the rounded boulder from end to end several more times, then at the sky, and then back to the sketches . . . And he broke out laughing, loud belly-laughs that exploded from his throat and bent him over.

"What are you laughing at, you fool," said Sveyin, who appeared out of the air wearing buckskins and a feather and a big smile on his face as if he'd been there all along.

"Come here and look," Sigurth said, or seemed to say.

"You mean, look at those sketches we used to make, that you were never smart enough to figure out by yourself?"

"Just listen to you . . . If you're so smart you'd see what I see from here."

"And what do you see?"

"Well look. It's not only the sketches. See the setting sun . . . It's low now so you can look at it without burning your eyes out and see that it's round. Now look to the east and see the rising moon . . . and *it's* round.

"And guess what? Remember that edge I kept looking for?"

"Are you kidding, you damn near killed us."

"Well, we were never going to find it," Sigurth said, pointing back at the sketches on the boulder, *"because the earth is round!"*

Sigurth returned to his favorite spot, continuing to chuckle . . .

"Did you hear that?" Gunnar said.

"Hear what?" Garth asked.

They'd snaked their way up the back trail, then half way down the far side to where another trail cut left leading to the *Sea Eagle*. They knew they'd guessed right when well before they got there, they saw Sigurth's horse. Dismounting at the ship, they saw that the stones were cleaned and readable, if they could read runes, that is, and also saw there was blood wherever Sigurth had been, including amounts streaking the flanks of his horse.

"It sounded like someone laughing," Gunnar said.

Seeing nothing like Sigurth in the vicinity, they grabbed the reins of all three horses and hurried up the slope and along the flattened area that defined the plateau.

"I see splatters every few feet," Garth said.

"Ya."

Near the far side of the flats, Gunnqr said, "I see him . . . He's just where we thought he'd be."

They came loser, dropping reins and walking around the boulder on which the sketches were displayed.

"Pa . . . You've scared the family half to death, and you're just sitting with a grin on your face . . .

"Pa?"

Gunnar knelt down, moving in to look into Sigurth's eyes, his voice breaking . . ."*Pa?*"

The two grown men were in each other's arms for a good long while, crying and blubbering unashamedly. Finally, they composed enough to go about doing what they had to do.

"We'll take him home first," Gunnar said, his voice shaking for control. "But I think he'd want to be buried beside Orm and Thora."

"Ya," Garth said in almost a whisper as he collected the sketches from the rock and rolled them up. "We never really understood what all of these meant."

"Ny . . . But they meant a lot to him. They reminded him of his travels, I guess."

"Ya . . . When we bury him in the *Sea Eagle,* we'll put these beside him, along with all his weapons."

"And all his tools . . . He loved his tools."

"Ya."

Afterword

Historians generally consider that the "Viking" Period began with the attack on the Monastery at Lindesfarn in 782, and ended with the battle of Stamford Bridge in England, and Harald Hardraada's death, in 1066.

Unfortunately history, as it is often portrayed years after the events occurred, can be misleading. For example, the term "Viking" wasn't used during the period in question, and no one has established when or why or by whom it was first used. Some speculate the term was later derived from the Vik, the most prominent fjord in Norway; while others suggest it came from the term a-viking, which meant to go pirating. What *is* clear is that pirates were bad people, with raids including robbing, killing, raping, enslaving and destroying without conscience; and further, that they were prevalent, not only among Scandinavians, but also among others all around the coastal areas of Europe, Africa and Asia from times prior to recorded history, continuing in places of the world even today.

What we think we know about this period in the Scandinavian countries is mainly derived from the amazing chronicles and sagas written by Icelandic authors a few hundred years after the events occurred, the most noteworthy being "Heimskringla" (History of the Kings of Norway) by Snorri Sturluson, from which many of the events herein were taken. The extent to which these writings are true in all regards is therefore reasonably to be questioned.

Another thing is clear, and that is that remarkable things happened during this subsequently defined period, and that most of it was by the 80 to 90 percent of the people—farmers, craftsmen and tradesmen—who lived their lives as peaceably as the times would allow. Farmland in Norway was limited because of deep, rugged fjords that characterize its coast; therefore growing populations, which were prevalent, had the effect of prompting people to move to wherever they could find opportunity.

What made this time as unique as it was, and as impactful as it was, were the remarkable Scandinavian ships that allowed what happened to come about. The ships—longships and knorrs—were shallow-drafting, allowing them to navigate rivers throughout the continent; they were light, allowing them to be portaged on rollers amazing distances and connect one river to another; and they were strong, allowing them to sail open seas.

What is known as the Viking Period eventually drifted into obscurity, which even the amazing stories out of Iceland couldn't revive. Part of this was the change in society influenced by its conversion to Christianity, and the growing prominence of the wealthy. A few hundred years later in Norway, the King, the great men, and the church owned over half the cultivable land, putting the small farmers and the common men almost into servitude.

Then came the Black Death, which ravaged Europe in 1349 and was particularly tragic in Norway, where as many as two-thirds of the population were erased. The impact was so severe that farmers didn't have the numbers to cultivate their lands, and kings, nobles and the church lost their means of livelihood. The country's economic foundations collapsed; and families of the royals were unable to find suitable partners, leading to a political mixing with other Scandinavian countries, and diminishing Norway as a nation for several more centuries.

An aside to this time is a crude depiction of the known world drawn by a Swiss monk in 1430. It was called the Vinland Map because it showed an island beyond Greenland that could be that discovered by Bjarni Herjolfsson. This part of the drawing, which later proved to be fraudulent, nonetheless showed the primitive development of cartography at the time, with the possibility that around the year 1000, the word "map" was not used and the skill in making them in infancy.

We recognize that in 1492, Columbus sailed to and "discovered" what became known as America, a dynamic event changing the world forever.

In 1607, a colony in Jamestown, one of the first settlements in North America, began with three shiploads of people. As in other early attempts, like that in Plymouth in 1620, initial mortalities were heavy with less than half surviving the first year, underscoring the difficulty of starting in the new world. Over the following years, Jamestown required many shiploads of settlers before stabilizing, especially after the massacre in 1622 of 347 people by what were erroneously called "Indians."

In the early years of those colonies, there was a unique situation unlike any other experienced, as settlers from different nations meant that English, French, Dutch, German, Scotch-Irish, Scandinavian and Swiss were among the languages in use given the diverse nature of the immigrants. At some point, in order to move forward with a common language, a vote was taken with English being selected; but this selection was only by a margin of one vote over the next most popular.

In the 18th and 19th centuries, the story of successful colonies in the new land proved to be a siren song to many in the European countries, who were drawn, not only to escape religious and governmental tyrannies, but also to take advantage of the freedom and economic opportunity the new lands represented. People came as individuals and families, and, as happened on occasion in Norway, as entire communities.

We may never know how near the colonizing efforts around the year 1000 came to being successful. But the possibility is there, that if everything had gone right, if Karsefni had not given up, if Freydis had not been a monster, or if a certain ship on a critical mission had not been caught in a storm, with valuable sketches unthinkingly buried, we, in the United States, could be speaking, not English as determined by that vote years ago, but the same language spoken in Iceland today . . . Norwegian from the "Viking" period.

FROM BIRD MOUNTAIN, is a narrative about a family that lives during a central part of what's been defined as the Viking Period, and tries to do so peaceably. But members of it are periodically drawn into historical episodes that confront it. They also become involved in a particularly astounding adventure that cannot be accurately defined because little evidence from one thousand years ago has been found. There is a possibility, however, that that adventure is as realistic as is written in the narrative.

To give the story an appropriate feel, names have been drawn from the chronicles, mostly indiscriminately and without historical relevance. But in some instances the names are true, and the incidences in which they're used are as accurate as the chronicles from which they're taken. Some of these are:

Earl Hakon: King from 960; killed in 995 by his slave while hiding in a pig sty on a farm near Nitharos.

Olaf Tryggvason: AKA as Crowbone; King from 996: killed in the sea battle of Svolth near Wendland in 1000.

Einar Thambarskelfir: Noted person; supposedly Norway's greatest archer at the time; fought at Svolth.

Earl Eirik and Earl Svein: Sons of Earl Hakon; victors at Svolth; subsequent rulers for a time after 1000.

Olaf Haraldsson, aka **Olaf the Stout** and **Saint Olaf:** King for a time after 1015; fled to Garthariki, tried to return but killed at Stiklastad in 1030.

Harald Sigurthason, aka **Harald Hardraada:** Half-brother of Saint Olaf; wounded at Stiklastad fighting alongside Saint Olaf (*he is the young, tall man mentioned in the battle*); fled to Garthariki, then to Micklgard. His lengthy story is not pertinent to this narrative; but he returned, became King from 1045; was killed at Stamford Bridge in England in 1066, supposedly ending the Viking Period.

Eirik the Red: Banished from Iceland for several murders; left for islands to the west, which he explored until his banishment was over; called the land "Greenland", and enticed its settlement in 985.

Bjarni Herjolfsson: Lost his way to Greenland while trying to follow Eirik, and discovered new lands (The American Continent) in 986.

Leif Eiriksson: Explored these new lands; established the first colony there (exact location unknown) in 1000, calling it Vinland.

Thorfinn Karsefni: From Iceland; sailed to Greenland where he met and married **Gudrun Thorbjarnardottir.** Beginning around 1003, explored new lands beyond Vinland, including far flung places like Hops and Straumsfjord, spending several years doing so. Their son, Snorri, is considered the first person from Europe born in the new land. They returned to Iceland where Gudrun is known for her three sons who became Bishops.

Freydis Eiriksdottir: Made last known attempt to colonize Vinland in 1010.

GLOSSARY OF PLACES

Fishook of Sands: Cape Cod
Garthariki: "Land of Forts"; Europian Russia
Hjaltlands: Old Norse name for Shetland Islands north of Scotland
Hopps: New York City area
Large Waterfall: Montmorency Falls east of Quebec City
Large Twin Falls: Niagara
Micklagard: "Great City"; Constantinople
Narvesund: Straits of Gibralter
Nitharos: Present day Trondheim
Oresund: Two mile wide narrows between Sweden and Denmark
Straumsfjord: Bay of Fundy area . . . Maine to Nova Scotia
Sentinel Rock: Perce Rock offshore of Quebec's southern peninsula
Way Station: L'Anse Aux Meadows . . . Norse settlement in Newfoundland; the only one in the new world of which ruins have been found.

Wendland: A country of Slavic people on the southern coast of the Baltic Sea

GLOSSARY OF TERMS

Berserkers: Fierce warriors in trancelike state

Byrding: A small ship used for coastal traffic

Byre: Barn or animal shelter

Byrnie: Mail shirt

Danegeld: Tribute paid to Vikings for peace

Family Cliff: Part of Norse lore where the old and infirm were taken to lessen the burden on younger family members; more a joke than actual practice

Flyting: Ritual exchange of insults, normally at a feast

Hel: *(Myth)* The underworld of ancient lore to which people who didn't die in battle were destined

Hird: The warrior retinue of a powerful chieftain or king

Hnefatafl: Game played on a checkered board

Holmganga: Dual fought on an island to settle a dispute

Knattleikur: game played with a hard ball and a bat

Knorr: A ship with deeper features than the sleek longship, making it better for both transporting cargo and cross ocean travel

Leidang: A naval levy . . . a requirement for an area or district to provide a fully manned ship for an excursion or battle

Midgard Serpent: *(Myth)* The giant snake called **Jormungand** that surrounds all lands and waters at the Edge of the world upon which humans reside

Moors: Islamic people in southern Spain

Niding: Disgraced person . . . a nothing

Norns: *(Myth)* Female deities who determine the fates of people

Runes: Early writing system mainly used for names and simple statements

Sigurth: *(Myth)* Son of Sigmund of the Volsung. Finest of warrior kings; slew the serpent (or dragon) Fafnir; upon tasting its blood, became able to understand the language of birds

Skerries: Off-shore rocks

Skoggangur: The ultimate banishment for a person deemed guilty; anyone so judged can be killed on sight if he should return

Suttung's Mead: *(Myth)* A mixture of blood and honey that made the drinker a poet or scholar

Thing: An assembly of freemen where disputes and issues of law and politics were settled

Thrall: Slave

Valhalla: *(Myth)* Hall of the slain . . . a delightful afterlife of fighting and feasting while awaiting the final battle of **Ragnorak**

Valkyries: *(Myth)* Superhuman female warriors in Valhalla

Wergil: Compensation paid to an injured party by the one deemed responsible

Yule: Scandinavian midwinter feast

RECOMMENDED READING

The Viking, by Tre Tryckare, Cagner & Co, Gothenburg, Sweden, 1966

Age of Exploration, by John R. Hale, Time-Life Books, 1971

The Vikings, by Else Roesdahl, Penguin Books, 1987

The Viking Art of War, by Paddy Griffith, Greenhill Books, 1995

Historical Atlas of the Vikings, by John Hayward, Penguin Books, 1995

Viking Designs, by A.G. Smith, Dover Publications, 1999

Viking Age, Everyday Life During the Extraordinary Era of the Norsemen, by Kirsten Wolf, Sterling Publishing, 2004

The Vikings, The Last Pagans or the First Modern Europeans, by Jonathan Clements, Running Press, 2005

Viking, The Norse Warrior's Manual, by Thames & Hudson, 2013

Norse Mythology, by Neil Gaiman, Norton & Co., 2017

Vikings, by Heather Pringle, National Geographic, March 2017

Heimskringla, History of the Kings of Norway, by Snorri Sturluson, University of Texas Press, 2011

King Harald's Saga, Harald Hardradi of Norway, by Snorri Sturluson, Penguin Books, 1966

The Prose Edda, Norse Mythology by Snorri Sturluson, Penguin Books, 2005

Other Classics by Penguin Books

The Vinland Sagas

Egil's Saga

Nyal's Saga

The Saga of King Hrolf Kraki

The Saga of the Volsungs

Seven Viking Romances

Laxdaela Saga

The Nibelungenlied

FAMILY TREE

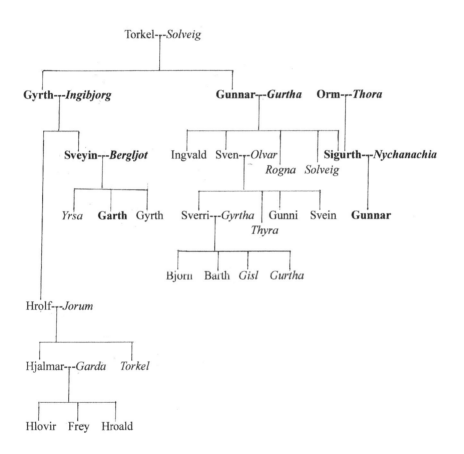

About the Author

Lyle Fugleberg, the founder of an award-wining architectural firm, retired in 2008 after 45 years of practice. Still active with sports and community service, he has also taken to write in fictional form about special issues and interests. This latest is from his heritage, which is being a third generation Norwegian who spent much of his early years on North Dakota farms in the company of highly-spirited, hard-working people—immediate descendents of the original sod-busters—who still preferred the mother language. His extensive research in preparation for this writing led to the unique and surprising interpretations included herein.

CPSIA information can be obtained
at www.ICGtesting.com
Printed in the USA
BVHW041355291021
620191BV00010B/18/J